The Mysteries of Heaven: Book 1
The Joy of the Lord

Mark Andrews

Published by Amar Patel at Createspace

The cover art was painted in 1344 by Ambrogio Lorenzetti. The original is housed in Siena, Italy.

To my wife and kids,

Thank you for putting up with my disappearance during the writing process. Your love made Regina's story possible.

To my mother who gave me my life,

Your tireless love and devotion to me gave me great insight into how Our Lady loved her Son. Thank you for saying yes to my life, may I cherish you for the rest of yours.

To my mother who gave me my wife,

You always treated me like a son, if not better. The grace you displayed during the hardships you endured taught us all about faith. Thank you for your intercession from heaven. We miss you.

Preface

When people ask me why I wanted to write a novel, I answer, I didn't. I was teaching second grade religious education to a bunch of eager and rambunctious eight-year-olds when I found myself frustrated with the proscribed curriculum. The lesson plans in the textbook left the kids bored and disinterested. My co-teacher and I decided to liven up the classroom by having the students act out the scriptures to make the stories come alive. This sparked a thrill in the students that kept them asking for more. Children and instructors alike came to look forward to the time we spent together on Sundays.

When I offered up thanksgiving to Our Lord before Mass one day, the story of The Joy of the Lord came to me in a flash. I knew that God wanted me to share this story despite my complete lack of a background in writing. I often prayed that He would turn this project over to someone who could surely do a better job, but still the inspiration kept coming and I continued to pluck away.

This is certainly not a theological treatise and I am no theologian. I simply did my best to play my small role in God's plan and I pray that in reading about Regina Marie's adventures you continue to do yours. The stories from the past come from scripture, tradition, and artistic license. I hope that readers avoid dwelling on the authenticity of the events and focus on how the Holy Spirit wants to touch their lives through meditation on the mysteries described.

May God bless the truth contained in this book and forgive me for any error my failings may have added. May the reader of this book feel as challenged by meeting Regina Marie as I was. I will pray for you. Please pray for me.

M. A.

The Joy of the Lord

Chapter 1
Thunderstruck

Saturday, November 30th
10:03 AM

In a modern school building, a man sat at a desk and stared at the stack of papers teetering before him. The students' desks sat empty on this Saturday morning, but it didn't stop him from talking to unseen students.

"What were you thinking?" He glared at the exam in front of him. "We just went over that!" He shook his head and marked several problems wrong. A large calendar hung on the wall behind him. All of the topics covered on the test were clearly labeled, along with examples and practice problems which could be found in the textbook. Large, carefully constructed posters also covered the walls. He wrote on one test, "More time studying, less time texting."

He dropped his red pen and sighed. "What am I doing, Lord?" Looking at the tiny crucifix attached to the rosary sitting on his desk, he closed his eyes.

A man, wearing a Roman collar, sat in front of a computer screen. The display contained a spreadsheet with column headings *Church Attendance* and *Sunday Offering*.

"Why did I ever get a commission together to track this information?"

"What was that?" a voice said from another room.

He didn't answer. A few moments passed. "How many pennies did we collect last week?"

3

"A couple of dollars' worth." A chair creaked and an elderly woman appeared at the door. He looked at the woman and shook his head. "Don't let it get you down, Father."

"I'm trying," he said. "Could you close the door, please?"

She closed the door and left him alone. He glanced around the office. Dozens of pictures of him with parishioners graced the walls, shelves, and desk. Each one was filled with smiling faces.

His eyes turned to the painting of John the Baptist on the wall. The inscription underneath read, "Prepare ye, the way of the Lord."

"Lord, I know you call me. Show me the way."

A woman bathed a filthy boy. "How did you get mud on your hands and feet?" she asked. "Weren't you wearing your mittens and boots?"

"I needed to take my mittens off to wipe my nose," the boy said with a grin.

"That explains your hands. What about your feet?" She frowned and shook her head. She opened the drain to release the brown water in the tub. Muddy footprints streaked the tile of the bathroom.

"You told me to take my boots off outside, so I did."

She chuckled at the child's response. "I did say that. Well, how much longer will you need your mother to give you a bath?"

He shrugged and took the wash cloth from her hands. He began scrubbing himself with the dirty water. His mother turned the handles and tested the water with her hand. She closed the sliding door after she was satisfied with the temperature and began wiping down the floor with another cloth. As her son played in the fresh water, she prayed, "Lord, what will I do when they don't need me anymore?"

A young woman, curled in a fetal position, lay weeping on a bed. She caressed her large belly with one hand as she wiped away tears with the other. The cream color of her waitress outfit matched the dinginess of the sheets on the bed. A barely closed suitcase sat by the door of the room. Several items of clothing poked out through the seam. An ancient television sat across from the double bed. The five button remote control sat on a table by the bed next to a full ashtray. A Gideon Bible was the only item in the room that appeared less than a decade old.

The woman got off the bed, grabbed her purse, and fumbled through it. She pulled out a photograph of herself with a good looking young man. Glaring at the picture, she tore it in half and threw it in the trash. She looked at herself in the spotty mirror and once again put her hands on her protruding midsection. She glanced at the garbage can again.

"We don't need you," she said. She looked at the mirror again. Tears welled up in her eyes. "Oh God, help me."

A woman surveyed the mess in her kitchen: two broken dishes, school books scattered everywhere, and an overturned chair. She grabbed a broom from the cupboard and began to sweep the pieces of glass. She struck one of the books with her broom and it fell out of her hand. She kicked the fallen broom and sent it spinning across the tiles. Picking up one of the chairs, she sat down at the table and put her head down in her folded arms.

Her body shook with sobs for a few minutes. Finally, she looked up and saw a picture amongst the collage of family snapshots that hung on the wall. She pulled it out from the others and studied it. A cute little boy in a soccer uniform and a man with his hand on the boy's shoulder smiled happily at her.

"What can I do to make you happy again?" she asked the picture. She stroked the cheek of the little boy. Her eyes moved to the man. "I can't do this without you."

She put the picture back in its place and another one caught her eye. She held a baby and stood by the man from the first picture. Two little girls were in the picture, as well as a priest. They all stood by a baptismal font with candles.

"God, why did you abandon us?" She pushed away from the table and began to finish cleaning the mess.

5

A gleaming, immense building stretched on in all directions. The architecture of every nation could be seen in its design, somehow set in harmony, the styles not clashing. White robed figures bustled in through the multitude of doors surrounding the large hall. From within, songs of praise rang out. The chatter of many voices could be heard discussing the needs and petitions of many souls across the earth.

A sudden brightness filled the air and silence accompanied it.

"Lord, you have heard your people call and have brought us here. What is thy will?" a figure asked into the infinite brightness that emanated from the sacred mount within the building.

"It is time," a resounding voice said. Everything in heaven and on earth stood still.

Out of eternity, an enormous thunderclap sounded. The entire earth shook from its might. Every person around the world stopped in place, frozen for a moment in time. Workers in the fields looked up at cloudless skies in wonder. Children lazing through chores became attentive. People staring at computer screens shook off their haze. Millions sat up in bed, wakened from their peaceful dreams.

Thunderstorms frighten many people with bright flashing lightning and roaring thunder, but not here. Every soul on earth united through the sensation brought by the thunder. The call touched believers and non-believers alike. Deep down in the core of their beings every man, woman, and child knew the thunder meant something monumental. The raging echo shaking the air announced the approach of something the senses could not discern. No horn declaring the start of a battle ever had this intensity.

Then, it ended. Billions of people, stunned with a profound clarity, returned to the blinding haze of their lives. The event stirred the world, but the web of deceit woven by the king of lies once again recaptured everyone. However, very soon, the web would unravel because of one little girl.

Chapter 2
The Letter

Saturday, November 30th
10:04 AM

"Regina, was that thunder?"

The thunder ended but Regina remained motionless. She held a pair of scissors and felt in her hands. Patterns, more felt, and glue sat on the table in front of her. She wore pajamas and slippers. Milk and cookies sat within her reach.

Her eyes locked on Da Vinci's depiction of the Last Supper in her dining room. She couldn't take her eyes off Jesus amongst his apostles. The sound of the thunder had vanished but something still gripped her.

"Regina, say your prayers," her mother had told her as a young child.

"Does God hear me?" Regina asked.

"Yes, and if you listen carefully enough you can hear him."

"Does he love me?"

"Yes. I like to imagine him hugging me when I am sad. He gives great hugs," her mother said.

Regina closed her eyes. "I can feel it." She had smiled.

After the thunder, Regina sat entranced by powerful emotions it brought about. The trance might have lasted forever if her mother didn't persist, "Regina Marie Andrews? Are you there?"

Her mother's sweet voice cut through her daze.

Regina regained her senses. "Yes, mommy."

"Was that thunder?"

"Yes."

"That's so strange," her mother said.

7

Hearing thunder in November was unusual in the cold air of their northern state. In addition, after a recent snow storm, which dumped several inches of snow on their suburban town, the sun shined every day in a crystal clear sky. The nice weather had melted the snow leaving a muddy mess outside.

Regina returned to her craft. The dining room cupboards contained more art supplies than plates. Samples of artwork sat all around the large, glass dining room table. She heard the sound of water rushing from the bathtub drain down the pipes behind her in the wall. Then it sounded like the faucets had been turned on to fill the tub again. She listened to the soothing sound when the doorbell interrupted.

Regina hopped up to answer it. She ran to the bathroom first and looked at herself in the mirror. After running a brush through her hair a few times, she went to the front door. Through the frosted glass she could see an adult standing there. Her shoulders slumped and she frowned.

"Don't answer the door for anyone you don't know," her father had told her. "Come get me or your mother."

Regina turned from the door and looked up the stairs. The door at the top was closed and she could still hear the sound of running water. She walked over to a side window and slid the curtain over very slightly. She saw a mailman waiting there.

"Mommy, the mailman is at the door!" Regina called out to her mother. She waited for a response but figured the water drowned out her shouts. She fidgeted in place. She put a foot on the stairs and took it back. She went back to the curtain and slid it only enough to expose her eyeball to the outside world. This time the mailman flashed a wide grin and looked right at her spying on him. Regina pulled her head back and gasped.

She backed away from the window. Her eyebrows expressed concern. She took a deep breath and walked around to the other window. She carefully slid the curtain back and found him facing her again. He winked in a delightful manner and held up an envelope with her name written on it. He ran his fingers under her full name like a jeweler displaying a watch. He put the envelope down and backed away from the porch. Her eyes opened wide and she cautiously made her way to the door.

She slid over to the door and cracked it open. The mailman stood several paces from the porch. She opened the front door and checked the lock on the screen door. It was engaged. Regina stared at the mailman who bowed to her, spun around, and walked away without a word. Regina lips parted and she tried to speak, but no words came out.

She watched him walk away. He didn't turn back or go to any of the neighbors' houses. He simply walked down the street. Regina unlocked the door, stepped outside, and picked up the envelope. It didn't have her address, a return address, or a stamp on it. Her eyes remained fixed on her name, which shimmered in beautiful calligraphy in the center of the envelope. She looked up again but couldn't see the mailman anymore. She craned her neck and looked in the other direction as well. "Where did he go?"

Regina went back inside and locked both doors. She stared at the spotless white envelope with black letters that she could now see were highlighted in a splendid gold outline. She ran her hands over the envelope and examined its every detail.

Suddenly, she looked up to the door at the top of the stairs and then back to the envelope. Regina slowly walked up the stairs. She carefully stepped over the seventh step from the bottom and went to the bathroom door. She heard her mother's voice over the sound of splashing water. She nodded and seemed satisfied.

Regina went into her room and closed her door. Princesses covered the walls of her room and the sheets on her bed. The posters clearly showed effects of aging.

Her father had asked her the previous summer about her room.

"Do you want me to repaint your room, G?"

"No. It's okay. It reminds me about when I used to dream of being a princess."

"You're still my princess, kiddo."

"Thanks, daddy."

Regina sat on her princess blanket and held her treasure in her hands. She studied the envelope, shaking it, sniffing it, and even touching it to her cheek. She looked at her own name. For a moment the letters glowed. She blinked and shook her head. Regina tilted the envelope to see if it had been the reflection from the lights. After failing to reproduce the glow, she turned the envelope over, opened it, and pulled out the paper within.

Midnight. Nativity

A knock came at her door.

"Regina? Are you in there?"

Regina's eyes flashed wide and she looked up at the door. She quickly scanned the room. She pulled away her blanket and as she went to put the envelope and paper underneath, they turned to dust, which then vanished into nothing.

She stared at the spot in wonder for a moment, then remembered to answer, "Yes, I'm here."

Her mother opened the door. "Are you ready to work more on our craft?" Regina could only see her mother's pretty face smiling at her through the crack she made in the door. She had her hair pulled back in a ponytail and had no makeup on.

"Sure," Regina said. She hopped off her bed and walked out of her room. Her brother was shaking his naked butt at her, standing outside his bedroom at the end of the hallway.

"Emmanuel Joseph Andrews, get in your bedroom."

He scampered into his room and closed the door, giggling.

"Mommy?"

"What dear?" her mother said, shaking her head at her son.

"Will I be as pretty as you someday?"

"Regina, I'm a mess." Her mother touched her hair and looked at the sweat suit she had on.

"No, you're not. You look great."

"Thanks, sweetie. You know what? Everyone says you look like me, so I guess so." She smiled.

Regina followed her mother down the stairs. When she reached the bottom of the stairs she paused and looked at the front door. Her mother walked to the dining room leaving her standing there in her own thoughts. "Midnight, Nativity," Regina said.

"What?" her mother said.

"Oh, nothing."

Regina excused herself from family activities by asking for reading time for the rest of the afternoon. She spent that time in her room repeating the words, *Midnight, Nativity* and lying quietly on her bed. However, she would not get out of eating dinner with the family.

"Anything interesting happen today, G?" her father said looking at her.

Their eyes met. She turned to her food and said, "No, nothing."

"Oh." She felt her father's eyes on her.

"Mark, did you get all of your grading done?" Regina's mother asked.

"Yes. I just need to go to the store for a few things. Since we don't have R.E. because of Thanksgiving, I can go before Mass tomorrow. We can go to noon Mass instead of ten o'clock," Mark said.

"Good." Regina's mother looked at her. "That will give *us* some time to clean up the mess *we* made during the break."

"That's good sarcasm, Katherine. Almost as good as these Thanksgiving leftovers," Mark said, putting more stuffing on his plate.

She smiled before Emmanuel said, "I didn't make a mess."

"What are you talking about? I spent an hour cleaning up your mess in the bathroom," Katherine said.

"Oh yeah," Emmanuel said. Regina and Mark looked at each other and shook their heads. Everyone laughed.

Later, Mark came to kiss Regina goodnight. "Is everything alright, G?"

"Why?"

"It seemed like something was bothering you at dinner." He sat down on the bed. His brown eyes looked into hers. She didn't look away.

"Daddy, when you asked if something interesting happened today, I felt like I lied when I told you nothing."

"Did something happen?"

She shrugged her shoulders. "I don't know, I'm not sure."

"What do you mean?"

"I think I daydreamed receiving a letter from a mailman."

"Do you still have this letter?"

"No, it vanished."

"Well, sounds like a dream to me." Mark kissed her on the forehead. "You don't have to feel bad about that." He walked to the door. "Good night." He turned off the lights and left her alone with her thoughts.

Regina looked at the clock; it read 9:04. "I have to stay awake for three more…" Sleep consumed her.

Regina's eyes popped open and she drank in the darkness of the room. She sat up with a gasp and looked at the clock. The bright red numbers of the digital clock read 11:56. She threw down the covers, rolled out of bed, and crept to the open door. She poked her head out and listened for any sounds. Her room stood next to the stairs and on the opposite side of the upstairs hallway from the rest of her family. She slipped out of her room and slinked down the stairs. Then she stepped on the seventh step and it creaked loudly. She winced and froze in place.

"Come on, Regina, you know about that step," she said. She waited for a few seconds then continued down. At the bottom of the stairs, she looked at front door where she got the letter.

"Midnight, Nativity." The image of the letter burned in her mind.

Regina turned to the right to enter the family room where the family's Nativity scene sat on top of a short bookcase. The shelves held story books and a children's encyclopedia set.

She fixed her gaze on the Nativity, barely visible in the moonlight. Mary, Joseph, and a few animals occupied the manger. The shepherds stood watch outside. The baby Jesus would remain hidden behind until one of the children placed him in the cradle on Christmas Day, and the wise men lined up on the far side of the room waiting for the Solemnity of the Epiphany to make their arrival.

As Regina stared at the little statue of Mary looking at the cradle where Jesus would soon lie, an ethereal light entered the room. Regina's heart started to pound in her chest. She turned to the see the source of the light.

A glorious creature stood before her. No image created by man could rival this marvel. Regina fell to her knees and bowed her head, averting her gaze.

"Ave electa," the creature said. The words echoed in Regina's mind. They freed her to look up and behold the spectacle of an angel of God. She stared right at him, able to witness his brilliance without squinting or needing to look away. The angel had long, brown, flowing hair and wore a simple, white robe. His wings splayed out to his sides and fluttered hypnotically.

She couldn't see the angel's face, which glowed brighter than the rest of him. "Ave electa," he said again.

Regina heard the words exactly as he spoke them but this time she replied, "Hail, chosen one?" Concern crept onto her face. "How can I understand you?" Her hands clasped in front of her.

He continued to speak in Latin but she understood him in English. "Do not be afraid, Regina Marie. You hear me speak in the language of Heaven and understand because the Lord wills it." His words barely eased her confusion so he continued. "Regina Marie, the Father has chosen you to play an important role in his holy work."

The angel's light filled the whole room. Regina remained transfixed in complete awe. The angel made no indication he would speak again.

"Who are you?" Regina whispered when she gathered up the courage.

"I'm sorry. Where are my manners? I am Gabriel, Messenger of Heaven." The light keeping Regina from seeing his face diminished. Regina's eyes opened wide.

"You? You're Saint Gabriel? The Archangel?" The angel had the same face as the mailman who delivered her mysterious letter.

"Oh good, you've heard of me," Gabriel said. He released his formality which calmed Regina. She smiled and her body relaxed. "Since we know each other so well, you won't mind if we get down to business?"

"What business can you have with me, Saint Gabriel?"

"Come child, get off your knees and sit with me." He moved to sit on the couch and the brightness coming from him diminished further. He still glowed, but only faintly. Regina obeyed and sat next to him on the couch. He held out his hand and she took it.

When they touched, she smiled and sat up tall. She took a deep breath and seemed more alive. "Why have you come?" Regina said. The volume of her own voice surprised her and she looked at the ceiling.

"Your family will not wake while I am here Regina, and you can decide what you tell them about my visit. I have important information for you, and then you must make a difficult decision."

"Okay."

Gabriel looked at Regina and paused for a moment. His expression turned from jovial to serious.

"Regina, the Most High loves all his creatures but on some he places special favor; some people excel in beauty, some in strength, and some like you in gentleness of spirit and faith."

"Like me? Are you sure, Gabriel?"

"Yes. The Lord gave you the gift of faith and your parents have nurtured it with their love. You have done well in pleasing the Lord."

"Thank you, but I am far from what you say, I don't deserve your praise." Her cheek flushed. She rubbed her hands together in her lap.

"The Lord gave you these gifts from his flowing generosity and you have pleased him in your actions. He knows your weakness but he also sees your strength," the angel said. He leaned forward. "But now, he asks for more if you are willing."

Regina pondered his words for a moment. "What can he want from *me*?"

"Regina, throughout the ages God has called his people to serve him. He calls some to religious life, others to marriage, still others to live as single people. In addition to these vocations, the Most High called some to come forward when the world most needed them. You read of these holy people in the Scriptures, and you can find their stories in the lives of the saints. The world needs someone to inspire them, to learn and live the faith. The Father has chosen you to be that person."

It took her several seconds before she managed to speak. "I don't understand how I could do anything like that. I am only twelve and really shy. How could I inspire anyone to do anything?"

"God knows you better than you know yourself. He would not have sent me here if he did not believe in you, so now you must believe in him." Regina seemed overwhelmed; her eyes shone with fear. "However, before you think about it further, I could show you something from the past that may strengthen your spirit. Would you like to see it?"

"Yes, please." Hope swept away some of her consternation.

"Close your eyes child and pray with me; you will see something so many in the world have forgotten and need to remember. Let us pray as the Lord Jesus taught us to pray. Our Father, who art in Heaven …" As Regina joined in the Lord's prayer she felt her body become heavy and fall away from her soul, leaving the world behind her.

Chapter 3
Betrothed

The sun faded beyond the horizon, leaving a beautiful, purple glow in its wake. Night fell upon a bustling ancient city; the locals finished their outdoor tasks and prepared for the desert night. Men secured animals for the evening, women emptied waste water and shook dust out of bits of clothing, and children returned home after hours of carousing. Families prepared to rest after a long day of labor.

Regina glanced around in all directions. Her eyes could not have opened any wider. She looked down at her hands. She could see through them. To her side stood a similar ghostly image of Gabriel, still in the simple white robe he wore in her house.

"Pretty neat, huh?" he said.

She continued to examine her surroundings. Crude houses made of stone and wood circled them. They stood together on an unpaved street made of dirt and gravel. The few people milling about wore plain cloaks and sandals on their feet.

A man walked right by them and didn't change his gait at all.

"They can't see us," Regina said. She looked at her pajamas and then at the archangel next to her. He smiled at her and nodded.

Regina tilted her head back and sniffed the air. "I can smell food cooking." She made a face. "I think it's food."

"They didn't use the same spices that your mother uses," Gabriel said.

"Where are we?" She thought about her question and followed with, "And when?"

"Technically? We are still sitting on your couch; as for the vision, you can see the holy city of Jerusalem two thousand years ago."

"But I can feel the chill of the night and the gravel under my feet." She reached down and tried to pick up a small stone. Her fingers passed through it.

"You can move around the scene God wants you to see and observe what happens, but you cannot interact with everything."

Regina and Gabriel walked over to the wall of a house. She put her hand on it and felt the smoothness of the stone. Two children came running down the street and, before she could react, ran right through her. She looked at Gabriel. He laughed.

"Come, see why you are here." She watched the children run down the street as she walked towards him. He put his arm on her shoulder and the scene blurred and shifted.

"What happened?" Regina held her head with her left hand and her stomach with her right hand.

"We will need to change locations and points in time to see what you must. You may feel unsettled; try to enjoy the ride."

"What is this place? It's beautiful!" Regina asked. She looked around at the tall columns, crafted doorways, and enormous central structure.

Gabriel held his hand out toward the magnificent building. "Behold the Great Temple of Jerusalem! The Holy of Holies is there behind a great veil."

"What's that?"

"It is the dwelling place of God which once housed the Ark of the Covenant. Have you heard of that?"

"Yes, I saw a movie about it. It held the Ten Commandments, right?"

"Very good. Once a year, on Yom Kippur, the high priest was allowed to enter the Holy of Holies and offer a sacrifice for the atonement of sins."

"Only once a year?"

"Yes, but then the Ark disappeared when the Babylonians came and conquered Jerusalem six hundred years before the time of Jesus."

"What happened to it?"

17

"I don't have clearance to tell you that," Gabriel said. "I can tell you that you will soon see the Ark of the New Covenant."

Before Regina could ask the question that came to her, the scene changed again. She stood in the corner of a very small room. A tiny cot sat in the opposite corner, a small, lit lamp sat by the door, and an old man wearing formal vestments paced back and forth in the center of the room. He muttered to himself.

"What's wrong with him? He looks upset," Regina said.

"Behold Simeon, one of the temple priests. God has blessed him in life and spoken to him on many occasions. Now, the King of kings calls him to a very difficult task," Gabriel said.

"How can I tell her?" Simeon said in a strange language. Regina clearly understood him in English.

"Who is he talking about?" Regina said.

"Our Father called him like he has called you," Gabriel said. "His parents wanted him to marry when he turned eighteen, but he chose to answer the Lord's call and serve in the temple. At this point, years later, the Lord called him to tell one of the maidens of the temple some bad news."

Regina opened her mouth to speak again, but Simeon interrupted her continuing his planning. "What will I say?" He raised both of his arms and looked upwards. He brought his arms down, fists clenched. "What will she say?" He shook his head.

"Who?" Regina asked. She looked at Gabriel. He put up a finger and motioned towards Simeon.

"Her vows mean everything to her." He covered his face with his hands, fell to his knees, and put his head down on his bed. He ran his hands through his hair, pulling at it. He rubbed his face in the plain blanket for a few seconds and then remained motionless for longer. One deep breath later, he said, "Lord, help me." He got off the ground, grabbed the lamp, and walked out the door of his room.

"Where is he going?"

"To talk to *her*," Gabriel answered. "Come on."

Regina followed Gabriel as he drifted after Simeon down some stairs to an open space. Simeon stopped after a few steps. Over his shoulder, Regina could see a lone figure sweeping in the distance.

Simeon took another step and the light of his lamp signaled to the sweeper his arrival. "Is there something I can do for you, rabboni?" she said. The girl turned and exposed her face to the light of the lamp.

"Mary, why do you stay up late and continue your work after the others have gone to bed?" Simeon said.

"Is that the Virgin Mary?" Regina asked. She stepped forward to get a better look. Mary and Simeon froze in their position when she asked the question.

"Yes, Regina."

"What happened?" Regina glanced back and forth between Mary and Simeon who had stopped moving.

"Feel free to ask questions during your visions. If you might miss something important the scene will stop. If the action is not significant it will continue," Gabriel said.

"Wow," Regina said. She studied Mary's face and tears filled her eyes. "She is so beautiful."

"Yes. Yes she is," Gabriel said. He nodded and the scene came back to life.

Mary smiled at Simeon and bowed her head.

"My child, I need to talk to you."

"Speak, your servant is listening," Mary said.

"I loved when she did that," Gabriel said.

"Did what?" Regina said. Simeon and Mary froze again.

"Mary quoted scripture in response to Simeon," Gabriel said.

Regina thought for a second. "Didn't people think that was weird?"

"The other temple workers jealously thought Mary used her knowledge of scripture to show off, but she simply preferred the Word of God to her own," Gabriel said.

Simeon continued. "Mary, do you remember why your parents brought you here to live in the service of God when you were three years old?"

"Yes. My parents told me that they promised the Lord they would consecrate a child to the temple if only he would grant them one in their old age. My mother told me every day that I was never hers to keep and how God blessed her with my being, if only for a short time," Mary said.

"What do you think about what she said?"

"I believe the Lord blessed me in allowing me to spend those few years with my holy parents," Mary replied.

Simeon nodded and seemed impressed. "Joachim and Anne were saintly people and true to the Lord in their word. Anne told me the Angel of the Lord appeared to her before your conception and told her she would bear a daughter who would be greatly blessed and exalted among all of God's creatures."

"Was that angel you, Gabriel?" Regina said.

He winked at Regina. "Guilty as charged."

Mary replied, "I have been blessed, by having holy parents whose love prepared me to serve the Lord, but I only seek to exult the Lord and remain in his shadows." She lowered her head and turned away from the light.

"What does Our Lady feel about being loved by millions of people like she is?" Regina said.

"Very perceptive, Regina. From heaven, she continues to serve the Lord by guiding souls to Jesus. People who mistakenly devote themselves solely to her and miss Jesus make her sad. Some people manage to do it, despite the difficulty," Gabriel said.

"According to custom, any girl serving in the temple from the House of David must leave and enter into a suitable marriage when she comes of age. As long as Israel waits for the Messiah, this tradition must be followed because any girl could be his mother," Simeon said.

Mary stood silently and thought about Simeon's words. Several moments passed before she could respond. "Rabboni, I am certain the

Lord called me to consecrate myself a perpetual virgin here in the temple." Tears welled up in her eyes. She did not raise her voice.

Regina looked at Simeon. He walked to Mary and placed a hand on her shoulder. "I know you made a sacred vow never to wed. I would not ask it of you for the sake of tradition alone, but the Angel of the Lord appeared to me as well."

Mary spun to look at him. "God's messenger told me the Lord decreed that you must be given to the care of a spouse to fulfill your service to him on earth. He told me you would trust that God would provide you with a spouse who would honor your vows."

Several moments passed. Mary held her eyes to Simeon's feet. Regina moved closer and tried to see Mary's face. Mary slowly slid down to her knees. Regina joined her. Mary lifted her eyes to Heaven and began to pray.

"Eternal God and incomprehensible Majesty, Creator of Heaven and earth, you can do with me what you will, but my good Lord, I confirm and ratify anew my desire to remain chaste and have Thee for my Spouse alone. If it remains your will to do as you have ordained I put my trust in your servant Simeon." Tears fell down her face as she spoke, but she remained composed through her prayer. Regina didn't look away from Mary's face for a moment.

"Young lady, the strength of your faith does you great honor," Simeon said.

"It is my honor to serve the lord, rabboni," Mary said. Simeon helped her up and hugged her before leaving.

Suddenly, a host of angels materialized around Mary. Regina saw them and looked amazed.

"Gabriel?" Regina said.

"Ah, these are, let's say, the Holy Queen's attendants," Gabriel said.

"Does she know they are there?"

"Yes, she does. We angels are always around, Regina, but we can only be seen through the eyes of faith and by the will of God. Mary has known them since her youth. They are as natural to her as breathing," Gabriel said.

A new phenomenon occurred. Gabriel held Regina's hand while many hours passed quickly.

"Simeon will send messengers out to invite suitors from the house of David to call upon Mary. Another angel will tell Simeon that someone in Jerusalem will be the one chosen by God to be Mary's spouse. Rumors will spread of her beauty and bachelors will quickly come in hopes of marrying her." When Gabriel finished speaking, he and Regina stood outside, amongst a throng of men.

A man dressed in an elegant tunic climbed on the first temple step and turned to look at the crowd. "I should get her, I am the wealthiest. She will live like a queen." Many of the men booed.

A large man stepped forward. "Step down, fancy boy. At least I could protect her in the face of danger. I am the strongest one here." No one agreed, but no one dared to boo.

"As a servant of the temple, she needs a man of God. I am the holiest," a third said.

"And the humblest," the rich man replied. The crowd laughed. The strong man slammed his hand down on the "holy" man's shoulder and he crumpled to the ground. The crowd roared again.

Simeon watched this display from the shadows. He shook his head and walked back into the building. Regina followed him to his small room. He knelt beside his bed and hung his head.

"Are any of these men worthy of your precious servant?" He looked up and waited.

Gabriel took Regina and joined Mary in her room, which was even smaller than Simeon's.

"Lord, I accept the judgment of your servant, Simeon. I have faith you will guide him to provide for me. I pray you give him peace," Mary said.

Regina looked at Gabriel with amazement in her eyes. He nodded and they returned to Simeon.

Regina saw a little angel fly to Simeon's ear and whisper something. Simeon's expression changed from pained to hopeful. He got up and rushed from his room. Regina and Gabriel followed him to Mary.

"Mary, a heavenly voice assured me that the Lord has heard your prayers. He will provide your heart's desires and a husband to care for you as well."

"Blessed be the Lord," Mary said and a weight seemed to lift from her shoulders.

The vision shifted again and Regina joined Gabriel at the temple steps. Simeon walked before the multitude of suitors and raised his hands to get their attention. The oldest of the men had clearly seen many, many harvests while the youngest had not even left his parents' home.

"Gentlemen, the Lord has given me instructions for the selection process of a husband for Mary, the temple servant," Simeon said.

The men stopped their chatter and listened to the priest.

"If you do not have a walking staff, you have not been chosen by the Lord. You may go," Simeon said. Several shouts of protest went up.

"I wasted my whole day here," Regina heard one man say. She couldn't see who spoke, but others joined in his complaint.

"I am sorry, but the Lord has spoken," Simeon said. His voice rose over the protests and dozens walked away. When only men with walking sticks remained, Simeon continued. "Brothers, please hold out your staff and offer a prayer to the Most High for his will to be done."

The men shared confused looks but one after another held out their sticks.

Simeon looked up and down the row. He seemed to be looking for something. After several moments he frowned. Nothing unusual happened and the crowd began to murmur.

"What is this old fool looking for?" one man said.

From the distance, one of the men without a staff yelled out, "You made me leave for that?" He shook his head and walked away.

"What *is* he looking for?" Regina asked.

"The angel told Simeon to look for a sign from God. The Lord will mark the man chosen to marry Our Lady," Gabriel said.

Simeon continued to scan the crowd and began to pace. He scratched his head then rubbed his hands together. The shouts from the crowd began to grow louder. Some children had come to watch the spectacle. Their mothers came, collected them, and walked away in haste.

Then Simeon noticed something that moved him into action. Regina followed as Simeon walked to a man standing in the distance. The man watched the spectacle of the crowd from a dark corner of the temple square. Simeon looked at the face hidden behind the hood of his cloak.

"Joseph? Is that you?"

"Yes, what's happening here?"

"Suitors from the house of David are gathered here to marry a young maiden in service of the temple. You have a walking stick. You may join them, son of David." Simeon seemed to gain hope.

Joseph turned away from the watching crowd. "Rabboni, I have only by accident come into this assembly. I am here from Nazareth to make my annual thanksgiving and consecration to the Lord. Twenty years ago on my thirteenth birthday, he healed me of a grave illness after I prayed for deliverance. From the brink of death he raised me, and in return, I vowed to live chastely and offering my earnings to the poor. So you see, I do not wish to have the hand of your maiden in marriage."

"Please Joseph. The Lord promised to choose one of the men in this assembly to marry this girl and he has denied the rest. Only you remain to stand the trial. Can you deny the will of God?" Simeon said.

Joseph looked at the stares of the other men who failed in receiving the sign of favor from God. They whispered to each other as they glared at him. Joseph closed his eyes and bowed his head. After a lengthy silence, Joseph looked to Simeon. "What do you want of me?"

"Raise your staff."

Immediately, as Joseph raised his staff, a white lily sprang forth from it.

The crowd gasped.

"The Lord let me pick that miracle myself," Gabriel said.

"Cool! So, that's how God chose Joseph to be Mary's husband," Regina said.

"Actually, God chose Mary and Joseph for their roles long before this moment, he simply revealed it to Joseph right now."

Joseph and Simeon both gazed at the flower in wonder. Neither man moved at first, but finally, Simeon took Joseph by the elbow and had him climb the first step of the temple.

"Behold, the Lord has chosen his man," Simeon said.

Joseph remained silent while the crowd dispersed amidst grumbling. Regina watched the men depart after receiving the disappointing news, but she soon noticed the emotion on Joseph's face.

"What's wrong, Joseph?" Simeon said. "It looks like you have been sentenced to death."

"Rabboni, I told you, I have consecrated my purity to the Lord. I don't understand how this can be," Joseph said.

"Joseph, look at this lily. Its whiteness is a sign of the purity you and your future bride have both committed yourselves to," Simeon said.

"What do you mean?" Joseph said.

"Mary has also consecrated her virginity to God. She has no greater desire than to maintain this vow. The Lord has honored both of your wishes and fulfilled the tradition of the House of David."

"God be praised," Joseph said.

"I don't know what God wills for your future, but he has great plans for you," Simeon said.

"I will take Mary into my care and will honor what you have said all my days. May this great sign remind me always of the power of God."

"Thank you Joseph. I must tell Mary the good news," Simeon said.

He ran as quickly as he could into the living area. He found Mary cleaning the floor of the dining area.

"He is telling her the whole story of the lily," Gabriel said. Simeon continued talking to Mary in the background but Regina could not hear him.

"Why can't I hear what he's saying?" Regina said.

"There will be times when the scene will continue while we are talking. You will not miss anything important while we talk," Gabriel said.

Simeon finished telling the story. The expression on Mary's face did not change.

"The Lord is my shepherd, I shall not want," Mary said.

"Mary, you have always been like a daughter to me. I am happy the Lord will allow me to see you get married," Simeon said, his eyes filling with tears. She smiled and embraced him.

Regina stood and watched the happy scene. Then a thought struck her. "Gabriel, I feel like I should remember something about Simeon and what the Lord will…" Regina did not finish her thought before the scene changed.

Chapter 4
The Annunciation

Regina and Gabriel stood outside the Great Temple. The sun rose over the horizon.

"What were you saying?" Gabriel asked.

"Huh? I don't remember," Regina said. She furrowed her eyebrows and closed her eyes, trying to bring back her last thought. It didn't come. "Gabriel, I know where we are, but when?"

"I see you are getting good at figuring out the lay of the land," Gabriel said. "Tell me, do you know what an engagement is?"

"Yes, I remember when my uncle proposed to my aunt. They recently got married."

"And how was that?" Gabriel said.

"It was so much fun. I don't think I ever stopped dancing at the reception."

"How about your uncle and aunt?"

"They looked really happy," Regina said.

"I'm sure they were. Well, a few days have passed since the miracle of the lily. Simeon performed a betrothal ceremony for Mary and Joseph," Gabriel said.

"A what?"

"In their custom, betrothal would make couples legally married, even though they would live apart for months until the night of the wedding banquet. Joseph will now escort Mary back to Nazareth where she will stay with one of his family members until they are finally married."

"So that's what 'a virgin betrothed to a man named Joseph' means," Regina said. (Luke 1:27)

"That's right. Come, let us join them on their journey."

They stood outside the Great Temple for only a few seconds when the large outer doors opened and Mary and Joseph came out. Mary carried a small bag while Joseph had a large pack on his back. Simeon walked with them.

"May the Lord bless you both and keep you safe on your journey," Simeon said. He took Joseph aside. "I gave up a life of riches when I chose to serve the Lord, but he gave me one great treasure late in my life. Now, I give her to you. Guard her well, Joseph."

Joseph put his hand on Simeon's shoulder and looked him in the eyes. Nodding, he turned to rejoin Mary and they set out on their journey. Regina and Gabriel remained with Simeon as he watched them depart.

"Lord, I feel like my joy goes with her. When will you bring an end to my days and bring me home?" Simeon said, looking up to the sky.

A beautiful, white dove descended from the sky. It fluttered before Simeon and allowed him to catch it. It sat on his hand and looked at him. Simeon seemed to be entranced.

"It looks like it's talking to him," Regina said.

"Watch this," Gabriel said.

The dove took off. Simeon fell to his knees and began sobbing. "Thank you, Lord. Thank you." Tears fell from his smiling face as the scene changed.

"What happened with Simeon?" Regina asked. They traveled with Joseph and Mary on a dirt road. Another strange phenomenon occurred. Regina saw the vision like someone had pressed fast forward on a video machine. "And what's happening now?"

"You will have to wait and see what happens with Simeon, and you will see events unfold like this when they take a long period of time," Gabriel said. "It will only take a few seconds for Joseph and Mary to get to Nazareth, even though the trip would normally take several days. Despite the shortened time, you will remember everything that they said and did. You will probably feel disoriented afterwards."

Gabriel didn't exaggerate. The scene returned to normal speed and Regina had to put both of her hands to her head and close her eyes. She teetered almost to the point of falling.

"How did you like that ride?" Gabriel's call helped her regain her senses.

"Are all angels as cheery as you?" Regina said.

"Perhaps you will find out," Gabriel said. Regina made a sour face at the noncommittal answer.

"Oh, lighten up, child. If I revealed everything to you at once, what fun would that be?" Gabriel said.

"It would make things easier."

"Easier is not always better."

"I guess so," Regina said.

"What did you find interesting about the trip from Jerusalem?" Gabriel said.

Mary and Joseph continued to walk before them. Regina said, "I found it beautiful how much they wanted to serve one another. Mary kept offering to help Joseph with his load. He would decline and ask if he could carry her bag."

"Anything else?" Gabriel said.

"Their prayers amazed me. They praised God and shared so much of their interior lives. How could they be so holy?"

"Regina, you know what God chose them for. Do you think he would have entrusted the care of his son to ordinary people?"

"No, it wouldn't make sense," Regina said.

They entered a small town.

"Welcome to Nazareth, my lady. I left this town poor and return a rich man in your company," Joseph said. Mary blushed and lowered her head. "The treasures of your insight on the love of God have touched me. I do not mean to embarrass you; I only wish to express my gratitude for your company."

"My lord, I too wish to express my gratitude to the Almighty for providing me with such a devout and amiable spouse. I am thankful that your heart burns with love for the Lord like mine," Mary said.

Joseph smiled and they continued to walk through Nazareth. "Here is the house of my cousin Rachel," Joseph said, coming up to small building. "I think you will be able to stay here until the wedding."

The door opened and a woman came out of the house. "Joseph, I thought I heard a familiar voice. How was your trip?" She embraced Joseph, looked at Mary, and turned to Joseph with an inquisitive expression.

"Rachel, this is Mary." Mary looked up briefly to make eye contact and then returned her gaze to the ground. "Is Malachi here? I would like to ask a favor of you."

"Sure, he should be out back in the garden. I'll get him," Rachel said. In a few moments, she returned with a man who made Joseph look small. Dirt covered most of his clothing, but a large smile was on his face.

"Joseph, good to see you, and you must be Mary," Malachi said.

Again, Mary shifted her weight and barely looked up to see Malachi.

"Yes, she is my wife," Joseph said.

Rachel and Malachi exchanged a glance. Malachi opened his mouth to speak but hesitated.

"I was in Jerusalem on my pilgrimage, as you know, when Simeon, one of the temple priests, asked me to join some suitors for the right to take Mary, a temple maiden, as my wife," Joseph explained.

"I thought you would come to your senses one of these days," Rachel said.

"Why did she say that?" Regina asked. The scene froze.

"In those days, society expected men and women to get married. Even most of the temple priests married and had children. The people of Nazareth respect Joseph for his holiness and generosity, but they still cannot understand why he would choose to remain single," Gabriel said.

"Even his family?"

"Especially his family. Let's see what Joseph says."

Joseph continued. "I actually declined his invitation, but he insisted, saying the Lord had not bestowed a promised sign upon the others. He asked me to raise my walking staff. When I did, a beautiful lily sprouted from it. It appears the Lord chose me to be Mary's spouse."

"That's incredible," Malachi said. He looked back and forth between Joseph and Mary. Mary remained silent.

"We completed the betrothal in Jerusalem, but I hoped Mary could stay here until the wedding. Her parents have passed and she has no kin here," Joseph said. Mary slid closer to him, almost imperceptibly.

Malachi and Rachel turned to face each other. Rachel nodded slightly while Malachi showed hesitation. After a few moments, he pursed his lips and relinquished with a single nod.

"We will make room for you, Mary," Malachi said.

"We have a storage area that I can make into a bed chamber for you. Come with me, I'll show you," Rachel said.

"Thank you for your kindness," Mary said. She picked up her bag and followed Rachel into the house. The men remained outside.

"Thank you for taking Mary into your home," Joseph said.

"For you, brother, we will make it work," Malachi said. He chuckled and continued, "Maybe we will both have children soon so they can play together."

Joseph nodded and looked into the distance. "Yes, maybe."

The men engaged in small talk until the women returned.

"Mary is all set. She is in good hands with us, Joseph," Rachel said.

"Thank you, Rachel." Joseph turned to Mary. "I am sorry to leave you so soon, but I need to leave town to get some supplies."

"The Lord honors our work," Mary said. "I wish you safe travel."

Joseph made a slight bow and left on his errands.

Mary turned to Rachel. "Mistress, please allow me to serve you for your great generosity. I am at your disposal."

"Thank you, Mary. I don't have anything for you to do right now." Rachel thought for a moment and said, "You could go to Joseph's house and see where you will live when you get married. It's the only house with a wooden roof on the other side of the well, which you can find in the middle of town. I'm sure it could use a good cleaning. Joseph has been gone for several days."

"Do you have a broom I can take with me?"

"Sure." Rachel went into the adjoining room. She returned with a broom and handed it to Mary.

"Are you sure I can't help you with anything," Mary asked.

"No, not right now, dear. You can help clean up after dinner."

Mary took the broom and started to follow Rachel's directions to Joseph's house. A woman drew water at the well as and fixed her gaze on Mary as she approached and walked by. Mary flashed a small smile, but quickly bowed her head when the woman continued to glare at her. She hastened her pace to Joseph's house.

"Regina, here comes the moment that changed the fate of the world."

Joseph had crafted a small but sturdy house with a wooden roof Rachel described. Mary went inside and began sweeping the dirt that blew into the house during Joseph's pilgrimage to Jerusalem. She quickly finished sweeping and found little else to do. Joseph had everything in its proper place. Mary examined her future home and found a little niche Joseph made for prayer. Here Mary knelt and closed her eyes. Regina walked over and joined Mary in her posture. She listened to the young virgin's words.

"Father, I thank you for the fellowship of Joseph and for allowing me to live out my vows.

For you make me glad by your deeds, O Lord;
I sing for joy at the works of your hands.
How great are your works, O Lord,
how profound your thoughts!" (Psalm 92:4-5)

"I loved when she did that," Gabriel said.

"Did what?" Regina asked.

"She quoted the psalm that perfectly fit the situation. Knowing the scriptures makes your prayers more perfect," Gabriel said.

"Really?"

"Your Heavenly Father loves any prayers, Regina, but he honors those who honor him in knowing his inspired word."

Mary spent a long time in prayer. The sun disappeared from the sky, leaving the dark night in its wake. The sounds of the town quieted as the citizens of Nazareth prepared for bed.

Suddenly, Regina sensed something different. She opened her eyes and a sudden brightness descended from the darkening sky. Mary also became aware of the light and turned to behold a dazzling figure dressed in white. Upon taking a glimpse of the wonder, she gasped and prostrated herself before it. She remained on the floor for a few moments, before she raised her eyes to take another look. She barely made it past his feet before he spoke.

"Ave, Gratia Plena, Dominus te cum, benedicta tu in mulieribus." Regina heard the strange words through her ears, but in her mind she knew the stranger had said, "Hail! Full of Grace, the Lord is with you, blessed are you among women." (Luke 1:28) Then, she recognized him.

"It's you, Gabriel," Regina said.

"Yes."

"Did Mary understand you?"

"She understood me in her own tongue like you do in yours."

"You said 'Full of Grace' as a name, not a description," Regina said. She found it odd.

"Yes, watch, it troubles our humble maiden as well."

Regina turned and saw Mary maintaining her gaze on the angel's feet. The Blessed Virgin looked concerned. "Why do you call me Full of Grace? Only the Father in heaven deserves such accolade." (Luke 1:28)

"Fear not, Mary, for you have found grace with God," the old Gabriel said. His words freed Mary to look up at him. "Behold, you will conceive in your womb, and bring forth a son, and call him Jesus." Regina understood his name meant *God saves.*

Mary's eyes opened wide but she could not yet speak. Gabriel gave Mary a moment to absorb his words before he continued.

"He shall be great and shall be called the Son of the Most High. The Lord God shall give him the throne of his father David, he shall reign over the house of Jacob forever, and of his kingdom there shall be no end." (Luke 1:30-33)

Mary's look of awe changed to concern.

"How can this be, since I have not known man?" (Luke 1:34)

Gabriel seemed to grow in size. His presence filled the room, yet he spoke gently. "The Holy Spirit shall come upon you, and the power of the Most High shall overshadow you. Therefore the Holy One that will be born of you shall be called Son of God. And now, your cousin Elizabeth in her old age has also conceived a son; and this is the sixth month for her who was said to be barren. For nothing is impossible with God." (Luke 1:35-37)

Tears began to fall from Mary's eyes. The color left her face.

"What is she thinking?" Regina said.

"Do you really want to know?" Gabriel said. Regina knew this was a very serious question. She looked again at Mary and knew she never wanted something more in her life.

"Yes," Regina said. Gabriel nodded and something changed in Regina's mind. It felt as if Mary was on a stage and someone had flipped a switch on a spotlight focused directly on her emotions. Regina felt them as certainly as she knew her own.

"She's terrified, Gabriel," Regina said. She began to choke up herself. Her eyes filled with tears as she shared in Mary's fears.

"Do you know why?" Gabriel asked.

"She believes what you told her, but feels unworthy of the task. She knows how important being the mother of the Son of God would be, but she doesn't understand why God chose her," Regina said. She

34

thought about what she said and asked, "But I thought God created her especially for this very purpose. Why didn't you tell her that?"

"He did, but he also created her with free will like all other human beings. Even though the Father perfectly created Mary, her humility keeps her from believing it. She needs to accept this without any divine assistance."

Regina gasped. Something changed within Mary.

"She is making the connections of the amazing events within her life. The miracle of Joseph, the dreams of Simeon, all of it is coming together," Regina said. Regina's connection to Mary broke.

The fear left Mary's face and she once again turned to Gabriel. Regina had never seen such joy. She felt Mary release herself into the purpose the Father created her for.

"Behold the handmaid of the Lord; let it be done unto me according to your word." (Luke 1:38)

Gabriel smiled and bowed deeply before disappearing. A white dove flew onto the window sill. Mary looked at the beautiful bird. A moment passed in which the whole world became silent. Regina felt a chill in her spine. She looked to Mary and a more powerful sensation came over her.

Mary kept the radiant smile on her face as she closed her eyes and relaxed her body. Regina saw Mary rise off the ground and remain suspended in mid-air. She began to glow from head to toe in a radiant light. Then the light slowly receded from Mary's body but remained emanating from her belly. Regina saw Gabriel fall prostrate before Mary and joined him. Regina looked up and saw many angels appearing. They all fell in adoration as well. Mary opened her eyes. The dove had disappeared.

"Does she see these angels?" Regina said.

"Yes. Some are hers, but the others came from the heavenly court of Our Lord."

Regina made a connection to something Gabriel said earlier.

"The Ark of the New Covenant," Regina said.

"The first tabernacle of Jesus," Gabriel replied.

Regina's connection to Mary's emotions returned. She felt Mary's whole being sing glory to God and she could hear the angels reply in song.

"Why did I lose the connection you gave me?"

"The Holy Spirit did not want you to share in the emotions of the moment of the Incarnation, but now you may once again share Mary's mind," Gabriel said.

Suddenly, Mary heard a shrill scream come from the depths of some untold distance, speaking volumes of anger and hate. Regina shuddered, feeling Mary's fear over its meaning, but the joy of the presence of Jesus washed away Mary's concern.

"What was that horrible scream?" Regina asked.

"You heard Satan, cast into hell for the pride that kept him from serving man. The same arrogance blocked him from noticing God had created the very woman he would one day enter the world through. Satan felt the spiritual power of the moment of the Incarnation. It basically slapped him in the face. Now Satan knows the Christ child lives inside Mary," Gabriel said.

"Why? Why doesn't the Father keep them hidden and protected with an army of angels?" Regina said.

"Regina, God has begun his life on earth and intends to share the struggles and pains all people face. His mother accepted this too, and while she carries him for nine months, she mystically carries the Cross with him."

"She knows about the cross?"

"No, that would be too much for her heart to bear." Gabriel paused to let Regina reflect. "She simply knows that she will suffer while playing the role the Father calls her to in his saving plan."

"To be the mother of Jesus?"

"Yes, God made her the perfect vessel for his Son to enter the world through, but he also made her for you."

"For me?"

"For all humanity. She lived her life in complete service to God. He created her to model perfect faith to the world. He creates all people to join in his divine life and Mary will blaze a trail for all who wish to be disciples of Jesus," Gabriel said.

"This is all so much," Regina said. She stared at the Blessed Mother with her company of angels rapt in prayer.

"But Regina, the story has only begun. Mary left the Great Temple to become a greater temple. Now, she will witness to how one's faith must stand up to the darkness of evil."

"What do you mean?" Regina said. Gabriel's words frightened her.

"The devil will not rest now that he knows Mary is his greatest enemy. He will be on the attack," Gabriel said.

Regina looked at Gabriel. Her eyes open in fright. She turned back to Mary. "When will it start," Regina asked.

"Tonight," Gabriel answered. Darkness came.

Chapter 5
Mary and Joseph

Now I see you, you will never be free…

Regina heard the words and chills tore through her body. She regained her sight and looked around in desperation to figure out her surroundings. She found she knelt with Gabriel in Mary's tiny bed chamber. Rachel had cleared out her storage space to give Mary a private place to sleep. Regina could see she couldn't even stand up in the cramped quarters.

Now I see you, you will never be free…

The cold, dark voice whispered again.

"Is it …," Regina said. She couldn't finish the question.

"Yes, it is," Gabriel said.

"Can I hear her dreams?"

"You can do more than that. Close your eyes and tell me what you see," Gabriel said.

Regina closed her eyes.

"Mary is running with a baby. I am running with her. Something chases us. I can't see it." Regina kept her eyes closed, but wanted to open them. "I don't want to see it. Mary has never been this scared. She can't find her angelic company. She feels abandoned."

Mary stirred in her sleep. Her breath changed its rhythm.

"Please continue," Gabriel said.

"She holds the baby tighter. Now some people surround us. They mock her and call her names. Someone screamed 'Stone her!'" Regina gasped and shook her head. "I want this to stop, Gabriel."

"No, you need to see this," Gabriel said. His voice reassured her.

"Rocks are flying. Mary tucks the baby like a football and runs." Regina winced. "I can feel the pain as the rocks strike her. Wait! I see someone ahead."

"Who is it?" Gabriel said.

"I think it's Joseph. Yes, it is Joseph. We are getting closer. Why is he looking at the ground and ignoring us? Help us Joseph!" Regina begged. She couldn't speak anymore. She was breathless.

They got near when Joseph looked up. His eyes burned red and terrified Regina. His face seethed with contempt.

Joseph will NEVER believe you!

Mary awoke shaking and rolled onto her knees. Regina came to and moved to the side, waiting to see what Mary would do. Regina's heart pounded in her chest and she could see Mary in distress as well.

She watched as Mary remained focused in her prayer. Her lips quivered.

"I wish I would turn to God so easily when I need him," Regina said.

"Maybe you will," Gabriel said.

"Is that what you meant about the devil attacking?"

"Yes. When Mary said she would do God's will, she did what Eve could not do against the serpent. This means she fulfilled the ancient scripture: *'And I will put enmity between you and the woman, and between your offspring and hers; he will crush your head, and you will strike his heel.'"(Genesis 3:15)*

"I still don't understand why God didn't keep her hidden? Look at her suffering." Regina's eyes brimmed with tears.

"Regina, it was important that she faced this challenge and that you witness it." Gabriel failed to elaborate.

Regina thought about what the angel had said. She did not understand.

Gabriel answered her unspoken questions. "The king of the universe chose to send the Prince of Peace into the world, and he created his queen not as man would. He didn't make her a noblewoman, resplendent with riches. He made her a humble worker despite her royal lineage. He didn't want her to be free from the difficulties of life, living in ease and comfort. Why do you think that is?"

Regina relaxed as the answer came to her. "Because we are supposed to learn from her example?"

"Yes. She literally carries the Good News within her as his first disciple. As a disciple, she must endure hardship, first with him in her womb and then as his primary companion in life. No one will ever have the intimate connection Mary did with Jesus, but all can use her example as a model for how to love the Lord," Gabriel said.

Regina nodded. This girl would lead the way for millions, if not billions of Christians.

"*Blessed be the Lord, for he has heard the voice of my supplication,*" Mary concluded her prayer. (Psalm 28:6) The scene changed and Regina found herself in the main room of the house.

Mary entered in the faint glow of the first light of morning. She still looked shaken.

"Mary, awake already?" Rachel said, causing Mary to tense up. Regina saw the momentary panic on Mary's face and the subsequent relaxing of her shoulders when she recognized Rachel's voice. Without saying a word, Mary turned and gave Rachel a tiny smile. "Poor thing, you don't look like you slept well. I will try to make your bedding more comfortable. Okay?" Rachel said.

"No, no," Mary said. "I will get used to it. Can I help you with anything?" Regina could tell Mary's mind still had not put aside the nightmare they shared.

"You can get some water from the well. Take the jug on the shelf." Rachel pointed to a short shelf with a jug, some cups, and bowls on it. Mary walked over and stopped to examine the small structure. She ran her hand along one of the edges. Rachel added, noting Mary's admiration, "Joseph made it."

Joseph. Regina felt the darkness of the night return to dim the light of the morning. "I have to talk to Joseph," Mary said to herself. Regina heard the words as if Mary spoke them out loud. Mary turned her face from Rachel, unable to conceal her worry. "Of course. I will be right back." Mary grabbed the jug and hurried out of the house.

On the short walk to the well, Regina listened to Mary petition the Lord for strength. "Lord, what will I tell him? How can I make him see?"

The angels from the night before reappeared and travelled with them on their way to the well.

"Gabriel, I don't understand how I can see them," Regina said.

"In the Incarnation, the Word became flesh. The True Light entered the world. Witnessing this event, even as a vision, removed a curtain from your eyes that keeps people from seeing the world in its true form. The spiritual world remains hidden because the whole truth would overwhelm you," Gabriel said.

As they approached the well, Regina could see a woman drawing water with her back turned to them. A little girl, maybe four or five years old, played on the road between them and the well. She picked up small stones and piled them together. Regina thought she looked like her brother playing with his building blocks. The sound of Mary's footsteps caught the girl's attention and she looked up.

Mary continued walking until the girl stood up and ran toward her. Mary froze and watched as the child approached her without any caution. Mary smiled at her. The girl rolled her head side to side like a puppy. She looked into Mary's eyes for a moment but had her focus on Mary's midsection. The girl squinted for a moment. Suddenly her eyes popped open and she went down on one knee in a profound genuflection.

Mary turned to see if the girl's mother saw this strange behavior. She still had her back to them while she continued working at the well. Scanning the street, Mary saw no one else around. She turned to the girl, reached to pick her up, but hesitated.

"This child's complete innocence allows her to recognize Jesus through Mary as if she were made of glass. She innately knows how to behave before the King," Gabriel said.

"My father told me that's why we genuflect when we enter the church," Regina said.

"Really, what did he tell you?" Gabriel said.

"He told me, in the past, people would kneel when royalty passed by, but we don't have kings or queens in the United States, so we genuflect to the King of kings present in the tabernacle," Regina said.

Gabriel smiled and gave Regina a slight nod.

"Oh, I get it." Regina looked at the little girl and understood.

Mary's cheeks flushed and she motioned frantically with her hands. "Please little girl, get up."

The child stood up as the woman drawing water finished her work and turned to look at them. Mary's tension disappeared. She breathed a sigh of relief, but then, the girl ran to her and hugged her tightly around the waist. Startled, Mary put her hands up, shrugged her shoulders, and gave the mother an awkward smile.

The girl's mother took a quick step toward, clapped her hands once, and said, "Ruth! Let go of her!"

The girl held on tightly to Mary. "Lord, I don't know what this girl wants, but please help me," Mary prayed.

Regina felt her distress and in the next moment she felt a warmth radiate out from Mary's belly. The little girl's body shivered and she released the Blessed Mother. She started walking towards her mother, but stopped and turned back to Mary. "Bye, bye, pretty lady."

"Bye," Mary said. Regina thought the strange situation had ended until she saw the look on the mother's face.

Immediately upon hearing her child's parting words, the woman fell to her knees, with eyes and mouth wide open, waiting for her daughter to come to her. She wept openly as she held Ruth in her arms. Mary and Regina both thought she cried tears of joy, but Mary had to be certain.

"Mistress, I didn't do anything. What is it?"

"God be praised!" The woman mixed her tears with laughter. "Ruth has never spoken before. Her father and I thought she never would. We gave up hope that she would live a normal life, but now, now..." She pulled Ruth away from her to look at her. The woman held Ruth's smiling face in her hands and then pulled her back in a stronger embrace.

"What happened?" Regina asked.

"Our Lord answered his mother's prayer," Gabriel said.

"What?"

"She asked for help from Our Lord and he granted it." Regina's heart skipped a beat as she considered what the angel had related to her.

"I learned Jesus's first miracle occurred …," she left the sentence unfinished searching to make a connection.

"At the wedding feast in Cana? Our Lord chose that occasion to begin his *public* ministry. Did you think God would restrain the power of his love for thirty years? Just as he worked wonders in the Old Testament and privately touches people in your own time, he has always touched the hearts of the faithful."

"Cool."

"Did you notice anything else significant about this scene?"

Regina thought about his question. "No."

"That's okay, it can wait," Gabriel said.

Mary waited patiently as the woman took some time to regain her composure. The woman finally asked, "Who are you, stranger?"

Her joy put Mary at ease. "My name is Mary and I am betrothed to Joseph."

"The carpenter?" Mary nodded and gave a smile which Regina knew was forced.

"She feels uncomfortable talking about Joseph," Regina said. She could feel Mary's unease about the secret she hadn't shared with Joseph yet. Gabriel nodded.

The woman returned Mary's smile and released Ruth from her tight embrace. She stood and stepped closer. "The nicest man in town is finally getting married? I can see he waited for the right person." Mary blushed at the compliment. "Welcome to Nazareth, Mary. My name is Judith. You are staying with Malachi and Rachel, I assume?"

"Yes, Judith. I think I will stay with them until the wedding."

The little girl tugged on her mother's robe. "Let's show daddy, mama."

43

Judith started to become emotional again. She looked one more time at Mary. "I hope to see you again soon, Mary. The Lord be with you." They left Mary at the well and walked away.

"If she only knew," Regina said.

Gabriel laughed.

Regina watched as Mary retrieved the water and returned home. She didn't share the story of the girl at the well with her hosts. She managed to pass the rest of the morning and afternoon without complication. As evening approached, she began to feel anxious and Regina shared her stress with her.

After she ate dinner and helped Rachel clean up, Mary excused herself to go to Joseph's and pray. Mary walked away, but Gabriel held Regina at Rachel's house.

"I can't believe Joseph found someone as devout as he is," Rachel said.

"I didn't think it possible," Malachi said.

Rachel watched Mary in the distance. She turned to Malachi and said, "Pray with me."

"What? Now?"

"Yes. Let us pray that we may have the faith of Joseph and Mary."

Malachi also looked at Mary, barely visible in the distance, and shook his head. "I don't know."

"Just hold my hands, then," Rachel said.

Malachi turned toward Rachel and saw the passion in her eyes. He took her hands and Regina and Gabriel moved to Joseph's house.

Mary immediately knelt, closed her eyes, and began to pray.

"My friends, I know you are here. Pray with me, that I may know how to tell Joseph the news of the messiah."

She opened her eyes and her angels appeared around her. Some appeared to be male and others female. They joined Mary in her prayers.

"You are all so beautiful," Regina said.

"Thank you," Gabriel said.

"Why doesn't Mary just tell Joseph the truth?"

"What would she say? That I appeared to her and then the Spirit of God conceived a child in her womb? Joseph is a holy and devout man, and he believes miracles have happened in the past, but it would be very difficult for anyone to accept."

"But he has to accept it eventually, right?"

Gabriel answered her with a couple of nods and then gestured back towards Mary. Another angel appeared before them. Her lips moved but Regina could not hear anything. Mary appeared to hear something and listened intently.

"I understand. I will do as the Lord wills," Mary said to the new angel. The angel bowed to Mary and then disappeared.

"What does that mean?" Regina asked.

"You'll see," Gabriel said

Some time passed before footsteps sounded on the gravel road outside. "Mary?" a male voice called.

"Yes, Joseph," Mary said.

"Rachel said you were here," Joseph said entering. "How are you?"

"I am well. How was your trip?"

"Good. I got the supplies that I needed. Did anything interesting happen?"

Mary paused. Regina didn't think Joseph noticed. "I received word that my cousin Elizabeth is expecting a child and is in her sixth month. I have nothing against Rachel and Malachi, but if it doesn't trouble you I would like to spend the time before our wedding attending to her needs before her delivery."

Joseph raised his eyebrows. "Elizabeth? She is the wife of Zechariah, the old priest, right?"

"Yes, they say the child is a miracle," Mary said.

"I believe it," Joseph said. "Yes, of course, I will accompany you there as soon as possible."

"Thank you, Joseph, for understanding," Mary said. She closed her eyes and prayed.

"I am at your service, my lady."

Regina smiled at his devotion to Mary and the vision ended.

Chapter 6
Chosen

Sunday, December 1st
12:30 AM

Regina's sight returned and she recognized her living room. She looked at the digital clock on the stereo.

"Twelve thirty? How can only thirty minutes have passed during the visions?"

"Your mind experiences things differently when freed from your body," Gabriel said. "How does it feel to be back?"

"Strange and sad."

"How so?"

Regina looked into the distance. "I started to get used to being back in that time. I liked it. Everything moved slower and more relaxed. Coming back here ..., I can't explain it, I feel ... pressure," Regina said. She turned to Gabriel. He didn't offer any assistance.

"And the sadness?"

"I got to know Our Lady and Saint Joseph so closely. I miss them already."

"I understand. I always wished I could have visited them more myself. That brings us to the next step." Gabriel paused and grabbed Regina's hand. "I visited Our Lady and she accepted the Lord's will at an age only slightly beyond yours. Go has a great plan for you, but you need to accept it to proceed."

"Proceed with what?"

"I can't give you any specifics, only that his plan will be revealed to you over time."

"I saw Mary's response to your call, and I want to have her courage. I believe what you say, but I don't see what kind of plan God can have for me? I am only twelve years old. How can I do anything for him?"

"Regina, do you know what happened in the village of Fatima in Portugal in 1917?"

"My father told me that the Virgin Mary appeared to three children. I remember thinking how amazing it would be to see Our Lady."

"And...?"

"It was pretty amazing."

"Well, you remembered correctly. First, one of my fellow angels visited a young girl, Lucia, and her two cousins, Jacinta and Francisco, to prepare them for her visits. Then, Our Lady appeared to them before they even reached your age of twelve. She came once a month for six months, bringing a message of conversion for the world. God gave the children the strength to stay faithful amid ridicule and slander."

"My father said people didn't believe them so Our Lady promised a miracle during her last apparition."

"Do you remember what it was?"

"At her final vision, seventy thousand people saw the sun dance and spin in the sky. Many atheists in the crowd had come to mock the believers who were there to worship. They saw the miracle too." Regina surprised herself with her memory of the story.

"Then what happened?" Gabriel said.

"It had rained the whole night before and all morning before the apparition, so everyone was soaked. The sun fell from the sky and came crashing down to earth. Everyone panicked. People screamed out to God for mercy. Then it all ended and everything everywhere was dry."

"Good job Regina. You know what the most important part of this story for you right now is?"

"What?"

"Lucia, Jacinta, and Francisco were younger than you and they were simple peasant children. They had little formal education and little understanding of church doctrine. Despite this, Our Lord chose them to send his mother to, in order that his will be done. He helped them persevere; don't you think he will be there for you?"

A flood of emotion rushed inside Regina as the events of the night flashed through her head. She experienced more excitement in the last thirty minutes than in all of her life. She looked down and the carpet became blurry through the tears welling up in her eyes. Regina felt her heart pounding in her chest. She envisioned Mary hearing Gabriel's words and thinking about her own response. She thought of the look in Mary's eyes before she opened her mouth to reply. Regina saw so much faith, so much trust.

"Fiat," Regina said. As the word escaped from her lips, she knew it meant *let it be done* in the language of heaven, and it made her declaration more official. Suddenly, many angels appeared in the room.

Gabriel smiled widely. "I have more information for you. God will bless you with tremendous graces to aid you on your journey, and you will witness many marvels. The Joy of the Lord will be your strength. Still, the forces of darkness will gather against you when you begin your mission. Satan, in his arrogance, never sees who God chooses as his emissaries, but once you start to make some noise, the devil's spies will find you."

A familiar chill went down her spine. "What happens then? Can they hurt me? And what is the Joy of the Lord?"

"Your primary adversary will be your tempter; a demon specifically assigned to steer you from friendship with God. This vile creature knows your weaknesses very well and will use them to lead you to sin. This will take you off the path God wants you on."

Gabriel waited for Regina to think about what he said. "The Lord will not allow demons to hurt you physically, but they are experts at playing with your doubts and fears. They can also manipulate your emotions, for example, leading you to anger when God wants you to love. You must stay watchful and recognize their tricks."

"So, when I get angry at my brother, it's a demon's fault?"

"No. You have free will to make every final decision in your life. Angels and demons can only influence you partially."

"Will you always be with me, Gabriel, to help me see their tricks?"

"No, but I have someone here who will. I think you already know her." Gabriel gestured and Regina turned to see an angel step from out of the crowd. She emitted an increasingly brighter glow. She appeared to be about Regina's own age. Regina had never seen the angel before, but her soul recognized the angel's spirit.

"Lucy?" Regina spoke the name she had forgotten since her childhood. As a toddler, Regina amused her parents with her talk about her imaginary friend. She spent many hours a day with her friend. They shared tea parties, bubble baths, and sleepovers. At age five, she believed in the reality of her friend when everyone else called her "imaginary." Now she knew the truth.

"Regina, meet your guardian angel." Joy and sorrow hit Regina together. It brought her great happiness to be in the company of her lost friend again. At the same time, she felt deep sorrow that she forgot about Lucy as she grew up. She learned about guardian angels from her mother but had already stopped playing with Lucy by then.

"How could I have forgotten you?" Regina asked. Tears trickled down her cheeks.

Lucy glided over to Regina. "Don't be sad. In your youthful innocence you knew me, but as children grow older they lose touch with their angel. Some people keep their relationship with their angel through prayer, but humans can only see or hear us through the will of God."

"I am still sorry I forgot you. You were such a good friend and I ignored you until you left." Regina looked away from Lucy, unable to make eye contact.

"I never left you, Regina." Lucy smiled widely, warming Regina's sadness. "A guardian angel never abandons their charge. Despite your sins and your flaws, we always keep trying to lead you on the right path. Some people make it harder than others, but you can't shake us. Remember how you woke up today right before midnight?"

"Yes, I couldn't believe how lucky that was."

"Not quite. Even though you couldn't sense me anymore, I still could call to you in your dreams. I can usually do the same thing every morning before school, yes?"

"I hardly ever need my alarm. You wake me up two minutes before it goes off?" Lucy smiled. "So, if my tempter comes after me, you are going to protect me?"

"Yes," Lucy said. "I know the demon well. He doesn't know about your mission yet. Gabriel has managed to make his way around here unnoticed."

"How can he do that? Don't the demons always know where the archangels are? They have to be noticeable," Regina asked.

"Darkness has difficulty entering the light," Lucy explained. "After all of these years, the devil still doesn't understand the Father. He is always taken by surprise when the Lord sends children or the meek to speak his word. Throughout history, he has raised them up, free from the demon world, because they never expect it. Before God became incarnate through an obscure maiden, Satan had no idea how the Messiah would come." Regina looked around and saw the other angels had left. "The Creator of Heaven and Earth took flesh in a human's womb and hell still looked for a triumphant appearance in a majestic form. The evil one could not foresee the King of kings beginning life as a helpless baby."

"He figured it out though, right?" Regina already knew the truth, thinking back to horrible scream she heard and the frightful voice that said, *now I see you, you will never be free.*

"Yes, the dark one eventually figures out who God has chosen to do his work, but his misunderstanding of God's love keeps him from stopping the Lord's will." Lucy paused.

"So, evil will find me?" Regina asked. Her lips quivered. She could not control them.

"Not before we can prepare for it."

"I don't know if I can do this." Regina didn't mean to speak her thoughts out loud. She didn't want Lucy to think she was a baby.

Lucy became alert. "It has begun. Your tempter sensed weakness in you and planted a little bit of doubt to see if you would turn against what you know is good and right."

Regina marveled at how Lucy sensed her thoughts. "Is that how he will attack?"

"Yes. Right now, he still doesn't know about the Father's plans for you."

"Neither do I," Regina said.

After a beat, they both laughed at the situation. Lucy continued, "You will in time. For now, your tempter sensed your distress and knew something about your faith caused it. He tricked you into doubting yourself, that's all."

"Why shouldn't I doubt myself? I'm not Our Lady. She showed great courage and greater faith. I am afraid I won't be able to live up to the Lord's expectations."

"Do not be afraid, Regina. As one of your favorite songs says

If you pass through raging waters in the sea you shall not drown
If you walk amid the burning flames you shall not be harmed
If you stand before the fires of hell and death is at your side
Know that I am with you through it all."

Lucy held Regina's hands.

"I feel a lot better knowing I have you with me," Regina said.

"Unfortunately, you won't always be graced with the ability to sense me, so you must be prepared to battle the dark forces on your own," Lucy said. "Your training begins tonight."

"My training?" Regina asked.

"Yes, pray with me," Lucy said. The angel slipped onto her knees. Regina did the same, and once on her knees, entered another vision, different from the earlier ones.

She saw herself in a room with various weapons on the walls. Swords, staffs, spears, and clubs hung all around her, shining in the light of the torches that stood in several spots in the room. The place reminded her of the hall of weapons at the museum. In addition to the weapons, three suits of armor stood in the corners of the room. They appeared lifeless, but ominous, nonetheless.

"What is this place?" Regina said.

"You tell me. I wanted your mind to think about battle and you brought us here. When you imagine warfare, why do you think of this?" Lucy said.

"I guess because my family and I recently saw the *Lord of the Rings* movies."

"I understand. Take the sword off the wall at your left."

Regina looked to the left and saw an enormous sword with a large handle. "It must weigh a ton," Regina said.

"It would, if it were real," Lucy replied, smiling.

The sword rested with the blade pointing downward on an elaborate hook dangling from the wall. Walking closer, Regina realized the sword stood as tall as her. Lucy's order seemed certain, so she grabbed the handle and tried to lift the sword from its housing. She couldn't move it at all.

"It's ... too ... heavy," Regina said, puffing between each word.

"Regina, we are in your mind right now, the sword doesn't really exist," Lucy said.

Still unclear of the situation, Regina said, "Okay, but you told me to take it from the wall."

"One thing you need to understand about human existence is you are mind, body, and spirit. All three are interconnected. They can work together to make you stronger or against each other to break you apart."

Regina shook her head to show Lucy she didn't follow.

"The devil wants your soul, but he assaults it through your body and mind. You will need your body and mind to fight back."

Regina thought to a similar lesson her father had taught her. "The posture of your body helps your mind focus on what your spiritual goal is at any given time," he told her. "We sit while learning about

God's word, stand when listening to the words of Jesus, and kneel in adoration of God."

She heard her father's voice say, "Always begin your prayers…"

"In the name of the Father, and of the Son, and of the Holy Spirit," Regina proclaimed, making the sign of the cross in her vision and in real life. The sword leapt from its station, spun in the air, and fell into her waiting hands. The light gleamed off the marvelous blade. She examined it closely and swung it freely as if it were made of cardboard.

"Wow!"

"Very good!" Lucy replied. "You are a natural."

Regina smiled and began to swing the sword around wildly. Suddenly, the weight of the sword became immense and she dropped it with a clang.

"What happened?" Regina asked.

"You forgot the nature of this spiritual exercise. This imagery exists only to help your mind focus on fighting evil through your prayers. You let your mind wander, thinking about the fun of swordplay instead focusing on the power of God. You can use your own words or rehearsed prayers, but when you battle the darkness, you must remember to pray."

Regina realized she had forgotten that a prayer had gotten the sword from its rack. She decided to start over.

"In the name of the Father, and of the Son, and of the Holy Spirit," Regina said. The sword again leapt into her hands. This time she continued, "Lord, help me understand this new meditation Lucy has shown me. I want to do your will and be strong when the enemy pursues me." Speaking these words, she twirled the sword like a great warrior in a movie.

"Yes, that's it, now continue with your favorite prayers," Lucy said.

"Our Father, who art in Heaven, hallowed be thy name." Regina felt strength in her limbs she had never felt before. She tried to jump and flew through the air so quickly that she stunned herself and barely landed without tumbling over. She kept praying and tried a flip. She over-rotated and fell forward on her knees.

"You'll get used to it. Keeping focused in prayer takes time and discipline. You won't always need this image for spiritual battle, but for now, let it help you," Lucy said.

Regina spotted a small shield hanging from the wall in front of her. "Hail Mary, full of grace, the Lord is with thee…" She held out her hand and the shield released from the wall and came to her. She came to a full realization that prayer could act as a weapon and a defense against the enemy. With a sudden clanking noise, the suits of armor came alive and moved towards her, wielding small swords.

"Regina, feel the power of the Holy Spirit!" The angel knew Regina's pounding heart filled her ears.

Regina rushed at the first soldier praying, "Glory be to the Father." She slashed her sword, taking off its arms. "And to the Son," she took out the next dummy's legs, making it fall over helpless. "And to the Holy Spirit," she said as she lopped off the final dummy's head, leaving it once again lifeless. The vision drifted away and she finished, "As it was in the beginning, is now, and ever shall be, world without end. Amen." She opened her eyes and found herself back in her house with Lucy.

"Cool," Regina said.

"Yes, but you must remember you pictured the battle in a way that helps you focus. If you dwell on the violence you imagined, you will lose that focus. Instead, meditate on the peace that comes from ridding yourself from the effects of the evil one. The real battle occurs in the spiritual realm, which you cannot see. As you grow in spiritual warfare, you will visualize this world differently, but the Joy of the Lord will always be your strength when you fight," Lucy said.

What is the Joy of the Lord? Regina wanted to ask the question but another one raced its way to her lips.

"How will I know when that is?"

"Your tempter won't come at you like those suits of armor. He will attack you in subtle ways: when you doubt yourself, when you feel angry, and when you feel lonely. When your thoughts turn away from God and to some pointless distraction, know he is working. For now, the time has come for rest."

Regina's eyes opened wide. "How will I tell my parents?"

"Which parent would be most receptive?"

"I guess my dad. He always tells me stories about stuff like this, but I still think he won't believe me."

"Don't worry, simply tell your story, and if your father still is unsure, tell him …" Lucy told what to say to her father as her weary mind and body began drifting to sleep.

That's such a strange thing to say to him, she thought as she fell asleep.

Chapter 7
Angels and Demons

Sunday, December 1st
6:00 AM

"God bless her sleep," Lucy prayed. She moved swiftly away from the Andrews' house in the spirit plane.

What does heaven want with me right now? Time and space mean different things to purely spiritual beings, but they still mean something. *I need to get back to her.*

She continued on her brightly lit path. In the distance, a greater brightness glowed. Suddenly, a fog cut through her path, bringing a shadowy darkness with it. She slowed her pace and cautiously came to a stop. She scowled as she looked around. "I know you are there."

"Hi, Lucy," a gruff voice said from out of the shadows.

"Right on time to ruin my good mood, Tenebraus," Lucy said.

Hearing his name, a tall, skinny boy stepped out from the heavy mist to the right of Lucy. He wore a sleeveless black tee shirt and ripped blue jeans. His shoes might have been white at one time but now looked grey and tattered. One had a hole where a toe with a long dirty nail poked through. Lucy glanced at it and felt sickened by its grotesque, reptilian look.

"Why so happy?" The voice spoke with an eerie calm. "Something going on with … our little friend?"

"She is not your friend."

"I'll know soon enough, so you might as well tell me now."

"It is none of your business." Lucy went to walk around him, but he stepped to block her path.

"Your business is my business. Save me some time and tell me what the deal is."

"Why would I help you?" Lucy glared at the demon.

"Admit it, you like me," he said. He smiled and nodded, trying to charm the angel.

"I'm not a human. Your tricks don't work on me. I can see right through you," she said. The smile dropped from his mouth and his appearance changed. Only a dark silhouette of his previous form remained. Lucy pushed through him. The shadow broke as she walked through and reformed on the other side.

"Since you have somewhere to be, I'll drop in on a little someone who is unattended."

Lucy froze in her tracks and turning her head to the side said matter-of-factly, "Go ahead, she just said her prayers before bed. See how far you get."

Lucy continued on her way, leaving Tenebraus behind. "You have it easy right now, Lucy. Wait until she becomes a teenager! I'll have my day. She will be mine," he said. Lucy disappeared before he finished his rant. He turned to look in the direction of the Andrews' house. He shook his head, cursed, and slunk off, dejected.

"Lord, watch over Regina in case that sneak tries to torment her while I'm away," Lucy said as she hurried on her way. She approached heaven quickly.

"He won't bother her tonight," a voice said. An old angel appeared before her.

"Consua, you old sneak. What are you doing here and why do you look older every time I see you?"

"I want you to think I am really wise."

"I already believe you are wise. You don't need to look like an old man."

"Okay, I just like it," Consua said. Lucy laughed. "So, this assignment is different, yes?"

"I was just thinking that." Lucy nodded. "I loved all of my humans. Only a few of them ever knew me, but I fought my hardest for each of them." Lucy turned her head down and started to cry.

"Forgive yourself, Lucy. We have all lost people to the darkness."

"The humans say there is no greater sorrow than a parent burying a child," Lucy said.

"Yes, I have heard that," Consua replied.

"But a parent gets to see their child again in heaven, but when we lose a human, we never ..." Lucy couldn't finish her sentence.

"Regina will not fall," Consua said.

"I am afraid I will not be strong enough to help her," Lucy said.

"We are all cheering you on. The guardians of those the Lord chooses for greatness get to experience the best and worst of what we can face. You can do it."

"Thanks Consua. It helps to know you believe in me."

"As the Lord chose Regina to spread his message, he chose you to be her guardian. Be honored, but be prepared. You know how they will test her."

"Thank you for your advice. You have always been such a great teacher," Lucy said. "Do you know why I have been summoned here?" She looked up at the heavenly edifice stretching forever in every direction. It mesmerized her.

"You really do enjoy beholding the marvel of heaven, don't you?" Consua asked.

"I can see God's perfection in it. It appears different every time I come back, but always more beautiful."

Consua smiled. "Yes, I understand." He reached into his robes and produced something. "I have this to give to you," Consua said, handing Lucy a small plastic card reflecting the light around them.

Lucy examined the simple prayer card. "What am I to do with it?"

"You need to place it on Regina's father's dresser so his guardian can guide him to it, when the time is right."

"The Lord works in mysterious ways." She nodded. "Is there anything else?"

"No, God be with you," Consua concluded and he faded from her view.

"Thank you," Lucy said. She bowed before heaven and turned to leave.

Tenebraus sat in a dingy waiting room. He glanced around at the grime and filth surrounding him on the chairs, countertops, and walls, with a sneer on his face. He tried to stop his bouncing knees with his trembling hands but couldn't. He took in several deep breaths and exhaled forcefully through his mouth. The receptionist watched this display and shook his ugly head.

"Come in," a coarse voice said. The office door had swung open on its own. A foul stench wafted out. Tenebraus walked through the door and it shut itself behind him. Every disgusting detail of the previous room intensified here. Roaches flirted with the edges of the shadows and flies buzzed around the few lights adorning the ceiling.

"Sit." The being across the desk glared at Tenebraus. The nameplate on the desk read Miseros. He appeared to be more of a giant slug than a humanoid.

"What do you want? I'm kinda busy out there," Tenebraus said. His bravado lacked conviction. He tried to look comported but his hands continued their shaking.

"Silence!" Miseros snickered as Tenebraus flinched. The minor demon's shoulders slumped and he averted his gaze. "You have accomplished nothing with your human."

"I... I... I've gotten her to yell at and strike her brother. She has thrown tantrums at times."

"You offer me child's play?"

"She's only twelve."

"Other tempters get their twelve year olds to steal, swear, and even sacrifice their innocence."

Tenebraus remained silent at first, but suddenly realized something. "Wait, she broke a commandment. She lied today. I could sense it."

"You could sense it? You didn't see her lie?"

Tenebraus turned white. His eyes opened wide. "No."

"Why not?"

"I couldn't get inside the house to see her."

"Had the family prayed together that day?"

"No."

"Did they have the house blessed recently? Don't lie to me. You know I will check on this with my special agents."

"No."

"So, you are saying without any special spiritual protection on their house, you couldn't get in and YOU DIDN'T BOTHER REPORTING THAT!" Miseros rose to his full height with his voice.

Tenebraus, trembling, couldn't answer, and Miseros didn't care to hear his response. He slowly oozed back into his chair and continued, "Something is going on there, Tenebraus. Something good and righteous and I don't like it." Tenebraus relaxed a little. "You need to find out what is going on or I will find someone who can." The door swung open, and Miseros swung his chair around. He left the dark office speaking under his breath, "I hate humans."

Chapter 8
Father Knows Best

Sunday, December 1st
9:12 AM

Regina's eyes popped open the next morning to sunlight pouring into her room. She stretched and rolled out of bed, ready to start her day, until she looked at her clock. It reminded her of the previous night. She wondered out loud, "Lucy? Are you there?"

Regina heard no response. She decided to try something different. "In the name of the Father, and of the Son, and of the Holy Spirit." Crossing herself, she continued, "God, thank you for last night and for the gift of my angel."

"You're catching on," a whisper spoke in her heart.

Regina smiled and continued to pray. "Will I not see or hear you anymore?"

"Maybe, but most of our relationship will be like this." Regina braced herself for this answer, so it didn't bother her as much as she thought it would.

"As long as you are with me," Regina said as she hopped out of bed.

"Always."

Regina got out of bed and took her church clothes out of her dresser. She began to take off her pajamas, but stopped halfway. She poked her head out of her room and sniffed the air. Smelling something cooking, she laid her clothes out on her bed and headed downstairs. She found the table set for three. Her brother already sat at his spot and her mother continued her cooking in the kitchen.

"Mommy, where's daddy?" Regina's mother finished making a special breakfast treat of French toast and sausage. Breakfast usually consisted of cereal or frozen waffles.

"He went to the store to get some things for school, honey. He should back around ten thirty or so. Why?"

Her mother couldn't see her grimace in the kitchen. Her brother wouldn't have cared, even if he wasn't completely engrossed in trying to cut his French toast with the wrong end of his butter knife.

"Oh, no big deal," she lied. Regina felt badly, but she had felt peace about her decision to speak to her father, and she didn't see how she could tell her mother, *I have some huge news for him I don't want to tell you.*

"God knows your sorrow. It's alright Regina," Lucy let her know.

"How many sausages do you want?" her mother asked her, not noticing Regina's anguish in the least.

Regina answered, "Two please," and then wondered, *did you have something to do with my mom not noticing?*

I had a little help from a friend. Regina sent a prayer of thanks to her mother's guardian angel and prepared herself to feast on her mother's cooking.

"How about you, Manny?" his mother said.

Regina's brother, Emmanuel, didn't hear her. Through the big sliding glass door, he had spotted a squirrel crawling on the back porch. He grinned from ear to ear as he tracked the creature on its journey. It didn't take much to distract his eight-year old mind.

"Manny?" her mother repeated a little louder.

"What?"

"How many pieces of sausage do you want?"

"Two please," he mimicked. He smiled at Regina, enjoying himself. Regina often felt God created Emmanuel to annoy her, but she would have to admit that his following her lead touched her. She found a sense of responsibility for her little brother and felt pride that she usually did a good job of keeping him out of trouble.

Her mom gave them their food. "Now, after you eat you need to finish all your schoolwork, pick up your rooms, and clean the living room. You guys left all your toys out yesterday. We will go to church at noon when daddy gets back."

"Can't we relax," Emmanuel said.

"You already got to sleep in, Manny. Religious Ed usually starts at eight-thirty and it's already an hour past that."

"Okay," he said, resting his head on his left hand and pushing his sausages around with his fork.

"Hurry and eat it while it's still hot," his mother told him.

Regina did just that and finished her homework quickly and went up to her room to clean up, leaving her mother to help Emmanuel with his reading. After putting her dirty clothes in the hamper, making her bed, and straightening up her desk, she left her room to go downstairs. By this point, her brother was cleaning his room while his mother supervised. Regina began putting her toys away. She only got through a fraction of the work when she heard the garage door open and her father's heavy footsteps above her.

"Katherine? I'm home," a voice called out. A few seconds later, footsteps began to sound on the stairway.

"Hi daddy."

"Hey G, how's it going?" Her father stood six feet tall, had broad shoulders, and a broader smile. This smile comforted the nerves rattling within Regina. He took the two bags in his hands and placed them in his office before he turned to wait for her response.

"Fine. Just doing some work. Did you get anything for me?"

"No, sorry, I only got some supplies for school."

"What did you get?"

"We are studying the Pythagorean Theorem next in class and I needed some cardboard to use for demonstrations."

"Cool," Regina said.

"Any exciting news?"

"Not today…," Regina said, looking down at her toys. She turned to her father who had caught her words and looked at her waiting. "Something happened last night. I think."

Her father's smile straightened and concern spread across his face. "You think? Are you alright?" he sat down on the couch and Regina joined him.

At first, she thought of how she would break down the story, but as soon as she began, the whole thing came out, seemingly in one breath. She lost the awareness of her own speech the deeper she got into her visions. Her father listened with a look that went from concerned to curious to awestruck. He didn't speak throughout her entire speech, and when she finished, he sat on the couch like a stone, frozen in wonder. Several agonizing moments for Regina passed and she feared he would never speak again. Then, the words Lucy told her the night before as she fell into sleep came back to her clearly. "Oh, and Our Lady really wants you to be her knight again." She finished her words and shrugged her shoulders.

Her father's eyes showed his shock and began to moisten with tears. "Wha…?" Tears began to fall from his eyes.

Regina sat motionless, stunned by this sudden change. She didn't know what to do as her father worked through his emotional burst.

"I believe you, Regina. I believe you." He pulled her close in a tight hug. At first, she only thought to hold on tightly to him, as his sobs frightened her, but then she could actually feel the joy radiating from him.

"What is it daddy? What did I say?"

"I didn't know what to think at first. I thought maybe you simply had a marvelous dream, but when you told me about Our Lady wanting me back as her knight, I knew everything you saw must have come from heaven."

"Why?"

"Back in college, I became a member of the Militia Immaculata. It helped me picture myself as a warrior for God. Saint Maximilian

Kolbe started this special movement in Poland many years ago. You remember him, don't you?"

"Not really."

"He was a Polish priest who spread the faith in innovative ways, fought the enemies of the church, and resisted the Nazis during World War II."

"Oh, didn't he go to one of those camps?"

"Yes, the Nazis sent him to Auschwitz, one of the most notorious concentration camps, for harboring Jewish refugees at his church. Father Kolbe ministered to everyone there, Jews, Christians, and non-believers alike, keeping their spirits up despite the hopeless conditions. One day three people escaped and as a warning to those who remained, ten men were selected to die of starvation."

"Didn't he take the place of one of the men?" Regina asked.

"Yes, the man begged the prison guards for mercy because he had a wife and children. Fr. Kolbe volunteered to take the place of the man. He encouraged the men, for two long weeks, to stay strong in their faith and remember that a better life awaited them. At the end, only he remained. He raised his arm to his jailor to calmly accept the lethal injection which ended his life."

"Whoa," Regina said. "Is that why you always take the name Max when we play computer games?"

"Yes. I chose Maximilian as my Confirmation name. Every day before Mass, I would kneel in prayer and renew my vows to Our Lady, to fight for her Son, in the example of her faith. I would say, 'Your knight awaits his orders,' and feel her call me to persevere in the battle against the devil."

"So that's what that means." Regina thought about her own training in spiritual battle. She felt proud she would be following her father in this tradition.

"I never told anyone about my devotion, not even your mother. Over the years, I forgot about this important part of my prayer life. I don't even remember when. It slipped away without me noticing.

When you reminded me of that special time, I felt the joy of all those memories and the sorrow for disappointing our Lord and Lady."

"My guardian angel told me you would believe me when I said that."

"I do." Her father smiled at Regina. Suddenly, he jumped up off the couch and went over to the phone. He dialed a number and waited for someone to pick up on the other end. He drummed his fingers on the table top as he waited.

"Hello, Father Joe?" Regina had never seen her father's face shine the way it did at this moment. He seemed like a child. "Yeah, it's Mark. I wouldn't think of calling you before Mass, but this is important." Regina listened as her father explained her whole story to their priest. After several minutes he stopped talking and listened for the response. It took some time before Regina heard a voice begin through the receiver. Mark's face strained with concentration on the priest's words. Regina waited without moving a muscle.

"Uh huh, uh huh," her father said before he ended with, "Thank you, Father. I will." He hung up the phone and turned to Regina. "He says he wants you to stay after church today and talk to him."

"Okay."

"Why the sad face?"

"I'm not sad. I just don't know how I am going to make it through the next two hours."

"It's alright, your mother and I…" Her father gasped. "We should tell your mother."

"Can you tell her?"

"Why?"

"I don't know what I would say."

Her father looked at her for a moment and said, "Okay. Wait here."

"What do you think she will say?"

"I have no idea," he said, smirking.

Regina's parents talked for a while in their room before they came out. Her mother came downstairs and gave Regina a hug and a kiss. When she pulled away, she smiled. Regina knew she had nothing to worry about.

The family remained silent on the short ride to church. Regina did not find this awkward, instead, she felt peaceful. Even Manny didn't engage in his usual car ride chatter.

As she got to the top of the stairs of the parish meeting hall, she saw Father Joe wearing his purple Advent vestments and shaking hands with parishioners entering the church. Waiting in the line going in, she expected something special to occur when she finally got to him. Instead of some special recognition or even a wink, he gave her his usual warm welcome of "Good morning, Regina" and a hand shake. A little disappointed, she lumbered slowly to the pew her mother had chosen and sank to one knee in a deliberate genuflection. She stared at the tabernacle, dwelling on what she had seen the night before. She felt if she stayed there long enough, Jesus himself would come and answer her endless set of questions. Instead, her father got to the pew and upon kneeling, knocked Regina out of her trance. She got up and settled in for the opening song.

She kept thinking at some point during Mass, Father would look over and acknowledge the secret appointment they had. This never happened. Father behaved normally and nothing he did led Regina to believe he had talked to her father that morning. She didn't know how he could be so calm because she felt a fire raging inside her. Dwelling on this, she spaced out through the Liturgy of the Word, missing all three readings and Father's homily.

Her lack of focus continued until the Nicene Creed. Since she did not have the words memorized yet, she began reading from the Missal as usual, "I believe in God, the Father Almighty, maker of heaven and earth, of all things visible and invisible." This broke the haze a little. *Lucy is invisible.* She continued reading, starting to think about the words until she said, "For us men and for our salvation, he came down from heaven. And by the Holy Spirit was incarnate of the Virgin Mary, and became man."

As she spoke those lines, she remembered the Annunciation from the night before. The power of the visions enveloped her and drew her into participating keenly for the rest of Mass in a way she had never thought possible. She said all of the prayers with fervor, sang the songs in a beautiful voice that didn't seem to be hers, and after she received Holy Communion, she felt like she floated back to her pew. While she knelt in thanksgiving, she could feel her body and her soul in union with Jesus. She looked around and saw many different families leaving church right after Communion and felt a deep sorrow in her heart.

When Mass ended and Father walked down the aisle away from the altar, he finally looked at Regina and made a head motion to her towards the vestibule. She looked at her father.

"You'd better get going."

They walked out together and waited on the side as Father Joe shook hands with people as they left. When they were finally alone, Father Joe called Mark Andrews over and whispered something to him. Her father nodded, came to take Emmanuel and Katherine's hands, and announced, "Father said to pick you up in two hours. He will meet you in the front of the church in two minutes." When Regina looked up, she saw Father had left the vestibule. Her family left and she waited for a moment before heading back into the chapel. She walked to the front and sat in a pew in front of the tabernacle. She felt herself falling back into a trance when she heard a familiar voice.

"Are you ready?" She turned ready to tell her story but stopped when she saw the priest carrying some rags and spray bottles.

"I guess so," Regina replied, confused.

"Good." He handed her the cleaning supplies and said, "You can clean the candle holders and bottom windows on the north side of the church, and I will take the south."

Stunned, she took them without saying a word, and headed over to the votive candles she had lit many times growing up. She cleaned the bronze holders at the feet of the Mary and infant Jesus statue. He held his little hand up in a blessing.

"Blessed Mother, how many times did you do work like this in the temple when you were my age?" Regina said. She cleaned a whole row before she stopped and turned to look at Father Joe, who still worked on the other side of the church. He seemed to be humming a tune and keeping to his business. Though confused, she didn't think she should question her orders. Still, when would he talk to her about her visions? At long last she finished her cleaning. She looked over at Father Joe, who knelt in a pew in front of the altar.

She walked over to him and said, "I'm done, Father."

"Already? I should call your parents to pick you up since you are done so early." He reached into his pocket and pulled out his cell phone. She watched in shock as he dialed her parent's number slowly, one digit at a time. *What was happening?*

"Don't say anything," Lucy's voice spoke. "Don't complain he hasn't heard your story yet. Just wait." Regina didn't understand but she followed her instructions.

When Father Joe finished dialing the number, he let it sit there on the screen, his finger resting on the green call button. He seemed to be waiting for something. Slowly he moved it away and said, "You have passed my test, Regina."

"Excuse me Father?"

Looking directly at the tabernacle he began, "For a while now, I have felt I would soon be helping someone on their spiritual journey in a very special way. I fasted and prayed to prepare for that person when he or she came. When your father called me this morning, I thought you might be the one, but to be sure I prayed for the Lord's guidance."

"I don't understand."

"He responded to my prayer with the test of humility you just passed. Someone who would make up visions to get attention would not have the humility to do the menial work you just did, let alone not say a word when I prepared to call her parents. I knew what your father told me had to be true and you are the one I've been waiting for." Father Joe finally looked up at her and smiled.

Regina smiled back and began to tear up out of happiness. Father Joe moved over, giving her space to sit down next to him. She took a deep breath and began to recount the whole story to Father Joe while he listened with great interest. When she finished, he sat quietly for some time.

"I would like to tell you I know exactly what we should do next," Father Joe smiled in a friendly way that Regina had seen for years, "But I can't."

"Should I be frightened, Father?" Regina asked.

"No, child. Trust in God and have no worries. The Joy of the Lord is your strength," Father Joe said.

What is the Joy of the Lord?

Before Regina could ask, the priest spoke, "I wish I could tell you more than this Regina. I feel both of our spiritual lives are about to become very interesting. You have obviously been blessed, but now you will need even more grace to move forward. Your prayer life will need to intensify. Let's start now."

"Yes Father," Regina replied. They prayed together for a few minutes.

"We need to keep this quiet for now. Some people would make you uncomfortable with questions or odd behavior if you spoke of this, so it is better to keep it under wraps," Father Joe said.

"Okay, should I let you know if something else happens?"

"Absolutely. Until then, you will be in my thoughts and prayers and I hope I will be in yours."

"Thank you, father."

"No, thank you, Regina. Something has changed inside me. I don't know what, but your story did it."

Regina called her father to come pick her up, and then continued praying with Father Joe while they waited. When Mark arrived, he saw them kneeling. Without a word, he walked over to them and joined in. All three remained silent for several minutes until Father Joe rose and stepped out of the pew. Regina and her father looked at him with interest to see what he would say, but instead, he simply smiled at them and left.

After a few moments, Regina's father said, "Let's go home G." They got up, genuflected, and left.

Chapter 9
School Daze

Regina woke up Monday morning one minute before her alarm went off. She preemptively turned it off and said, "Thanks for waking me up, Lucy." She slid out of bed and fell to her knees. She prayed a morning offering her father suggested.

"Father, care for me. Jesus, be with me. Holy Spirit, burn in me. Blessed Mother, pray for me." Although Regina did not hear her, she felt Lucy join her in prayer. She finished and stood up when a knock came at her door.

"G? You awake, kiddo?"

"Yes, daddy."

"Can I come in?"

"Sure." Regina started thinking about what outfit she would wear to school. *School!* This would be the first time she would go to school after her visions. She would need to interact with someone outside her own family. The thought made her nervous. The torrent of emotion began to swell, but her father's entrance broke her fretting.

"Are you nervous about school?"

How does he do that? She nodded. "A little bit."

"Well, I found something on my dresser that may help. It's the strangest thing I don't remember where or when I got this." He handed her a prayer card, at which point Lucy and Thomas, the guardian angel of Mark Andrews, exchanged a high five. The front of the card had a beautiful image of an angel talking to a girl. The back of had some prayers.

"The Angelus. It's an ancient prayer of the Church," her father explained. "We would pray it before noon Mass back in college. Almost a thousand years ago, monks used it as a simple devotional to remember the Resurrection in the morning, the Suffering of Our Lord at noon, and the Incarnation in the evening. The powerful words of the prayer come from the visions you had about the Annunciation."

"Really?"

"Yes, let's do the morning version."

"Okay," Regina said. Her curiosity shined in her face.

"If you pray it with more than one person, you can have a leader and a response, like we do with other prayers. I will lead, since you haven't done it before. Read the responses and you'll do fine. Oh, and remember to meditate on the Resurrection."

Mark Andrews began.

"The Angel of the Lord declared unto Mary."

"And she conceived by the Holy Spirit," Regina said.

"Hail Mary, full of grace, the Lord is with thee, blessed are thou among women, and blessed is the fruit of thy womb Jesus," Mark prayed.

"Holy Mary, Mother of God, pray for us sinners, now and at the hour of our death. Amen."

"Behold the handmaid of the Lord," Mark said.

"Be it done unto me according to thy Word," Regina said.

They both said their parts of the Hail Mary.

"And the Word was made flesh."

"And dwelt among us."

They said the Hail Mary for the last time.

"Pray for us, O Holy Mother of God."

"That we may be made worthy of the promises of Christ," Regina concluded her part.

Her father finished. "Let us pray. Pour forth, we beseech thee O Lord, Thy grace into our hearts; that we, to whom the incarnation of Christ, Thy Son, was made known by the message of an angel, may, by his Passion and Cross, be brought to the glory of his Resurrection, through the same Christ our Lord. Amen."

All of what she had seen and felt in the last few days seemed to have been encapsulated into this one card. She felt a lot better about going to school.

"Thanks daddy."

"You're welcome, kiddo. Have a good day, I love you."

"I love you, too."

Her father left for work and Regina finished getting ready for school. She slipped the prayer card into her pocket. It helped her get ready to face the day.

Regina did not know what made her dread the thought of school, but she found out very quickly. Only a few minutes into her first class, she started to feel a strange disconnect from her surroundings. She felt like she didn't fit in. She felt like Gabriel revealed the beauty of the real world to her, and this mundane existence had become a jail cell for her spirit.

"Regina Marie Andrews? Are you with us today?" Mrs. O'Connor asked. Regina's disturbing feelings had nothing to do with Theresa O'Connor's class. She usually liked reading class and her teacher, but she felt like a blind person who obtained sight and then got stuck in a darkroom.

"I'm sorry, I'm a little out of it," Regina answered, shaking her head. She tried to return to her work. The lessons her teachers could show her could not compare to the truth of the glory of God. *How can I keep from singing?* She finally understood one of the songs she liked at church. Her soul wanted to burst from her body and dance to heavenly music, but she felt stuck. *I have to fight through this.* She made it through that class and the rest of the morning by periodically sneaking a glance at her Angelus prayer card. It gave her enough strength to make it to lunch, when she could meditate on the cross.

Regina sat down and took the sandwich her mom prepared out of her lunch bag. She took huge bites and chewed while she watched the long line of kids waiting for hot lunch. She gulped down some water to help her swallow the sandwich, and then took out her card to start her quick prayer. She glanced around and got ready to begin.

"Whatcha got there?" a voice said.

Regina turned to see a girl with short auburn hair and piercing green eyes.

"Oh, hi Mary. It's nothing." She put the card back in her pocket.

"It looked like a prayer card. Remember when we would get one at the beginning of every month back when we were at Saint John's?"

"Yeah. I still have mine in a drawer at home. I wish we still went there. It was fun having twelve kids in class," Regina said. "Why aren't you getting hot lunch?"

"My mom said we have to eat this left-over turkey. I don't mind," Mary said, taking out her lunch. "Pleasant Hill Elementary wasn't so bad, but junior high has been harder to get used to."

"My mom warned me that kids could be meaner in junior high, and she was right," Regina said.

"Yeah. So, let me see your prayer card."

Regina took it out again. "Do you want to say the prayer with me?"

Regina stunned herself with the question and Mary shocked her even more with, "I'd love to." Their guardian angels rejoiced.

"Really?"

"Yeah, why?"

"You don't say much at Religious Ed, I thought you didn't like churchy stuff."

Mary smiled. "No, I just don't like Sunday mornings."

Regina laughed. She explained the prayer like her father did and then they began. They whispered their lines back and forth, not wanting to draw attention to themselves, when Regina felt her peace get cut by an icy sword. Something bad approached.

"Are you two praying?" a mocking voice asked. Regina looked up to see a tall, scowling boy standing across from her.

"Frank Roland, leave us alone," Regina said.

Saying his name brought her mother's words from earlier in the year back to her. Her parents didn't know she overheard their conversation from the other room.

"Guess who I ran into at the Halloween party?" Katherine said, as she had walked in the door.

"Who?" Mark asked.

"Ann Roland, Louise's sister-in-law."

"How is she? And how is Louise?"

"Ann is fine, but Louise is still struggling after Tim's death."

"I bet. I haven't seen her in... I don't know how long. Did she move?" Mark asked.

"Regina and Frank were in second grade when Tim was killed. She pulled Frank out of Saint John's when she couldn't pay the tuition. She had to move to an apartment but is still in town."

"I remember offering to help her out at the Mothers Against Drunk Drivers benefit she invited us to, but she never called. What else did Ann say?"

"She said that Alice had to leave Notre Dame and go to community college, and Karen was doing well in high school, but Frank is really having trouble coping. Louise tried to keep bringing the family to church, but Frank refused because he said God took his father away. Ann said Louise tried leaving him at home but he destroyed the living room in a fit while she was gone. He is having a really hard time with all of it."

"I can't bear to think of not being here for you and the kids. Missing a father can lead to a lot of problems for children, especially boys," Mark said.

"That's true for Frank. He gets into a lot of trouble in school and has really taken the life out of Louise. Ann says Louise is depressed and worn out."

Regina had felt sorry for Frank that day.

"I asked you if you were praying!" Frank's voice changed to anger.

"What's it to you?" Regina said, trying to be brave. She looked to see if the lunchroom supervisors could see them. The two women talked in a corner on the other end of the room. No luck there.

"Hey, everybody look! Sister Regina and Sister Mary are saying their prayers. Isn't that cute?"

Tell him to shut up. "You shut your mouth Frank!" Her anger released a little and she felt powerful. *No Regina. Stand up and get the adults.* She felt confused by the conflict in her mind but didn't have a chance to think about what happened.

"Oooooh, Churchie's getting angry. Maybe you should pray to God to make me." Frank had gotten the attention of the tables in their immediate vicinity and now many students watched their exchange.

Yes Regina, pray. Pray for peace. Another voice tried to cut through Frank's jeers, which echoed in her head like a gong. *He deserves to be yelled at. Think of all the things he's done to you and the other students. Have no mercy.* She felt dizzy. *No, Regina. Fight your temptation.* Regina could not speak, she could not think straight, and her head hurt from the turmoil.

His eyes bored into her like drills. He looked feral as he growled, "Don't waste your time! There is no God!"

Liar! The dam holding back Regina's flood of emotions burst and she screamed at the top of her lungs, "I don't care what you think! Just because your dad is dead doesn't mean you can be a big, fat, stupid jerk to everyone!"

The whole room froze. Regina could only hear the pounding of her heart in her chest. She looked at Frank's face to see her piercing arrow had hit its mark. Regina watched in horror as Frank's eyes told her his father had died for him all over again. This time, she killed him. *Regina, beg for forgiveness. Do it now.* She clearly felt Lucy guiding her now. The other voice left. So did her anger; now only regret remained.

"Oh, Frank. I'm so …" She didn't get to finish. Frank Roland roared like a lion at Regina. She cowered and stepped back but, instead of leaping over the table at her, he made a wild swipe and threw all of the trays of food off the table and into the aisle. Tears ran down his blood-red face as he dashed toward the outside door that led into the playground. The crowd of students blocked the adults from getting to them in time to stop their argument before it reached its horrible conclusion. They desperately chased Frank out of the building where snow had started to fall.

Mary saw the devastated look on Regina's face and tried to console her. "Regina, it's not your fault." Regina finally realized the chaos in her mind had been a spiritual battle that Lucy couldn't help her win. She clutched her prayer card tightly as she ran from the lunchroom.

Tenebraus danced his way back to Miseros' office. He felt invincible. He reveled in his triumph over Lucy. His human had taken part in a verbal assassination. He planned with the Roland boy's tempter to get the two children into an embarrassing verbal altercation that erupted into some delicious sin. He licked his lips as he tasted Regina's wrath. Still enjoying the feast, he entered the disgusting waiting room he despised. Nothing could spoil his mood, nothing.

The door slowly opened and Tenebraus got ready to gloat before his master who had so rudely dismissed him the last time they met. He never got the chance.

"Sit down you idiot!" The force of Miseros' shout threw Tenebraus into a chair.

"What?" Tenebraus said. "Don't you know what I managed to do?"

"Of course I do. Do you?"

"I defeated that angelic pain, Lucy, and guided my charge to feel Wrath. I would hope you would show me some gratitude for committing one of the Seven Deadly Victories."

"Gratitude? What exactly am I supposed to be grateful for? You got to taste the puny fruits of your precious victory but we want a soul to feast on."

"Exactly. Now she's one step closer to our banquet hall. A big step, I might add." Tenebraus displayed his anger at the lack of appreciation from his boss.

"Have you learned nothing from your training?" Miseros had not moved from his chair, but now got up and slid over to a chart on the wall.

"What are you talking about?" Tenebraus asked, his voice failing.

Miseros glanced at Tenebraus in disgust. "The humans you brought down to us in the past must have been genetically disposed for trouble or surrounded by people with gifted tempters, because I can't see how you could have ever succeeded on your own."

"How dare you? I have won many souls for Our Father Below."

"Tenebraus, save your pathetic pride for some other demon. Don't you know the first rule of effective tempting is not to shove your patient off the edge of a cliff into the abyss? You are supposed to ease them slowly down the slippery slope. Try to remember your most basic training. I know it has been a long time. What does an innocent soul, who is not calloused to sweet sin, do when she jumps headlong into a serious sin and immediately sees its consequence?"

Suddenly, Tenebraus began to feel ill. His victory turned quickly to defeat as he realized his mistake with Regina. He thought about what would happen to her next. She had clearly displayed wrath and deliberately broke the heart of another person. He thought it would lead her to despair and eventually loss of faith. *No, you idiot. She has a loving family who will guide and support her through this.*

Reluctantly, Tenebraus answered, "She might show remorse?"

"She's already done that, you fool! She may be on the way to contrition." Miseros stopped examining his chart of elite tempters and turned to stare icily at Tenebraus. "You better hope for your sake this doesn't lead her to …" Miseros looked like was about to wretch. He regained his composure and finished, "Confession."

Tenebraus gulped at the naming of a sacrament. "She wouldn't."

"Why? It's true our elite forces have done a tremendous job getting these foolish humans to abandon the abundant graces that come from this vehicle our Enemy created. We have even coerced the priests to stop preaching about it or offering it regularly in their parishes. Despite this, there are many wretched humans who utilize its power against us, and we rarely bring them down to our furnace."

"Her parents don't go regularly, so maybe they won't take her."

"Have you conferred with their tempters? They don't go because their tempters skillfully make them too busy at the scheduled hours of confession or forgetful about their intent to go. They still believe in its power."

"I'll go back and make sure she doesn't go," Tenebraus said.

"No, I've already assigned someone else to the case."

"What?" He thought about fighting it, but realized it would not get him anywhere. "Fine, who do I start on now?" He hoped for someone with lax parents who lacked discipline.

Miseros pressed a button on his desk, opening a door that Tenebraus never noticed. Two huge, gruesome demons walked in and stood on both sides of him. "We are going to wait and see how your debacle turns out. In the meantime, we will find a way to make you actually useful."

The two demons grabbed Tenebraus, who shook violently at his boss's words. "No! I can work harder! Please, give me another chance!" he screamed as they dragged him through the door.

Miseros shook his head and said, "At least someone will satisfy us with their suffering." He licked his lips.

Regina Marie raced from the lunchroom and ran straight into the first bathroom she found. She sat on the toilet in the last stall and sobbed. She grabbed handfuls of toilet paper to wipe her tears and blow her nose. *Do the right thing. Tell the principal the truth.*

"Lucy?" She didn't feel her angel's presence.

Tell the truth and it won't be a big deal.

"It sounds like good advice," Regina said to herself. The look on Frank's face vaguely crossed her mind, but it vanished when she thought of going to the principal's office. "I'll tell Mrs. Winters the whole story and accept my punishment." She did.

"You did the right thing, coming to tell me what happened." Regina felt proud and vindicated. "I am going to let you off with a warning. I don't want any more shouting matches in my school, young lady."

"Thank you, ma'am," Regina said and walked to her next class.

The rest of the day passed without incident. Strangely, Regina felt emotionally numb all afternoon. Whenever her mind moved back to the lunchroom incident, a guiding voice would say *focus on school work, the past is the past. You did the right thing.*

The evening seemed to fly by. Her father frantically graded tests he wanted to hand back to his students the next day. Her mother caught up on housework and made dinner, while Regina helped Emmanuel with his homework and did her own. The memory of the lunchtime confrontation faded as the quiet voice in her mind kept repeating her principal's words, *you did the right thing, you did the right thing.* Regina wondered if she should have done more, but again, *you did the right thing* rang in her mind. She thought she felt peace, but something did not sit right with her.

After Regina's family ate dinner, her mother said, "Let's play a board game."

They played for over an hour and Regina felt like her usual self. The confrontation with Frank left her thoughts completely. A little past seven o'clock, the phone rang and Katherine Andrews got up to answer it.

"Hello?" Regina watched her mother smile in her usual way. "Hi, Ann, how are you?" her mother said, smiling even wider. She continued listening and her face fell. She became very serious. The call lasted several minutes, at which point Katherine Andrews said, "We will pray for him right away."

"What was that about?" Mark said.

"That was Ann Roland. She's calling people to pray for Frank. It seems he stole a car and crashed it earlier today." Regina's heart started to race. "He is in critical condition at Good Shepherd with several broken bones and internal injuries. They are waiting for the chaplain to come and anoint him in case…" Her mother looked up at Regina and Emmanuel and did not complete the sentence.

Regina finished it for her. "He dies."

Chapter 10
The Prodigal Daughter

Monday, December 2nd
7:04 PM

Lucy battled the darkness before her.

"Who are you?" The demon did not respond. "What happened to Tenebraus?" No response.

The spiritual struggle continued. The demon threw Lucy back.

"You are the reason Regina has not turned to prayer."

The demon remained silent. Lucy knew she couldn't defeat the monster on her own. She left.

A general alert from Frank's guardian angel found its way to Lucy. She found his angel.

"What do you need?" Lucy asked.

"My human may die and his soul was…" The angel frowned and continued, "Not in the best state."

"How can I help?"

"Here is his mother's guardian." Another angel arrived. "His mother has been away from the church and sorrow has rendered her helpless."

"I need Louise to call the chaplain to anoint her son, but her fear and anger is keeping her from prayer."

Lucy thought about this. "Let us pray." The angels prayed together for guidance and an answer came quickly.

"I have an idea," Lucy said. "Let's go to Louise."

Frank lay in the bed motionless and broken. His mother wept with her head on the bedside by his arm.

"Help me," Lucy said. The angels worked together in Louise's mind.

Frank's accident had brought back the images of her husband's death. She recalled the horrible pain of the tragedy. Her family still had not recovered from that trauma, and now she wondered how they would survive.

"What got her through her pain last time?" Lucy said.

"She spent hours before the replica of Michelangelo's Pieta in the chapel," Louise's guardian said.

"That's perfect," Lucy said.

Her mind already thought back to those days in the hospital with her husband. Lucy and the others guided her mind back to time she spent in the chapel. Louise pictured the Pieta. The Blessed Mother holding the lifeless body of her Son, taken down from the cross. She remembered the anguished expression of Mary.

"She is making the connection to her sorrow with Frank," her guardian said.

"Blessed Mother, help her turn to the Father like you did," Lucy prayed. The others joined in.

Louise opened her eyes and looked at Frank. She realized where she could find help. "Oh God, help me!"

The angels rejoiced and watched as the cascade of events unfolded. The Father showered Louise with many graces from heaven. She asked the nurse to call a chaplain to minister to Frank. She then called her sister back to ask as many people as she could to pray for her son. Afterwards, she began to pray quietly, having done all she could do.

"She is at peace for now," her guardian said.

"Her sister will call the Andrews for prayers soon. When that time comes the demon will weaken and I will get back to Regina. Thank you guys," Lucy said.

"Regina, don't think the worst. I'm sure he will be fine," Katherine said. She looked at Mark for support.

"Yeah, Good Shepherd has the best doctors. They will take care of him," Mark said.

Regina didn't hear them. *You did the right thing Regina. You told your principal and resolved the issue. She said you did the right thing.* The voice in her mind consoled Regina in the face of the terrible news about Frank. She heard the words, but they felt so empty. The myriad of emotions battling in Regina's mind left her confused and full of questions. *Should I tell the truth? Will I get in trouble? Will Frank die? Will my parents still love me?* Her tempter's lies continued, *you don't need to say anything, you already did the right thing.* It didn't help.

"Let's say an Our Father for Frank," Katherine said. She began to pray and Mark joined in. Emmanuel took a moment to start, but Regina remained lost in her mind. The power of the family prayer weakened Regina's tempter.

Pray Regina! In her heart, a familiar voice returned. *You must battle!* Regina suddenly remembered the training Lucy gave her two nights before. She began to pray. The effect of this first step back to God could not be overstated. It stunned her tempter and released the dark grip on her mind long enough for her to feel an emotion she had been denied.

"I'm sorry!" Regina got up from the table and ran from the room in the middle of their prayer. They could hear her sobs over the pounding of her feet up the stairs.

"I'll handle this one," Katherine said. She got no argument from Mark who shared her confused look. Emmanuel had already attached himself to his father's side when Regina left the room. The little boy muffled his whimpers in his father's shirt.

Katherine went to Regina's room and found her curled up in a ball on her bed. She buried her face in her pillow and could not control her wailing.

"Regina, what's wrong? Why are you so upset?"

Through her sorrow, Regina stayed in a prayerful state. She did not say any specific prayers, but her soul cried out in supplication. She envisioned battling her tempter.

"You got me to ignore God at lunch, didn't you?" Regina prayed to lift her sword at the dark menace. Despite her desire for him to appear in a threatening form she could fight, he looked like a movie star wearing a stylish suit.

"It wasn't me, I'm trying to help," her tempter replied. He held his empty hands up in innocence.

"You made me think I could stay quiet and everything would be okay."

"Telling your mother won't make Frank better. You will get into trouble. It will only make it worse for you." The demon's voice soothed and confused Regina. She had her sword ready to attack, but the demon did not come at her. He didn't threaten her at all.

"Regina," Lucy came into her meditation like before. "Don't fall for his deception. He wants you to think that forgetting about the incident will heal your soul from the damage of your sin. Hell removed your original tempter and sent a nastier one," Lucy said.

Regina understood. The tempter's outfit changed to a suit of black armor. He held a sword before him. The demon realized his deception had failed. His eyes flashed red with fury and he came at her. Her heart spoke out in sorrow, *have mercy on me Lord Jesus, I have sinned against you*. The simple act of love allowed her to fend off his sword slashes. With the help of Lucy, Regina quickly turned the attack on the demon, forcing him into a hasty retreat. She freed her mind of his lies.

"It's my fault! Frank's dying, and it's my fault!"

"No it's not dear. He got into an accident. You had nothing to do with it," Katherine said.

"No, it really is." Regina explained the whole scene at school. It took a long time because she stopped frequently to cry. She explained the battle she had in her conscience to keep her culpability to herself and her ability to come clean with the whole story. Her mother listened in astonishment. "I felt horrible for yelling at Frank in the first place, and now even more since he's badly hurt, but that's not the worst thing."

"Oh?"

"I am mostly sorry because I feel like I have let God down. I feel terrible about that."

"Why?"

"Because after he gave me the gift of my visions, I feel like I wasted it."

Katherine looked at Regina for a moment. "Perfect contrition?" She didn't say it to Regina, but seemed to ask herself.

"What, mommy?"

"Huh?" Katherine's mind went somewhere distant. "Oh. Let me tell you a story I think you have heard before."

"Which one?"

"The parable of prodigal son."

"I think I remember it."

"Good. I think it will help you right now."

"It starts with two brothers, right?"

"And their father, yes. Jesus spoke of a loving father who had two sons. The younger son asked for his inheritance up front and his father granted it to him. He then proceeded to move to a town far away and spent up all of his money in sinful ways. After he used up his father's money, he needed to work like a slave to eat scraps unfit for the pigs he slept with. Does that ring a bell?"

"Yes, I remember."

"You are very much like the prodigal son, Regina."

"What? How?"

"Think of it this way. God gave you a special gift in your visions. You kept those gifts at home for a whole day, but then what did you need to do?"

"I had to go to school."

"Right. You left the safety of your father's care. Away from home, the prodigal son had a chance to choose to spend his money for good or evil purposes. After God granted you the gifts of your visions you also had a chance to make the same choice."

Regina understood she had been given a chance to witness to God's glory and had instead turned to walk in the opposite way. "I wasted my gifts like the son," she said. Her eyes moistened.

"Sweetheart, don't feel so bad. There is more to the story. So, after the son spends all of his money, he has to work for practically nothing and almost starve. He suffers like you are suffering now. Some people who sin feel its effects for a long time without ever addressing the problem. You at least confronted the problem right away."

Regina thought about how her tempter wanted her to ignore the issue. She would have, too, if Lucy hadn't helped her fight her way out of his grasp. She could have suffered from the guilt and the numbing loss of God's friendship for a long time.

Katherine continued, "Within his suffering, the son came to his senses. He felt tremendous sorrow. He planned on returning to his father to say,

Father, I have sinned against Heaven and against you. I am not worthy to be called your son. Treat me as you would treat one of your servants. (Luke 15:18-19)

He was contrite, Regina. He knew he offended his father, he hated the deeds he committed, and offered to work as a servant to make amends."

"Mommy, you said perfect contrition a while ago. What did you mean by that?"

"Imperfect contrition is feeling bad because you are getting punished for your actions. Perfect contrition is when you are sorry for your sins because you have offended your Father in Heaven, whom you should love above all things. When you said you felt bad because you let God down, I sensed you might have perfect contrition."

"Is that good?"

"Yes. Actually, it's beautiful. It's a sign of a soul in love with God."

"What happens now? What should I do?"

"Do you remember when you first heard that parable?"

"In Religious Ed."

"More specifically," Katherine said.

Regina thought hard about when she learned that lesson. She frowned. "When we were preparing for first Reconciliation."

"That's right. I think it may be time for all of us to go Reconciliation together. We have not come close to our desire of going once a month. I think you could really use the grace to heal from your wounds, kiddo." This idea did not bring comfort to Regina.

"Mommy?"

"Yes dear?"

"I still don't like it."

"What do you mean?"

"You said when I got older, I would like going to Confession, but I still don't like it."

"What don't you like about it?"

"You know how you always point out how angry I get at myself when I don't get things right the first time?"

Katherine laughed. "Yes."

"I don't like doing things wrong in the first place, and I especially don't like talking about my mistakes."

"Like your father and I have told you before, mistakes are how we grow. If you don't ever mess up in life, you probably aren't challenging yourself enough."

Regina nodded. "I guess so, but I still don't see why I have to go to a priest. I remember someone said sin hurts your friendship with God. Why can't I simply tell him I'm sorry?"

"You can, Regina, and you should, but in Jesus, God became a human being. He lived as one of us and knew our likes and dislikes, strengths and weaknesses. Jesus knew his Father created people with a body, mind, and spirit. So when he gave the power of forgiving sins to his apostles, he trusted they and their successors would establish a way for people to receive the grace of forgiveness that cares for their complete person."

"What do you mean complete person?"

"Hmmm… I have an analogy which may help. I've told you not to play catch with Manny in the house, right?"

"Yes."

"Let's say you did anyway, even though you know it's wrong, and you break my favorite vase. Would it be fair for me to be upset?"

"I would be."

"Exactly, that is what happens when we break one of God's commandments. I tell you not to play catch in the house because you can break things. The Ten Commandments exist to help us from breaking our souls. When you sin, God is upset, but he still loves you like I would love you."

"Okay, that makes sense."

"Wait, there's more. Now you've broken the vase, and I assume you feel sorry. Should you leave a note for me to find or call me on the phone?"

Regina thought about this for a second. Neither of those options sounded right. She figured the right answer and said reluctantly, "I would find you and tell you in person."

"Why? Wouldn't I know about your disobedience and your sorrow either way? What difference does it make?"

"It means more if I come to you."

"Yes, Regina. It means more to both of us. You show me your love and respect for my authority by taking your time and energy to come and see me and ask for forgiveness. I see that you put aside your fear and trust in my love. Being together physically allows you to express your sorrow with your voice and hear my words of forgiveness with your own ears. I could even give you a hug to physically show that I take you back. Do you see?"

The concept started to click. "So Reconciliation at church gives me a chance to physically go to God to say sorry for breaking his vase?"

Katherine Andrews laughed. "Kind of, but there's still more."

"Really?"

"Yes. Why would you feel bad in the vase situation?"

"Because I broke your favorite vase and I would be in trouble?"

"That's true, and not bad, but that isn't perfect contrition. You said you would be sorry because you would get punished, but I would like you to be sorry for something more important," Katherine said, wanting Regina to figure it out for herself.

What else was there? *No playing ball in the house.* "I should be sorry for disobeying your rules."

"Yes, and now the big question. Why?"

"Because I love you and I should do what makes you happy."

Katherine smiled and nodded. "Very good, Regina. Perfect contrition is when you repent of your sins because of your love of God. You impressed me when you said you felt so bad about your fight with Frank because you had let God down after he had entrusted you with your visions. Many people spend their entire lives never having that feeling."

"Really?"

"Oh yes, and there is still more to Reconciliation."

"What?"

"Do you know how your basketball coach asked you to shoot twenty free throws every day in the offseason and write down the results in your journal?"

"Yes. He said we should be getting at least 10 out of 20."

"Right. How do you feel when you don't make at least ten?"

"I feel like I'm not doing something right."

"I know. You've told me that. You also told me you wish that..." Katherine waited for Regina to finish the statement.

Regina thought about what her mother wanted her to see. It took her a moment, but she figured it out. "Oh yeah, I wish I could see coach so he could give me pointers on how to get better."

Katherine smiled again at her daughter. She raised her eyebrows at Regina, asking her to make the connection herself.

"Confession is like coaching?"

"That's right. You can feel sorry to God for your sins, but how much better is it that you can have a coach tell you how to avoid the sin in the future?"

"That's cool!" Regina saw the beauty in the Sacrament of Reconciliation where she had once seen a chore. "I want to go to Confession."

"Great. Let's see if Father Joe is free right now." Her mother went downstairs to inform everyone to get ready to go to Confession if Father Joe could fit them in. She called him and he agreed to see them right away. Everyone got ready and went over to the church where Father Joe had already set up in the Confessional.

Her mother went first, followed by her father. Regina had gone to Reconciliation with them before and usually they were in the booth for only a few minutes. It took her by surprise when they both took about ten minutes to come out. They both smiled when they came out and knelt in pews apart from each other, to work on their penance, Regina supposed. It came time for her to go in.

"In the name of the Father, and the Son, and the Holy Spirit," Father Joe said as she entered her booth.

"Bless me Father, for I have sinned, it has been …" She thought about it. She went at the beginning of the school year with her Religious Ed class. "Three months since my last Confession." Regina proceeded to explain to Father Joe the Frank Roland situation. She felt the weight fall off her shoulders as she spoke. She also mentioned some other sins that occurred to her doing the Examination of Conscience while she waited for her parents to finish. She felt like she had talked forever when she finished.

"Regina, Jesus told us to love our enemies and to pray for them. He knew this wouldn't be easy, as you've found out. In the past, I have given you a basic penance of an Our Father and a Hail Mary. We can never earn God's forgiveness. He offers it freely, so any penance is only a token of our love and intention to turn our hearts back to his Will. This being said, I feel called to give you a special penance that will help you heal and grow in your mission."

Regina felt excited and scared at the same time. Father Joe continued. "I want you to visit Frank Roland in the hospital. Tell him you are sorry in person, and regardless of what he says, tell him you are praying for him."

"Yes, Father. I'll go soon."

"Now, say an Act of Contrition."

Regina panicked for a second but spotted the helpful prayer card to her left.

"My God, I am sorry for my sins with all my heart.

In choosing to do wrong and failing to do good,

I have sinned against you whom I should love above all things.

I firmly intended, with your help, to do penance, to sin no more, and to avoid whatever leads me to sin.

Our Savior Jesus Christ suffered and died for us.

In his Name, My God, have mercy."

Father Joe responded with,

"God, the Father of mercies, through the death and resurrection of your son, you have reconciled the world to yourself and sent the Holy Spirit among us for the forgiveness of sins. Through the ministry of the church, may God grant you pardon and peace. And I absolve you of your sins, in the name of the Father, and of the Son and of the Holy Spirit. Amen."

Regina made the Sign of the Cross and said, "Thanks be to God." She felt a happy lightness and said, "Thank you Father." She left the Confessional and went to pray in thanksgiving. This allowed Emmanuel to take her place. He came out a few minutes later. Father Joe came out of his booth and motioned for Regina's parents to come see him.

"It's getting late, but I need to see you all tomorrow again, if possible," Father Joe said. He smiled from ear to ear.

Mark looked as confused as the rest of the Andrews, but he spoke first. "Why don't you join us for dinner?" he looked to Katherine, who nodded in agreement.

"Fabulous. I'm sorry I can't be less mysterious, but I need to pray about something first. I assure you, I will explain."

"No problem, Father. Thank you so much for seeing us tonight on such short notice."

"You're welcome, and thank you for having me over tomorrow." Father Joe led them to the door and bid them good night.

No one talked on the ride home. Regina noticed everyone had a smile on their face, even Emmanuel. "I need to go see Frank in the hospital for my penance."

Katherine looked at Mark. "What an interesting penance."

"Yes, interesting," Mark said. He smiled at Katherine.

"Of course, Regina. I'll take you as soon as possible. I'll call his mother tomorrow morning."

Regina thought about the way her parents spoke to each other as she got ready for bed. As she fell asleep, she said, "God, help me understand adults. They're so weird."

Chapter 11
Vocatio et Missio

Monday, December 2nd
9:54 PM

After Father Joe escorted the Andrews out of the church, he picked up the phone and dialed a number.

"Hello?"

"Father Pat? It's Father Joe Logan. I'm sorry to bother you so late," Father Joe said.

"Father Joe? It's nearly ten o'clock. Is everything all right?"

"Could you hear my confession tonight?"

"Can't it wait? I have the early Mass tomorrow morning?"

Father Joe thought about it. "If you can do this for me, I will say Mass for you in the morning."

"You? Do early Mass? This must be serious. I will be ready for you when you get here."

Father Joe ran to his car and drove away. Nine minutes later he pulled up at Holy Family church.

In the church, Father Joe found the "Priest" lamp lit on the confessional. He went into the side booth and knelt.

"Bless me Father, for I have sinned. It's been one month since my last confession. Thank you for ministering to me tonight." Fr. Joe paused for a moment to collect his thoughts. "I have not lived my vocation to its fullest. During formation in seminary and my early years as chaplain at the high school, I felt the call to be as Christ, ministering to people who came to me in need. I responded with constant prayer and fasting. I saw each day as an opportunity to die to myself like Our Lord and to offer those graces to others. Now, I perform my duties like I am working a job. I perform tasks on time and efficiently, and I feel prideful about it. I haven't let God work through me as his instrument."

"You are too hard on yourself Joe. You are a great priest. I have heard it from my parishioners, your parishioners, other priests, even Bishop Roberts. You serve God and his people well. Don't beat yourself up so much."

"Father, do you ever get the feeling the Lord is calling you to be his Apostle?"

"Of course, that is why I became a priest," Father Pat replied.

"No, I mean, to follow him even to death? His voice is ringing in my heart. I don't wish to beat myself up. I just want his healing grace so I can have the strength to live and serve as he wants."

Father Pat remained silent. It took him a moment to respond. Father Joe heard the tremor in his voice when he did.

"Father, I am touched by your passion. For your penance, I ask you to pray that the Lord may bless me as he has clearly blessed you," Father Pat said.

"Of course."

They completed the rite. When they stepped out of their respective booths, Father Joe extended his hand to the old priest. Instead Father Pat embraced him.

"Father Joe, I know it's late, but… would you mind hearing my confession?"

Father Joe had not expected the request. After a few moments he said, "Oh, yes, yes, of course."

Father Pat gave him his stole and they switched booths.

When the old priest was done, they came out and embraced again.

"Do you want to give me the keys to open the church or will you be up tomorrow morning?" Father Joe said.

"Forget about it. You have done me a great favor by coming here tonight. We are definitely even. Good night, Father," Father Pat said.

"Good night and God bless you," Father Joe said.

Father Pat closed the door to the church and smiled. He looked at the crucifix. "He already did."

Tuesday, December 3rd
11:54 AM

Mark Andrews sat at his office desk staring at his computer screen. The man sitting across from him looked up.

"Mark, you alright? You have been staring at your screen for the last five minutes."

"Huh?" Mark said.

"Are you okay?"

"Yeah, I'm fine, Rick. Just spaced out, I guess."

"I'm still exhausted from the weekend. I can't wait until winter break," Rick said.

Mark nodded. He didn't reply.

"Hey, do you want something with a little caffeine? I'm going to the caf," Rick said.

"Yeah, maybe that will get me out of my daze. Could you get me a Diet Coke?"

"No problem." Rick walked out of the office, leaving Mark with a few other teachers. Everyone worked in silence.

Mark looked over at a sticky note he had left for himself. *You are a knight. He* pulled out a piece of paper that had the Angelus printed on it. He looked at the clock. *Close enough,* he thought to himself. He held the picture of Regina he had on his desk as he said the prayers and meditated on the Crucifixion.

"Hi Regina, how has your day been," Mary Murphy asked. She placed down her lunch on the lunch table and plopped herself onto the bench.

"Quiet, like yesterday morning. I hope lunch stays that way," Regina said. She knocked on the table and the girls shared a forced smile.

"Do you know how Frank is doing?" Mary said.

"Oh, you heard about it? No one else has mentioned it today, so I assumed only my family knew."

"No, my mom is good friends with Frank's aunt. She called us yesterday," Mary said.

"Oh. No, I don't know how he is." Regina looked at the door which Frank had run out of the day before.

"Do you want to pray the Angelus again?"

Regina touched the card in her pocket. "I don't know. I don't want to get in trouble," Regina said. She looked at the lunch ladies who focused on monitoring the lunch line.

"I told my mom what happened yesterday and she said Frank's outburst was a sign we did the right thing. She said the devil worked through Frank to try to stop our devotion and that we should definitely keep doing it," Mary said.

"Wow, she said that?"

"Yeah, I think she always has a Rosary in her hands. 'Just in case,' she says." Mary laughed. "She makes me carry one." Mary pulled a beautiful Rosary made of silver links and red crystal.

"Pretty," Regina said.

Regina pulled out her Angelus and they prayed.

"I hope my dad is praying right now, too," Regina said.

"You think he is?"

"I don't know. I hope so. It's been hard to concentrate on school since..." Regina stopped herself.

"Since what?"

"Since fighting with Frank and then finding out he got hurt." Regina felt she had covered her tracks. She wanted badly to tell Mary about her visions, but understood why Father Joe suggested she keep quiet about the issue.

"Oh. Yeah, I get it."

I hope Daddy is praying for me.

Open your drawer. After Mark finished the Angelus, he clearly felt the voice in his heart. He opened his top left desk drawer and rummaged around through some of the junk he had accumulated throughout fifteen years of teaching: a deck of cards, jump drives, assorted pens and pencils, and random service awards.

He wondered if he had imagined the voice in his spirit until he stumbled across a book, The Way, The Furrow, and The Forge by Saint Josemaria Escriva. He opened it to the index to find some words of wisdom about work. He found a reference and went to the correct page. He read:

That supernatural mode of conduct is a truly military tactic. You carry on the war— the daily struggles of your interior — far from the main walls of your fortress. And the enemy meets you there: in your small mortifications, your customary prayer, your methodical work, your plan of life: and with difficulty will he come close to the easily-scaled battlements of your castle. And if he does come, he comes exhausted.

"Perfect." Mark said out loud.

"What?" Rick said. He placed a can of Diet Coke on Mark's desk next to the Angelus prayer card. He looked at the card for a moment and then returned to his seat.

Mark realized he had thought out loud. "Oh, sorry. I was just reading something. Never mind."

Rick prepared to speak to say something, but then went back to work. Mark opened his pop, took a sip, and went back to his vocation with a new energy.

Regina came home after school to find her mother sitting at the kitchen table. A plate with peanut butter crackers sat ready for Regina. Across from that sat an empty plate with crumbs all around it.

"How was school *today*, Regina?"

"Fine." She looked at the empty plate and got lost in thought for a moment. "Where's Manny?"

"Downstairs playing. Why?"

"Should I tell him? You know, about the visions?"

"What would you tell him?"

"I don't know."

"Do you think he would understand?"

"I don't even know if he could sit still long enough to listen to the whole story."

Katherine smiled and shrugged her shoulders. Regina gathered that her mother did not intend to solve this issue for her.

"What if I tell him about seeing an angel? He probably already knows something special happened. I don't want him to feel left out, in case he hears us talking about it, you know?"

Katherine smiled wider.

"What?" Regina asked.

"You care about your little brother," Katherine said. Her tease found its mark.

"Stop it," Regina said. She tried to keep a frown on her face to show her mother she didn't appreciate the teasing, but couldn't. She relinquished a smile. "Fine, okay, I love him, does that make you happy?"

"Yes."

"I think you should tell him, but you'll have to come up with your own words for this one," Katherine said.

"Okay, I'll tell him right now."

Regina found Emmanuel playing in the living room with his cars. He raced them around and smashed them together. He made them scream as they crashed.

"Hi, Manny."

"Hi." He didn't look up. His imaginary car war didn't skip a beat.

"I need to tell you about something that happened to me. It's kind of important." She didn't really know what else to say, but she hoped something would come to her.

"You talked to an angel and he showed you stuff," Emmanuel replied matter-of-factly, still without looking up from his cars.

This stunned Regina and she stared at her little brother in silence. He continued his game. Finally she regained her speech. "Did Daddy tell you that?" She assumed her mother hadn't told him a word since she hadn't mentioned it moments before.

"Nope." Cars continued to crash and burn.

"How did you know?" Regina confusedly asked.

He paused his play long enough to look at her briefly and shrug his shoulders. He gave a quick grin and went straight back to his car game.

"What does that mean?"

He didn't respond and Regina realized she had gotten everything she could out of him. She backed out of the room wondering what it meant. He knew about her visions, but her parents hadn't spoken to him. It gave her another thing to ponder and pray about in her strange new life.

Three hours later, Katherine worked on dinner in the kitchen while Mark helped the kids finish their homework at the dining room table. The doorbell rang. Regina ran to the door. Mark cleaned up their school books and put them aside.

"Hi, Father." Regina moved aside to let Father Joe come in.

"Regina, how are you?" He had his usual casual outfit on: black pants, black shoes, a sweater on top of a black shirt, and his roman collar poking out on top. He also had a black bag with him.

"Fine, how are you?" She led him to the dining room. Mark finished clearing the table and pulled a chair out for the priest.

"I am well and excited to be with you and your family tonight."

"Dinner will be ready in a little bit," Katherine said from the kitchen.

"Okay, honey. Have a seat, Father," Mark said.

"Actually, since we have a few minutes, do you mind if I bless the house?"

"That would be fantastic," Mark said. "Where do you want to start?"

"Right here will be fine." He took his stole out of his bag, kissed it, and put it around his neck. He also took out a vial of holy water and a book of prayers. "Katherine, can you join us for a few seconds?"

"Sure, Father," she said and came into the dining room. Father Joe started the blessing rite with the whole family present. He then moved around the house sprinkling holy water in each room and saying a prayer. By the time he finished, dinner waited on the table. They all enjoyed some light conversation about school and the sports the kids played. After dessert, Mark and Katherine cleared the plates and returned to the dining room table.

Mark asked the question the Andrews all wondered. "So, what did you want to talk to us about, Father?"

"Yes, to the business at hand. I want to talk to you about Vocatio et Missio."

"What?" Regina said.

"Sorry. It's Latin for 'Vocation and Mission'. One of my favorite teachers in seminary, Father Albert Lemarque, used to use the expression when he talked about Our Lord's ministry." Father Joe looked up at the Andrews family, Katherine and Emmanuel to his left, and Regina and Mark to his right. They all gave him their full attention. "Jesus first called the apostles to him, and then sent them out into the world to spread his word. Vocatio means 'a call' and missio means 'a sending.'"

"Okay, Father. I think we are with you," Mark said. He looked around to see nodding heads.

"I called Father Pat McNulty at Holy Family yesterday and went to Reconciliation after you all left last night, and I want to share why. During your family reception of the sacrament, I realized I have not lived out my vocation as fully as I could. God called me to be another Christ, and I have been satisfied giving less than my best. Despite not answering his call completely, the Lord has seen fit to send me this mission." He gestured to Regina and the rest of the family.

"The Seal of the Confessional prohibits me from sharing what any of you said yesterday, but it doesn't restrict you. No one needs to speak, but I think it would benefit everyone to consider what God has intended for their vocation and mission." Father Joe looked like he finished what he had to say. He expected a response, but appeared satisfied he had said his peace.

Mark Andrews cleared his throat.

"Ever since Regina reminded me of my consecration to the Militia Immaculata, I have prayed with more conviction and felt drawn to the Sacraments." He reached into his pocket and pulled out a Rosary. "I started to carry this with me at all times, like I did in college. I feel like I am carrying a holy sword with me."

Regina thought of her training meditation and wielding the huge sword against the wooden dummies. Her father continued, "I don't know what this means exactly, but I know I have to share Saint Maximilian Kolbe's military spirituality with others in some way."

Father Joe nodded his head in agreement, happy someone had shared. He looked at Katherine.

"I told Father I had felt a call to use my counseling skills at the Women's Crisis Pregnancy center for a long time. I confessed I had avoided answering Our Lord's voice with many different excuses. Helping Regina through her grief over Frank Roland's accident reminded me of how much I enjoy helping others talk through their problems and find comfort." As she spoke her words, Katherine's face shined like she had opened a Christmas present.

Regina felt left out. Father Joe and her parents could explain what missions they felt called to, but she didn't feel having visions could count as a mission. She didn't do anything, they just happened. Gabriel did not setup an appointment for a future vision. He possibly could never return.

"What about me?" Regina asked.

"You? It's too early to tell exactly, but all of this has come from you," Father Joe said.

"But I didn't do anything."

"Oh, but you did," Father Joe said.

"What?"

Father Joe smiled. "You said 'yes.'"

Regina's face showed her confusion.

"God called you, and you said 'yes'. You took a heroic first step on a journey in a scary situation. We are all very proud of you," Father Joe explained. Her parents nodded in agreement.

"Don't forget, God called us to our missions through your faith. That is a big deal," Mark said.

The dinner party ended shortly thereafter. The whole family escorted Father Joe to the door to bid him goodnight. Afterwards, realizing the time, everyone started their preparations for bed. Mark came to his daughter's room to tuck her in.

"Daddy, what should I do about school?"

"What about it?"

"It seems so unimportant now."

"I know exactly how you feel, G."

"Really?" Regina sat up.

"Yes. Since you told me about Our Lady's desire for my knighthood, the thought is always on my mind. I couldn't focus on doing my job."

"What did you do?"

"To be honest, a bad job. I owe my students my best effort and I wasn't giving it, but then I found something that really helped me."

"What?"

"A book of inspirational quotes from Saint Josemaria Escriva."

"Who's that?"

"A very wise and holy priest. He founded a group in the church called Opus Dei."

"That means the work of God, right?" Regina asked.

"How did you know that?" Mark said.

"I have no idea. I just did."

Mark gave her a quizzical look.

"Saint Josemaria taught us that doing daily tasks, no matter how plain, sanctifies you."

"I've heard that word before, what does it mean?"

"In other words, you can become a saint by working to be the best daughter, student, piano player, athlete you can. Do your best to respect the gifts God gave you. The work you do is the work of God."

"So, by doing my work in school and paying attention, I am both praying and becoming more holy?"

"That's what he taught."

Regina thought about this.

"I have started to feel like school is a prison where I am locked away from God. This helps me see it in a whole different way. Thanks, that helps a lot."

"Great, anything else?"

Regina thought again.

"Yes, what is the Joy of the Lord?" The question left her lips before she fully thought about having it.

"What do you mean?"

"You know, like from the Bible? The Joy of the Lord is my strength." (Nehemiah 8:10)

"I don't know. I guess true joy comes from God. You need it in your heart to be strong in your faith. What makes you truly happy?"

Regina thought about the shows she watched and her favorite music, but figured she only liked those things. "I don't know. What gives you joy?"

"You." Her father smiled and paused. "And Manny, and mommy. I am happy for the gifts God gives me. Sometimes I take you all for granted, but I am truly joyful for my family. Does that help?"

"Yeah, I guess so."

"Sweet dreams, G." He kissed her and left.

"Lucy? Do you have anything to add?" Regina asked out loud, remembering to make the Sign of the Cross.

"Continue to pray about it. You will find your answers, Regina."

Regina felt the warmth of her angel's embrace. She remembered her mother said Frank's mom invited them to see him the next day. She fell asleep, giving thanks for the family who brought her joy and strength.

106

Chapter 12
Muted

Wednesday, December 4th
9:12 AM

"A girl in my parish had a vision of Saint Gabriel," Father Joe said out loud as he drove down the highway. He shook his head. "No, that's not good."

"Your Excellency, God is blessing my parish in a special way." This time, he pounded the steering wheel lightly. He pulled into the parking lot of the cathedral. He got out of his car and looked at his watch. "I still have some time to figure out what to say."

He blessed himself as he entered the beautiful church and found a pew to kneel in. He didn't have much time, so he began his prayers in earnest. *Lord, give me strength. Holy Mother, be with me.* He focused his thoughts on these two intentions.

He looked up to the crucifix. His church had a resurrected Jesus on the cross, with his hands held upwards and his holy body healed from the pains of his Passion. The cathedral had a traditional corpus that showed Christ's wounds very realistically. Father Joe looked at the eyes of Jesus. He could see the love of God there. His spirit stirred.

Are you ready to suffer with me? The question came softly but with a substantial weight.

If it is your will, Lord. The priest resolved to go where this mission led him.

Pray for your Bishop. He realized he prayed for himself but not for his superior. He began when a familiar voice called him.

"Father Logan!" The bishop entered from a side entrance. "I thought I saw you from my office."

"Your Excellency, I arrived early, and I elected to wait here. No offense to your waiting room." Father Joe smiled, hoping to be diplomatic. He got up and greeted the prelate by kissing his ring.

"None taken. I often hear, 'Bishop Roberts, you need more comfortable furniture in your waiting room,' so I understand."

"Someone actually said that to you?"

"No, I'm just kidding." He laughed. "Please, come with me."

They walked quickly to the bishop's office, making some small talk about the traffic and the weather. Coffee was offered and declined, and both men made themselves comfortable in their seats.

"So, what is so important it dragged you all the way out here to see me?"

"Your Excellency, I have to tell you about something of a very mystical nature that occurred in my parish." The bishop looked intrigued. "A young girl told me Saint Gabriel, the archangel, showed her visions of Our Lady and Saint Joseph."

Bishop Roberts thought for a moment.

"Please, tell me what she said."

Father Joe told the bishop exactly what Regina had told him. It took several moments for Bishop Roberts to respond. He looked intently at the younger priest. "Do you believe in the authenticity of these alleged visions?"

"Yes, Your Excellency, I do."

"And what supports your belief?"

"There are several things. I have felt something big for my ministry coming my way for the last few months. I prayed and fasted in preparation, waiting for this opportunity. I can't see how it could be anything but this. Also, the girl has no interest in making a spectacle of herself or making the news public. She has followed my commands to keep the events secret. Only her family and I know about this. Then there are the fruits of the Spirit I have seen."

"What fruits?"

"The girl's parents have each become energized in their faith. The Holy Spirit is calling both of them to service and prayer. I myself feel like I am on fire. I want to bring this fire to my parish. I feel called to preach the truth to the people. My prayer life has never been as engaged as it is now. I know God is calling me to a radical evangelization of my parish, then who knows."

"This is not like Fatima, Lourdes, or even Medjugore. The girl described images from the past but did not get a message to share. You are sure she would have no way of knowing the details of the locations and traditions she described?"

"I am sure."

"I see," the bishop said. Father Joe sat silently, waiting to see what his superior would say. The bishop took some time before speaking. "Father, you were wise to keep the visions quiet. We need to wait for them to play out before we make official pronouncements on them. Have the girl continue to speak only with you. It sounds like her parents can be trusted to keep silent as well. I will trust you to decide whether you need to contact me about the content of future visions."

"I agree, Your Excellency."

Bishop Roberts went back to his thoughts.

"And about your mission…"

"Yes," Father Joe answered. He felt a chill go up his spine.

A demon and angel grappled in battle.

"Leave him alone you dog," the angel said. "Behold his prayers."

The demon fell backward but got right back up.

"Impressive, but I offer you his fear that his authority be questioned." The angel reeled from the attack.

"Faithfulness to the church," the angel said, battling the demon back.

"Concern for money," the demon replied. The devastating blow severely wounded the angel and left the demon in charge.

"Father, many people come to church only during the Advent and Christmas season. You should hope they stick around. You don't want to scare them away. Plus, you can't risk scaring away your regular parishioners. Think of the mortgage on your new school addition that you are already behind on."

"With all due respect, Your Excellency, I really feel the Lord wants me to bring his word to my people." Father Joe felt a strange coolness in the room.

"Father Logan, I do not disagree with you, but now is not the time."

"As you said, many people only come to church at this time. There can't be a better time."

"Father Logan, I am not going to censor you, but I want you to consider your debts and the fact that the diocese has to often make up the difference in your weekly budget. The bishop did not raise his voice, but he remained stern. He felt he made his point. His demon smiled with the success.

Father Joe badly wanted to argue, but the bishop thought correctly. He understood the threat. The collection basket often fell short of parish expenses and bishop's willingness to support him financially could not be argued. Angry thoughts swirled in his head but he battled them with prayer. He heard in response, *forgive him, he knows not what he does.* Father Joe conceded, "Yes, Excellency." He laid down his pride and prayed he could do God's will. This seemed to be it.

The bishop's tension released and he said, "Thank you, Father Logan. Please let me know if anything else occurs."

"Thank you for your time," Father Joe said. He left the office and began the long, lonely drive home. He did not know how he would contain the demands of the Holy Spirit within him, but he prayed the Lord would guide him. Soon, he would.

While Father Joe had his appointment with the bishop, Regina spent another uneventful day at school. She followed the advice her father gave her and found it really helped her get through the day. She felt closer to God through her attention to her daily work. While she had her mind set on school, her spirit itched to make amends with Frank Roland.

She walked in from school and threw her backpack on the couch. Her mother put down her book.

"Can we go see Frank now?"

"Fine, thank you, how are you Regina?" Katherine said.

"Oh, sorry. How was your day?"

Katherine smiled. "Great. I just got back from the shelter a little while ago. Let me call Frank's room. His mom is probably there."

It took her a few seconds to look up the number for the hospital and get the room number from the receptionist. She got connected and Regina could hear the phone ringing.

"Hello, Louise?" Regina guessed a woman must have answered. "Oh, hi Ann. This is Katherine Andrews. Is your sister there?" Regina's excitement for doing her penance after Reconciliation and making up with Frank began to deflate as she watched her mother desperately try not to cry as she listened on the phone. She didn't say a word until Frank's aunt finished. "I'm so sorry, Ann. Send Louise our best. Yes, we will say a prayer right away."

Regina could not help thinking the worst. "Is Frank …" Regina could not finish the question.

Her mother looked at her warmly, her eyes glistening with tears. "No, Regina, no. He's still with us. He needed to be rushed to surgery because of complications. His aunt says it's pretty serious and she asked us to pray for him." Regina could do nothing more than fall into her mother's arms and cry.

"Christina, honey, you haven't touched your dinner."

"I'm sorry mom. I don't have much of an appetite," Christina Wilde said, pushing her carrots around her plate with her fork.

"What's wrong? Did something happen at work?"

"I got written up."

"Oh my goodness, for what?" Her mother put down her fork.

"You know my friend Matty?"

"Yes."

"Well, we were talking at lunch about what we do at our lab stations, and I guess someone overheard us and reported it to our supervisor."

"What did you say?"

"Nothing really. We talked about the kind of stuff we do every day."

"That's it? You got written up for that?"

"Mother, calm down." Christina looked up and saw her mother's concerned look. "I guess I didn't read the employee contract when I started working. They highlighted for me how I was not supposed to tell anyone what I did in my lab."

"You told me," her mother said.

"Are you going to report me, too?"

They both laughed.

"It's not a big deal. I just have to be more careful in the future."

"It's not right. I told you there is something wrong with that place. Maybe some techno-bio places do some good work, but I've heard rumors about PermaLife."

"Mom, it's called bio-tech, and the rumors you've told me about are crazy talk. My supervisor explained to me how there is a lot of competition in the industry and all of these companies have hush-hush policies to make sure no one steals their secrets. I only wish I had read the contract closer."

"I wish you would quit and find a new job."

"What if I couldn't? Would I just move back in with you forever?" Christina looked at her mother.

"You know you could." Tears filled her mother's eyes.

"Thanks mom," Christina said. She took her mother's hand and held it.

Later that night, the Andrews prayed together for Frank. Afterwards, they played a game to try to lighten the mood. It worked, but Regina continued to pray while they played.

She fell asleep quickly after being tucked in but woke suddenly in the middle of the night. She looked around in the darkness.

"Lucy," Regina whispered.

Her angel shimmered in her room and Regina jumped out of bed. "You're back. I mean, I know you are always with me, but I can see you again." Regina's smile hurt it stretched so wide.

"Yes, Regina. You are receiving many graces right now. Come on, we are going back to the Nativity downstairs."

"Is Saint Gabriel coming back too?"

"Let's go, Regina!" Lucy drifted out of the room and down the stairs. Regina sneaked down after.

Downstairs, Regina found Lucy on her knees before the Nativity. Regina joined her. Only a few moments passed before the archangel appeared. Regina bowed deeply, awestruck once again.

"Regina, come sit with me again."

Upon his invitation, Regina jumped up and went to his side.

"I am so glad to see you again," she said.

"Do you have something to ask me?" Gabriel said. Regina knew he had read her mind.

"Is Frank going to be alright?"

"You have much to see and do before you find out, my dear," Gabriel said.

"I … I really want to say sorry to him."

Gabriel smiled, comforting Regina.

"Come, hold my hands. You have accepted your mission, now it continues."

She reached for his hands, anticipating the odd sensation of her mind and body separating through time and space. Regina found herself back in time once again. She looked around and saw the beautiful architecture of the Great Temple off in the distance.

"That's Jerusalem, right?"

"Very good, child. We are in the hill country south of Jerusalem. You could call it a suburb. It is actually several months before the last visions you saw of the Annunciation. If you look over there you can see the house of Our Lady's cousin, Elizabeth. Here comes her husband, Zechariah, now."

Regina looked over to see an elderly man walking with difficulty up the hill on a road from Jerusalem. She walked toward him with Gabriel to get a better look.

"His robe looks kind of like the one Simeon wore," Regina said.

"Yes. Zechariah is a priest of the division of Abijah. There are twenty four orders of priests who take turns performing certain religious duties in the Great Temple on a rotating cycle. He is about to begin his two weeks of service."

Zechariah reached his house and entered. Inside, a woman, as old as Regina's grandmother, greeted him.

"My love, why do you look so upset?" The woman came up to Zechariah and embraced him. She pulled back and caressed his cheek with her hand.

"Will we ever find peace, Elizabeth? Will we greet the kiss of death still forsaken by our own countrymen?" He looked into her eyes with tears in his own.

"Why do you let them bother you so?"

"It isn't fair. We both come from priestly families. We have always followed the Lord. We have given our lives to his service, but they talk about us like we are sinners. They do it in my presence."

"It's just talk from fools with only their gossip to keep them company. Let them think God curses us. What can we do but continue to pray he give us a child, as he did to Father Abraham and Sarah."

"Your wisdom has been my foundation for all these years, dear wife. I am sorry I troubled you with my complaints."

Zechariah took Elizabeth's hand and kissed it. She held his and pulled him with her.

"Come; let us thank the Lord for the food he has given us. Then you can eat to regain your strength. Tonight we can raise our prayers for a child again like we always do." They walked further into the house and out of sight, leaving Regina and Gabriel alone.

"What are they talking about Gabriel? I don't understand what's happening," Regina asked.

"Regina, throughout the ages, people have been cruel to each other for so many reasons. Many have suffered for things such as the color of their skin or the land of their birth. In Our Lord's day, married couples without children were ridiculed. People assumed the barren had been cursed or offended God in some way to live a fruitless life. Not only did they have the sorrow of being childless, but they also had to face the shaming of their peers. Zechariah and Elizabeth never had children, so they are scorned."

"That's terrible."

"Times have changed. In your day, people blessed with many children get ridiculed and many couples go out of their way to reject God's plan of parenthood for them," Gabriel said.

"Can we go inside and see them?"

"No. As I said, Zechariah will soon begin his turn in the temple. You needed to see the holy couple in their sorrow. Now we will move to Jerusalem a week into the future." The scene melted away.

Once she regained her focus, Regina recognized the familiar setting of the Great Temple. She saw many priests dressed like Zechariah. She searched the faces and finally found him. The priests seemed to play some kind of game.

"What are they doing?" Regina asked.

"They are casting lots to see what roles the priests will have during their time in temple service. There are many sacred duties to perform and chance will decide who gets to do what," Gabriel answered.

Regina watched as they decided who would kill the animals, capture the blood, trim the wicks of the candles, and perform several other minor duties. Several priests were left when they began the process of deciding who would bring the sacrifices into the temple.

"We will now cast lots for who will offer the incense in the temple," one of the priests said. (Luke 1:9) The group started to murmur amongst themselves.

"Why are they acting like that?" Regina asked.

"The incense offering is considered the best and most honorable duty for the priests. This is a special moment."

Zechariah, who still had no assigned duty, cast his lots with the rest of the remaining priests. Regina could not figure how the process worked, but she watched as the men examined the results. One priest stepped forward to examine the results.

"Zechariah is the winner. He will offer the incense." Immediately, whispers went through the crowd. Regina could not hear what they said, but by the look on Zechariah's face, she could tell it upset him.

Regina and Gabriel watched as the priests bustled about doing their appointed tasks. Many of them stole nasty glances at Zechariah.

"They do not feel it is right Zechariah got the best job. Remember, they feel he has no children due to some hidden sin," Gabriel said.

Regina stared at the other priests with a dark scowl. They went about lighting candles, slaughtering sacrificial animals, and catching the blood.

"The time for the offering has come. Let us approach the sanctuary and Brother Zechariah will enter and burn the incense to begin the ceremony."

Regina and Gabriel walked with the crowd up the temple steps to approach the mount. Zechariah ignored the dirty stares of his peers and solemnly passed beyond the curtain to the inner sanctum. The others waited outside and chanted prayers.

"Come, let us follow," Gabriel said.

"Is it okay?"

"This is why we are here."

They passed behind the curtain to see Zechariah preparing to burn the ceremonial incense. He prayed and gestured according to his custom. Regina watched with interest.

"Here we go again," Gabriel said as a bright light startled both Regina and Zechariah. Zechariah shielded his eyes with his arms. Regina looked at the source of the light and recognized a familiar face.

"It's you again!"

"I was pretty busy back then. Well, I am always busy, but I don't always get to reveal myself to humans. God gave many holy people special graces to see me like you can. Scriptures do not record all of these visits."

Regina turned to see fear replace shock on Zechariah's face. He saw the old Gabriel and fell prostrate, unwilling to raise his eyes.

"It's like the Annunciation," Regina said.

"Yes and no. Watch," Gabriel said.

"Fear not, Zechariah, for your prayer has been heard." Regina looked at the old man and saw him raise his head at the sound of his name. "Your wife Elizabeth will bear you a son, and you shall name him John. You shall have joy and gladness, and many shall rejoice in his birth. He shall be great before the Lord; and he shall drink no wine nor strong drink: and he shall be filled with the Holy Spirit, even from his mother's womb." (Luke 1:13-15)

"He will drink no wine, what does that mean?" Regina said.

"It means he will be a Nazarite, like Samuel and Samson from the Old Testament. Zechariah and Elizabeth will need to consecrate him to God in a special way," Gabriel said.

Regina nodded and continued to watch Zechariah stare at the angel as he prophesied about a child of wonder.

"He shall convert many of the children of Israel to the Lord their God. And he shall go before him in the spirit of Elijah; that he may turn the hearts of the fathers unto the children, and the incredulous to the wisdom of the just, to prepare unto the Lord a perfect people." (Luke 1:16-17) Gabriel finished his words and waited on Zechariah's response.

Zechariah finally lowered his head and remained deep in thought.

"What is he thinking about?" Regina asked.

"The same kind of thing Our Lady did. I just gave him a lot of life changing information, but now his guardian angel and tempter are battling to direct his thoughts. His doubt and fear are overtaking his faith." Regina could see the battle on Zechariah's face. He shook his head and prepared to speak.

"How shall I know this? For I am an old man, and my wife is advanced in years." (Luke 1:18)

The angel's eyes closed to slits.

"Why were you mad?"

"Zechariah asked me for proof. He prayed for a child his entire life, but now God answered his prayer and he wanted assurance. His tempter made his trust in God to waiver. When I came to you Regina, you doubted yourself but you trusted that I came from God. Watch what I said."

The old Gabriel appeared to swell in size and regained his heavenly aura. His words roared like thunder in the room.

"I am Gabriel, who stand before God. I was sent to speak to you and to bring this good news. And behold, thou shall be dumb, and unable to speak until the day until these things take place, because you did not believe my words, which will be fulfilled at their proper time." (Luke 1:19-20)

Zechariah grabbed his throat. He tried to plead with the angel but found his sentence had already been carried out. He fell to his knees and wept in sorrow. The old Gabriel disappeared.

"Let us go outside and wait for Zechariah to finish his prayers for forgiveness," Gabriel said.

Outside the sanctuary, the other priests started to grumble.

"What is he doing in there?"

"We have so much more to do!"

They all started to chatter amongst themselves to pass the time. Regina kept thinking about Gabriel's words about John and tried to fully grasp their significance. Zechariah pushed aside the veil hiding him from everyone's sight. He ran into the middle of the crowd and began to gesture frantically.

"What? What is it, Zechariah?"

Zechariah pointed to the sanctuary and to the sky trying to convey what happened. He grabbed his throat and opened his mouth trying to speak.

"He lost his voice," one priest said.

"He lost his mind," someone else responded. Many laughed.

"I think he saw something in the sanctuary," the high priest said.

Zechariah nodded and pointed at the high priest.

"You saw the Lord?"

Zechariah shook his head.

"You saw a ghost?"

Zechariah didn't quite shake his head.

"An angel, perhaps?"

Zechariah nodded. He gestured with excitement.

"And the angel took your voice? Sounds more like a demon," one of his detractors said and, again, many laughed.

Zechariah looked at them in disgust and bolted from their midst. As the vision started to fade, Regina saw him run for the hills.

"He will write down what he saw for his holy wife," Gabriel told Regina. "And when he does, she will believe."

Chapter 13
The Visitation

Regina did not get to see Zechariah return to Elizabeth to share his story of Gabriel's visit. Instead, she found herself outside Joseph's house. The door of the house opened and Mary walked out. Regina thought she glowed even brighter in the morning light. She had a bag in her arms.

"Are you ready to go?" Joseph said. He carried several bags across his shoulders as he stepped out of the house.

"Yes, whenever you are," Mary said.

"I'm good. Let us be off."

Regina and Gabriel joined the Holy Family on their journey. Mary's prayers inspired and awed Regina. She saw that they moved Saint Joseph as well.

Mary and Joseph, once again, spoke at length about the majesty of God. They prayed the Psalms and sang hymns together. The time travelling to Judea passed quickly this way. Regina and Gabriel would fast forward in time whenever the couple spent their time in silence.

Although she witnessed a multitude of prayers and conversations between Mary and Joseph, when Regina finally saw Zechariah's house at the top of a distant hill, she felt like the whole trip had only lasted a few moments. They made their way up the hill and reached the front of the property. A servant greeted them.

"Are you expected by the master of the house?"

Joseph answered, "No. I am Joseph and this is my wife, Mary. She is cousin to Elizabeth. She has come to aid her during her pregnancy."

"Very well, sir. Please come with me. I will show you where you can place your bags. Madam, come in and I will find my mistress."

Joseph nodded to Mary and left with the servant. Mary waited in the large entrance hall that could have fit Joseph's entire house. In a few minutes, Elizabeth appeared in the doorway.

"Mary! I am so glad you came, what a pleasant surprise." Elizabeth made her way across the space between them. She shuffled her feet and kept one hand on her back as she walked. Mary walked to her and they embraced. When they parted, Mary spoke for the first time.

"I am so happy for you, sister."

Elizabeth shuddered and gasped. She touched her belly and looked at Mary, astonished.

"Blessed are you among women and blessed is the fruit of your womb. Why am I so favored, that the mother of my Lord should come to me?"

Mary stepped back, stunned. She touched her own belly and looked at Elizabeth in wonder.

"As soon as the sound of your greeting reached my ears, the baby in my womb leaped for joy. Blessed is she who has believed that the Lord would fulfill his promises to her!" (Luke 1:42-45)

Mary's eyes welled with tears. She embraced Elizabeth again.

"What is she feeling?" Regina asked.

"Since the Annunciation, Mary has kept her miraculous condition to herself. Imagine the burden this must have been," Gabriel said.

Regina realized Mary's spirit probably burned with this information on their whole trip from Nazareth. She looked at the Blessed Virgin and saw the Holy Spirit shine from her.

"My soul proclaims the greatness of the Lord;
my spirit rejoices in God my savior.
For he has looked upon his handmaid's lowliness;
behold, from now on will all ages call me blessed.
The Mighty One has done great things for me, and holy is his name.
His mercy is from age to age to those who fear him.
He has shown might with his arm,
dispersed the arrogant of mind and heart.

He has thrown down the rulers from their thrones but lifted up the lowly.
The hungry he has filled with good things;
the rich he has sent away empty.
He has helped Israel his servant, remembering his mercy,
according to his promise to our fathers,
to Abraham and to his descendants forever. (Luke 1:46-55)

"That was beautiful!" Regina said.

"We call that the Magnificat, or the Canticle of Mary. The church considers it a profoundly important prayer. People around the world recite it every night in the Church's official evening prayer."

"Her soul and spirit were bursting with the love of God. That's amazing."

"Yes. Remember, God always blessed her with special graces throughout her life, but at this moment he is truly present within her. She speaks with the power of the Holy Spirit coming from Jesus in her womb."

"Generations have called her blessed, but she gives all of the credit to God. The Mighty One did the greatest thing ever to her," Regina said.

"The Father allowed Mary to bring Jesus into the world and give him to the rest of us. She considers herself his handmaid for doing this work. The greatest job anyone ever did," Gabriel said.

Regina's understanding continued to grow.

"Too often, people go to God only with petitions, praying for things they want. Mary turns to God in praise and thanksgiving for what he gave her out of his love," Gabriel said.

Regina vowed in her heart to be more thankful. "She says God's mercy is to those who fear him. What does that mean?"

"You see fear as a negative thing?"

"I think of monsters and ghosts when I hear the word fear."

"The world makes you think that way, but Fear of the Lord is one of the seven gifts of the Holy Spirit."

Regina wanted to ask about the others but Gabriel did not give her the chance.

"Do you fear punishment from your parents, Regina?"

"Yes."

"Of course you do, but tell me, what do you fear most with regards to your parents?"

Regina thought. "I don't know."

"Let me help you. Picture yourself in a crowded public place. What would be the most fearful thing that could happen to you?"

Again Regina thought, but this time she had an answer. "Losing my parents in the crowd!"

"What do you fear more? Punishment or losing your parents."

"Losing my parents."

"Can you tell me why?"

"I can stand receiving a punishment for something I've done wrong, but I couldn't bear being apart from my parents."

"Exactly. Do you understand Fear of the Lord now?"

"I think so. You fear losing your relationship with God, so you do whatever it takes to stay close to him."

"Right. Very good, Regina. What do you think about the might of his arm?"

"He uses it to take down the arrogant, the mighty, and the rich. He lifts up the lowly and tends to the poor."

"You heard Mary's philosophy of the love of God. Where else have you heard the same kind of talk?"

"Jesus always preaches like that in the Gospels!"

"The voice of the Father speaks to Mary through Jesus. As a young boy, he will hear these lessons from his mother and they will shape his philosophy."

"Wow!"

This touched Regina deeply. God gave her this role from the beginning. "She was always a vessel for God."

"Yes, and she ends her song with an acknowledgement of God remembering his promise to save Israel with the Messiah. She knows who she carries in her womb and what he will become."

All of the things they discussed inspired Regina to plan on meditating on the Magnificat when she got a chance.

"Our Lord gave a preview of what his divine message would be thirty years in advance. Saint Joseph and Our Lady will repeat this prayer to Jesus as he grows up. He will hear the words he inspired his mother to say over and over, until they become his refrain throughout the Gospels."

Regina accepted the angel's words and returned to the scene. Mary and Elizabeth had not moved as Regina and Gabriel discussed the significance of the Magnificat. Regina also noticed that Zechariah stood in the doorway, frozen. The scene continued.

"Oh, Mary. Your mother, Anne, shared my childless sorrow for years. It gave me so much consolation when God answered her prayers with you, the miracle child. Fourteen years later, you come to me, after the Lord blessed me with the miracle I so desired, to feed my spirit with the graces from your Divine Infant. My body is old and tired, but you have renewed in me the spirit of my youth. God *is* great. And holy is his Name."

Mary regained her senses completely after losing herself in the ecstasy during the Heavenly speech. She looked up and saw Zechariah as well. He approached her. He took her hand, kissed it, and placed it on his own head.

"What's he doing?" Regina asked.

"Zechariah wants Mary to bless him. Her words moved him to deep remorse for doubting my words in the temple. He recognizes Mary's incredible role as the Mother of God. Mary would never have dared to place her own hand on Zechariah's head to bless him, because only an elder possessed that right. She does so because he insists."

Mary allowed Zechariah to hold her hand on his head and Regina saw them both slightly shiver. Mary reflexively took her hand back and Zechariah recoiled. Gabriel answered Regina's question before she spoke it.

"Jesus forgave Zechariah. In his heart, Zechariah begged God to accept his apologies with a truly contrite spirit. The Father of Mercies heard his plea and through his unborn Son, forgave the father of the man who would eventually herald his coming."

Zechariah looked at Mary with profound happiness. He puts his hands together and bowed repeatedly to show his thanks.

"If God forgave him, why can't he talk yet?"

"He still has to do his Act of Contrition," Gabriel said.

"I suppose you aren't going to tell me what that is." Regina guessed correctly. Gabriel smiled.

"Please don't speak of this," Mary asked.

"You haven't told Joseph?" Elizabeth said.

"The Lord has told me to wait," Mary replied. Elizabeth and Zechariah looked at each other and nodded.

Joseph walked in.

"I have prepared your room and put away your things," he said.

"Thank you Joseph."

An awkward silence filled the room.

"Joseph, even we in the hill country heard of the miracle of the lily. Would you please tell me about it?" Elizabeth said.

Joseph eyes lit up. Mary showed relief as he shared his story. When he finished, Elizabeth shared Zechariah's story. They shared a meal and pleasant conversation. Soon, the two couples prepared for bed.

The scene jumped to the next day and Regina found herself watching the end of Mary and Joseph's goodbyes.

"My soul will weep for the loss of your fellowship, Mary."

"Mine too, Joseph. Be safe."

He bid her farewell and began the long journey home.

"There goes a true manly man, Regina. He is known as Saint Joseph, the Worker, for this reason. God chose him to be the step-father of his only son. He showed Jesus the holiness of hard work. Joseph, in his own way, prepared the way for Jesus like John the Baptist," Gabriel said.

Regina thought of her father going to work. She understood the sacrifice he made so he could continue his vocation. She prayed her father would have the strength to answer God's call to the personal mission he shared at dinner with Father Joe. With these thoughts, the vision ended and Regina returned to her own time.

"Is that the end of this story?"

"No, my dear. The Lord has decided you will see the rest of this story when you complete your Act of Contrition," Gabriel answered.

"So, I need to see Frank?"

"Yes. Then you will see the rest of the vision."

"Okay. I hope I will be able to go tomorrow."

"Good night, Regina." Gabriel faded into a blip of light.

"Good night, Gabriel."

Regina returned to her room and tried to go to sleep. Thoughts of the vision continued to swim in her mind. She began to replay all of the events in her head but got stuck when she remembered how Zechariah's peers mocked him.

Regina got angrier and angrier as she thought of the looks on the faces of the priests who cruelly spoke of Zechariah. She thought of the sadness Zechariah and Elizabeth felt, and it reminded her of how she felt when Frank accosted her in front of everyone in the lunch room. She recalled it as the straw that broke the camel's back. All of the bullying from Frank finally caused her to boil over, and she began to dwell on her fury. The combination of her fury at Frank and her anger at the detractors of Zechariah clouded her mind from love. She fell into wrath, only for a moment, which was all the waiting demon needed.

Suddenly, Regina felt a darkness enter the room. Her heart began to race and she felt frozen in time. She couldn't open her eyes to look at the presence but she felt it. She never knew this kind of terror before. At first, she could only hear the sound of her own heart pounding while she felt a crushing force pressing down on her. Then, a grisly voice spoke in the darkness.

"So, your God has chosen you for an important mission. My lord chose me as well. Your angel cannot protect you from me. I can taste your fear. I have so much more torment to bring you."

The room seemed to shake around her as she heard the pounding of her heart as it attempted to break free of her chest. Regina wanted to cry out for her mother at first. Then, she wanted to call out to her father. That reminded her of her training. She didn't need *her* father. She needed …

"Our Father, who art in Heaven," Regina began in desperation. The darkness recoiled a little and a familiar voice cried out to her.

"Regina, I'm here," Lucy said. She too, seemed out of breath.

Regina continued her prayer confidently with her guardian angel at her side. The demon wavered. Its grip on her mind relaxed. Regina thought she had gained the upper hand, but the evil surged back long enough to give her one final spine tingling chill.

"Next time I'll bring friends." It left.

A second passed before copious tears began to fall from her eyes. Her heart beat slowed, her breathing returned to normal, and she spoke out loud to Lucy.

"What happened?"

"I'm so sorry Regina," Lucy began. "A group of tormentors, under the supervision of your new tempter, trapped me. They call this beast, Atramors. It appears your old tempter has been punished."

"Don't be sorry. I was too busy being angry that I forgot to turn to prayer when the demon came upon me."

"Don't beat yourself up, Regina. You will take many wrong steps on your journey, but God believes in you. You will make it. Let us pray for strength again."

They prayed together and Regina felt better. The terror of the spiritual battle began to dissipate. While calm enveloped her, she knew she would not forget the events of that night. Lucy prayed a Rosary with Regina until she could fall asleep. She kept wondering when they would come again.

Chapter 14
A Voice Cries Out

Thursday, December 5th
6:58 AM

When Regina opened her eyes, she immediately looked around her room. She still carried some of the fear that strangled her the night before. Although she could no longer feel the suffocating pressure from the new tempter, the memory replayed in her mind. She said a prayer to set her thoughts straight and got prepared for school.

"Mommy?" Regina asked when she finally got downstairs to eat the breakfast that awaited her. Her father had already left for work. She really wished she could have talked to him about the demon's attack. She again feared her mother would not take it well.

"Yes, dear?"

"Are you going somewhere?"

"Why do you ask that?"

"You look very nice," Regina started. "Not that you don't always look nice."

"I am going to work at a shelter when you guys go to school. I've been doing it all week," Katherine said.

"Oh yeah, I forgot."

"I'm sure you've had a lot on your mind."

Emmanuel stared out the window as he ate his breakfast. He didn't pay attention to their conversation at all.

"Saint Gabriel showed me another vision last night, but he said he wouldn't complete it until I go see Frank."

Her mother stopped what she was doing and looked at her for a moment. "What was the vision about?"

"I saw Zechariah lose his voice and Our Lady visit Saint Elizabeth."

"Interesting." Regina could tell her mother thought of something she didn't share out loud.

"What?"

"Oh, nothing. I did talk to Frank's mother about visiting. It lifted some of the sadness in her voice. The doctor's say he's stable and she invited us to come as soon as we could. I need to go to a parent-teacher conference at Manny's school tonight, but I will take you to see Frank tomorrow right after school. I think Emmanuel can stay at Johnny's house."

Emmanuel seemed excited at the prospect of going to his best friend's house. It meant playing with toy cars or video games. He talked about it all the way to school. It would be complete enjoyment either way.

The day rolled along as normal, but then Regina started to dwell on her battle with the new tempter and her visit to Frank and lost focus on her studies. Then her thoughts drifted away from her visions into other things in her life, until she heard Lucy's voice barely break through.

Regina, focus on school. The nudge helped her shake her distraction.

What happened to me? She hoped Lucy would respond.

Your tempter slowly led you to think wasteful thoughts. You have not been doing the daily work God wants you to do.

Regina accepted her fault and spent the rest of the day dedicated to her school tasks. She did them with a prayerful spirit and found it gave her great strength to keep the demon at bay. She thought of her father's words about the holiness of her studies and daily work and attended to them with purpose.

Nothing happened that evening, but the next day at school Regina had the same problems focusing on her studies. Her tempter constantly distracted her from her duties.

At the end of day, Regina left school and found her mom in the usual spot. She always parked under a tree at the end of the parking lot. She opened the backdoor and threw her backpack into the car.

"Hi, mommy."

"Are you ready to go see Frank, Regina? Manny went straight to Johnny's house."

"Yes. I've been thinking about it a lot today."

"Okay, let's go." Regina hopped into her seat and they made the short trip to the hospital. On the way, Regina tried to think of how she could apologize to Frank for her part in the fight. She played over several different versions until she settled on *Frank, I am so sorry for what I said to you about your dad. I wish I could take it all back and keep you from your accident, but I can't. I can only hope you can forgive me.* She hoped Frank would be merciful enough to accept her apology.

They arrived at the hospital and asked the receptionist for Frank's room number. The woman told them, 832. They thanked her and took the elevator up to the eighth floor. When they stepped out, the first thing they saw was the empty nurses' station, so they decided to find Frank's room for themselves.

As they approached the room, Frank's mom stepped out. She looked up to see Regina and Katherine. Regina felt frightened. She expected to be yelled at, but instead she saw a big smile form on Mrs. Roland's face.

"Katherine, Regina, I'm so glad you came. No one but my daughters have come to see Frank. Thank you."

"You're very welcome," Katherine said. "Regina would really like to tell Frank she's sorry for their fight. She is hoping to make amends with him."

Louise Roland looked at Regina with deep concern.

"Oh, I'm sorry, dear. Earlier today, the doctors felt the pressure on Frank's brain was so great they decided to induce a coma. He hasn't been conscious since then." The last few words were muffled with tears. Regina watched her mother go to embrace the rattled woman as she shook from the grief. Numb from the news, Regina looked around the hospital hallway. Her eyes came across a crucifix on the wall. She looked into the eyes of Jesus and saw the sorrow in them mirror her own. She continued to stare and unconsciously fell to her knees.

"Oh Lord, help me." Another vision overcame her.

When Regina's vision returned, she recognized Elizabeth and Zechariah's house. The house looked the same, but she saw Elizabeth's belly now protruded much further than it did during her last vision.

"Mary?" Elizabeth called for her cousin as she shuffled across the room. At her age and in her condition she moved very slowly.

Mary entered from another room and rushed to her cousin's aid. "Cousin, why are you out of bed? You should be resting."

"I didn't want to lie in bed all day, but as I reached this room I felt my labor pains begin. Can you help me get back to my bed?" Mary led her back to her room and rushed to call the midwife. She told all the servants to get ready and explained to a distraught Zechariah that everything would be alright.

Regina watched as the servants whirred about in fast forward as the ordeal of the labor lingered on and on. Mary comforted Elizabeth in her pains with soft words and prayers. Elizabeth stayed calm but Regina could see her discomfort.

"I think this is a sign, dear cousin, that my child is destined for the discomfort of many," Elizabeth said with a sly smile, between shallow puffs of breath.

"I'm sure his day will come, but he will be a comfort to his faithful mother and father, I'm sure," Mary said. She wiped Elizabeth's brow and massaged her back.

Suddenly, Mary swooned and collapsed into the arms of the servant standing next to her.

"What happened?" Regina said.

"Mary worked so hard to keep Elizabeth comfortable that she neglected her own nutrition and health. Her body gave out on her," Gabriel said.

Elizabeth managed to command some servants to carry Mary to a bed in a nearby room. Zechariah saw the servants bring Mary out of the delivery room and helped them take her to a room to rest. Regina and Gabriel followed them. Regina saw the worried look on Zechariah's face as he left Mary unconscious on the bed.

Regina spent more time watching the frantic activity around Elizabeth as servants continued to bring fresh towels and clean water into the room.

"The child is coming," the midwife said.

The servants picked up their activity. One went out to inform Zechariah and the male servants waiting with him that the birth approached. They all smiled and began to pat Zechariah on the back and congratulate him.

Regina returned to Elizabeth's bedside.

"It's a boy," the midwife said. The same servant ran out to announce the news to the men. Regina heard cheers from the crowd. Moments later, she saw the look on the midwife's face change from excited to terrified.

"He's not breathing!" she exclaimed. All present let out a worried gasp. Zechariah, who had crept up to doorway to hear his child's first cries, instead heard the horrible news.

Gabriel, who had remained strangely silent, finally spoke. "You are going to like this." Regina, forgetting this story had a happy ending, felt frightened for the newborn child. She looked at Zechariah's face that showed a pain far worse than what he felt when his peers mocked him. To almost have a son to hold, but then lose him, would be too much for his old heart to bear.

Then Regina saw a flash of revelation come across Zechariah, who hurried off from his waiting room. Regina followed him to the room where Mary rested. She still slept on the bed. Zechariah ran up to her unable to speak. He gently but firmly shook her shoulder until she came out of her slumber.

Coming to, she saw the look on Zechariah's face and said, "Cousin? What is it?" Zechariah stood up and motioned for her to follow. Sensing great need, Mary raced after Zechariah, who didn't wait for her. They both ran into the delivery room where the servants cried and Elizabeth sat in shock.

"Mary, my son is not breathing," she finally cried out, with a look of desperate anguish. Regina could tell it was a plea for her help.

Mary went over to the child, turning blue, and picked him up. She cradled him in her arms and prayed. Regina saw a flash of light as the Son reached through his mother, and spiritually touched the infant John, saving his life.

The child cried out with a loud shriek, filling the house with a heavenly sound. Everyone exhaled in relief and the babe continued to bawl at the shock of the new world he had entered. Zechariah left the delivery room as custom required.

Elizabeth knew her closer kin surrounded her, but she fixed her gaze on Mary and her child, who the young virgin still held. "Thank you, Mary. Blessed are you, and blessed is the child within your womb," she said, repeating her earlier words.

Mary smiled and handed the baby to his mother. Others swaddled the baby and he quickly calmed long enough to nurse. Elizabeth smiled proudly and said, "I am so glad you are here Mary." Looking at Mary's belly, she added, "Both of you."

The scene changed and Regina found she had moved to the living room, still in Elizabeth and Zechariah's house. Many days had passed, the color in Elizabeth's face had returned, and she could walk about comfortably. Many new people graced the crowd, men and women alike, all dressed up for a special occasion.

"What is happening here, Gabriel?"

"This is now the eighth day after the baby's birth. It is time for his circumcision, according to Jewish custom. He will also be given his name," the angel said.

Regina walked over to a group of women waiting with Elizabeth and Mary.

"What are you going to name him, Elizabeth?" one woman asked. She appeared to be about Elizabeth's age.

"We will call him John."

"John? Zechariah does not have anyone in his family named John. Surely he will want to name him for his father or grandfather." The woman scowled and walked away. Elizabeth did not seem to care in the least bit. She fixed her attention on the miracle child in her arms. He slept through all of the commotion of the guests. Regina followed the woman to see where she went.

She walked straight into another room where Zechariah sat with some men. The woman whispered something into the ear of one of the men. Her husband, Regina assumed. He listened to what his wife told him and said, "Zechariah, will you name the child after yourself, or perhaps your father?"

Zechariah looked at the man and shook his head.

"My wife says Elizabeth wants to name your son John. Surely you would honor one of your ancestors by naming him after them." Again, Zechariah shook his head and forced himself out of his seat. He walked over to a table to pick up his writing tablet. He grabbed a pen, scribbled something on the tablet, and handed it to the man.

The man read the tablet. "His name is John."

"Here we go," Gabriel said to Regina.

As soon as the man read what Zechariah had written on the tablet, Zechariah's eyes opened wide and he clutched his throat. He hummed for a moment, cleared his throat, and then spoke in a loud booming voice, which caused everyone in the house to come running.

"Blessed be the Lord, The God of Israel;

He has come to his people and set them free."

Zechariah paused for a moment as the gathered crowd all gasped in alarm. He continued looking intently at Mary. No one but Elizabeth, Mary, Regina, and Gabriel could tell Zechariah fixed his gaze on her.

"He has raised up for us a mighty Savior,
Born of the house of his servant David.
Through his holy prophets he promised of old
That he would save us from our enemies,
From the hands of all who hate us.
He promised to show mercy to our fathers
And to remember his holy Covenant.
This was the oath he swore to our father Abraham:
To set us free from the hands of our enemies,
Free to worship him without fear,
Holy and righteous in his sight
All the days of our life."

Zechariah paused again to take the infant John into his arms. He carefully held him aloft as an offering to heaven and said,

"You, My child shall be called
The prophet of the Most High,
For you will go before the Lord to prepare his way,
To give his people knowledge of salvation
By the forgiveness of their sins.
In the tender compassion of our Lord
The dawn from on high shall break upon us,
to shine on those who dwell in darkness
And the shadow of death,
And to guide our feet into the way of peace."

Many of their guests exchanged questions of amazement.

"What does this mean?" one man said.

"What will this child become?" another asked.

Regina smiled to herself and looked to Gabriel.

"Before John the Baptist became the voice crying out in the wilderness, his father cried out in faith to atone for his doubt. He completed his penance of silence and God graced him to speak the amazing words you heard. It's time for you to go back and do your penance. Speak with faith Regina, what you need to say."

Regina barely had a moment to think about what Gabriel meant before the vision finished and she fell harshly back into the real world. She realized she still knelt in front of the crucifix.

"Regina, are you alright?" Katherine asked. She heard her mother speak but continued gazing on the face of Jesus. She remembered Gabriel's parting words and set her heart on the sorrow she owed Frank and God, whom she loved above all things.

"I'm sorry." She spoke the simple words barely above a whisper intending for only Jesus and Frank's spirit to hear.

"Regina!" The desperate and shocking voice came from the hospital room behind them. Regina turned quickly to see the look of shock on Mrs. Roland's face. She gasped and turned to run into her son's room.

"Frank?" Louise disappeared around the corner. Regina got off her knees and went to her mother. Together, they entered the room to find Mrs. Roland stroking her son's bandaged head, hoping for some more words. They didn't come.

"Franky? Franky?" She looked up and saw the Andrews waiting in the doorway. "Come in, come in. He is supposed to be in a drug induced coma to help his brain remain stress free. I don't know how he just spoke."

Regina stepped forward, unsure of what to expect. Several machines pumped life into Frank's heavily bandaged body. Wrappings almost completely covered his bruised eyes.

"I'll go get the doctor and tell him what happened," Louise said. Katherine Andrews waited at the door. Regina went and touched Frank's hand, afraid of what might happen. Suddenly, his eyes fluttered under their swollen lids like someone within a dream. A few moments of this passed until he became still and rigid again.

Suddenly, his eyes shot open, startling Regina. Just as his mother and doctor entered the room, he looked right at Regina and said with an exhausted voice, "I forgive you, pray for me." His eyes closed and his body relaxed into the familiar deep sleep.

Everyone in the room looked at each other without speaking. Frank's doctor stared at his patient in shock. He moved to the bed to examine Frank. Regina went to Katherine's embrace. They all waited to see what the doctor would say.

"All vitals are normal. I can't explain what happened," the doctor said. Louise Roland exhaled.

"Louise, I think we should go. Thank you for having us. We will keep you in our prayers," Katherine said.

Louise nodded her head in response, but did not take her eyes off her son. Regina surprised herself by asking, "Mrs. Roland, could I come back and visit Frank again?"

This broke her focus on Frank and she turned, eyes full of tears, and moved to hug Regina. "Yes, of course dear. Please come whenever you want."

Regina smiled and after taking one last look at Frank, walked with her mother out of the room and back to their car.

Right after the car crash, Frank wondered if he would ever escape the blackness he found himself steeped in. Time meant nothing in this empty space. His mind had plenty of time to reflect on his life and his heart broke from the grief he caused his loved ones, especially his mother.

When he felt like he couldn't take any more of the darkness, a flash of light broke him out of the pitch. A marvelous being in dazzling, white robes stood before him. Even though his body lay broken in a hospital bed, he felt free to move in his mind and fell to his knees. Frank never saw anything as beautiful and frightening in his life.

"Arise, Francis. Do not be afraid. I am Raphael." When Frank heard the angel speak the name Raphael he heard both the actual word and the words *God heals*.

"Am I dead?"

"No my child, you still live. Your body is in a hospital. Your mother weeps at your side."

Frank pictured his mother crying over him and his heart broke again.

"Where are we now?"

"I am speaking to you in your soul. Your mother remembered me from her youth. Her grandmother would always tell her when she was ill to pray to Saint Raphael, the archangel. She told your mother I would raise her prayers up to God."

"I don't believe in God," Frank said. He still held onto the anger that he knew put him in this position.

"Really? Why not?"

"I don't know. I just don't."

"I think you do know and I can't heal your body until you choose to heal your soul." The angel spoke with a soothing voice.

Frank never discussed why he resented God; he simply liked to express it. The angel challenged him with this ultimatum and forced him to drag the deep, buried pain up to the surface.

"He killed my father!" Frank yelled throughout his soul. He convulsed with sobs. "He was my best friend and God stole him from me!"

The rage had filled his soul for many years. The pain of his father's death haunted his every step and now, like a volcano, the emotions spewed from him. The angel did nothing to stop his furious explosion. After finishing his rant, Frank felt exhausted.

"I have someone for you to meet," Raphael said. From behind the angel's aura stepped a man.

"Dad!"

The spirit moved to embrace Frank. The son fell into the father's embrace and emptied the tears he had saved over the years. The man held his son and allowed him to shed his pain.

"Son, do not be angry with God. I am always with you," Tim Roland said.

"But you aren't! Mom and the girls don't understand me. I feel so alone." Frank vented what he wanted to say the last few years.

"I am always with you: when you sleep, when you are awake, and if you can find it in your heart to pray."

"I don't know if I can," Frank said.

"I know you can, son. Offer your anger and sorrow to God. Ask him for forgiveness and to take you back as a spiritual son. He will be your Father as I was. We will both be with you as go through life."

Frank's tempter urged him to hold on to the anger. *If you hold onto your hate, it will protect you from being hurt.*

Frank's guardian simply allowed his father's words to echo in his heart. *I know you can, son.* The words broke the dam within him. His love for his father allowed a torrent of remorse for the petulance he displayed towards the Lord to spill out. Again his soul sobbed, but this time for his sins.

Raphael, who waited in silence, spoke now. "The Lord accepts your contrition, Frank Roland. He rejoices in you as a shepherd rejoices in finding a lost sheep. You have been saved from death for a special calling."

It took Frank some time to recover from his outburst and subsequent reconciliation.

"What special calling?"

"Your healing has already begun, but is far from complete. The Lord wants you to suffer to save those who have hardened their hearts against God. Everyone has had the seeds of faith planted within their hearts and you will water those seeds with your pain. After this time, you will bring them God's word, so the fruits of the Spirit may shine forth through their lives." The angel's beautiful language confused Frank.

"I'm sorry, Saint Raphael. I still don't understand."

"You hardened your heart to the Lord because of your father's death. People turn away from God for so many reasons. There are so many excuses people use to build up walls to block out the love of Jesus. These walls cannot be torn down without prayer and sacrifice, both from the wounded souls and from those who love them. You will have to bring this message to the world."

Frank thought about the wall of anger he built up around his heart since his father's death. It almost led to his death. It should have. Why did he survive? Was it really for this purpose? How did God get through? The answer came through like a lightning bolt.

"My mom!"

"Very good, keep going."

"My mom's prayers, she never gave up on me. She told me so many times over the last few years she prayed for me. I got so angry and told her to stop wasting her time, but I saw her, night after night, on her knees."

"Yes Frank, your mother's love and devotion eventually broke down your wall. She especially invoked the intercession of Saint Monica, the mother of Saint Augustine. Augustine lived a life of sin that made a wall so large and thick, it would make yours look like paper, but Saint Monica never gave up hope and continued to pray and suffer for him until God tore down his wall. Augustine became one of the most brilliant theologians of all time. Her prayers in concert with your mother's helped you out of your darkness."

Thinking about his past, Frank returned to sadness. "I kept my mother from church. I kept her from God."

"When the Lord determines the time in your current state is over, you will be able to make amends to your mother. Know that he has freed your heart from the oppression you placed it in. Now, you must focus on your mission and pray."

Frank nodded in agreement. "Will you help me?"

"Of course, and I will soon send you an advisor as well. Together we pray, *Our Father ... *"

They prayed together and Frank wondered what Raphael meant about an advisor. His soul melted into an ecstasy he could have lived in forever, while his body remained shattered on the hospital bed.

Misero paced furiously in the space behind his desk while a cowering tempter sat quivering in the chair across from him.

"How could you let this happen? We had that boy! We had him set for a lifetime of sin."

"It wasn't my fault, boss. I tried manipulating him in his coma, but our enemy sent in some serious help. I can't say for sure, but it might have been an archangel," Frank Roland's tempter said. "I've never seen a conversion like that. Please, have mercy."

"Mercy? I don't know the meaning of the word," Misero said. The smaller demon closed his eyes and winced. Misero made a fist and appeared ready to strike, but changed his mind.

"Get out of my office, you fool! I don't have time for you." The trembling monster opened his eyes and quickly ran from the room.

Left alone, Misero sent objects flying around the room without touching them. He swiped everything off his desk and then proceeded to overturn it and his chair. The chaos ended and he surveyed the mess.

"If I don't get a handle on this soon, the Master will feast on my suffering." He realized something. He righted his desk and rummaged through a drawer. Pulling out a book and rifling through its pages, he arrived at what he wanted.

"Ah, yes. The Job Rule." He bared his hideous smile. "That should work very nicely indeed."

The next morning, Regina awoke to the sound of her father's voice in the distance. She checked her clock and saw her alarm wouldn't buzz for over an hour. She decided to investigate and found her father sitting in the living room reading out of a red book.

"Daddy, what are you doing?"

"G., I didn't wake you up, did I?" Her father looked concerned. "I thought I kept my prayers quiet enough."

"No. I woke up on my own, but then I heard your voice and wanted to see what you were doing." Regina thought maybe Lucy woke her up to talk to her dad. *Thanks, Lucy.*

Mark Andrews looked relieved. He motioned for Regina to sit by him on the couch. She joined him.

"This is a breviary." He showed Regina the book, which had several multicolored strings dangling out of it. "It contains prayers for different points in the day."

"Like the Angelus?"

"Yes, but here you pray using mainly the psalms. The church requires priests and religious to offer these prayers every day, but anyone can join them as a personal devotion. We call them the Divine Office."

"Do you do this every day?"

"I used to, again, back in college. I fell out of practice and didn't even remember I had this. I guess you could say I have you to thank again for bringing me back to it." He smiled at her and she smiled back.

"How does it work? I mean, what do you do?"

"Well, it is kind of like the Liturgy of the Word at church. There are psalms, a reading, responses, a Gospel Canticle, pray-," he explained before Regina cut in.

"Canticle? Is that like the Magnificat?"

"I'm impressed you know that word. Do you remember that from R.E.?"

"Oh yeah, you came home late last night. I didn't get to tell you about my latest vision."

Mark raised his eyebrows and waited.

"I saw the Magnificat and I know it is called the Canticle of Mary. Then Gabriel showed me the birth of John the Baptist and the Canticle of Zechariah."

"Wow, tell me more."

She told him the whole story of the visions and Frank's speaking from the coma. Her father drank in her words. When she finished, he said, "We will have to call Father Joe and see if he can see you soon, so you can update him on your visions." He looked at the clock. "For now, I will simply tell you the words of Mary and Zechariah are so important, people pray them around the world every day. The Canticle of Zechariah for morning prayer and the Canticle of Mary for evening prayer."

"That is a lot of devotional prayers. The Angelus, the Divine Office, the Rosary…"

"Well, you eat three times a day don't you?" Mark asked.

"Yes."

"The Lord in his wisdom has given us structured ways to feed our soul throughout the day as well. Hundreds upon thousands of Saints have used these devotions to prepare their souls for heaven."

The explanation made a lot of sense to Regina. She thanked her father, kissed him goodbye, found she could still use some more sleep, and headed back up to her bedroom.

Chapter 15
Life

Saturday, December 7th
9:14 AM

After breakfast, Regina went to her room to clean up. When she came back down, she found her mother sitting on the couch reading a book. Katherine did not look up, even as Regina sat beside her.

"What are you reading now?" Regina asked.

"Huh?" Katherine said, not breaking her focus.

"What are you reading?"

Katherine looked at Regina.

"Oh, sorry, it's called *Left to Tell*."

"What's it about?"

"It's about a woman named Immaculee Ilibagiza, who had to hide in a tiny bathroom with seven other women for three months."

"What? Why?"

Katherine Andrews measured her daughter with her eyes. "I guess you are old enough to know, Regina." She paused for a second, thinking of how she would begin. "Men were hunting her."

"Hunting her? Like an animal?"

"Yes."

"Why would they do that?"

"Basically, because she was different from them and they feared that."

"That's it?"

"It's worse than that, Regina. Some of these people were her neighbors and friends. They also killed her parents and some of her siblings while she remained hidden."

"That's awful." Regina tried to make sense of this. "But how could they kill their own friends?"

"It's a sad story that has happened over and over throughout history. Bad leaders made their followers think others were less human than them."

"How?"

"With their words."

"That's it?"

"Yes. In Africa, there is a country called Rwanda. In Rwanda, there are two different tribes of people, the Hutus and the Tutsis."

"Tribes? Like Cherokees and Seminoles?"

"Like that, yes," Katherine said. "Germany originally controlled Rwanda as a colony, but then the Belgians took over. When they did, many years ago, they placed favor on the Tutsis because they looked more European. The Belgian governors gave people with Tutsi heritage positions of authority and more opportunities for education and advancement."

"Didn't that make the Hutus angry?"

"Of course. Not only was it unjust, but very dangerous and foolish, because the Hutus outnumbered the Tutsis."

"Did the Hutus fight back?"

"Not at that time, because the Belgian soldiers had far better weapons and training. They could not win that battle."

"Then what happened?"

"When the Belgians left Rwanda, the Hutu majority won the fight for supremacy and took power. The Hutu government oppressed the Tutsis as payback, but most people lived their lives ignoring the differences between themselves and their neighbors from the opposite tribe. The Tutsis took their turn as the inferiors in the country, but life seemed to go on. Then, things changed."

"What happened?"

"Hutu extremists took control of the government and started to broadcast on radio and television, day and night, that the Tutsis were not to be trusted. They claimed Tutsis were trying to take control of the country so they could be in charge again. They provoked the historical anger the Hutus had for the Tutsis. The extremists called the Tutsis 'cockroaches' over and over. Like cockroaches, they said the Tutsis needed to be exterminated."

Regina gasped at the language her mother used. "What happened then?"

"The bloodthirsty Hutu government formed death squads to hunt down all the Tutsis. The gangs murdered those they considered cockroaches and any Hutus who didn't support their tactics."

"They killed Hutus too?"

"Yes. They considered them to be Tutsi supporters, making them enemies of the state."

"I would never kill anyone. Even my life depended on it," Regina said.

"I hope your conviction is never tested, dear. Fear can be a powerful motivator, even stronger than anger. It is more primal, more animal."

"So this girl, Im.., Im…"

"Immaculee," Katherine said.

"Immaculee. She found a place to hide?"

"Not easily. Her parents literally had to beg a neighborhood Hutu minister to take her. He finally agreed and hid her in a tiny bathroom with seven other Tutsi women. They stayed there for three terrifying months."

"They never left?"

"Not once. The minister managed to bring them scraps of food every so often, but they had to stay there the whole time. She went from one hundred fifteen pounds down to sixty-five. When she got out of the bathroom, she found out almost all of her family had been murdered."

Regina felt rage well up inside her. "Was she angry?"

"That is the amazing part of this story, Regina," Katherine replied. The clenching tension binding Regina dissipated.

"What do you mean?"

"At first, she felt great wrath, but all she could do in the cramped bathroom was pray. She said constant Rosaries for herself and her fellow prisoners. She prayed all day and night until at one point, she started to have visions of Our Lord."

"Jesus came to her? What did he say?"

"He told her to pray for his Divine Mercy, not only for her but for the killers in the streets. She hated them and didn't want to, but since the Lord demanded it of her, she did. Hour after hour, and day after day, she continued. She gained a great knowledge about evil and its power over the world."

"Did the others pray with her?"

"Not at first. They called her crazy and resented her at first, since she came in last making the bathroom even more crowded. However, eventually, her loving care for them in their sickness won them over."

"How did they get rescued?"

"The violence ended and the United Nations negotiated peace talks. The women left their bathroom and excitedly headed to a UN safe zone, but then, a wandering Hutu death squad captured them."

Regina gasped, but her mother continued, expecting her fear. "The killers taunted them and threatened their lives, but Immaculee knew Jesus had not saved her only to be killed. She yelled out, 'Go away, evil!' A machete wielding killer was ready to strike but paused. He looked like he saw a ghost and then simply walked away. His comrades did the same."

"No way!"

"Immaculee found out only one of her brothers had survived the massacre. Jesus told her to personally go to prison and forgive the man who killed her family. She did."

"That's amazing!"

"She now goes around the world telling her story of forgiveness in the face of hatred."

"I don't know if I could do that," Regina said. "I'm so glad that kind of killing could never happen in America."

Katherine Andrews had been smiling about the positive ending to Immaculee's story, but the smile fell off her face. Regina noticed the change.

"What is it?"

Her mother wrestled with something else in her mind. "Regina, you know how I've been volunteering at the Crisis Pregnancy Center?"

"Yes."

"Do you know what I do there?"

"You counsel women on how to take care of babies." Regina felt pretty confident in her response.

"No, Regina, I counsel women to have their babies."

"What do you mean?"

Katherine paused. "I think you are old enough to know this, sweetheart. There is a slaughter happening in this country that I find as horrifying as Rwanda's."

Regina's curiosity piqued. She had to know what her mother meant. "What could be that bad?"

"In Rwanda, you understand how the Hutus used dehumanizing words to make it easier for people to kill the Tutsis, who they considered a problem and a threat to their way of life?"

"What do you mean, like cockroaches?"

"Exactly. Well, in the United States, many people have done the same thing, with babies in their mother's wombs."

"What?" Regina did not understand her mother's point. "How can anyone feel threatened by a baby?"

"Do you know what abortion is, Regina?"

"No, but I know we pray to end it at church. Is it a disease?" She couldn't think of what else it would be.

"No, it is when a doctor kills a woman's baby before it is born."

Regina's horror must have been evident in her eyes because she could see the regret in her mother's face in an instant. Regina could tell her mother wished she hadn't taken the conversation in this direction.

"That's impossible!" Regina thought of the many baby showers she had been to. Everyone congratulated the expecting mothers who seemed so happy. She then thought of the baptisms she attended. The celebrations could not have been happier.

"It's not. Unfortunately, it's very real and how it happens is very much the same as what happened to the Tutsis in Rwanda."

Fighting back tears, Regina asked, "How?"

"In 1973, the Supreme Court of the United States, based upon the evidence of the time and terrible logic, decided that an unborn child was not a person, but actually part of the mother's body, like an organ or a bone. They stated a woman can do what she wants with her own body. So women can choose to kill their own child growing inside them." Katherine tried to explain it as plainly as possible, but her adult mind did not realize Regina didn't care about the history or legality of the procedure. She had one simple question.

"Why would anyone want to do something so horrible?" Regina felt her world crumbling. She always believed in God, and the events of the past few weeks made her believe in the Devil, but she wouldn't have needed the visions to tell her evil was real, if she had only heard this about the world she lived in.

"No one."

"What?" None of this made any sense to begin with, and her mother didn't help things with her confusing answers.

"Any woman that I counsel at the center doesn't want to kill their own 'child', but she could get 'rid of a problem' or an 'unplanned pregnancy' or a 'fetus'. This is what people who support abortion do. They use words to dehumanize the baby. If you hear those words enough, you lose your touch with the truth. A frightened mother won't kill her baby; she will be making a 'choice'."

Katherine watched her daughter struggle with this startling revelation. She continued, "Regina, the Hutus could see the Tutsis with their own eyes. They had known them as friends and neighbors for years. They had laughed, played, and even prayed with them, yet when they heard the Tutsis were cockroaches for long enough, they ignored their humanity and killed them. Unfortunately, an unborn baby has little hope when visible people have been killed throughout history."

"Can't we do something?"

"You can pray," her mother said. "Pray for the intercession of Our Lady of Guadalupe. Her feast day is coming soon."

"Our Lady of what?"

"Guadalupe."

"Why?"

"Over five hundred years ago, before Europeans fully conquered North and South America, many native civilizations existed. One of them was the Aztecs. Their brutal power struck fear into their opponents. Everyone knew that they used human sacrifice in their religious rituals."

"Real people?"

"Yes, thousands of people would be killed a year. One day, a native named Juan Diego, who had converted to Christianity, walked on a path outside what is now Mexico City, but was the capitol city of the Aztecs back then. A vision of Our Lady stopped him. She asked him to go to the bishop and have a church built for her."

"Did the bishop believe him?"

"No. He went and told the bishop, but he didn't believe him and asked Juan to come back with a sign. So, he went back to Mary, who told him to take a bunch of roses, which miraculously appeared on the rocky mountainside, to the bishop. Mind you, that type of rose didn't grow in Mexico. He gathered them up in his apron, called a tilma, and set off for the bishop's house. He opened up his tilma to drop the roses he gathered as a sign."

"Let me guess, the bishop believed him when he saw the roses?"

"Not quite. When he opened up his cloak and threw the roses on the table, the men gathered there were not really impressed with the roses."

"Why not?" Regina thought miraculous roses would be pretty cool to see.

"Because when he threw down the roses, everyone saw the beautiful image of Our Lady imprinted on his cloak. The same image you see every time we go to church. The one you called the 'Colorful Mary' when you were little."

Regina knew exactly which one her mother meant. The image of Mary looked like a young, native-American girl. She stood on a moon with the rays of the sun behind her. The painting hung in the alcove by the entrance to the crying room, on the opposite side of the painting of the Sacred Heart of Jesus.

"What happened then?"

"The bishop believed the story and had a church built upon the spot Our Lady requested. A bigger church stands there today. It houses the tilma of Juan Diego, which still miraculously exists, five hundred years later, with the same image."

"Still? How could it?" Regina thought of her own favorite clothes that had worn through in less than a couple of years. She didn't see how a piece of clothing could last for that long.

"It truly is a miracle. Scientists have studied the image for many years and can scientifically say it should have disintegrated long ago. The image has many other miracles associated with it, but most importantly, the human sacrifice ended soon after the apparition. In addition, Our Lord depicted his Mother as pregnant on the tilma. We call Our Lady of Guadalupe the Patroness of the Unborn. We pray for her intercession to help end the human sacrifice of abortion happening now."

The amazing story helped to subdue Regina's fears and anger. "Okay, mommy, I will pray, but what else can I do?"

Katherine thought for a few moments about this, wanting to help her daughter find some way to satisfy her conscience. "I know. You can come with me to the Crisis Pregnancy Shelter today and sit in the break room and pray. There may even be some envelopes for you to stuff. You could say I am doing this work because of you and your mission, Regina. I feel like God called me there. It would be good for you to go and see the place."

"Okay."

Regina went with her mother to the small office building. She brought her backpack full of school work to keep busy in case she couldn't remain focused on prayer. Her mother's shift went from noon to five and Regina wanted to be sure she had enough to do. When they arrived, Katherine showed her to the little break room where she unpacked her things and made herself at home.

"If you really need something, come and get me, but otherwise hang out here and I will stop in to check on you."

"Okay." Regina took out her Rosary and felt confident she would be able to keep herself occupied while her mother helped people in the office down the hall.

Katherine Andrews headed down the hall to sit at the phone banks. It took her some time to get used to the process of being a volunteer counselor at the center, but she felt like she had it down.

"Hi, Katherine," a woman in a business suit said.

"Hi." Katherine looked at her own clothes and forced a smile.

"What is it?"

"I feel a little under dressed," Katherine said.

"Don't be silly. The person on the other end of the line will never know what you're wearing. I dress this way because I have a wardrobe full of stuff that I will never wear now that I am retired, unless I force myself."

"Thanks, Mrs. Marcos."

"You're welcome, and call me Susanna, please."

"Okay, Susanna," Katherine said. They both smiled.

"Could you do a huge favor for me?" Susanna said.

"What is it?"

"Our face to face counselor called in sick today and I have a meeting I have to go to with a potential donor. Could you counsel a walk-in if we get one?"

The color left Katherine's face.

"Face to face?"

"Sure, you told me in your interview that you looked forward to that role."

"I assumed that would take months. I've only been volunteering here a week."

"You know I've been monitoring your phone calls, since you are new," Susanna said.

"Yes."

"Well, I can tell you are a natural. You will be fine. If you feel something is too much for you to handle, you can call Carla Banks. I'll leave her number, okay?" Susanna's encouragement found a home.

Katherine smiled and nodded. Susanna led her to a desk at the front of the office where Katherine could answer calls but also receive anyone who walked in for help. Putting on her coat, Susanna said, "I will be gone for a few hours for my meeting. Good luck."

"Bye," Katherine managed. Her confidence waned as she watched Susanna leave. She walked back to the break room to check on Regina. Regina prayed with her eyes closed and hummed a tune Katherine couldn't quite recognize. Katherine smiled and returned to her desk.

She straightened up the desk and then continued reading *Left to Tell*. She received two phone calls in the first hour. One woman didn't have enough money for groceries and hoped the center also acted as a food bank. Katherine apologized, but knew the number of the food bank, having volunteered there before. The second caller, a man, wanted to order a pizza. Katherine told him he had the wrong number and laughed to herself, because it happened several times before.

A few minutes into her second hour in charge, Katherine checked on Regina and returned to her desk. Moments later, she heard the ring of the bell on the front door. She looked up to see a visibly pregnant girl, in her early twenties, walk in. A frown strained her pretty face.

"Hi, my name is Katherine Andrews. Welcome. How can I help you?"

The girl looked at the smile on Katherine's face and returned her own nervous version. "Hi, I'm Maggie Rowen. I need to talk to someone."

Katherine stood up and escorted Maggie to a small room next to her greeting station. "Come in here and make yourself comfortable. I need to take care of something real quick and then I will be right with you."

Maggie went into the little room that had two comfortable leather chairs and a couch to settle into. Katherine went to Regina and said, "I am talking to someone in the meeting room in the front. I may be with her for a while so stay put and come get me only in an emergency. Okay, sweetie?"

"Okay."

"Regina, this is a chance for you to help through your prayer."

"Oh, okay. Thanks." She perked up.

Katherine smiled and returned to Maggie, who awkwardly shifted her weight around in the chair.

"It's hard to get comfortable, huh?" Katherine said.

"You have kids?" Maggie asked.

"Yes, two. I remember never being able to sit for more than a few minutes at a time in the same position."

Maggie laughed. Her tension eased.

"Do you want to have any more?"

Katherine's smile soured. "I had some complications with my second one. My doctor said I probably wouldn't be able to have any more. That was eight years ago." Her eyes took on a distant look as she finished her sentence.

"I'm so sorry, I didn't mean to…" Maggie didn't finish.

"It's okay, you couldn't have known." Katherine returned to the present. "How about you? How is your little one doing?"

"Fine, I guess. I don't have insurance so I haven't seen a doctor since I found out I was pregnant."

"Goodness, well we can certainly help you with that." She wrote down a note to get the forms for pre-natal care. "What else can we do for you?"

Tears began to pour down Maggie's face.

"I don't know where to begin," she said.

"Take your time." Katherine got up and got Maggie a box of tissues.

"I didn't know where to go. My boyfriend and I had a huge fight so I left him, and my mom moved to Florida to take care of my grandma." The words flowed like her tears and ended with sobbing.

They sat close enough together for Katherine to reach over and put her hand on Maggie's knee. "Why don't you take a minute and tell me your story from the beginning?"

Maggie wiped her eyes and blew her nose. She composed herself and began.

"I met my boyfriend a couple of years ago. I lived with my mother and she didn't like him. She said he bossed me around too much. It's funny because I could say the same about her. Anyway, I was taking nursing classes at the community college and working as a waitress at Ricky's, the steak house at the mall."

"Oh yeah, I've been there," Katherine said.

"It's good, right? So after constant fighting with my mom, I decided to move in with him. I knew I shouldn't have. My mom raised me to wait until marriage before living with someone, but I excused myself because of the fighting. My mom taught me that, too. My family would go to church every Sunday, but during my senior year, my brother died of cancer. Not too long after that, my father disappeared and left me and my mother alone. She responded by excusing us from going to church. She said God didn't care about her. She never let go of the hurt."

"What about you?"

"I don't know what I thought. I counted myself lucky because I could have gotten my brother's disease, too, but I didn't. I missed my dad but I still had my mom. We didn't fight all the time." Maggie paused for a moment deep in thought.

Katherine let her have a second. "So you moved in with your boyfriend?"

"Oh, yeah. Things were great. He has a good job and took care of me real well. We talked about getting married. Last year, my mom moved to Florida because my grandma got sick. The last thing she said to me is 'I'm going to live by grandma, because I guess *you* don't need me anymore.' She doesn't even know I'm pregnant." This brought more tears from Maggie.

Katherine got out another tissue and gave it to Maggie.

"When the pregnancy test turned up positive, I was terrified, because things were going so well. When I told my boyfriend, Paul, he tried to deny it. Then he told me I should get an abortion. I think it was the first time I told him no. I think I shocked him, but I knew I had to keep the baby. He tried to convince me, but something deep inside me kept me strong in my conviction. He said fine, we would work it out."

"What happened then?"

"Little by little he started to change. He would have bursts of anger and get a crazed look on his face when we argued. I thank God he never hit me, but he looked like he wanted to, and then recently he got worse."

"How so?"

"He pressured me to have an abortion again."

"What? Now?"

"Yes. He said our state allows late-term abortions and that the baby would ruin us. He said he didn't want to be tied down by an intruder. He called our baby an intruder. I came here because I don't know what to do. I don't think Paul would ever hurt me but I don't know what he might do to my baby." Maggie lost her composure and Katherine tried to console her.

In the break room, Regina prayed a Rosary with fervor. She had started the Second Joyful Mystery, The Visitation, when she heard Lucy's voice.

"Regina, go to your mother. She needs you."

"But she told me not to come unless it was an emergency."

"This is an emergency."

Regina had no reason to doubt Lucy but she wanted to honor her mother's wishes. "Are you sure?" She did not feel a response.

Regina got up and started to walk down the hall. As she left her room, she felt a voice stopping her.

Your mother said to stay where you are. You shouldn't bother her. Honor your father and mother.

Regina shook her head. She knew Lucy wanted her to go, but the new voice mentioned the fourth commandment, which she would be breaking.

She took a few more steps.

You don't want to disobey your mother. Go back to the break room and do what you are supposed to be doing.

Lucy's voice broke in. "What did your mother say you should be doing?"

Katherine told Regina to pray.

"Lord Jesus, help me!" Regina cried out. She recognized the darkness that slyly gripped her and felt it lifted. She took a deep breath.

"Your tempter used his cunning again," Lucy said. "Without fighting him with prayer, he can divert you from your mission in clever ways. He tried to use God's laws against you. The devil does not want you to go see your mother right now, so let's go."

Regina hurried down the hall to hear the steady crying coming from the room where her mother had to be. She poked her head around the wall to see the two women sitting next to each other in their chairs. Katherine spotted her and gave her a stern look.

Regina gave a sheepish smile. "Hi, mommy. I thought you might need me."

Maggie jumped at the sound of Regina's voice. She grabbed her large belly and a strange look came over her face. She turned to Katherine.

"Is this your daughter?"

"Yes, her name is Regina."

"Please come here," Maggie said, motioning to Regina. "Regina, may I hug you?"

Regina looked at her mother, who gave her the okay. Regina embraced Maggie for several moments. When they released, Maggie had a huge smile on her face, leaving both Katherine and Regina perplexed. Tears of joy replaced her tears of sorrow. They both awaited an explanation.

Maggie laughed and settled herself back into her chair. She couldn't contain her giddiness.

"I can't explain it. A few seconds ago, I had no idea where my life was headed, but when Regina spoke ..." Maggie laughed again and hugged her unborn child tightly. "My little girl jumped up and wanted to be with her. I felt my baby call me to hug Regina."

Katherine and Regina looked to each other in wonder. Regina thought of the Visitation

Maggie continued smiling.

"Then what happened?" Regina asked.

"When we touched, something happened in my heart. My spirit changed."

"Really? How?"

"I have no idea. I feel like God touched me in a special way through you. Suddenly, I am not terrified anymore. I still don't know what will happen to me, but I have hope. All I want to do is sing. Is that crazy?"

Regina thought of the Canticles of Mary and Zechariah and said, "No, that's not crazy at all."

Chapter 16
The Homily

Saturday, December 7th
6:03 PM

Later that night, family dinner buzzed with the relating of Maggie's story. Regina raced through, trying to get to the end, but Katherine reined her in, making sure to supply enough details for it to make sense.

Mark Andrews waited until they finished. "So what happened after that?"

"I didn't know what to say for the longest time, but after Maggie finished telling us what she experienced, we talked about some other plans for her. You know, ways to get her on her feet before the baby comes." Katherine gave Mark a funny look.

"Oh? Like what?" Mark asked, as if he knew something.

"Well, first I had her sign some forms to get her prenatal care, then I got her some short term housing, and we also arranged for her to meet with our financial counselor."

"And…?" Mark smiled at his wife.

Katherine gave in. "And, I invited her over for dinner tomorrow night."

Mark Andrews nodded his head and grinned even harder.

"Stop it," Katherine said, smiling as well. "You knew, Regina told you."

"No she didn't, but I know you." He chuckled and said, "Can't wait to meet your new friend."

"Daddy? Did you talk to Father Joe about meeting him?"

"I didn't get a hold of him earlier. I'll try him again after dinner."

After dinner, Mark called Father Joe and gave him a brief run down on some of the amazing things that happened since they last saw him. Regina listened to her father set up an appointment for the next morning and couldn't help but notice a strange look on her father's expressive face.

When he ended the call, she asked, "Daddy, what's the matter?"

"Father Joe sounded a little off. He didn't sound like his usual, upbeat self, but he did agree to see you tomorrow at 7:45 before R.E."

The evening passed quickly to bed time. Before Regina could drift into sleep, Lucy spoke to her while she prayed her evening Angelus.

"Regina, you must pray for Fr. Joe."

"I know. Daddy said he didn't sound well when they talked on the phone. Is he ill?"

"No, you know how your tempter attacks you?"

"Yes."

"There are more powerful demons the devil can employ called tormentors. They are making your priest suffer horribly. You must pray for him."

"I will," Regina said. She thought about what Lucy told her. "These tormentors will come after me too, won't they?"

Lucy did not respond. She didn't need to.

"Stay with me, Lucy," Regina said.

"Of course."

Regina prayed for Father Joe until she fell asleep.

Father Joe's Saturday did not pass as smoothly. The bishop called in the morning to discuss minor financial details for the parish. Tormentors tried to use the conversation to distract Father Joe from his mission, but God continued to speak to his heart.

He decided to take a walk in the local forest preserve to clear his head. He remembered the first conversation he had with Regina about her visions. She described the visualization her angel gave her for spiritual battle.

"My guardian angel told me to think about some kind of battle."

"What do you mean?"

"I saw a vision where I fought some dummies dressed as knights. I had to say prayers in order to use my sword. Saying Our Father's and Hail Mary's allowed me to cut the dummies apart."

Regina's simple understanding of spiritual warfare amazed Father Joe. He knew demons attacked his spirit now and decided to ask his guardian angel to help him battle them like Regina did.

"Peter, my guardian angel, you've always been there for me and I've neglected you. Please, join with me now, be my right hand, and help me fight in this war." God heard his prayer and gave the priest the grace to sense his angel more clearly than he ever had before. He couldn't see his angel like Regina, but he had no doubt of his presence.

Father Joe took out his Rosary. He thought of Saint Louis de Montfort's preaching of the Rosary as a weapon against evil.

"In the name of the Father…" He crossed himself and kissed the body of Our Lord before starting the first Our Father. What happened next, he could never explain.

The path before him changed before his eyes. What had been a defoliated forest covered in a small blanket of snow transformed to a scarred battlefield. Fighting raged all around him. He could hear the clashing of swords, the explosions of bombs, and the tormented screams of people. This new landscape confused and frightened him. He did not know what to make of the change in perception.

"Behold the spiritual state of the world," a voice behind him said.

Father Joe turned to see who spoke and beheld a beautiful young woman dressed in ancient clothes shining brightly. He fell to his knees. Tears of joy of this gift and sorrow for his sins poured from his body as Mary showered graces from her Son upon her priest.

"Rise, my son." Father Joe rose to his feet and wiped his face with his hands, but could not make himself look up.

"Look at me." He turned his yes upon the image and his heart melted with love. "My Son and Lord gave you a mission and you accepted it. The enemy will not let you progress without a fight. You see around you the state of mankind. You must prepare your flock. They have to know the real dangers of this world. Many risk the loss of their souls and have been given no chance to fight back."

"Mother, what if I frighten them away? The bishop has kept this parish running with financial support. If people leave because they don't want to hear the truth, he'll stop or maybe even remove me."

"Pray for your bishop. He has been given a very powerful tempter, one who has confused him about what his role as a shepherd should be. He is a good man. I will intercede on your behalf."

Father Joe realized his moment had arrived. He looked at the woman who accepted a much more difficult mission than his and drew strength from her. He knelt and closed his eyes.

"Hail Mary, full of grace, the Lord is with you. Blessed are you among woman, and blessed is the fruit of your womb, Jesus. Holy Mary, Mother of God, pray for us sinners, now, and at the hour of our death. Amen." He opened his eyes. The vision ended. On the snow where she stood sat a single, red rose. He picked it up. It warmed his hands.

He prayed many Rosaries that day. His mind and spirit came together as one. He envisioned the spiritual attack upon him as a war in his mind. He could see he had more than one tempter and several tormentors as well. The tempters kept trying to dissuade him from speaking the truth to his people and the tormentors barraged his mind with a range of dreadful thoughts and feelings. They forced upon him many emotions, like anger, jealousy, and lust, all leading him away from the love of God. Still, he battled on.

Luckily, I don't have 5 o'clock Mass, he thought to himself. He didn't see how he would be able to make it through. His battle raged on through dinner time into the evening. The phone ringing broke his deep, prayerful trance.

"Hello?" he answered.

Who is calling me at this hour? The anger in his own thoughts startled him. He looked at the caller ID.

It's the girl's father, the one who started all of this trouble, if only she hadn't had these visions, life would be so much simpler for me. Great! She had another vision. Don't meet with her.

He fought through the attack.

"Have her meet me in the morning at 7:45 at the school," he said tersely. He wrote down the appointment on a pad of paper. His demons continued to attack him. His head pounded with doubt and frustration with his mission. Minutes passed into an hour. He paced around his office, trying to clear his head. Finally, he happened to look down at the name he had written down. *Regina Marie.*

"Queen Mary!" The name broke through the deception his tempters worked on him. The battle ended for the time being. He got ready for bed, able to think clearly and thank God for the gift of Our Lady and the little girl who prayed for him at that moment as she fell asleep.

Regina didn't know that her priest's torment ended a short distance from her home but she did sense a vision coming as she lay in her bed.

She walked with Joseph as he walked alone along a road she recognized. "Joseph is getting close to Zechariah's house. I remember this path," Regina said. She assumed Gabriel stood beside her.

"Very good," Gabriel said.

Joseph made his way through the hills. In the distance, a lone traveler wearing a dark cloak walked towards them. The hood on his cloak hid his face, and he clearly had trouble walking. It didn't look like he carried a great load, but it seemed to burden him heavily.

As they neared each other, the stranger staggered and fell. Joseph ran forward to help him. The man's hood fell back as Joseph assisted him to his feet. He had long, stringy, gray hair and a shaggy beard. His leathery skin had more wrinkles than Regina could count and his eyes seemed impossibly black.

"Thank you, kind sir. May blessings be on you and your family."

"You are welcome. Are you alright?"

"Yes, yes, don't worry about me. Your children are probably waiting for you. Hurry home and see them," the old man said.

"Actually, I don't have any children," Joseph said.

"Surely an excellent fellow like you is married."

"Yes, well, soon. I am betrothed to a fine and faith-filled woman." Joseph helped the man gather the belongings he scattered in the fall. Regina felt Joseph's thoughts.

"The thought of Mary makes him happy. They spoke of making the poor their spiritual children on their travel to Elizabeth's house before," Regina said. She looked at Gabriel and saw he glared at the stranger. "What's wrong?"

The old man displayed a set of rotting teeth as he grinned. "It is good when a man has a wife who he trusts. A faithful woman is the greatest grace a man can be given, but a wayward wife can drive a man to ruin. Don't you agree, Joseph?"

Regina felt a strange sensation. The strange traveler's final words burned into her mind. She looked at Joseph, who shared the weird feeling. Joseph closed his eyes and shook his head trying to relieve himself of ringing which filled his head.

Joseph stumbled a few steps down the path; his eyes still closed. He opened them, remembering he hadn't said farewell to the old man. He and Regina were surprised to see he had disappeared.

Did he call me Joseph? How did he know my name?

"Where did the old man go?" Regina said.

"Not a man, a serpent, and he left his venom in Joseph," Gabriel said.

"What?"

"Joseph met a demon, one of the enemy's finest. You will soon see how his words poisoned Joseph."

Regina felt a chill. Time passed and they arrived at Elizabeth's house. Evening had already arrived. A servant met Joseph at the door and took his things. Zechariah came and said, "Joseph, you are here. Welcome."

"You have your voice again, praised be God," Joseph said.

"Yes, but despite having my voice, I don't have the words to express my joy at what the Lord has done for me." Zechariah explained all of the wonders surrounding the birth of John.

"He is so happy, Gabriel." Regina beamed as she listened to his story.

"Well, that's enough for tonight." Zechariah motioned to a servant who waited nearby. "We can talk more tomorrow when everyone is awake. Take Joseph to a free bedroom." The servant took Joseph's things and they tiptoed through the house.

The servant put Joseph's things down and turned to leave but stopped. "You are Mary's husband?"

"Yes," Joseph said.

"We all love her here." Joseph smiled and nodded his head, but before he could respond, the servant continued. "And congratulations to you."

"For what?" Joseph asked.

"For the coming of your child." The servant looked confused, but Joseph looked worse.

"What?" Joseph asked. He forgot the time of night.

"I know I shouldn't have been eavesdropping, but I heard my mistress and your wife discussing it." Joseph could not have opened his eyes any wider. "You didn't know. I'm so sorry, congratulations anyway," the servant said as he dashed from the room.

A wayward wife can drive a man to ruin. Joseph cringed and fell to his knees. Regina felt his pain.

"His heart is breaking," she said.

Joseph could do nothing for several moments but shake his head. Regina felt the demon's words echo over and over as Joseph thought about his conversations with Mary.

"How? Who? When?" The questions came out of Joseph as whispers but he screamed them in his mind. Regina felt the whirlwind of emotions inside Joseph. Somehow, he managed not to unleash the fury of his feelings. The storm would have awakened the neighborhood.

Joseph fell onto the bed and cried with his face buried, muffling the sound. "Father, I thought you called me to care for this girl. I thought we had the same values and dreams, but now I find her with child."

Regina thought her ability to feel the emotions of others in her visions had been a great gift, but now she felt cursed.

"What is he thinking, Regina?" Gabriel said.

"He imagines what will happen when the townspeople find out. He knows he will be humiliated, but Mary…" Regina said. She paused with a sudden gasp.

"They will stone her for sure," Joseph said. "I can't let that happen. Lord, what should I do?"

"No, Joseph, no," Regina said as Joseph relaxed.

"I will take her back to Simeon. He will hide her in the temple. I can say I divorced her for some reason and she will be safe." He nodded, satisfied with his plan. Regina shook her head.

"Relax, Regina. You know how this story ends," Gabriel said.

Regina thought about it. Her emotions had clouded her memory of scripture. "Oh, yeah."

Joseph fell into a troubled sleep. Even though he had a plan, his soul could not rest. Regina watched Joseph toss and turn in his sleep.

"Watch this," Gabriel said.

"Joseph, son of David …," a familiar voice called out.

"You *were* really busy back then," Regina said.

"The work of the Lord is never done," the angel replied.

Joseph, startled awake, sat up in his bed and looked around. This time Gabriel could not be seen, but Joseph heard his melodic voice clearly. "Do not be afraid to take Mary as your wife; for the Child who has been conceived in her is of the Holy Spirit. She will bear a Son; and you shall call his name Jesus." (Matthew 1:20-21)

At the name of Jesus, all of the darkness in Joseph, sown by the demon, disappeared. Joseph felt sorrow for his doubt. "Father, forgive me for doubting the righteousness of Mary, your servant. I will honor and serve her all my life and her child I will care for as if he were my own."

As Regina heard these words, she finally could see how Mary and Joseph became the Holy Family. Gabriel smiled when she glanced at him. The vision pulled away and full of warm thoughts, she found herself back at home.

The next morning Regina waited with her father to meet Father Joe before Sunday morning religious education classes. The school building adjacent to the church housed Sunday school and several of the offices of the church staff.

"Regina, Mark, good morning," Father Joe said when he came in and saw them. The troubles of the day before seemed far away.

"Good morning, Father."

"Are you joining us, Mark?"

"No, I will get my room set up for class. Regina has a lot to tell you."

"Let's sit right here. No one will disturb us for a while." Father Joe pointed to a wooded pew that he converted into a waiting area for kids and parents outside the office.

Regina and Father Joe sat down and she told him how she saw Zachariah lose his voice, Mary's visit to Elizabeth, and the birth of John the Baptist. She also explained her own visit to see Frank Roland and what happened there. Father Joe listened to her whole tale. When she finished, he folded his hands and thought for several minutes.

"Regina, I think I have an idea of what Saint Gabriel is showing you. I may even have a guess at why."

"Really? What?"

"I think he is showing you the Joyful Mysteries, one at a time. First, you saw the first Joyful Mystery, the Annunciation. Now you have seen the second Joyful Mystery, the Visitation. If my guess is correct, you will see the Nativity next. With Christmas approaching, it only makes sense."

Regina followed Father Joe's logic. She felt childish for not seeing it herself.

"Your parents and I both thought it might be the case after the Annunciation, but I asked them not to say anything until you had one more vision to see for sure."

"You said you might also know why I am seeing these particular visions?" she asked.

"It's an educated guess, really. The Mysteries of the Rosary tell the story of Jesus. The Rosary provides not only a simple guideline for prayer, but also a way to meditate deeply on the most important moments of his life. The world needs to hear that story and the Lord is making it come to life through you."

"What should I do?"

"I don't know," Father Joe confessed. "For now, you can only pray and wait."

Regina wasn't exactly satisfied with that answer, but she nodded her head and accepted it. They separated with Regina going to her classroom and Father Joe going to prepare for Mass. Regina remained free of attack but Father Joe was not so lucky.

On his short walk back to the rectory, it began. Regina's latest visions and experiences emboldened him to follow the Spirit and tell the people something more than what he had planned for his sermon this weekend. This prompted his demons to move.

You are a good priest. You have always followed the orders of your superiors. Your parishioners love you the way you are. They are happy with you. He felt the love and respect of his flock and the comforts of a content parish. His tempters had skills.

Still, the Holy Spirit continued to call him to his mission. God placed Regina in his care. She accepted her call, and he could see the amazing results that choice already had in his people. The Spirit had powerfully touched her father and mother. The incidents with Frank Roland and Maggie Rowen astonished him. *What about me?*

The tormentors countered with doubt. He turned to prayer and paced the rooms of the rectory, needing to clear his head before church. In the end, the demons won this battle by deluding him into a particularly dangerous sin, procrastination.

You should wait and see what happens with Regina's next vision. It will lead you in the right direction. The demon's logic sounded so good he believed he found his own solution and was clever for doing so. He went to the church holding the printout of the basic homily he prepared.

Father Joe liked to get to church ten minutes early to greet as many people as he could. He shook hands and felt great since he believed he had resolved his issues on his own. His tempter smiled.

Mark Andrews brought Regina and Emmanuel up from the school. They would meet Katherine at their usual pew. When Regina smiled at Father Joe, his false calm cracked for a moment, and his heart felt an ache for something, but the feeling quickly passed. As he continued to greet more parishioners, his tempter played at his pride. *You see? They like you the way you are. You are doing a great job already.*

Father Joe signaled the music director and the choir began to play. His tempter, unable to enter the sanctuary of the church, left him mental wounds that ensnared his mind. *The people are comfortable. You are comfortable. They like you the way you are. Why change things that work?*

He walked up the aisle and saw many people smiling as they sang. Some adults nodded their heads to him while children waved. He felt their friendliness. Mass continued and no one noticed their priest drifted through, barely present.

His mind remained in a fog until the Gospel reading about the Visitation of Mary. As he read the words of the Magnificat, the chains of his tempter's words began to release and the Holy Spirit flowed through him.

He read, "My soul proclaims the greatness of the Lord." At these words, his spirit freed itself from the tempter's snare. He forgot about Saturday's torment and finished the Gospel reading with a surge of energy. He took out the notes for the plain homily he had written.

Father Joe paused for a moment and looked over the congregation. Some people smiled and paid attention but others did not. Some read the bulletin, had muffled conversations, and sneaked looks at their cell phones. He turned to look at the crucifix and imagined Jesus preaching to the multitudes. This strengthened him. He braced himself to speak.

"Brothers and sisters, we are at war!" The strength and force of his voice stunned the congregation to attention. He continued.

"We are at war, and we are losing the battle. The Church entrusted me to lead you in this war, and I confess to you I failed at my duty, but not anymore!" People looked at each other.

"The greatest trick the devil plays is to convince people he doesn't exist, but I tell you the Enemy is real, and he sends out his army to lead us away from God. Demons from hell swarm around you, attack your conscience, and lead you to sin."

Regina sat in wonder as the Holy Spirit consumed Father Joe. His words ceased to be his own. He had opened himself to the heavenly will, and he could not turn back. She looked around at people who shifted in their pews uncomfortably.

"But … we are not alone! Oh no. Not by a long shot. Our army is righteous, stronger, and we know we will win in the end. We have the Lord Jesus Christ on our side, and if God is for us, who can be against?" Regina listened intently as Father Joe spoke about the triumph of Jesus over sin and death, the institution of the Church and the Sacraments. The congregation devoured his words. No one could take their eyes off the emboldened priest. Regina marveled at his discourse on the Eucharist and his desperate plea for a return to Reconciliation. No one noticed how much time had passed.

"At the cross he entrusted his Immaculate Mother to us, to be our guide as she was for him as a young man. You can turn to her love as a shield against the stoutest of demons." Father Joe spoke of the Rosary as a weapon and described the battle that lay before the people. Regina could see tears on some faces, tears and smiles.

"Now, you must take a stand." He walked back to his chair and sat down. He bowed his head and closed his eyes.

Then it began. One man began clapping. Others joined in, and shortly so did everyone else. It moved Father Joe. After the applause died down, he prayed for guidance and felt his guardian guide him to say, "I will hear Confessions after Mass, who would like to come?"

Immediately dozens of hands shot into the air, soon hundreds. The sea of arms told Father Joe he had followed the right path. The enemy did not want this mass return of sheep to the shepherd. "I will give a General Absolution and we will say of an Act of Contrition together, but you will still need to confess your sins to me after Mass. Please be patient."

Men, women, and children who rarely participated exuberantly prayed and sang like they never had for the rest of Mass. Father recited the rite with a deeper focus. When he raised the host during the consecration, one could have heard a pin drop.

When the time came to line up for receiving Communion, a tiny fraction of the congregation came forward. Father had said during his homily, "lines for Communion are 100 times longer than lines for Confession. If you really believed in whom you received, it would be the other way around."

After Mass, Father went to the sacristy to call Father Bob, the traveling priest who would also say mass at the parish, to ask him to come and hear confessions to lessen the load. He then went to the confessional and stayed there for three hours.

Although Regina had gone home hours before, Father Joe's thoughts went to her throughout the marathon Reconciliation session. *What have you started, Regina?* He smiled and focused on his returning flock. Satan screamed.

Chapter 17
Aftermath

Sunday, December 8th
11:47 AM
The Feast of the Immaculate Conception

"Well, that was something else," Mark said, on the short ride home from church. He had a huge smile on his face.

"Yes," Katherine said. "I don't think I have ever heard a homily like that. I felt like he had me in a trance."

"I know. I had no sense of time. I could have sat there all day listening to him preach," Mark said. Regina watched her parents prattle on like teenagers talking about a pop star. "What did you think guys?"

Before Regina could describe her thoughts, Manny jumped in. "Pretty cool."

Regina didn't think to check if Manny paid attention during Mass, but she figured he must have.

"I felt like he spoke directly to me, like his words went straight to my heart," Regina finally said after some thought. Her parents looked at each other.

"You said it better than I ever could," Katherine said.

"Yeah," Mark said. They remained quiet until they got home.

Once alone, Regina had some time to herself to pray in thanksgiving for Father Joe's homily. She knelt by her bed and offered up her joy to God.

"You are right to be glad, Regina," Lucy said. Regina did not see her angel but felt her presence.

"Lucy, were you at Mass with me?"

"Of course, I always am. Guardian angels love going to Mass with our people. We get to adore Our Lord without having to leave your side to go to Heaven."

"Father Joe's homily was amazing!"

"Yes, it was, but he also drew a line in the sand for the devil to cross."

This puzzled Regina. "What do you mean?"

Lucy explained. "Father Joe struggled between answering God's call and taking the easy road. Now that he accepted the challenge, hell will not back down on its assault."

"More demons will attack?" Regina felt a cold chill on her spine. No matter how much time passed, she could still feel the terror of her encounter with her tempter in the night.

"We don't know, Regina. There is still much for you to learn about how the spirit world operates. Some things I am not free to tell you, others you are not ready to know. But I will be here to help you through."

Regina nodded, confident that following God's call put her on the right path. She couldn't help wondering if life wouldn't be a whole lot easier if she hadn't.

Lucy sensed her thoughts and said, "Taking God's path will be more difficult, but your reward will be great Regina. The sleeping world is counting on you."

"The world?"

"I'm sorry, I've said too much. Let's pray and focus on the task before you."

They finished their prayers and Regina spent her Sunday playing with Emmanuel, reading, and watching television. She also helped her mom with dinner preparations. The excitement of Maggie coming to dinner started to build as they cooked.

A little after five in the afternoon, Emmanuel shouted, "She's here."

The family gathered at the door to greet their guest. Maggie came up to the door and smiled at the Andrews, who crowded around.

"Please, come in," Katherine said.

Maggie smiled and stepped into the house. Katherine and Regina both gave her hugs, while Emmanuel stood shyly behind Mark's legs. Katherine introduced Mark and Emmanuel and everyone went over to the dining room table. The food sat on the table, ready to be passed around. It didn't take long before the conversation began.

"How's your baby treating you?" Mark said.

Maggie beamed, happy to be thinking about her child. "Good. She is getting big. I can tell when she is awake and when she is sleeping. I can't wait to meet her."

Katherine looked at Emmanuel. "Manny kept me awake and I couldn't wait to see him so I could scold him for the first time." Manny saw his mother's smile and replied with a sheepish grin.

"Thank you all so much for inviting me into your lovely home. I can't tell you how much it means to have someone's support right now as I try to get my life in order."

"It's our pleasure. I tried to explain what happened yesterday to my husband, but I was hoping you could do a better job," Katherine said.

"I haven't stopped saying prayers of thanksgiving since yesterday. God touched me through Regina, and I have not been the same. I feel like I am being called to something."

Mark and Katherine looked at each other first and then at Regina.

Maggie caught the silent exchange and asked, "What? Am I missing something?"

"The Holy Spirit has been working in amazing ways around here for the last week. Starting with Regina, God has called us all to do… something," Mark said. "What do you feel called to do?"

"I'm not exactly sure. I feel like I need to tell my story to other women. Maybe I could help others in my situation. Do you know what I mean?"

"Yes. I do. Well, let's enjoy our meal, and we will pray that God will grant you the clarity to do what he wants." The hungry people around the table all agreed and the evening passed very enjoyably.

Unfortunately, Father Joe did not enjoy the rest of the day. After hearing confession for several hours, he spent about an hour in the chapel before the tabernacle. He offered thanks for the strength the Spirit gave him at Mass. At the end of his prayer, he felt the voice of Peter, his guardian angel.

"Joseph, the Lord thanks you for the trust you put in him to go forward with your call, but remember, the road is difficult."

"I know, Peter, my heart is ready."

"Despite the great steps you took today, the Enemy made some gains in his plan as well."

"What do you mean?"

"You are about to find out."

At that moment, Margaret Bower, the church receptionist, called out from the entrance to the church, "Father? I'm sorry to disturb you, but Bishop Roberts is on the phone." She paused for a moment, uncomfortably, and finished, "He sounds angry."

The priest made the sign of the cross. "Thy will be done."

He walked toward the doorway where Margaret stood. She looked worried; he smiled at her. He took away her anxiety but kept his own. He walked to the office to get the phone, preparing himself for a battle.

"Hello," Father Joe said.

The bishop did not waste any time. "Father, I thought we understood each other." Father Joe did not respond. "Imagine my displeasure when I received a call from one of your parishioners who told me he was going to leave your parish because of your preaching."

Tell him about the applause. Tell him about the supportive crowd. Tell him your parish is alive. He listened to the voice. It wasn't Peter speaking to him. The evil ones tried to start a fight. Father Joe begged his angel to help him hear God's will.

Don't say a word. It won't help. Pray for the Bishop. His tempters have won his mind for now. His guardian angel needs your help. This time, he could hear

175

his angel's voice. He did not understand why he should remain silent, but he knew he should obey.

"Well, what do you have to say for yourself?"

"I am sorry, the Spirit moved me and I..."

"I can move you, too."

"With all due respect …," Father Joe began.

"If you want to show me respect, heed my words. I don't want you preaching again until further notice. I will arrange for a deacon to come and say homilies at Sunday Mass."

A flood of sound, logical objections came to the embattled priest, but he knew this was not the time to voice them. He knew he needed to pray and let the spiritual battle raging for the bishop's soul play out. He needed prayer, not logic, to get over this obstacle.

"We will revisit this in a few weeks," the bishop said.

"Yes, Excellency." The phone call ended. Father Joe felt the opposite of the joy he felt a few short hours before. Still, even in his devastated state, he felt called to return to the chapel. He walked out of the office and reentered the church to find it empty. A strong force brought him to his knees.

"You have done well, my son. The Lord has heard your prayer and knows your sorrow."

Father Joe recognized the soft voice. "Thank you, mother." He did not look around, but held his head down.

"There is much work to be done. Heaven is with you, listen to the Spirit and heed his call."

"I will. Thank you." The heavenly encounter ended as quickly as it had begun. Father Joe spent a long time in prayer before returning to his chambers to think about what he would do next.

Miseros sat at his desk furiously writing. He wrote for some time before calling a secretary with his intercom.

"Putridus, come in here now and type up this form for me."

A smaller demon crept into the office and took the paper from him. He glanced at it. "The Job Form? I've never seen one of these before."

"We don't use them that often," Miseros replied. "Now go and type it. The higher ups are not happy when they receive requests with mistakes on them." The large demon swiveled around and faced away. Putridus took the paper and left the office. He returned to his work space. Dozens of other demons worked on their tasks around him. He walked up to one of them.

"Hey Insipidus, can I ask you a question?"

"Sure. Go ahead."

"What is the Job Form for?"

Insipidus look startled and took Putridus by the arm and moved him over to the side, away from the others. "Why do you want to know?"

"Miseros gave me one to type up."

"Can I see it?" Insipidus asked. He took the document, looked it over, and whistled. "I've never seen one of these before."

"I don't get it, what is the big deal?"

"Do you know the story of Job?"

"Of course, Our Father Below obtained permission to test Job's faith from Our Enemy a long time ago."

"Yes, that started as great fun, but it turned into a huge defeat."

"I know. That wretched creature Job, refused to give up his precious faith, even after what our friends put him through. We took everything from him and still he believed and did not curse The Enemy."

"Well, The Dark Lord made an arrangement with The Enemy that he be allowed to test certain souls from time to time in the same way."

"Like Job?"

"Not always. A demon needs to fill out the Job Form about a particular human and explain exactly what sufferings are going to befall them and why they should be tested. If the Enemy signs off, then we get to have our fun."

"Does it work?" Putridus asked.

Insipidus' look turned dour. "Not often, but it can, especially in those cases where we probably have no chance at the soul of the target. I think of it as a win-win situation."

"I don't understand."

"If the human turns from his maker because of his sufferings, then we get the soul to feast on down here, but even if he stays faithful, we get to taste their anguish, even if only for a short time."

"Oh, I see. Well I better get to work on this then."

"I didn't see who it was for."

Putridus looked at the paper having forgotten the name. Finding it, he said, "A young girl named Regina."

Chapter 18
The Dark Night

Friday, December 13th
7:00 AM

The alarm clock buzzed for the third time before Regina mustered up enough courage to reach over and turn it off.

"This has been the worst week," she said out loud. "Lucy, are you there?" No response came. "Where are you?"

She picked up the notebook sitting by her bed. She thought of her mother's words when she gave it to her.

"Write down your visions in this diary. You can also keep track of your thoughts and prayers in here as well. Many people find it helpful to keep track of their conversations with God." Katherine helped her decorate it.

She picked up a pen and wrote.

I cried myself to sleep again. That makes three nights in a row. God, are you there? I haven't felt you since Sunday. Please send Lucy to comfort me. What did I do wrong?

Regina picked up her Angelus card and recited the prayer. She waited for a moment, but nothing changed in her spirit. She started getting ready for school at a deliberate pace.

"Heavenly Father, I am sorry for whatever I did. I pray you will grace me with your Spirit or Lucy or Gabriel." Regina paused, thinking she should add some thanksgiving to her petitions. She prayed in thanksgiving for Maggie and for her family. She listened again for Lucy's voice but didn't hear her. Regina went downstairs and found her mother talking on the phone.

"I think I may have a couple of leads for you, Maggie. We'll get you out of the emergency shelter soon. Okay? Talk to you soon," Katherine said hanging up the phone. "Good morning, Regina."

"Good morning." Regina didn't think her mother recognized the lack of conviction in her response.

Emmanuel got up and left his plate of food behind. He went into the kitchen and came back with food for Regina, placing it in front of her. Katherine noticed the act of kindness and said, "How thoughtful."

"Thanks, Manny," Regina said, loud enough for her mother to hear. Katherine went back to work in the kitchen. "And for being so nice to me all week."

Regina realized Emmanuel had gone out of his way to bring her treats and help her out all week. He even avoided annoying her in his usual way. He hadn't said anything, but it seemed as if he knew she struggled with something and wanted to help out.

At lunch that day, she thought of Frank Roland again as she prayed the Angelus, but felt nothing in her spirit. She frowned to herself, or so she thought.

"What's wrong with you?" Mary Murphy said as she sat down with her tray, holding her hot dog, chips, and milk.

"I don't even know where to begin," Regina said.

"Try anywhere," Mary said, smiling.

"Okay. Well, I want to go visit Frank again, but my parents have been busy all week."

"You already visited him once?" Mary said.

"Yeah, when I got there, he came out of his coma all of a sudden. He told me he forgave me and to pray for him. Then he went right back into his coma."

"No way."

"For real. You should have seen him in the hospital. They have him wrapped from head to toe and he had wires and tubes going everywhere. He could barely breathe, but when he talked to me, he seemed full of life."

"It was a miracle!" Mary said.

"There is no doubt about it. So you see why I want to see him again soon."

"Do you think I could see him too?"

"Do you really want to?"

"Yeah. I have this feeling I should go see him too. Is that weird?"

"No, but I wish I could feel something."

"What do you mean?"

"Well, you know how I've told you about feeling close to God and how cool that is?"

"Yeah."

"I haven't felt anything in my spirit all week," Regina said.

"Some people feel like that all the time," Mary said.

Regina looked at her friend who shrugged her shoulders and continued eating.

"You're right. Thanks, Mary," Regina said. Mary's words made her feel better at the time, but as the day wore on, Regina felt more and more crushed by the loss of her connection with the Holy Spirit. She couldn't even feel her tempter trying to bring her down. She called out to Lucy for some spiritual companionship but found none.

When she got home she went to her room and grabbed her journal again. She started to write.

A month ago, I didn't recognize you in my life, but now without your love I am so lonely. I don't know how I ever lived without your touch in my heart. I feel so lost.

A tear drop splashed on the page. She closed the notebook and began to weep.

"Regina? Are you in there?"

"Yes, mommy." Regina wiped her face. Katherine came in.

"You came straight up here without saying a word. Is everything alright?"

The tears flowed even harder. Katherine sat down by her daughter.

"Is it possible I never had any visions at all?"

"What are you talking about?"

"I don't know. I can still remember what happened, but it's starting to feel like a dream."

"Why do you say that?"

"Because I don't feel God's love at all. At all!"

Her mother held her close and let her cry.

"You seem to be going through some spiritual dryness."

"What?"

"Spiritual dryness is when you don't feel the hand of God on your soul."

"Why do you get it?"

"It's hard to say, it could be many things. It could be fatigue clouding your spirit. It could be the devil getting between you and the Lord, or it could be the dark night of the soul."

"What was the last thing?"

"The dark night of the soul is a spiritual state described by Saint John of the Cross in a beautiful poem he wrote several hundred years ago. He compared missing God to waiting in the dark for someone to join you on a romantic outing. You wait for the person you love to come, but while you do, you are alone in the darkness. Many saints have said it is necessary to experience this to get closer to God."

"Why would you have to feel further from God to get closer to him?"

"I don't know. Maybe you learn to appreciate his love when you don't have it. People say you don't know what you have until it's gone. Many saints have written of this pain."

"Like who?"

"Saint Therese of Lisieux and Blessed Teresa of Calcutta are two famous ones who come to mind."

"Mother Teresa? She had this feeling?"

"What do you know about her?"

"I learned in Religious Ed class that she taught at a school in India when she became a nun. After several years, Jesus called her to serve him by ministering to the poorest of the poor. So she went to the streets of Calcutta to save the dying from starvation and illness."

"All of that is true. What else?"

"I know she also had her nuns wear simple white saris in the style of the Indians they served and her religious practice was very strict."

"Good memory. She also won the Nobel Peace Prize."

"Oh yeah, I knew that," Regina said.

"What you don't often hear is she spent most of her life suffering from spiritual dryness. She did not feel the presence of Jesus like she did when he called her to her amazing vocation."

"How long did she suffer like this?" Regina asked.

"Her superiors suspect she felt abandoned by God for forty years."

"Forty years? That's a lot longer than one week," Regina said.

"Regina, you have to remember while she no longer had the intense, direct connection to Jesus, her faith burned brightly for the whole world to see. I know you have been blessed in a special way, but you have to be prepared for that special feeling not to last forever. It is very much like being in love."

"What do you mean?"

"When you first fall in love, there is a time when you spend lots of time with the other person, and it's like no one else in the world exists. Then life has to go on, but all of those great feelings you had in the beginning help lead you to a much deeper relationship with your lover that allows you to feel him when he is not physically there," Katherine explained.

"So you are saying even though Mother Teresa couldn't feel Jesus, she remembered the power of his call and her faith lived on?"

"Yes, and not only that, when your love is great, all you want to do is be with that person again and make them happy. That is how she lived without the great gift that started her on her journey. It took a great marvel for her to start her mission, but greater faith to carry it out."

Regina gave a weak smile and leaned back into her mother's embrace. They stayed that way for quite some time.

Miseros smiled as he listened to Atramors give his report on the state of Regina's mind and spirit. Taking away her spiritual connection definitely had a shot at defeating her. His best agents had not been able to determine why the Enemy found this child so important, but he vowed to undermine his plans.

"Boss, do you think the child will maintain her faith under the Job Rule?" Atramors asked.

"Many saints have withstood the crushing effects of losing their friendship with the Enemy," Miseros explained, saying the words saints and Enemy with particular distaste. "But this girl is no saint. Many have fallen from grace without the love of the Enemy apparent in their lives. From what you are telling me, your charge seems to be taking this business hard."

"Yes, she has suffered for the last week, but I still cannot figure out more about the Enemy's plan for her. More than her guardian protects her from my attack," Atramors said.

Miseros nodded.

"I don't like this. It reeks of goodness."

Mark Andrews worked at his desk at school. He looked at the clock and pulled out his phone.

"Hi, honey. I'm done with my meetings and waiting for the Knights of Columbus business meeting. I don't have time to make it home for dinner. I'm going to catch up on some grading."

He listened to Katherine's response.

"I don't know what I'm going to say. I want to share what the Lord put in my heart about knighthood, but I don't know if the guys will take it."

Mark listened again.

"Okay, thanks, I'll see you after the meeting. Love you," he said.

Christina Wilde drummed her fingers on her lab desk. She looked at the stop watch, shook her head, picked up a novel, briefly opened it, and put it back down. She yawned and said, "This should be classified as torture."

The other technicians in her lab had already gone home for the evening. She needed to make up the two hours she lost taking her mom to the doctor. Boredom choked her.

Her phone buzzed. She checked the stop watch again, looked around, and picked up the phone. She began texting.

Matty: R u still at work?

Christina: Yes, flex time

Matty: How r u?

Christina: Crazy bored, waiting for the cycle to finish

Matty: I'm sorry I got us written up

Christina: Don't be, I was talking too

Matty: Make you sure you delete this thread. The KGB may be watching

Christina: LOL

Matty: K, take it easy

Christina: How many trials did you say you've done?

Matty: IDK, maybe 2000 in 2 years

Christina: I don't know how much more of this job I can take

Matty: Hang in there kid

Christina: Thx

She made sure to delete the message thread and put her phone back down. She looked at the stop watch. The ten minutes had elapsed. She opened the hood of the canister on her lab counter. She held her breath for a moment.

"Nothing," Christina said. She opened her lab notebook and wrote down the results. Removing the test vials, she threw them in the discard bin. She went to the fridge to take out the next blood sample. Only a few samples remained. *Maybe another hour.*

Christina went through her procedure again and prepared the test. Closing the canister with the test vials, she set her stopwatch and put it down. The provocative cover of the novel invited her to pick it up again, but when she did she looked at the calendar and then to her framed diploma. Tears welled up in her eyes. No one was around so she didn't hold back.

Mark pulled up at Saint John's and went to the parish center attached to the church. A smiling man stood by the door.

"Are you a member of the Knights of Columbus?"

"Yes," Mark said.

"Do you have a membership card?"

"Oh. Yes. One second." Mark took out his wallet and found the card. He handed it to the man who looked it over.

"Looks good. Are you new to the parish?" the man asked.

Mark felt his face flush.

"No, just haven't done much with the knights," he said.

"No worries. Welcome. My name is Tom Phillips." He stuck out his hand. Mark shook it.

"Mark Andrews. Thanks."

Mark walked in the room and saw about twenty men standing in groups talking. Looking around, he saw one face he definitely recognized.

"Mark, good to see you," a tall, hulking man said.

"Hi John," Mark said. They shook hands.

"You made it just in time. Please, take a seat." He stepped back from Mark and looked around. "Everyone, can I have your attention? We are going to begin. Please take a seat." John waited for everyone to sit before continuing. "Our first order of business is to welcome Brother Mark Andrews to our midst."

Mark smiled and nodded to the men who waved at him and smiled. He watched John and thought back to when they met.

Mark had approached the table where John sold tickets.

"Would you like to buy tickets for the Knights of Columbus pancake breakfast? All proceeds this year go to mentally handicapped kids." Mark found the large, smiling man captivating.

"When is it?" Mark asked, "I don't see a date."

"What?" John came running around to the front of the table and looked at his sign and shook his head, still smiling, despite his frustration. "Darn it, well, it is next Sunday, and the date is on the ticket."

"Sure, I'll come." Mark fished some money out of his wallet.

"Is that a K of C membership card?" John asked, having spotted the small piece of colored paper in Mark's wallet.

Mark looked down and saw the small card with the tell-tale Knight's insignia in the upper left hand corner and nodded. "Yeah, it's my card from college. I guess I never could bring myself to throw it away even though it expired years ago."

"Well, we will have to get you a new one," John had said. "Write down your name, address, membership number, and your old council number on this paper and I will mail you a new one … if you want to join our council that is."

"Sure, that would be great, but my wife recently had a baby so I don't know how active I can be."

"Don't worry, come when you can. I'm glad to have another brother in the family. I'm John Jameson, Grand Knight." Mark remembered the powerful handshake of the burly man.

They met more than ten years ago and Mark had barely done a few things with the Knights in all that time. He used the pregnant wife excuse for eighteen months and the two small children routine the rest of the time. In retrospect, he realized Katherine would have been more than happy to let him serve the parish for a couple of hours at a time, but he convinced himself his duties at home precluded him from service.

The secretary finished reading the minutes from the last meeting and Mark looked around at many familiar faces, few of which he could put a name to. His guilt continued to grow. He listened as they discussed the month's schedule and what to do with the leftover Tootsie Rolls from the annual donation drive. Things seemed to be winding down when John said, "Does anyone else have something they would like to address or bring up?"

The time had come. *You haven't earned their respect yet. Who do you think you are coming in here and asking these men to follow your leadership?* Doubt welled up inside Mark. He did not recognize his tempter's darkness. He still felt the call inside himself but it no longer burned brightly. He prayed for the strength but an evil voice tricked him further. *Spend some time with them. Do some service. Sell some candy, make some pancakes, then you will earn their respect and can share with them your mission.*

"Anybody else?" John asked.

Mark fell into the trap set for him. *I will go to the service projects this month. After that, I will share my mission. Once I gain their trust, I will be able to convince them to take on a deeper spirituality.*

His guardian angel could not counter. The demon won the contest.

Suddenly, a knock came on the door. The Inner Guard moved to the door and opened it to see who had come. After he confirmed the guest's ID, the Guard let the newcomer in. Mark recognized him from Mass and could see panic in his eyes.

The Grand Knight, who also saw his distress, arose from his chair. "Bill, what's the matter?"

Bill, out of breath, took a few moments to explain. Still gasping for air, he said, "Sorry ... I'm ... late. I had to ... hear the ... whole report." Bill obviously did not have occasion to run very often.

John Jameson replied, "Calm down Bill, take a deep breath. Somebody get him some water."

Bill took several seconds to catch his breath. "I was ready to leave my house to come here when I caught a news report about a law that the governor is trying to push through."

"What about it?"

"He wants to revoke the tax exempt status of any organization that takes official positions about political issues."

Murmuring filled the room. Mark felt a dark chill.

"What?" John exclaimed. "Are you serious? Did the report mention anything about churches or other religious institutions?"

"Yes. The reporter said the language of the bill doesn't mention religious groups, but clearly the wording applies to us. The governor stated non-profit organizations have no business in the political process." More grumbling came from the group.

"Gentlemen, gentlemen, calm down. I motion we all go home to learn all we can about this proposal and I will send out an email for another meeting date later in the week. Keep your wits about you. If what Bill says is true, then we will need to be studious and know what we are up against. Let's close with a prayer. There is nothing we can do about it now."

The grumbling ended as they stood and crossed themselves. Mark prayed the words to the Our Father, the Hail Mary, and the Glory Be, but his thoughts raced. *What does this mean about my mission?* He realized he missed an opportunity at the meeting and wondered how it happened. The meeting ended and he headed for home, frustrated at his cowardice.

Chapter 19
God and Country

Thursday, December 19th
8:12 PM

Dear God,

It has been ten days since I last felt your presence. I can still remember my visions but I am starting to doubt my mission. I feel like I didn't live up to my call and you have chosen someone else to send Saint Gabriel to. I understand if that is the case. I am sorry for having failed you.

Love,

Regina

Regina put down her pen and closed her notebook. She placed it on her nightstand and got ready for bed. She thought of the conversation her parents had in the kitchen after dinner. She pretended to read a book in the next room, but she heard every word.

"I have another K of C meeting tomorrow," Mark said.

"How is the political battle going?" Katherine said.

"We are trying to gather all the facts about this legislation so we can get people informed. The governor has not released the language of the bill yet so all we have are theories and conjecture."

"That has to be frustrating. You have been spending a lot of time on this," Katherine said.

"I know. I'm sorry. I've been neglecting you and the kids. How are things with Maggie going?"

"Remember how I said the Carters from down the street were looking for someone to rent their house to?" Katherine said.

"Aren't they going to Australia to live with their daughter for a year?" Mark said.

"New Zealand, and yes, she just had a baby. Well, they agreed to let Maggie housesit for them. I was amazed," Katherine said.

"Nice."

"And Susanna said she would be able to pay Maggie for some clerical work at the center. It will make a nice addition to her money from the restaurant."

"So, is she going to keep the baby?" Mark asked.

"I think she wants to, but she is afraid. Do you think we could help her do it, if she does?"

Regina held her breath as her father paused.

"I'm sure we could."

Regina got on her knees.

"Lord, thank you for helping my parents live out their missions. And my brother, I don't know what he's been praying about, but thank you for touching him as well." She had asked God enough times to come back to her so she didn't add that this time.

Regina thought of finding Emmanuel praying in his room. When she asked him what he prayed about, he responded with, "I dunno, wanna play?"

Katherine walked in. Regina still knelt.

"I'm sorry. I don't want to interrupt."

"No, I'm finished."

"Are you feeling the touch of God yet?"

"No."

"I'm sorry, sweetheart. Daddy and I will pray for you."

"Thanks, mommy."

Katherine looked into Regina's eyes for a moment and kissed her goodnight.

The next morning, Regina woke up with a pit in her stomach. She had dreaded school for the last two weeks, but she knew this day would be the worst. The last day before Christmas Break would have the rest of the kids excited and joyful. Regina knew she would find this annoying.

All morning, Regina forced polite smiles as people said, "Merry Christmas" or "Happy holidays." She secretly wanted to shout, "What's there to be merry about?"

At lunch, Mary Murphy saw Regina sitting at their lunch table with her head across her arms, staring at her lunch. "Why so gloomy, Gus? It's the last day before vacation."

"I know. I don't feel much like celebrating," Regina replied.

"Why? What's wrong?"

Regina had kept her struggles from Mary. Partially because she didn't think anyone else could understand, but also because her mother told her she could offer her suffering to God as a sacrifice for graces to be poured on others. She knew Jesus warned against putting on a show of one's suffering to make sure other people would notice.

"I am feeling very lonely."

"Hey! You got me, aren't we friends?"

"Of course, you're a great friend, Mary." Regina put on her best happy face.

"Hey Regina, have you ever gone back to see Frank Roland?"

"No, I haven't. My parents have been really busy. I have called Mrs. Roland a few times. She says Frank has been stable and his body is healing. I hope I can go over break."

"If you do, let me know. I am little nervous about going alone." They shared an awkward nod. "Are you doing anything fun for Christmas?"

"No, we are pretty much hanging around the house. I think we will visit my grandparents for Christmas. We do that every year."

"Yeah, us too. I hope it snows more so we can go sledding or tubing. I went a lot last year. There's a place, not too far, where you can rent a tube and go up and down all day. I think I did it twenty times before I couldn't make it up the hill anymore," Mary said.

"I know the place. They have really good hot chocolate at the tube rental booth, right?"

"I thought it was kind of watery."

"Maybe it tasted so good because I was so cold?" Regina said. The girls both nodded and giggled. "Thanks, Mary, you cheered me up."

"Good. Merry Christmas, Regina."

"Merry Christmas." Regina felt good that she meant it.

Regina went home after school and spent more time alone in her room. She remembered her conversation with Mary and thought about how her parents told her to remember to enjoy being her age, regardless of her mission. She decided to try to have some fun on her break and went downstairs to find something to do.

Her mother sat on the couch knitting.

"What are you making?" Regina asked, startling her mom.

"Oh, hi kiddo. I must have been in the zone. I am making booties for Maggie's baby. I have never made anything so small so I am not sure how they are going to turn out."

"Everything you make always turns out good."

"Thanks, sweetie."

"Can I do anything to help?"

"You can wipe my brow," Katherine joked.

Regina smiled. "I will, if you want me to."

"No, that's okay. You can sit with me and keep me company. Tell me how you are doing. Are you still having a rough time?"

"Yeah, I guess so."

"Hang in there. Do you remember watching the movie 'The Song of Bernadette'? I think we all saw it last year."

Regina remembered she played with Manny in the room but really didn't pay attention. "Sort of."

"Do you remember the basic idea?"

"Our Lady appeared to Saint Bernadette somewhere in France and a miraculous fountain appeared out of the ground. That's basically all I remember. Oh, and she became a nun."

"That's right. It happened in a small town called Lourdes, but a significant part of the story is Our Lady told Bernadette she would have to suffer much during her time on earth."

"That doesn't sound like fun."

"It wasn't, but Our Lady also told Bernadette she would receive her treasure and joy in heaven. Now, no one has told you that was your fate, right Regina?"

Regina thought back to her memories of the angel's visits, which seemed so distant now. She couldn't think of anything as dark as that. "No, I don't think so, but I would take a vision of Our Lady telling me that, if only to see or feel anything again, even for the last time."

Katherine gave Regina a compassionate glance. "Well despite never seeing the Blessed Mother again, Bernadette lived an extraordinary life as a simple nun at a convent far from Lourdes, where her visions occurred. She touched the lives of many people, even though God didn't touch her directly like he did in her youth. Don't feel down, I'm sure God has more in store for you, too."

Regina leaned her head on her mother's shoulder and said, "Thanks mommy. I guess I'll pray to Saint Bernadette to ask God to give me the strength she had to continue with her mission even after her visions ended. I really miss seeing Gabriel's face. I wish you could see his beauty."

"Me too."

"If he is only an angel, what will the face of God look like?"

Regina looked up during her lament and saw Emmanuel standing with only his head sticking around the corner. He had a sad and pitying look on his face. She assumed he heard her talking about her Dark Night and could see how it bothered him. Before Regina or Katherine could comfort him, he scurried off.

"Should I follow him?"

Her mother tilted her head listened. "I don't hear him crying. We'll let him be for now. I'll talk to him later, okay?"

"Okay." Regina let herself relax. She fell asleep almost immediately against her mother's warmth. The slamming of the door to the garage brought Regina out of her nap.

"Oh, I'm sorry G. Were you sleeping?" Mark held several bags in his hands. He had kicked the door closed with his foot.

"That's okay. It's probably getting close to dinner time, anyway." She could smell something cooking in the kitchen.

"The kids were crazy today at school," Mark said. "How about you? Are you excited to be off for a couple of weeks?"

"Yeah, I guess so."

"Still nothing, huh?"

"Yeah, but I talked to mommy about it. It's okay. Daddy?"

"What sweetheart?"

"Now, can you tell me what the governor is trying to do?"

"Oh my goodness, I totally forgot we never had that conversation. I'm sorry G." He thought about where to begin. "Do you understand how taxes work?"

"I know you have to pay some of the money you make to the government. We learned in school this is how police, fire fighters, and teachers get paid."

"That's right. People have to pay taxes and so do businesses, when they make money."

"That makes sense," Regina said.

"Well, some organizations receive money but don't have to pay taxes. The government classifies them as non-profit, charitable entities. This means they use their money to help people, so the government doesn't charge them taxes."

"Like churches?"

"Yes, also schools, mommy's women's center, the Salvation Army, things like that."

"Okay."

"Well, non-profit organizations are not supposed to support political candidates. For example, Father Joe can't tell people to vote against Governor Incredo during the next election. He can't put up voting signs on the rectory lawn or put in the bulletin the names of the people he wants us to vote for."

"What if he did?"

"The government could revoke the church's tax-exempt status, which means they would have to pay taxes on the money they collect. This would severely cut into the church's ministry."

"Okay," Regina said.

"Well, the governor is trying to write a law that not only prohibits campaigning for non-profits, but also prohibits the discussion of political topics in their official meetings."

"I don't understand."

"For example, this would mean Father Joe would not be allowed to preach abortion is wrong, or about the unjustness of war, or anything else considered a 'political' topic."

"But that could be anything."

"Exactly, but no one thinks the governor will go after every political thing a non-profit does. He will use the law to attack the organizations that block his agenda. We feel the number one target will be the Church."

"Why?"

"The governor doesn't believe in God but he does believe in the total power of the government. He doesn't think religious institutions should exist anyway, but since he can't change that, he wants churches only to be places where people pray and then go home unchanged. He doesn't understand our faith is what drives our actions."

"Do you think the law will pass?"

"People didn't think someone openly hostile to religion could be elected governor, so anything could happen."

"What happens if it does?"

Mark had a distant look in his eyes and thought for a while before he answered, "It is important we remember the government derives its power from God. Jesus reminds us of this in the Gospel of Saint Matthew. The Pharisees asked whether he and his disciples should pay taxes to Caesar. Do you remember what he said?" (Matthew 22:21)

"No."

"Jesus outsmarted them. He asked someone to show him a coin. Then, he asked them to declare whose face graced the coin. Someone replied 'Caesar's!' Jesus said, 'Then give unto Caesar what is Caesar's and give unto God what is God's'. Later, he told Pontius Pilate that he had no power over him except what his Father in heaven had given him. Jesus clearly taught God is above the government, even though we have to obey them both." (John 19:11)

"What does Father Joe think about this?"

"I still haven't heard from him. I left several messages. Maybe he took some vacation time before Christmas comes. He might have his phone turned off."

Father Joe stared at his phone lying on his desk. He scratched the heavy stubble on his chin. The hood on his sweatshirt covered his uncombed hair. His stomach rumbled.

"Lord, I offer you my hunger. Grant me the grace to follow your will."

Your bishop is holding you back. Disobey him and speak out against the governor. Tell your parishioners to fight back.

Father Joe shook his head. He grabbed his Rosary and crossed himself.

Pray for your bishop. His tempter keeps him from seeing the Lord's call for you.

The phone rang, disrupting the battle. He looked at the incoming number. Mark Andrews had called three times earlier, but Father Joe could not bring himself to answer the phone. *What if Regina needs me?* He had dwelt too much on his own struggles that he had forgotten his most immediate mission. He picked up the phone.

"Hello?"

"Father Joe, thank goodness. It's nice to hear your voice. How have you been?"

"Fine, how about you?"

The priest's response failed to convince Mark.

"I am well. Are you in town?"

"Yes. I'm just taking some personal time." Father Joe's terse response lacked his usual warmth.

"Oh, I'll be brief then. Some of the other Knights would like to hear your thoughts about the Governor's attempts to change the tax laws…," Mark explained.

"I have been told to not take an official opinion on that."

"By who? The bishop?"

No response.

"How about an unofficial opinion? Could you come to our next meeting?"

"I'm not supposed to go to meetings right now."

Mark paused. Father Joe didn't fill the silence.

"Is this because of your homily?"

"Mark, how is Regina?"

"Oh… she hasn't had any visions and is experiencing some spiritual dryness."

"Really? I will keep her in my prayers. I need to go. You take care, Mark."

"Wait, Father?"

"What was that about?" Katherine said. She had entered the room in the middle of the phone call.

"I have a feeling Father Joe is being censored."

"What do you mean?" Regina asked.

"Like someone has told him to not be so vocal."

"Why do you think that is?" Katherine asked.

"I have a guess."

"What?"

"Someone might have not liked his challenging homily and complained. He said he had been told not have an opinion about the governor's bill. Only the bishop would have that kind of authority," Mark said.

Regina wondered what her father meant. Katherine gave Mark a similar puzzled look. He saw both of their faces and explained, "We haven't seen or heard from him since last Sunday. Maybe Bishop Roberts found it too controversial. Father Joe told me before his boss did not like the boat rocked."

"Can we do something? I think most people liked his fire," Katherine said.

"Yeah," Regina said.

"I don't know," Mark said.

They all stood in silence for several moments. Something caused Mark's face to light up.

"If one negative phone call got him in trouble, maybe dozens of positive ones will straighten things out," he said.

"What if that isn't the issue?" Katherine asked.

"At worst, Bishop Roberts will know how much Saint John's Parish loves its priest," Mark said. He smiled and grabbed the phone. "I'll start a phone tree. Let's see what happens."

Mark walked into the next room.

"Why would the bishop be upset with Father Joe over a phone call?" Regina asked.

"Politics, Regina," her mother said.

"Politics? I thought that has to do with the government?"

"Well, that's how we usually use the word, but it also applies to people manipulating situations to get what they want."

"How?"

"Did you ever hear the expression 'the squeaky wheel gets the grease'?"

"Yes. That means whoever complains the loudest will get what they want." Katherine nodded. "That doesn't work with you," Regina said.

Katherine smiled. "Someday you will thank me."

Regina didn't see how.

"I can think of a few people in the parish who wouldn't like Father Joe's powerful homily. One of them may have called the bishop, while I bet no one who gave Father a standing ovation would have thought to call to praise him."

"Daddy told us in R.E. that people ask God for things all the time, but rarely thank him for what he gives us. Is that the same thing?"

"Yeah, kind of."

"So politics happen in church, too?"

"In church, at school, on sports teams, pretty much everything human beings are involved in. We are very political creatures, Regina. From the time you make friends on the playground you are trying to win people over to your side. God made us to *love* each other and to *use* the things he gives us. Unfortunately, people *use* each other because they *love* things like money and power."

"But why does that happen in the church?"

"Because people make up the church. Even though God has revealed his perfect truth, human beings administer the church's ministries. Humans, as you know, are far from perfect. Jesus knew from the beginning this would be the case. Who did he choose as the first pope?"

"Saint Peter."

"Exactly. What did Peter do when bystanders identified him as an apostle after Caiaphas had Jesus arrested?"

Regina had to think about what she learned in Sunday school. "Peter denied Our Lord three times."

"Right. In fact, he made a lot of mistakes, and despite them, or maybe because of them, Jesus chose Saint Peter to be the rock to build his Church on."

"But why would God entrust his Truth with people who can make mistakes and not be perfect?"

"Regina, the Church acts as a sign of how every person should live. The Church holds the truth and struggles to proclaim it using human beings. Despite their failings, all people can hear the truth and try to live up to it. If they fall short, they have the Sacraments to lift them up. Jesus knew we would need the Church exactly the way he set it up."

Mark came back.

"I called several people and told them to call the bishop to praise Father Joe for his awesome homily. I told each person to call three more people and do the same. Even it doesn't amount to anything, it's something we should have done anyway a long time ago. The bishop will know what we really think of our priest."

"I hope so," Regina said.

Chapter 20
The Nativity

Dear God,

Please take care of my grandparents. I am sad that we couldn't go to their house because of the snow storm that's coming. I always look forward to seeing them and having Grandma's cookies.

Take care of Father Joe too. I don't know why he couldn't be at Christmas Eve Mass. A lot of people told my dad that they called the bishop about Father Joe and wondered why he wasn't around yet.

I am sorry I gave up on my prayers for the last few days. I was just really sad and angry, I guess. I am trying to hang in there and would love an opportunity to make up for anything I might have done to upset you.

Happy Birthday.

Love,

Regina.

Regina put aside her prayer journal and covered herself with her blanket. Sleep claimed her quickly. As it deepened, a shadowy dream formed in her mind. She felt imprisoned in a black room with thick walls. "Help!" she yelled out, hoping for a response.

Nothing came. Instead, a deep cold invaded the space and chilled her to the bone. She felt the same crushing emptiness she felt all week, but it intensified in her mind. Her legs gave out and she fell to her knees. Tears poured from her eyes and her voice choked with sobs. Her soul reached out for God but the confines of the walls constrained her spirit, threatening to break it. She felt as though the pressure would kill her.

A crash sounded.

The change shocked Regina from her terror. She looked around but darkness remained. Again, the clang of a hammer sounded. The force of the blows should have scared her, but instead, they gave her hope.

Again and again, the thundering noise repeated until a crack appeared in the black wall. A few twinkles of light appeared. A few more smashes and large cracks began to form. A few more and the wall caved in. A figure stepped through the hole bathed in light pouring from behind. The sudden brightness blinded Regina, prohibiting her view of her hero. As she started to focus on the image, the dream ended, and she found herself sitting upright in bed.

Regina still longed for Gabriel to bring her a vision, but this dream filled a little of the emptiness in her spirit. It meant something. Still, in the quiet surrounding her, she resolved to never see him again.

"Don't give up, Regina; God will never give up on you."

"Lucy!"

"I'm back," the angel said.

Regina's heart raced.

"I'm so happy to hear your voice again." Something in Lucy's voice bothered Regina. "Why are you breathing like that? Are you alright?"

"I've been better." Lucy took a deep breath. "A lot has happened since we were last together, Regina."

"Not on my end."

"Yes. I know about your spiritual darkness. Hell has invoked the Job Rule on you."

"The Job Rule? What's that?"

"Do you know the story of Job?"

"Not really, I only remembered that he sat in ashes and talked to his friends." Regina felt embarrassed for not knowing the scriptures better.

"Job was a very devout man, who had great wealth. Arrogantly, the devil thought he could make Job curse God, if only God would allow all of Job's possessions to be taken away. The Lord agreed.

Despite losing everything he had, including his family and his own health, Job stayed faithful to the end."

"Why would God allow that?"

"You could think of it as another of his mysterious ways, but also because now everyone remembers the faith of Job amidst adversity."

"What does that have to do with me?"

"The Lord has allowed the devil to use the Job Rule on certain special people. If the Almighty grants permission, Hell can send special torment to the soul it chooses."

"Why would they choose me?"

"We believe that they have figured out that God has big plans for you. Even though the devil doesn't know what your mission is, he wants to keep you from it by making you suffer."

"I'm not complaining, but why did they take the Job Rule off?"

"Actually the Rule wasn't taken off. It is still in effect, it just isn't on you anymore."

"What do you mean 'not on me'? Who is it on then?"

"I don't know. I am not privileged with that information. My superiors told me that I could visit you again."

"Cool, but you still didn't tell me why you sound so distressed," Regina said.

"Well, after I got permission to see you, I came at once, but I ran into the demons assigned to enhance your suffering during your Dark Night. They hadn't gotten the message on the change of Job Rule. Let's say they didn't take my word that you were to be released from their torment. We fought for some time before a demonic messenger came and gave them the information. They left, angry and without apologizing. Typical."

Regina found it charming that her angel had a sense of humor about the abuse she had taken. She wanted to ask more questions about the Job Rule and angel battles, but a more important question came to her mind.

"Does this mean Gabriel will come see me also?" Regina said.

"His comings and goings are also above my clearance level, I'm afraid," Lucy said jokingly. "But my guess would be yes."

"It would be a great Christmas present, considering," Regina said.

"Definitely, but something else troubles you?"

Regina knew Lucy could read her mind but she answered anyway. "I haven't seen Father Joe in so long. Daddy thinks the bishop has told him to stay out of the public because of his challenging preaching."

"Let us pray for your bishop."

They prayed for Bishop Roberts by name and for Father Joe. When they were done, Lucy said, "Go to your parents, Regina, they have suffered with you during this dark time. No parent sleeps well when they know their child is in pain. You don't have to tell them much, only that you are better. I will be back soon."

"Goodbye, Lucy." Regina felt like begging her to stay. For a moment, she feared never seeing Lucy again, but then the Holy Spirit surged through her, quashing her doubts. She knew her dark night had ended.

"Good evening, Bishop Roberts," a man emptying a trash can said.

"Evening, Carl. You're working late, aren't you?" The bishop carried his briefcase in one hand and a travel bag in the other.

"Yes. I had to take my car in this morning for a repair. How was your conference?"

"Good. We accomplished a lot, but I am glad to be home."

"That's nice."

"Carl, go home. I appreciate your work ethic, but it's Christmas Eve. You shouldn't be here. That can wait until Thursday. I better not see you around here tomorrow."

"Okay," Carl said. "Merry Christmas, Bishop Roberts."

"Merry Christmas, Carl." Bishop Roberts unlocked the door to his office, put down his bags, and slumped into his chair. He pushed a button on his phone.

"You have three hundred twenty new messages," the robotic voice said.

"What?"

He pushed another button and listened to a parishioner from Saint John's express their love and appreciation for Father Joe Logan. He listened to the next message, which mimicked the first. He went to the next. *I love Father Joe's passion. His homily changed my life. The church needs more priests like Father Joe.* The message continued.

Immediately, his tempter roused his anger and suspicion. *I can't believe Logan got his people to call me. Who does he think he is?*

His guardian angel stepped forward to confront the demon. Drawing swords, they clashed. The angel used the bishop's prayers as protection for his spirit. The demon countered with the bishop's pride.

"He just won an award for financial leadership at the Bishop's Conference. He thrived off the admiration of his peers. I can make him feel threatened by this priest in multiple ways."

"It may work for now, but you know it won't work forever," the angel said.

"Maybe it will, maybe it won't. Either way, for now I will savor this sin."

The tempter overpowered the guardian.

Bishop Roberts sat at his desk and pondered his next move. He picked up his gold plated pen. Taking his notepad he wrote, pressing each letter forcefully into the paper.

Logan – Patience

He put down his pen and got up. Taking his bags, he left his office.

Regina went to her parent's room. Poking her head through the open door, she saw her mother sleeping and her father sitting, reading a book.

"Hi, daddy."

"Hi, G.," he whispered. He put his index fingers to his lips, made a silent shush sound, and pointed to his wife asleep next to him.

Regina nodded to her father and tiptoed to his side of the bed. "My guardian angel came to me again, daddy. I'm feeling much better."

Mark put his book down and smiled. "That's great." He hugged her. "Do you want me to come tuck you in?"

"Sure."

Her father got out of bed. When he lifted the covers, Regina saw Emmanuel wedged into his mother's side, holding onto her arm.

"What's Manny doing here?" she asked.

"I didn't even know he was there. I just sat down with my book a second ago. He must have had a bad dream or something."

"Are you going to take him back to his room?"

"I would try, but it would probably wake up your mom too, and then she would have my head." He laughed and led Regina back to her room. "You know, if it snows as much as they say it will, maybe we could go sledding or make a snow fort tomorrow."

"That would be fun. Can we go to the hill that rents inner tubes?"

"You mean the place with the hot chocolate, right?" He smiled at her. She replied in kind. "That's fine. Either way, it's off to bed for you."

"Okay." Her father took her back to her room, got her snuggled back under her covers, kissed her on the forehead, and left her for sleep to claim.

Regina woke to find herself back in time. Joy abounded in her spirit. She called out with confidence.

"Saint Gabriel, I'm so glad we are back here."

"Yes, dear child, we have returned. Your persistence has pleased the Lord." His voice soothed her.

"Don't get me wrong, I'm glad you are back, but Lucy said the Job Rule hasn't ended. Can you tell me what that means?" Regina hoped he would have an answer.

"No, but I can say you will know in time. Behold, the scene unfolds."

A man nailed something to the wall of a building. Regina looked around and saw people beginning to gather. She recognized one of them.

"It's Saint Joseph." She felt as if years had passed since she last saw him.

"Yes, and he is about to find out some very bad news," Gabriel said.

Joseph's face dropped as he read the paper on the wall. He didn't say a word. The other townspeople, however, begin complaining in earnest. Joseph walked through the crowd with his right hand covering his face. Regina and Gabriel followed.

"What does the paper say?"

"You'll see soon."

Joseph went into his house and approached a side room hidden by a curtain. "My lady, I have some bad news."

A second passed and the curtain pulled back. Mary, now clearly pregnant, looked at Joseph. "Dear Joseph, what is it?"

"Caesar has called for a census. Every man must register in the town of his birth. I thought, for a moment, we could get an exemption, but the decree says no exceptions."

"Then we must leave at once." She began packing. Joseph looked at his wife in awe.

"You are not upset about the news?"

"It is written

But you, Bethlehem Ephratah, though you are small among the clans of Judah, out of you will come for me one who will be ruler over Israel, whose origins are from of old, from ancient times. (Micah 5:2)

It appears the Lord indeed intends to fulfill this prophecy through us."

After a stunned moment, he joined Mary in the preparation for the journey. Regina took the time to ask Gabriel some questions.

"Gabriel, did Mary know they would have to go to Bethlehem?"

"She knew the scriptures and prepared for this one to be fulfilled. She knew the long, uncomfortable journey would mean suffering for her. She mystically accepted her own cross by carrying the infant Jesus in her womb."

"She knew about the cross already?"

"Not exactly. She knew she did the work of God and her Son would do his work as well. She offered herself to God as an aid to her Son's mission."

"So she doesn't know he will die on the cross yet, right?"

"It is difficult to explain. Our Lord protects her from the dark knowledge of his brutal death. She doesn't know she will have to endure watching all of it, but she knows pain and suffering lie ahead, for both of them. Humbly, she accepts all of it for the glory of God."

Regina marveled that the young girl before her, barely high school aged, had been entrusted with the greatest mission in all of human history, and she seemed to handle it with ease.

Regina watched the preparation in fast forward as before. She remembered Joseph leaving to find a caravan headed to Bethlehem. She saw Mary pause her packing to pray a beautiful prayer of trust and petition to God for a safe trip. The scene returned to its normal speed and Joseph returned. He looked worried.

"What is it?" Mary asked. He looked perturbed.

"I asked Malachi to borrow his donkey, but the poor beast can scarcely stand."

His sorrow shook Regina. "Why is he so sad?"

"This trip would have been difficult for Mary even if she had an animal to ride on. Now Joseph fears she will have to walk. The Father put him in charge of protecting his Son and he feels he will fall short of the challenge," Gabriel said.

"Take me to it," Mary said, throwing on a shawl.

"Mary, I saw it myself. It could barely lift its head off the ground."

"Please, Joseph." Mary's gentle insistence won him over, and they left for their friend's house.

They came to a house and found Malachi. "Back so soon, Joseph?"

"Um, yes. We thought we would take another look at your animal, if you don't mind," Joseph replied.

"Help yourself. Poor thing, I may have to put him out of his misery." Malachi walked them around the house to his meager stable. Regina could see the animal lying on a pile of straw.

Mary walked over to the animal and knelt down by its head. Regina moved closer. Mary stroked the donkey's head and spoke in a whisper only Regina and Gabriel could hear. "Poor creature, have strength, the Master has need of you."

The sickly animal opened its eyes wide and looked at Mary. To the amazement of Joseph and Malachi, it forced itself to its feet. Then, it took one step forward and appeared to bow towards Mary.

"Does it recognize Jesus?"

"The creation knows its creator," Gabriel said. Mary scratched its head as it nuzzled her.

"Can we take him now?" she asked a wide-mouthed Malachi.

It took a moment for Malachi to respond. "Yes, of course, but …"

"Thank you, Malachi. Please don't mention this to anyone," Joseph said.

"What would I say?"

Mary and Joseph left Malachi scratching his head.

"How did you know that would happen?" Joseph asked Mary.

"I didn't. I felt the call to go to Malachi's house. When I neared the animals, I felt words in my heart that I knew I needed to speak."

Joseph simply smiled, shook his head, and went about the business of preparing for the trip, leaving Mary to her own work.

The scene shifted to a sizable group of people traveling down a winding road. Regina glided along the middle of the caravan close to Mary and Joseph. Mary rocked on the back of the donkey as it made its way. She didn't look comfortable, but she didn't say a word.

The trip passed in a flash.

Regina spotted a town in the distance. "Is that Bethlehem?"

"Yes," Gabriel said.

Much of the caravan had broken off during the journey. The remaining few left for their own destinations.

"I know what will happen here," Regina said. "Joseph will not be able to find a room for them."

"That's true, but I think you will still find it very interesting," Gabriel said.

Regina moved with the couple as they went from house to house asking for lodging. Mary stayed with the donkey while Joseph's expression fell with each denial. Regina found herself surprised not by the rejection, which she expected, but by something else.

"Gabriel, why do they have that look on their face?"

"What look?"

"They're not simply telling Joseph no, they are completely dismissing him, as if he wasn't even a person," Regina said.

"They may be feeling the same thing in their hearts that made you act that way in the past."

"What are you talking about," Regina said. "I've never done that."

"You haven't?"

"No, never."

The present vision stopped and another took its place. Regina saw herself in a car with her father. He pulled up to a stop light. Despite the summer heat, a man wore a jacket and held a sign reading, "Out of work, please help family, God bless you." She saw her father fumble around in his center console. She looked up and made eye contact with the man. *Look away. If you don't look at him, it won't be awkward.* Regina saw herself look away, intent at not seeing the man standing there. Her father found some McDonald's gift certificates and rolled down the window to beckon to the stranger. Regina continued to try to look away as the man came up to the car to accept the offering. "God bless you sir. You too, miss." Her father thanked the man, but she said nothing. The side vision ended and she returned to Bethlehem.

Regina was speechless as the Holy Family continued its struggle to find lodging. She felt a stab of guilt every time another person denied Joseph. She couldn't tell if her mind was playing tricks on her, but she could swear Joseph looked more and more like the homeless man her father had helped.

"I was hungry and you gave me no food, I was thirsty and you gave me no drink, a stranger and you gave me no welcome. Do you remember the response of the goats?" Gabriel asked.

"Lord, when did we see you hungry or thirsty or as a stranger?" she whispered. She paused for a second, watching the scene continue. She offered contrition both for herself and those who sent the unborn Lord away. "I'm sorry I didn't recognize you, Jesus. Why is it so hard to see him in others?"

"It isn't," Gabriel replied. "You have to learn how to look."

Mary and Joseph reached one edge of the town and prepared to head down a different road when Mary spotted a tiny hut in the distance.

"Let's go to that house," she said.

Joseph looked at the forlorn shack and asked, "Do you think they would have room for us?"

Mary didn't reply. Seeing something in her eyes, Joseph guided the beast of burden carrying the Ark of the Covenant to the tiny house. An elderly man came out, hearing their approach.

"Hello stranger," the man said. He looked directly at Joseph, a large smile on his face. "You look weary. What brings you here?"

"My wife and I are here to register in the census. I was born and grew up here in Bethlehem until my father Jacob moved us to Nazareth," Joseph answered.

The man looked Joseph over carefully. "Jacob, son of Matthan?"

"Yes."

"I remember your father. Good man. Has he passed?"

"Yes sir, many years ago."

"I am sorry to hear that, but we can only offer you a warm meal." His wife had come out with some fresh bread. "This is my wife, Adina, and my name is Yigal. Please, have something to eat."

Joseph helped Mary get off the donkey. The elderly couple noticed, for the first time, Mary's pregnancy.

"Goodness, my child, you must stay in our house in our place. We will go up into the hills and find shelter in a cave. Yigal, we can use the one where you nap in the summer."

"Yes, we can do that. Please, you must stay here," he said.

The graciousness touched the couple and their unborn child. The love they showed these strangers moved Jesus to express his will through his mother.

"Thank you for your offer, but we will take the cave if you please," Mary said. Her words surprised Joseph, but he didn't object.

"I remember those caves. I used to play there as a boy. If I could purchase some food and blankets…"

"Nonsense," Adina interrupted. "You must accept our hospitality. What would my mother say about my hospitality?" She went into the house.

Yigal smiled and shrugged his shoulders. His wife soon returned with blankets and other supplies.

"May God bless you for your kindness," Mary said.

They shared a brief meal together and Joseph packed the provisions on the donkey at Mary's request.

"The Lord calls me to walk this final distance. I need to carry my Son to the place of his birth," she said.

"Remember what I said about Mary mystically carrying her cross?" Gabriel said.

Regina nodded. "She carries him to be born, but he will carry his cross to die."

"Miss Regina, I'm impressed."

"Thanks." Regina smiled. She could feel the bitter cold blowing in from the desert. It seemed much more real than any other sensation she had felt in her visions so far. She shivered in her vision.

They made their way up a narrow path into the hills. For the first time her bare feet felt the ground and the sand felt like snow. She thought for a second to ask Gabriel about it but the struggles of the Holy Family distracted her. They arrived with some difficulty at the ample cave Joseph remembered from his youth. He took Adina's little broom and swept out loose dirt and rocks. He lit a candle and prepared an area for Mary to sleep in the back.

"It looks like people use this cave," Regina said.

"Sometimes shepherds use this cave to shelter their animals during storms. See, Joseph is cleaning out the manger," Gabriel said.

"I will get fresh grass tomorrow," Joseph said. "You can lay the baby here."

Mary nodded. Joseph cleared a space for himself near the front of the cave. Mary retreated to her room and offered thanks for the shelter afforded them. As Mary entered deeper into prayer, Regina once again found herself joined with her thoughts. Regina felt the love of Jesus filling his mother from within. He vowed to protect her from bodily decay and pain as a sign of the heavenly promise awaiting all humanity through the power of God's redemption. Then, he gave her a glimpse of what it would mean when he left her virginal womb. Mary received a brief connection to his future anguish and her own sorrows. The sensation made her soul tremble and she cried out, "It is beginning."

Joseph heard her. "What should I do? Should I find a midwife?"

"Our Lord has assured me I will have no need. Please look to the heavens and pray for our child."

Joseph nodded and went out to pray. He wept at her saying, "Our child." They both knew he could not claim paternity, but his holy wife had made sure to include him in this mission. He offered his own petitions to God.

Regina stayed with the Blessed Virgin who remained on her knees. The torment of the knowledge of her son's future suffering subsided. The communion they shared for nine months neared its end and filled her with a new sorrow. Mary knew this day would come. She offered up her breaking heart. "Lord, let it be done to me according to thy word."

Mary's angel cohort became visible in their splendor. They gathered around and supported her as the same waves of ecstasy from the Annunciation returned. The angels moved to Mary's womb to adore the Lord and assist Our Lady. A brilliant light filled the room. Its intensity forced Regina to shield her eyes. She kept them covered until she heard singing in her soul:

Glory to God in the highest! And peace to men of good will! (Luke 2:14)

She opened her eyes and saw Mary holding the infant in her arms, reclining amongst the angels. Mary's small collection of angels now swelled to a great multitude, joined by legions who served the Son of God. Regina joined the angels in adoration of the newborn.

Joseph entered and saw the same scene. He fell prostrate as well. The angels ceased their praises and all creation took a deep breath in silence. Deep within this quiet, Regina sensed an explosion of anger much greater than the one she felt during the Annunciation.

"Satan raised his battle call. With the Lord revealed to the world, the enemy has realized the Lord's plans. He will attack in many forms," Gabriel said.

Joseph looked up and Mary beckoned him to come closer. The scene surpassed the beauty of any Nativity she had ever seen. Regina looked at Jesus, who, surprisingly, looked directly into her eyes. He called her to him.

Looking into the eyes of God brought forth tears of joy she couldn't contain. Gratitude for his love burst forth from her. She crawled closer, believing she could touch him if she tried.

As she gazed lovingly at Jesus, she heard a baby's cry. It wasn't him, but he raised his little hand out to her. She reached out to touch it, but as she got close, the vision ended. A tiny infant, covered in blood, replaced the image of Jesus. Regina looked around to recognize she wasn't in her bedroom. She realized she was in a bathroom, but not one in her house. She returned to the infant and finally turned to the woman lying beside her. *Maggie!*

Chapter 21
The Joy of the Lord

Wednesday, December 25th
1:37 AM
The Solemnity of Christmas

Regina stared at Maggie, struggling to make sense of the scene. She knelt on a bathmat wet with blood. Maggie lay on the ground, holding a baby wrapped in a towel. Regina looked at her red hands, stunned and confused.

Maggie eye's barely opened. "Regina, call for help."

Regina's focus returned. She managed to get up and stumbled across the slippery floor to find a phone. She ran to the kitchen to use the one on the counter. Grabbing it, she dialed the first number that came to mind, her own. It rang several times until someone answered.

"Hello?" her father asked in a confused voice. Regina realized the time of night.

"Daddy, it's me." Regina's voice trembled with her body.

"Regina?" Mark's voice became suddenly alert. "Where are you?"

"I am with Maggie, at her house. She had her baby, she needs your help."

"It's Regina. She's with Maggie. She had the baby." He turned back to the phone. "Regina, did you call 911?"

"No."

"Okay, I will and I'll come right over."

Regina put the phone down and returned to Maggie.

"My dad's coming."

"Good. How did you know to come here?" Maggie said.

Regina looked down at her pajamas and bare feet. *No wonder the cold seemed so real in my vision.*

"I don't know," Regina said.

Maggie started crying. "She's so beautiful." She looked at the whimpering infant.

"She's so tiny," Regina said.

"Regina, she came too early. We need to get to the hospital," Maggie tried to get off the floor. "Help me up."

Regina helped Maggie get up and get dressed. Maggie found boots and a coat for Regina to wear. The baby slept on the floor as they got ready. As they finished their preparations, the lights of a vehicle pulling into the driveway flooded the living room. Regina did not see flashing lights.

Mark Andrews came through the open front door. He had his coat unzipped and hat on sideways.

"The dispatcher said there were no ambulances left because of the storm. I borrowed Mr. Carlson's truck. Let's go."

For the first time, Regina saw the ferocity of the snow. They struggled to walk through the drifts to get to the truck. Mark helped Maggie and Regina into the car. Maggie clung to her baby, who cried from the bitter cold.

Mark jumped in and started driving the massive vehicle. Normally, it would take a few minutes to get to the hospital, but the weather hampered them. No one spoke as Mark concentrated on the treacherous road. He drove through two red lights after looking for oncoming traffic.

When they arrived at the hospital, they found emergency personnel waiting for them at the door. A couple of nurses took the baby and disappeared into the building, while Mark helped Maggie down from the truck and into a wheelchair. Another nurse pushed her away. Finally alone with his daughter, Mark asked, "How did you know to go to Maggie's house?"

"I didn't. I was sleeping in my room when I had a vision of Mary and Joseph travelling to Bethlehem for the census. I saw the Nativity and when I went to touch the Baby Jesus, I woke up and found myself in Maggie's house. I have no idea how I got there."

Mark did not respond. She could see by his expression he didn't know what to say. He parked the truck and ran back to the emergency room lobby.

The admission's nurse gave them a quizzical look. Regina remembered what she and her father must have looked like. Mark stepped forward. "Can you tell me where they took Maggie Rowen? She just came in with a newborn."

"Are you her husband?"

"No. We're her only family in the area," Mark said, shooting a look at Regina.

"They took the baby to the neonatal wing and Maggie to ICU. You can see her after they evaluate her and make sure she's stable. You can sit over there and fill out this paperwork." She pointed to the waiting room.

Regina and Mark sat down. He put aside the clipboard the receptionist gave him, pulled out his cell phone, and made a call.

"We made it. The doctors are looking at both of them." Mark looked at Regina. "Yes, she's fine too. I'll call you when I know something. Okay, love you too." He hung up and closed his eyes for a moment.

Regina took off the gloves Maggie gave her. Dried blood covered her hands. Instinctively, she went to put the gloves back on but Mark opened his eyes and saw them. He looked at her, about to ask a question, when a doctor walked up. Regina finished covering her hands.

"Good evening, sir. Miss Rowen is doing well. She's stable and resting. I have to say, I am very impressed with how well you helped in her delivery. Have you had some medical training?"

"What do you mean?" Mark asked.

"When I asked how the delivery went, she said was unconscious for most of it. It must have been difficult to deliver the baby without the mother's help," the doctor said.

Mark turned to Regina. "It wasn't me. It was my daughter."

"Amazing," the doctor said. "Were you scared?"

"I don't know, I don't really remember what happened either."

"Really? Well, whatever you did, I'm impressed. Good job. Someone will let you know when you can see Miss Rowen." The doctor walked away.

"Regina, do you remember anything at all?"

She didn't remember any of the delivery but explained all of her vision. Mark asked a few questions but mostly let her talk. She ended with her phone call to their house.

"I'm guessing that vision is not finished," Mark said.

"Me too," Regina said. "I feel like it got me to where I needed to be but was put on hold."

"Let's go get you cleaned up."

They used the family wash room to wash off the blood and returned to their seats. Regina dozed off until another doctor arrived.

"We have run some tests and determined that the baby needed to be rushed into surgery. There is something wrong with her heart. I'm afraid the odds are against her. I will keep you posted."

The doctor left. Regina felt tears welling up in her eyes. They had gone to all of this trouble and Maggie's baby still might not make it. "Daddy, what can we do?"

"Let's go to the chapel and pray."

At the chapel, they found a nativity scene by the altar. They went to the kneelers and began to pray the Apostle's Creed when Regina's vision continued.

She rejoined the holy family in the Cave of the Nativity. Mary and Joseph sat and watched the baby Jesus lying before them. They had the look of parents enjoying their newborn and devotees adoring their God.

"We have to go see something else, Regina. We will be right back," Gabriel said. The scene changed to a hillside. Sheep grazed around them.

"Where is the cave?"

"We are a few miles from Bethlehem."

Regina saw several men walking around, talking to each other and the sheep. A flash of light appeared in the sky, forcing everyone to shield their eyes. The shepherds stumbled about in a panic. They fell to their knees and cried out to God for mercy. The sheep did not seem to mind at all.

Regina gazed up and once again saw the old Gabriel. He stood with the same powerful presence he always had.

"Do not be afraid. I bring you good news of great joy that will be for all the people. Today in the town of David a Savior has been born to you; he is Christ the Lord. This will be a sign to you; You will find a baby wrapped in cloths and lying in a manger." (Luke 2:10-14)

Behind Gabriel, an angel choir appeared. They began singing their song of praise again, "Glory to God in the highest and peace to men of good will." The shepherds kneeled and bowed until the angels finished their song.

When the anthem ended, the angels disappeared. The shepherds said to one another, "Let's go to Bethlehem and see this thing that has happened, which the Lord has told us about." They left their sheep and set off.

"Gabriel? What about their sheep?"

"After what they have seen and heard, faith has drawn them to give up their lives to follow the path of the Lord. They accept the cost of discipleship. Some sheep will be lost, but they will find a far greater treasure in the cave."

Regina and Gabriel returned to the cave. Little had changed. Mary reclined on some blankets and Jesus slept in the manger. Joseph knelt and adored the babe.

"How much time has passed?"

"Several hours. Joseph ran down to Bethlehem and got more blankets and some fresh straw."

Mary got up and joined Joseph in his adoration. Regina recognized the look on their faces. Her parents looked the same during the Consecration at Mass.

"Behold! The Joy of the Lord," Gabriel said.

The Joy of the Lord? She looked at the scene to see what Gabriel meant.

"What? What is the Joy of the Lord?" Regina asked.

"This scene displays the Joy of the Lord. It is the deep grace that springs forth from following the will of God and the Love of the Father in response to his people's adoration. Mary and Joseph have followed the Father's will and now they bask in the glow of his presence. People feel this true Joy in small bursts in their lives but will only fully know it in Heaven."

The baby stirred. He opened his eyes and looked up at his mother. Mary moved closer to caress his face, a loving smile on hers. The obvious depth and intensity of their connection moved Regina to tears.

"Our Lady is the embodiment of the Joy of the Lord. She has been in constant contact with Jesus since the Annunciation and has known true communion long before the Apostles will at the Last Supper. No one in history has ever followed God's will as perfectly as his mother. Regina, your mission begins with bringing this knowledge to the world."

"What knowledge?"

"You have seen the first three Joyful Mysteries of the Rosary. In sharing your visions, when the time comes, you will advance an important weapon against the devil. Humanity needs to be reminded what it means to find God's will in their lives and then follow it."

"What do you mean?"

"People waste their lives seeking pleasure or accumulating wealth. As much as they try to find joy in these things, they find despair and loneliness. The Father sent a savior to teach mankind the way to true joy. Look how he came into the world." Gabriel gestured to the baby Jesus. The Almighty God, in all of his radiance and splendor, the Creator of the universe subjected to the body of a newborn.

"He came in the innocence of a new life to show humanity how to enter into new life," Gabriel said.

"People have to be like babies?"

"One must be willing to be helpless and humble before your life can truly begin anew. Look at Mary and Joseph. They did not know what to expect in Bethlehem, but they trusted in God and believed he would guide them on their journey. The peace you see right now will be short lived. Their faith and love will be tested, but they will find strength in the Joy of the Lord." Gabriel finished his explanation and voices sounded outside the cave.

Joseph jumped up. He grabbed his staff and headed for the entrance. Regina followed. Peering outside, Joseph could see a group of men approaching. They all stared upwards, forcing Joseph to turn and look. Regina looked as well and saw a star shining brightly as the moon directly above them. It seemed to project light directly towards the cave. Joseph overcame his wonder and returned to a defensive posture.

"Gentlemen, state your business."

The men stopped their chatter. They turned to their elder, who answered, "Please, sir. A messenger of the Lord told us that Our Savior has been born. This star has led us to this hillside. We mean you no harm. We only wish to worship the child. Are you his father?"

Joseph hesitated at first. "Yes." He looked at the number of men present and knew he couldn't stop them. He prayed for protection, beckoned them forward, and retreated into the cave.

"My lady, our child has visitors." Mary did not seem surprised at all. She simply nodded and picked up Jesus to make him clearly visible to anyone who entered. Joseph produced more light with extra candles. Footsteps closed in from outside.

"May we enter?" a voice asked.

Mary nodded and Joseph said, "Please, come in."

The first shepherd crossed the threshold and as his eyes beheld the infant he fell to his knees. He wept as he crawled closer. The other shepherds followed suit; a dozen men huddled close together on their knees adoring the child.

This fascinated Mary and Joseph. Regina, too, found the image powerful. She saw her own father cry, at times, and always found great beauty in it. She knew he had to feel deeply touched to evoke such emotion.

After some time, Jesus squirmed and managed to free a tiny arm that he held out toward his visitors. Mary gasped. She nodded to Joseph, who said, "Friends, you may touch him."

The shepherds smiled. The first to enter got off his knees and approached the child. He extended his right index finger until it touched the tiny hand of Jesus. He held it there for a few moments and then touched it to his own forehead. Closing his eyes, he stood frozen, relishing the moment. Finally, he turned and made his way out of the cave. The next shepherd stood to do the same. All of the men kept their eyes on Jesus until they left, full of joy.

She thought of this joy as the vision began to spin away. She looked one last time at the baby with his little hand out and wished that she could touch his hand herself. She reached out thinking, *If I could only touch him...*

"Regina? Regina?"

"Huh?" she said.

"Did you have another vision? You've been in a daze," Mark said.

"Yeah, how long was I out?"

"Maybe thirty seconds. I looked over and saw you with a blank stare. I called your name several times. When you didn't respond, I waited for it to end, but then you said something."

"I did?"

"Yes, it sounded like goodbye."

"That makes sense." She explained the whole story to her father.

"Father Joe didn't want to jeopardize the authenticity of your visions, but Gabriel confirmed his suspicions."

"I don't understand."

"Father Joe wanted you to experience your visions without any outside influence from anyone. He said we could answer your questions but not to give you any information about the Joyful Mysteries. If you continued to experience the rest of the mysteries, no one could say that we implanted the thoughts in your mind. Do you see?"

"Why would someone say that?"

"People have always been suspicious of young visionaries, probably because some unscrupulous people have used children to advance their own agendas. We wanted you to be completely free to see what God wanted you to see."

"I can't believe I didn't make the connection myself. I've learned what the Joyful Mysteries are before. Is that bad?"

"No, G, but I think Gabriel was telling you that God wants you to show us how to live the joy in the mysteries so we never fail to see their connection to our lives. Let's offer the Joyful Mysteries for Maggie's baby. She could use the prayers."

"Okay."

They prayed together and when they were done they headed back to the waiting room. A doctor approached after about an hour.

"We successfully repaired the baby's heart, but she is still in critical condition. We won't know for a while if she will make it through. You look like you could use some sleep. Go home. We sedated Miss Rowen. You can see her when she wakes up tomorrow."

"Thank you doctor," Mark said. He got himself and Regina ready to go outside. The storm had subsided. Plow trucks had cleared the roads, making the ride home simple. Once home, they both passed out in their beds.

Chapter 22
Emmanuel

Wednesday, December 25th
9:25 AM
The Solemnity of Christmas

Regina woke up to extreme brightness pouring in from the window. She turned to her clock and sat up in shock.

Why didn't anyone wake me up? I'm late for... Before she finished her thought she remembered the date. Then she remembered the snow. She walked to the window to see the massive white blanket that covered everything in sight. She began to make a list of snow activities in her mind. Picking out the clothes she would need, she spotted dried blood on her arm she had missed the night before. *Maggie!*

"How could I forget about her and the baby?"

"The brightness of the fresh snow distracted you. Don't feel bad. Shiny things tend to do that to humans," Lucy said.

"It doesn't even seem like it happened."

"Life's greatest moments are like that. At the time, your soul is on fire, but when the distractions of life hit, you return to your normal routine. It keeps people from living extraordinary lives because their habits hold them captive."

Regina thought about Lucy's words and her own journey, still at its beginning. School and friends made her forget about her vision on several occasions.

"Your parents are right. You should continue to be a twelve-year old girl. God wants you to bring his joy to the world, but he also wants you to live your life."

"But does he think I am being ungrateful when I forget about him and take his call for granted?"

"It happens to everyone. It only becomes a sin when you hear his call and actively go out of your way to ignore him."

"Okay, thanks. I'll go see what's going on at the hospital."

Regina felt Lucy leave. She walked down the stairs to find Emmanuel playing in the family room. He made toy cars talk and drive around.

"You can't steal that money. Yes I can. Get back here," he said in different voices.

Regina smiled and marveled at her brother's imagination.

"Hey Manny, where's mommy?"

"She went to visit Maggie," Manny said without looking up.

"What about Daddy?"

Emmanuel changed to a whisper. "Sleeping on the couch." He immediately returned to his raucous game.

"I'll let him rest," Regina said to herself. "Can I play with you?"

"Sure." Manny smiled and pushed some cars in her direction. She followed his lead until she got curious about what her brother had heard about the previous night.

"Do you know that Maggie had her baby?"

"Yes, mommy told me."

"Did she tell anything else about last night?"

"No, but daddy said we can go to the hospital too, after you wake up."

"What time did you get up?"

"I don't know; whenever mommy got up."

This reminded Regina that she had spotted Manny in her parents' bed. He slept in his own room, proudly, for years.

"Were you sleeping with mommy because you had a bad dream?"

Emmanuel looked at her like she had cursed and turned away.

"Manny, I'm sorry. Let's keep playing." She wondered why he responded like that.

"Regina, is that you?" her father asked from the other room.

"Yes."

"Do you want to go see Maggie?"

"Yes," she answered, jumping up to get her boots.

They got dressed and ate breakfast before heading to the hospital. No new snow had fallen, but drifts made travel slow. Mark called Katherine on the way over. She met them at the door. Both kids ran to hug their mother. She kissed each of them. "Maggie is sleeping again. I talked to her briefly and told her everything was alright. She is still a little loopy from her meds. Maybe you can see her soon." She looked right at Regina when she said the last part.

"What about the baby?" Regina said.

"A nurse told me the surgery was successful but she will have to stay in the intensive care nursery for a while. She did offer to wheel her into a family viewing window so we can see her." They followed Katherine to the elevator.

When they arrived at the right floor, Katherine explained to a nurse why they were there. The nurse nodded.

"Come with me," the nurse said. She led them to a window that looked into a small room. Leaving for a moment, she returned with a cart containing a tiny infant. A tube went up her nose and sensor pads covered most of her body.

Regina only had a moment to see the baby before Jesus took her place. Mary held him, stroking his cheek. Regina fell in love with him all over again. She found it incredible that she had forgotten what it felt like to be in his presence. Seeing him again, she wished the vision would never end.

"What are you thinking, Regina?" Gabriel asked.

"I don't know. I look at Jesus and I don't understand how he can be God, but at the same time, I know it's true."

"This setting frees your mind to experience the mystery of the Incarnation. The humility of the location and bodily form God chose to enter the world are both so unthinkable to the human imagination, yet give you a glimpse into his mysterious workings."

"What about the star? What about the heavenly angels? Doesn't everyone notice?"

"The Lord withholds the miraculous from some people, while he shows others signs and wonders. Only those he has chosen have beheld the spectacle of his birth. Here come some others now," Gabriel said. Someone approached.

"Please, announce yourself," Joseph said.

"It's Yigal and Adina. We both dreamt you had your child and he is the Messiah. Can it be true?"

Joseph didn't answer. Instead, he met them at the cave opening and escorted them in. Despite their age, they both fell to their knees upon seeing the child. They remained on the ground until Mary said, "Please rise and meet him."

Yigal rose first and helped his wife. He led her to the child who slept in the hay. Adina said, "Oh, my dear, he is so lovely. Never in my wildest dreams did I think I would behold the Messiah with my own eyes." Yigal nodded in agreement and together they adored him.

"Thank you for the help you gave us," Mary said.

"It was our pleasure. We only wish we could do more. Our Savior is here and we can only offer you a little food," Yigal said. He handed a sack to Joseph.

"Maybe you can help us with more," Joseph said. Adina and Yigal both looked at him with interest. "Do you know of a mohel? The eighth day will come too soon for us to find someone we know."

"Yes, of course. I have a close friend who has performed many Brit Milahs in his life. I will ask him to come. When will the eighth day be?" Yigal said.

"It will fall on the fourth day of the week," Joseph said.

"I will let him know."

"Thank you, Yigal," Mary said. "Would you like to stay for a while?"

Regina thought she probably had the same look on her face as Adina whenever a vision would end. Yigal answered, "Why don't you stay, my dear. I will obtain the mohel and then come back for you."

Adina smiled with gratitude towards Mary's invitation to stay with her divine infant. Yigal genuflected to the Christ child before getting ready to leave.

"Oh, Yigal," Joseph interrupted.

"Yes?"

"Could you keep this …" Joseph gestured towards the Holy Infant at a loss for words until he settled on, "Situation … to yourself? We would rather avoid unnecessary attention."

"I understand," Yigal said.

Regina followed Yigal down the hillside with Gabriel.

"Where is Yigal going?" Regina said.

"He knows a mohel, a person who can perform the ritual circumcision that Jewish males receive eight days after their birth," Gabriel said.

"Oh. What did Joseph mean about attention?"

"Mary and Joseph know the Lord will make his birth known as he wills, but they don't want to get swamped by gossip hunters."

"Do you mean how you called the shepherds to the cave?"

"Yes, the shepherds, Yigal and Adina, and you, Regina."

"Me?"

"Yes. God chooses certain people to see his glories directly. He calls them to special work, but others have to act on simple faith, without experiencing the wondrous. Everyone plays their own role."

Regina thought once again about being chosen by God. She still felt unworthy of this task, but watching Yigal as he slowly made his way down the mountain, she realized it was not for her to question the ways of the Lord. *The Joy of the Lord is my strength.*

Yigal approached a house and knocked on the door. After a few moments, it opened.

"Yigal!" An elderly woman appeared in the doorway. "What a pleasant surprise. How can I help you?"

"Bina, is Elad here?"

"No, he is performing his duties down the road. You can probably see the crowd gathered from here."

Regina looked in the distance and saw many people outside a home.

"Thank you, Bina. Good to see you." The old woman smiled, nodded, and closed the door as Yigal walked away.

As they arrived, a small group walked out of the house. An elderly man carrying a bag stood in the middle. He had a gruff look on his face. His companions gave him another bag and they bowed to one another. He walked briskly away and straight towards Yigal. He looked down, shaking his head.

"Elad?" Yigal called out.

"Hmpfh," Elad said. "Oh, it's you, Yigal. What do you want?"

"How was the bris?"

"Tiring. These people told me to be here at ten o'clock and I had to wait an hour before I did the circumcision. People can be so rude."

"My friend, you perform a great service to the people of Bethlehem. What would we do without you?"

"Ha, I know parents get mohels from other towns, so don't give me that. People don't like me, but I'm cheap and I'm convenient. That's why people hire me."

"No, no, no. You are a good man who uses his gifts to do the work of the Lord, and you will be greatly blessed for it."

"The work of the Lord? I used to think so, but now I am not so sure."

"Remember our father Joseph? The Lord gave him the gift of interpreting dreams. It got him into trouble with his brothers, but he continued to use his gift even when he was in jail. The gift brought him to ruin for a while, but he still honored God by using his skills. And what happened?"

"He waited years before his release, when Pharaoh's cupbearer finally remembered him. The ingrate."

"Yes, but Pharaoh did release him. Joseph used his gift to serve Pharaoh, who handsomely rewarded him. Sometimes you need to have patience with the Lord and wait for his plan to unfold."

"Yigal, you are always a pleasant fellow, but I sense you want something. Why did you find me here?"

Yigal hesitated and turned from Elad. Regina could see his worried expression.

"Why does he make that face?"

"He knows his friend struggles with his vocation and is not happy after the recent ceremony. Yigal doesn't think he should ask Elad to circumcise Jesus right now," Gabriel said.

Regina, worried now as well, continued to watch. Yigal clenched his fist and nodded. He turned to Elad as they walked.

"Elad, I do have a favor to ask of you. Another couple needs a mohel on the fourth day of the week," Yigal said.

Elad stopped walking, rolled his eyes, and sighed, "I guess I'm free. Who are they and where do they live?"

"They came from Nazareth for the census." Yigal paused. "They found shelter in a cave in the hills."

"Oh, that will be great on my knees. It will take me an hour to get there and back."

"Yes, I know, I'm sorry."

"What will they give as a … donation? My sacrifice will be great."

Again, Yigal looked worried.

"What donation?" Regina asked.

"It is customary for the family receiving the help of a mohel to give him a donation for his time. People still pay priests and ministers for their time when they do weddings and baptisms. Here, Yigal knows Joseph and Mary have little to offer to Elad."

"They don't have much, but …," Yigal said. Regina felt uncomfortable watching him struggle. He rubbed his hands together, but then suddenly stopped. "I will give you this ring." Regina looked at the hand that Yigal held up to Elad. She saw a beautiful ring there and beyond it, Elad's expression changing.

"Isn't that your father's ring. I feel like we have talked about it before?"

"Yes. It has been in my family for a long time," Yigal said.

"Yigal offers a great sacrifice here, his family's only treasure," Gabriel said.

"You have a deal," Elad said, holding out his hand. Yigal took off the ring, paused a moment, and gave it to his friend. Elad nodded and walked home. Yigal walked back to his own house. Once inside, he fell to his knees and wept.

"Father, forgive me. I have failed you twice in my life. I could not bring forth children to continue our lineage, and now I have relinquished your gift from our fathers. I pray I have done the right thing. O God in heaven, I live to serve you."

"It did mean a lot to him," Regina said, with tears in her eyes.

"Yigal and Adina are simple people. They live on very little and have few possessions. What they hold precious has great sentimental value," Gabriel said.

The scene changed and Regina knew days had passed. She remembered witnessing the Joy of the Lord in their love. Now, the day of circumcision had arrived. Mary and Joseph prepared for the ceremony. Yigal and Adina also helped.

Her vision blurred and she found herself outside Elad's house. He came out carrying his bag. He walked toward the hills with a scowl on his face. He remained silent until he reached the beginning of the climb.

"Oh Lord, why do you torment me with such tasks? Why must I suffer to serve you?" Elad said, looking up the path. Regina listened to him grumble unintelligible words as he made his way. Almost to the cave, he paused to catch his breath, and Regina heard him say, "This ring better be worth all of this."

"Hello?" Elad said as the neared the mouth of the cave.

Yigal went out to meet him. "Elad, we are ready for you."

"Good, I would like to do this quickly. I need a nap."

"Thank you again for coming," Yigal said, leading Elad inside.

Joseph met him. "Thank you, sir. You have blessed us with your presence." Elad nodded and grunted. Joseph led him towards Mary who faced away.

Regina could hear Elad's thoughts. *Why Lord, must I minister to poor fools in caves? Let's get this over with.*

At this moment, Mary turned around with the baby Jesus awake in her arms. Regina never saw Mary look as beautiful. Jesus looked directly at the newcomer. Elad saw his face and froze. His breath left him. He dropped the bag from his trembling right hand and fell to his knees. The others exchanged surprise glances.

Tears began to stream down Elad's face. Pure sorrow replaced the contempt he had when he entered. He dropped his head to the floor and stammered, "Forgive me Lord, forgive me."

"What's happening, Gabriel?"

"I think you know this feeling, Regina. Remember your sorrow for what happened to Frank?"

She did. She remembered her heart breaking when she realized her sin. She recalled the depth of her sorrow not only towards Frank but to God, who gave her a special mission. She failed him and then longed for redemption.

"I know he complained about coming here. Is that why he feels bad?"

"Wait for one moment and you will see," Gabriel said.

Elad remained weeping on the ground. Finally, Mary looked at Joseph, who went to the poor man, touched his shoulder, and said, "Brother, what troubles you in this way? This is a happy occasion. You honor us with your presence. Please, have comfort."

Elad made his way to his knees. "I apologize for my behavior, but my true apology goes to the Lord. When I received my sacred training for this ritual, I felt so strongly God called me to this service. I felt I had a great purpose. I remember feeling the promise of something special."

He looked at his friends, and then at the baby. He continued to confess to the child, himself. "As I performed each circumcision, my bitterness kept increasing. I thought my calling had turned into a meaningless job. Even recently, when Yigal reminded me that God gives us gifts to use for his service, like Joseph's skills with dreams, I felt bitter and didn't appreciate my vocation."

He paused, gazing at Jesus. "But, this child … I can see in him, my redemption. From the moment I saw him, I knew God had called me, all my life, for this purpose. Lord, I am sorry I did not trust in your goodness. Please forgive me, and allow me to serve you." He smiled, trusting in the mercy of God.

Mary held the babe out to the old man, who gladly received him. Jesus played with Elad's beard and the man overflowed, now with tears of joy. He handed him back to his mother and gathered his bag. "Shall we begin?"

Regina heard Elad begin to pray as the vision faded and she returned to her own time.

"Manny? Manny?" Mark Andrew's voice rang. Regina stood in the same place, but something had changed. She noticed the chaos around her. She looked to her side to find her parents bent down on the ground. To her horror, she saw her brother on the floor writhing. Only the whites of his eyes showed and he gulped short, quick breaths. Medical personnel rushed in.

"Stand back," a female nurse said, and the family obeyed. She held her hand to Emmanuel's forehead. "He's burning up. This may be a febrile seizure."

"What?" Katherine asked. Before the nurse could respond Emmanuel stopped shaking. Everyone exhaled.

"A febrile seizure occurs when a child's temperature spikes very suddenly. I can't say for sure that's what happened, but I would guess his temp is well over a hundred. We should get him down to the ER."

"Is he going to be okay?" Regina asked in a broken voice.

"He looks stable now, sweetie. We will do everything we can to make him better, okay?" the nurse said.

"Can I pick him up now?" Mark said.

"Yes, let me grab a gurney and we will take him downstairs."

The nurse ran around the corner and came back with a gurney. With Emmanuel safely strapped in, she escorted the Andrews family to the emergency room. On the way, Emmanuel opened his eyes briefly, saw his parents, smiled, and went back to sleep. The nurse wheeled them into an open stall and went to explain the situation to the admitting nurse. She came back to talk to the family.

"A doctor will come and examine your son shortly, but he told me to start him on an IV. It will allow us to give him some fluids and something to bring his fever down."

"Okay, thank you," Mark said. He and Katherine shared a look of relief. Regina wanted to do something for Emmanuel but felt helpless in the room.

"Can I go to the chapel? To pray?" she asked.

Katherine looked to Mark, who said, "She knows the way there. I think she's old enough."

"That's fine," Katherine said. "Come back every thirty minutes or so to check in. One of us will be here."

"Okay." This freedom allowed her to escape the claustrophobia she felt. She prayed on her way to the chapel.

"Lord, what is wrong with Manny? Please heal him." When she arrived at the chapel and knelt, she felt the world spin and knew she would soon have some answers.

Chapter 23
Vita et Mors

Regina found herself in the weapons room where she first trained for spiritual battle. She glanced around and saw the familiar weapons from her first experience. She also saw the beautiful face of her guardian angel.

"Lucy! It's so good to see you again," Regina said.

"Yes, it has been too long. God has allowed this meeting so I can prepare you for what comes next."

"What's coming?" Regina could not hide her worry. "Do I want to know?"

"Remember what I told you about the Job Rule?"

"You said something had changed but you didn't know what."

"Right. Job had many levels of suffering he had to endure during his test. He lost his goods, his family, his health, almost his sanity. You lost your connection with God, only for a short time, and see what it did to you?"

"It was awful."

"Why?"

"Because I became so used to the closeness I felt with God and you angels."

"Yes. That is why the devil chose to give you that suffering first."

"First?"

"Yes. He wanted to strike quickly and deeply, but you endured, and then, unexpected to the evil one, someone intervened."

"Who?"

"Emmanuel."

"What?" Regina replied in shock. "How? And why?"

"There is more to your baby brother than meets the eye, Regina," Lucy answered. "He offered himself to take on the Job Rule."

"He is even younger than I am. How could he know about the Job Rule? Is he having visions too? Something is different about him."

"That is why the devil didn't see it coming. Emmanuel lives a very spiritual life, in his own way. He has sensitivity to our world that he doesn't understand but simply accepts. You have seen it, you know it's true."

"I don't know what you mean."

"Haven't you ever watched him at Mass? One second he has tons of energy like any young boy, the next second he will be transfixed on the altar as if he sees something you can't."

Regina thought about the Lucy's words. She had seen that behavior.

"Remember how he knew about your visions even though no one told him about them?"

"Yes, I thought that was weird."

"He has seen and felt many things he can't explain, but when he saw you suffering from the dark night, he willingly took on your pain to allow you to continue your mission."

"How is that possible?" Regina asked.

"Our Lord showed you it was in the way of the Cross. Christ called humanity to this kind of sacrifice by his example."

"How does it work?"

Lucy laughed. "When you are with Jesus in heaven, you can ask him."

"Then why is Manny sick? I wasn't sick," Regina asked.

"First, think about what has happened. Without his normal connection with God, a simple nightmare terrified Emmanuel last night."

"That's why he was in my parents' bed."

"That's right. Despite the terror he felt, he offered himself for you again in the morning. This really angered hell. His heroic act would protect you from pain so the demons decided to change their tactics. They decided to go after you through Maggie."

"Maggie's baby is my fault?"

"No, Regina. You must never think that. The torments hell evokes on the world are no one's fault. Remember, they used the same tests on Job to lead him to despair. Bad things happen to good people because you live in a broken world. The enemy places obstacles in your way to cause you to stumble, but the Lord shows us that these occasions help people become saints."

"How?"

"The saints looked at suffering as a necessity in their lives. They needed it and wanted it to unite them with Jesus and his Passion."

Regina tried to make sense of this. Her thoughts went back to her brother.

"What about Manny?"

"Despite his spiritual dryness, when he saw the frailty of Maggie's baby in the incubator, he offered his health for hers."

Regina started to cry. "He is so much braver than I could ever be. He won't die, will he?"

"Even the angels don't know when people will die, but the Lord will honor his agony and send graces to the baby. You are all connected in a mystical way. Think of it as a spiritual economy, if you understand."

"I don't think I do."

"It is a mystery so no explanation could be fully complete, but I will try. God knew his children's suffering would eventually require him to send his Son to share in your humanity. Now, imagine that God owned a bank, and then that all of mankind owed Him debts for its sins, but Jesus paid all of humanity's debts at the bank. Through Our Lord's suffering, death, and resurrection he also opened something we can imagine as a bank account. Jesus enables you to access spiritual money to help yourself in times of need," Lucy said.

"Money?" Regina said. "What money?"

"Not really money, but like it in the spiritual world. We call it grace."

"I've heard of that."

"Right. Remember, I'm taking a holy mystery and oversimplifying it, but I think it will help you understand a little better."

"Okay."

"So, Jesus secured for you an infinite amount of grace."

"So, what then? Do we earn it?"

"Not exactly. The Lord gives it as a gift when you live in his love."

"How do I do that?"

"Jesus suffered and died so you might live in the light of God's love. So when Manny suffers …" Lucy held her word, trying to get Regina to finish her sentence.

"He is joining in Jesus' suffering?"

"Very good, Regina. Jesus said 'There is no greater love than to lay down one's life for a friend.' You can live in his love when you follow the Gospel message." (John 15:13)

"And that leads to grace?"

"God's grace flows upon the soul in love with Jesus. Those graces also proceed to the soul offered up by the one who suffers."

"Do you have to suffer to receive grace?"

"No, but suffering unites you to Christ. Anything that expresses your love for Jesus allows you to open your soul to his. In this state, you receive grace from Our Lord."

"How can Manny understand all this?"

"You don't have to understand it, Regina. Some people can just feel their spiritual connection better than others. Your brother is one of these souls."

"Okay, Lucy." Regina paused to reflect. "What next?"

"First, we must train again. You must remember to focus on the love of God while you face the growing darkness. Do not be afraid, Regina. Jesus has commanded many angels to fight by your side."

Regina thought about the terror she felt in the presence of the dark spirits. She didn't look forward to facing it again, but having Lucy back gave her confidence.

"Okay, let's begin," she said. The suits of armor came to life. She also felt the familiar chill of evil.

"I have made the training more challenging. You can use your visions to help you focus on the life of Our Lord. Draw strength from this," Lucy explained. The suits of armor held up their weapons but also taunted Regina.

"Your faith is too weak to carry out your mission," one enemy accused.

"Your brother suffers because of you," another said.

The Joy of the Lord is my strength, Regina thought. She continued her prayer and meditated on the Annunciation. The more she offered her battle to the will of God, the stronger she felt. The words of her challengers diminished.

"That's it Regina!" Lucy said. "Now, remember the Visitation."

More enemies appeared from a door in the wall and menaced with varying weapons. Regina meditated on the pregnancies of Elizabeth and Mary. She thought about the Canticles of Mary and Zechariah. This gave her strength to attack. She jumped around the room routing the empty knights.

"Very good. We will train using the Nativity soon. Now, you must return to your family," Lucy said.

"Okay, goodbye," Regina said before the vision ended.

Regina realized her father had joined her in the chapel. He remained in prayer until she sat back on the pew.

"They moved Manny to his own room. He is sleeping right now. Do you want to go see if Maggie is awake?"

"Yes."

"Let's go to Manny's room and mommy will take you."

"Okay."

They went to Emmanuel's room and found Katherine sitting in a chair by the bed where Emmanuel slept. Katherine got up and hugged Regina.

"How are you feeling, sweetheart?" she asked.

"Fine, I guess. How is Manny?"

"The doctor said he is stable, but he still has a bit of a fever. They drew some blood for testing. We should know the results in a few hours." She paused for a moment to let the news sink in. "Do you want to go see Maggie while daddy stays with Manny?"

"Yes, let's go."

They left Mark with Emmanuel and went to Maggie's room. They found Maggie with her eyes closed but clearly not asleep. She mouthed words they couldn't hear. When they walked in, she opened her eyes and seeing her friends, smiled warmly.

"I'm so glad you're here. I was praying for my baby, please join me." They did. Maggie fumbled to find the words to express her passion for her newborn.

Katherine rescued her. "Dear Lord, please bless Maggie's baby with your love and your light. Give her strength to grow into the person you have called her to be. Give Maggie the grace to be a strong mother and a witness of faith to her child. We ask this in your name..."

"Amen," they said.

"Thank you, Katherine," Maggie said.

"You're welcome."

"Katherine, do you think your priest would come and baptize my baby? The doctors don't know if she is going to make it." Her voice wavered. "The nurse told me the hospital chaplain is off for Christmas."

"I can ask. He has been hard to get a hold of recently. I'll go call him." Katherine stepped into the hallway.

The whole time Katherine and Maggie spoke, Regina stood beside her mother, quietly. She felt uncomfortable, both for being in a hospital room for the first time and because she didn't know what to say to Maggie. Maggie sensed this and said, "Regina, can you come here and give me a hug?"

She ran over and they embraced. "Regina, thank you so much. I don't know what would have happened if you hadn't come to my

241

house. I went to the bathroom in the middle of the night and suddenly I had this pain and my water broke. I slipped and fell. I think I hit my head on the edge of the sink. The next thing I remember is seeing you and my baby. How did you know to come? How did you do it? The delivery, I mean."

"I don't know, Maggie," Regina said. She realized she had never spoken to Maggie about her visions. She wondered if she should. Father Joe said to keep it between themselves and her family. She decided to wait.

Maggie looked confused but she let the matter go. "Well, I thank God you came when you did. Have you seen my baby? They told me I should be able to go see her as soon as the doctor clears me."

"She's beautiful," Regina said. "And so tiny."

Maggie smiled and started to cry. Katherine walked in.

"He still isn't answering. I left him a message."

Regina saw Maggie's disappointment and changed the subject. "What do you want to name her?"

"I don't know, I guess I haven't really thought about it."

"How about Vita Plena?" Regina said. She surprised herself and the others.

"That's pretty, what does it mean?" Maggie said.

"Full of life," Regina said.

"How did you know that?" Katherine said.

"I don't know."

Katherine saw Maggie's confusion.

"Regina, you can tell Maggie anything you want. Go ahead," Katherine said.

With her mother's permission, Regina told Maggie all about her visions. She also explained the missions of her family and Father Joe.

"That explains a lot," Maggie said. They sat quietly for a while. Maggie turned to Katherine. "Can I ask you for a favor?"

"Sure."

"Would you be my daughter's Godmother?"

"Of course, I would be honored."

Maggie turned to Regina and said, "I know this is not a normal thing, but I would really like you to be her Godsister."

She looked to Katherine, who nodded. "I would love to."

A knock on the door caused them to turn. A doctor stood in the doorway.

"Hi, Miss Rowen? I'm Doctor Phillips; I am here to examine you. May we have a moment?"

"We'll wait out in the hallway, come on Regina," Katherine said. She closed the door as they left.

The doctor checked Maggie and wrote on her chart. He looked over some other things. "You are healing up quite well."

"Can I see my baby?"

"That sounds fine. It's a long way to the neonatal ward, so you need to ride in a wheelchair."

"Thank you, doctor, how much longer do you think I will be in the hospital?"

"I would like you to stay another night or two at the most," he answered, smiling. She recognized something about Paul in the doctor and realized how much she missed him. She remembered the ferocity of their last fight, but she knew she still had feelings for him and wished they could have settled their differences.

"Okay, could you send the others back in, please?"

"Sure. I will probably be back tomorrow around the same time to see you. Good bye." He walked out and Regina and Katherine returned.

"Are you okay?" Regina said.

"Yeah, sweetie, I'm fine. He said I can go see Vita. I'll buzz the nurse for a wheelchair." She pushed her call button. They got a wheelchair and went down to the neonatal wing.

When they arrived there, they asked the nurse to wheel Vita's incubator into the viewing area again. After a short wait, Katherine and Regina helped Maggie stand up to see her baby. She put her hand on the glass barrier, longing to hold her child, but motherly love poured forth from her soul nonetheless.

"I could stand here all day." Something in her heart stirred. The Lord used this moment to nourish a seed in Maggie that would blossom over the coming days. He planted it when she embraced Regina back at the women's shelter. It took root and events in the upcoming days and Maggie's choices would determine if it would flower.

Regina glanced at the look on Maggie's face and remembered her mother's words years ago.

"When I looked at you for the first time, I had so much joy in my heart that I thought it would break. I would often cry when I looked at you sleeping."

Regina didn't understand what her mother meant at the time, but watching Maggie, it made more sense. She thanked God for the opportunity.

They stayed there for a while. Regina lost track of time. Katherine had to say, "Maggie, you should get some rest."

"I guess you are right," Maggie said. She struggled to turn away from the glass. She sat down in the wheelchair. "Okay, let's go."

Katherine and Regina wheeled Maggie back to her room. They got her back into bed and said their goodbyes. Katherine promised to return soon. When they got to Emmanuel's room, they found him sitting up in bed with a big, goofy smile on his face. Mark changed channels on the television manually because the remote control had stopped working. Emmanuel really enjoyed watching his father stand on his tiptoes to change the channel time after time. He didn't even check the show to see if he liked it. His father knew it but didn't mind being the entertainment for his ailing son.

Katherine and Mark started speaking. Regina heard Lucy's voice. *Don't bring up what you know about Emmanuel's sacrifice, he won't speak of it, and your parents won't understand. It is God's will your brother has accepted. You must pray for him and be strong.*

Regina nodded to herself and looked at Emmanuel. He turned to her with a toothy grin and opened his arms for a hug. In the past, this would make her uncomfortable and she would shy away, but her love for him compelled her to comply. Somehow, in their contact, she knew his suffering had only begun.

Regina began to pray. "Our Father, who art in Heaven."

Her parents heard her and stopped their conversation. They looked at Regina and continued with her. "Hallowed be Thy Name." They all joined hands.

Emmanuel smiled and joined in as well. "Thy Kingdom come, Thy Will be done, on earth as it is Heaven."

They also prayed a Hail Mary and a Glory Be. When their prayers ended, they enjoyed the silence together. Shortly, a doctor arrived to discuss the results of Emmanuel's blood tests. Regina looked at Emmanuel while her parents spoke with the doctor. She could tell by the look on his face that he knew more trouble awaited him. She took his hand and squeezed it. He smiled.

Chapter 24
Visionary

Thursday, December 26th
10:12 AM

"So, Father Logan, what I am trying to say is, I am going to give you a little freedom with your homilies. I do want my priests to listen to God's call, but I would still like you to avoid being too provocative," Bishop Roberts said.

"Thank you, Your Excellency," Father Joe said.

"And as I have told the other pastors, try to avoid political topics until the Governor's bill is sorted out. The church doesn't need to create negative publicity that will help his cause."

"I understand."

"Thank you, we will talk soon," the bishop said.

"Yes, goodbye."

Father Joe said a prayer of thanksgiving.

"Keep praying for the bishop," his guardian said.

He did and then picked up his phone.

"Hello? Katherine?"

"Yes."

"I got your message. How soon can we do this baptism?"

"Right away, I'm sure. Let me talk to my husband and call Maggie, but as soon as you can get to the hospital."

"I am ready now and have no other appointments."

"I'll call you back soon, okay?"

"Okay, goodbye," Father Joe said.

"Goodbye."

Father Joe smiled and decided to pray a Rosary in thanksgiving until Katherine called him back.

The Andrews chatted with Maggie when Father Joe knocked. He entered and embraced them all. Maggie remained in bed until Katherine realized they needed an introduction.

"Maggie, this is Father Joe Logan. Father Joe, Maggie Rowen."

"Before we do the baptism, will you hear my confession Father?" Maggie asked. Her tempter wailed in agony.

"Of course." He looked at Mark with raised eyebrows.

"Oh, yeah, we'll wait outside," Mark said, leading his family out.

Ten minutes passed before Father Joe came out with Maggie in a wheelchair. Regina could tell Maggie had been crying but she wore a large smile now.

At the neonatal ward, Father Joe had to sterilize his hands and put on scrubs over his vestments. He baptized Vita Plena with a few drops of holy water and a touch of sacred oil. Father Joe gave a beautiful sermon on the fullness of the Christian life through the graces of the sacraments. Even the attending nurse, bored at first, seemed moved by his words.

Once they returned to Maggie's room, Father Joe explained his struggles with the bishop. He asked them to pray for his boss, for the church, and for the governor. He explained that to live out his mission, he would have to suffer. They all would.

"Do you have more to tell me, Regina?" Father Joe said.

"Yes."

They stepped into the hallway and Regina told her about the newest visions. He nodded throughout her story as if he expected much of what she had to say, but he found the details fascinating.

"The Lord's birth brought joy to Mary and Joseph, but as you know, it also brought danger. You have seen that joy in the past and in your own life. I think you are only beginning to see the danger. Pray and remain faithful and know I am with you always," he said.

"Thank you, Father," Regina said. Lucy and Gabriel also warned her of the future, but she had confidence in the Joy of the Lord.

Sunday, December 29th
9:58 AM

Father Joe shook hands with every person who came to Mass. The choir sang a prelude as the church filled up. It looked beautiful for the Christmas season, especially the Nativity.

Regina looked closely at the Baby Jesus and thought of how much more beautiful he really was. *If only everyone could see him like I did.* She thought about her time with the Holy Infant and lost herself in the memories until the choir started to sing "O Come All Ye Faithful".

Nothing unusual happened until Father Joe finished proclaiming the Gospel. He delayed starting his homily to walk over and kneel before the Nativity. Everyone looked confused. Mark shrugged at his family and got on his kneeler. The Andrews followed his lead and soon everyone joined them. Regina continued to think of her visions. In a minute, Father Joe got up and remained by the Nativity.

"The savior is born," he said. "To a virgin, in the town of Bethlehem." He again paused and let his words fall upon the people.

"How much time have you spent meditating on this mystery at the core of our faith?" He paused. "How much time did you spend shopping for Christmas presents?"

"How much time have you spent thanking God for humbling himself before you as a helpless infant?" He pointed to the baby in the manger. "How much time did you spend decorating your house with lights?"

Many of the people nodded. Father Joe stepped aside to stand by the statuette of Mary.

"How many times have you said yes, with complete abandon, to do God's will like the Blessed Mother did in response to the Angel's call? How often do you neglect your loved ones because your earthly boss asked you to work more hours?"

No one looked away. Eyes stayed focused on the priest as he offered up the mysteries of the season to his congregation. Regina felt her heart flutter as he spoke of the things she had witnessed firsthand. She wondered if her visions had inspired the priest's words.

"How much time have you spent sharing the Good News of the Lord? How much time did you spend sending out Christmas cards?"

He paused after the last two questions, love burning in his eyes. "My brothers and sisters, I am guilty of the same shortcomings. That is why we need to turn to the Good Shepherd." He turned his attention again to the Nativity. "Like the shepherds who left their flocks and came to visit the Christ child, we must also listen to God's call. They left everything behind to see the newborn King. Will you do the same?"

Father Joe walked from the Nativity to stand before the altar.

"During the Christmas Season, we meditate on the Incarnation. God became man, to live as we live. On this Feast of the Holy Family, we contemplate the Almighty choosing to experience childhood in the care of a loving mother and father."

He walked up to a woman holding a sleeping baby. He smiled at her.

"A mother, who said, 'Yes', to life and the will of God. Facing the prospect of being stoned for adultery, Mary overcame her fears and agreed to lend herself to God's saving plan. Can you overcome your fears?"

Father Joe moved across the aisle to a man who sat by two teenage boys.

"God chose to subject himself to a father, who would raise him as if he were his own. We call him Saint Joseph, the worker. The Heavenly King wanted to learn what it meant to labor. Joseph taught Jesus the value of work and the importance of suffering. He taught him how to be a man. Men would do well to ask for the intercession of Saint Joseph in their prayers. Ask him for guidance, especially if you are a father."

"The world needs to know about these mysteries, but the message must go through you. The church waits to welcome back the lost sheep, but only through your love, your witness, and your sharing will they hear the Good News."

Father looked individuals in the eyes as he spoke.

"Our Lord spoke to many people who heard his voice, but many walked away unchanged." Father Joe walked up through the middle aisle of the church, squeezing the shoulders and shaking the hands of the people sitting there. "But those he touched, and those he healed, and those he loved, they were the ones who followed him."

"Friends, you must be Jesus to your neighbor. You must share his truth. As a Christian, it is a necessity, it is a duty, and it is a calling. We are not worthy of this mission, yet Our Father calls us anyway. What say you? Will you answer his call?"

Silence. *Are we supposed to answer?* Regina wondered if other people thought the same thing. Father Joe continued to wait.

"Yes," Mark Andrews said.

Father Joe smiled. "Can you answer the call?"

Many others replied, emboldened by their fellow parishioner. He asked again and now the whole church responded with an enthusiastic reply.

"Good, then you must prepare, and that begins with prayer."

Father Joe returned to his seat. He sat for five minutes in silence. Everyone remained focused in prayer. Then, Father Joe stood and Mass continued.

Regina prayed the words of the Sanctus.

"Holy, Holy, Holy Lord God of hosts. Heaven and earth are full of your glory. Hosanna in the highest. Blessed is he who comes in the name of the Lord. Hosanna in the highest."

The moment her knees hit the kneeler, Regina's vision blacked out. When she regained her sight, Regina stood high on a mountainside looking over a large valley. She felt a surge of anxiety standing so close to the edge of a cliff.

"Do not be afraid."

"Gabriel, where are we? What is this place?"

The angel appeared beside her. Regina looked around to find a decimated landscape with scarred terrain. Darkness filled the sky like a storm approached. She could barely make out figures in the distant valley through a smoky haze.

"This is no place. God wants you to see the spiritual world." Regina returned to her survey of the landscape and wondered what he meant.

"Regina, sin has ravaged humanity. The devil's forces have assaulted mankind in spectacular ways. Behold the result."

Regina found the disaster painful to see. "Is there anything that can be done?"

"At the end of the nineteenth century, Pope Leo XIII celebrated Mass when he suddenly stopped, his eyes fixed in the distance. His expression turned to horror," Gabriel said.

"What did he see?"

"Basically what you see here. He saw the way evil spirits attack men's souls and the need to stop them."

"What happened then?"

"He remained in his trance for quite some time. When he emerged, he asked for paper. Upon this, he wrote a lengthy prayer to Saint Michael the Archangel. He decreed that it be said at the end of every Mass, to call for his protection against the dark forces of the devil. Many people still recite a short form of the prayer to invoke the intercession of Saint Michael."

"Really? How does it go?"

Gabriel began to pray,

"Saint Michael, the archangel, defend us in battle,
Be our protection against the wickedness and snares of the devil
May God rebuke him, we humbly pray,
And do thou O Prince of the Heavenly Host,
By the Power of God, Thrust into hell,
Satan and all the evil spirits
Who prowl about the world seeking the ruin of souls. Amen."

A lightning bolt flashed by Regina causing the hair to stand up all over her body. She heard the powerful thunderclap but fought to regain her sight after the sudden flash. After she regained her vision, she beheld a creature as wondrous as Gabriel. This angel had the same long, flowing hair, but instead of soft robes, he wore gleaming armor and held a flaming sword in his hand.

"Michael, thank you for coming. I thought I had a flair for the dramatic," Gabriel said, smiling. He bowed slightly as he welcomed his fellow angel.

Michael bowed the same way. Regina noticed Michael did not smile.

"This is Regina," Gabriel said.

"Hello, child." Michael nodded to Regina.

"Hello, Saint Michael," Regina said, bowing deeply.

"The time has come for God's instrument to understand more of what she faces on her mission. I leave her in your care to show her the nature of this world," Gabriel said.

"Very well," Michael said. "Come, Regina," he said, holding out his hand.

Regina looked at Gabriel for reassurance. He smiled to ease her worry. She took the hand of the heavenly warrior. Immediately, they soared into the sky. Regina waited for terror to come but it never did. Michael took them on a controlled descent off the mountainside into the valley.

"First, we shall see our forces," Michael said. They moved quickly across the wasteland to a refuge in the darkness. Despite the desolate surroundings, the beauty present here lightened Regina's spirit.

Michael took Regina past hundreds upon thousands of angels, farther into the camp, where she saw countless people moving in spectral form. They looked like holograms she had seen in movies. The people appeared to be doing everyday activities. Some talked, worked, ate, or slept, but above each one stood an angel.

"Are those their guardians?"

"Yes, and as you can see, they stand ever vigilant against the tempter of their human."

The angels stood in a ready battle stance. She noticed several battles ensuing. The guardians fought monsters much smaller than themselves.

"Despite being in the camp of God, these souls still face temptation, but the love they have shown God has strengthened their guardians, so only the craftiest demonic attempts can make them slip into sin." Regina watched angel after angel defeat its demonic opponent, but a few imps did claim minor victories, causing venial sins.

"Don't let the size of these little demons fool you, Regina. Even a soul this close to God can fall. The evil one has many ways to capture souls."

"So, no one is safe from hell?"

"You know how fragile people's spirits are. Think of how many holy people have fallen into ruin. He'll never rest. Come; let us see the other side." Michael held out his hand. When she did, they lifted off and flew to the far front of the battlefield.

"The army of darkness," Saint Michael said.

Everyone in this small army had a large demon above them holding puppet strings. They controlled their human without any angelic intervention. Sorrow overcame Regina.

"Very few people completely abandon the Lord and forsake him openly in their life, but when they do, they find themselves here. Their demon has full control of their minds and leads them to believe they can live their lives without any regard for their souls. They hurt everyone in their lives and leave a trail of wreckage behind them."

"What about their guardian angels?"

"They still exist but have to pray for their human from heaven."

"So these people have no hope of salvation?"

"They still do, but it will take a heroic act of love to break through to them. Unfortunately, it is very rare that someone will take the risk to offer themselves up for a soul as cold as this, but it does happen. Often it leads to martyrdom," Michael said.

She watched the demons torture their humans by keeping them stuck in an endless cycle of self-gratification and despair. Clinging to false love, they hoped in power of earthly pleasure to find happiness. Michael reached for her again. Regina said a final prayer for these souls before taking the angel's hand.

This time, they headed directly to the middle of the battlefield. Here, millions of souls moved about. She could see, from their aerial perspective, people moving from the central camp to each of the other locations. The stream of movement never ended.

"These are the lost sheep." The angels and demons over each soul battled vigorously. "These souls oscillate between living virtuously and succumbing to sin. Believers are lukewarm, and non-believers ignore the voice of God in their hearts. These people don't form their consciences or prepare for heaven. They do works of mercy as easily as they fall into sin, because the world has blinded them to the power of the Holy Spirit. You have been sent to claim these souls, Regina."

Regina looked at the vast multitude of people in this space and the magnitude of the task overwhelmed her. "How could I touch this many people?"

"The Joy of the Lord will be your strength. You will share the mysteries of heaven with the world while angel armies battle to sow the seeds of Truth in the hearts of these lost sheep."

"Regina, this battle goes beyond the individual," Michael said. "It begins there, but the demon realm uses its skill to attack the family, the community, nations, and the world."

"How?"

"People do not live in solitude. You are social creatures. Demons collaborate to take individual sin and form it into social sin. They use the gifts God freely gives mankind against you in heinous and manipulative ways."

"Like what?"

"From the beginning of time, God's gifts like sexuality, bread, and wine have been abused, leading to fornication, gluttony, and drunkenness. As humanity progresses, so does the abuse of its own creativity."

Regina understood the angel's first three examples but didn't know what he meant by humanity's progress.

"All of earth's wealth and knowledge could be shared to guarantee the feeding, health, and education of every person in the world with ease, but instead demons use it to bring souls to hell."

"How?"

"God gave people intellect. One of the products of that intellect, for example, is the internet. This result of a gift from God has advanced sin more rapidly than anything in the past. Do you know what the seven deadly sins are?"

"I don't think I could name them. I'm sorry."

"That's okay, very few can. They are Lust, Sloth, Wrath, Pride, Gluttony, Envy, and Greed. I assume you know how Lust destroys lives?"

Regina nodded. Her mother had explained to her how she should protect her purity by avoiding the filth available on computers. She only had to think the thought before Michael continued.

"Have you ever wasted time on the internet, endlessly clicking from one website to another?"

"Yes. I often lose track of time watching videos or looking at pictures."

"Many people do. If you fail to live out the work of your vocation, then you commit the sin of Sloth. Next, think of the comments people make to each other on websites."

"I have seen some really nasty things," Regina said.

"We call it Wrath when you can't control your hate for someone. This anger people can have towards each other shows a sad state of someone's soul."

Regina thought of her anger towards Frank. She understood Michael all too well.

Michael continued, "People post their every thought and action on the internet. This can lead to the sin of Pride in one's self-importance. Hand in hand with Pride, the spreading of gossip through instant messaging creates Envy, which can destroy the spirits of your brothers and sisters."

Regina's principal gave them a long lecture on this topic when they were given their school-issued laptops. She knew several girls who had gotten in trouble this year talking about classmates.

"Greed leads people to accumulate things they don't need. People can obtain anything with a few clicks. Many love things more than they love the people in their lives."

"Yeah, I find I ask my parents for a lot of things that I see on the internet. They usually say no."

"That's good," Michael said. "Finally, every Gluttonous desire of an increasingly obese population can be quickly and cheaply satisfied, leading to a vicious circle of addiction."

"I understand," Regina said.

"Our Father in Heaven weeps for the blindness of his people. The path to sanctity sits on the internet, yet so few look to obtain that knowledge."

"Really? How can I use the internet to work against sin?"

"Every deadly sin has an opposite virtue associated with it. These virtues are Chastity, Diligence, Patience, Humility, Temperance, Kindness, and Charity."

"I've heard all of those except for Temperance."

"Good. Anyone with internet access can read the thoughts of the saints about how to live a virtuous life. Saint John Paul wrote thousands of pages on what he called The Theology of the Body. He explained how God created us to care for our bodies as temples of the Holy Spirit. The world would benefit greatly in Chastity if people would take time to read and meditate upon his writings."

The Theology of the Body, Regina made a mental note.

"People can achieve the virtue of Diligence by creating schedules, to do lists, and making reminders on their various technologies. Discipline is critical to promoting a healthy spiritual life."

"My parents always bug me to get more organized. I could use my computer to help me remember deadlines."

"Exactly. Also, the negativity you see on your computer requires the virtue of patience. You need to pray for people who offend you, instead attacking them with your keyboard."

"Or yelling at the computer screen?" Regina said, remembering her behavior.

"Absolutely. Next, we come to Humility, which opposes the sin of pride."

"Being humble, like Mary? Right?"

"Yes. Our Lady diminished herself to elevate the Lord throughout her life. People desire to be noticed by their peers, but saints live for the glory of God. Instead of sharing what you do with others, share what God does in your life. You said you never heard the word temperance?"

"Yes, I don't know what that is."

"Temperance is showing self-restraint and moderation. Most people in the world only consume a small fraction of what Americans do each day, yet health continues to decline in your country. Millions of people need medications to live because they can't practice temperance in their lifestyle. Could you sit in front of a chocolate cake and not eat it?"

"I love chocolate cake," Regina said, picturing her favorite treat.

"That's why I chose that," Michael said.

"It would be hard."

"Exactly. Tempters barely have to work to get people to fall into Gluttony. The last two virtues go together."

"Kindness and Charity?"

"Very good. They oppose Envy and Greed. Do you remember the story of the Good Samaritan?" (Luke 10:30-37)

"Yes, a Jewish man gets beaten, robbed, and left by the side of the road. Two religious people walk by him without helping, but a foreigner helps him."

"Right. The priest and the Levite could not be troubled by the man's difficulty, but the Samaritan showed him Kindness. He treated the wounded man like a child of God."

"How does that apply to the internet?"

"Technology makes it easier for you to go out of your way to show Kindness to others. You can send them kind notes or post nice messages to uplift your brothers and sisters. Many people are emotionally hurting and you need to be the Samaritan."

"I understand, and for Charity I have seen lots of places to click to donate money on websites," Regina said.

"Yes, technology has made giving money to those in need very easy, but you must remember Charity comes from the root word *caritas*, which means extending your love for God to your neighbor."

"How do you do that?" Regina said.

"Jesus made it very easy. He said 'Whatever you do for the least of these brethren, you do it to me.'" (Matthew 25:40)

"He was talking about feeding the hungry and clothing the naked, right?"

"Any act of love, whether physical, emotional, or spiritual, answers Our Lord's call," Michael said.

Regina nodded and thought if people treated each other like Christ, instead of objects, the world would be a better place.

"What does this all mean for me, Saint Michael? I mean, what am I supposed to do with this knowledge?"

"Hold it in your heart. Meditate on what you have seen and share it with Father Joe and your parents. Your full mission will soon be revealed and you will know how to proceed. Pray and do not be afraid. May the peace of Our Lord Jesus Christ be with you," Michael said.

"And with your spirit," Regina said, with many voices around her.

"Now share with each other a sign of peace," Father Joe said.

Regina turned to her father. He hugged her and saw her concern.

"What's wrong?"

"I'm okay, I'll tell you later," she answered. She gave her mother and brother a sign of peace along with the people around her.

The rest of Mass passed. When Regina walked out and shook Father Joe's hand, he held it a little longer than usual.

"We need to talk, don't we?"

Chapter 25
We Three Kings

Monday, December 30th
6:42 AM

Regina made sure to add the Saint Michael prayer to her morning offering before going downstairs for breakfast. She could hardly wait for Father Joe to call her. He said he would be in touch first thing in the morning. With no one else around, she sat on the couch and opened a book. Moments later, she felt the familiar pull to the past.

Regina stood outside a large tent guarded by two men wearing desert clothing.

"Do you think the master has gone mad?" one man whispered in another language Regina never heard before, but she still understood all of the words in her head.

"He doesn't act like he lost his mind, but why else would he have dragged us out here?"

"Everything he does follows some calculation. Has he told you what his reasons are?

"No. Did he tell you?"

"No, but earlier I heard him repeat to himself, *Follow the stars, follow the stars.*"

"Ha! He studied them for so long they started speaking to him."

The men laughed, but stifled themselves quickly. Regina thought about entering the tent.

"Go ahead, child. Enter," Gabriel said.

"Who's in there?"

"Let's find out," the angel said. They walked through the door.

A dark skinned man with a gray beard wearing formal robes and a turban knelt in front of a small table. He feverishly wrote on a parchment. Regina moved closer. She saw a strange script, but as she looked at the paper, the meaning of the words jumped into her head.

I have spent my life learning about the truths science has to offer humanity. I have accumulated knowledge of physics, chemistry, surgery, astronomy, and astrology from the four corners of the earth. I have tried to become a master of science so I may control my own destiny and help mankind, but another truth has been revealed to me. A power higher than science orders the universe, and that power draws me through the stars to the fulfillment of a prophecy. Where do I go? My books have no answer but my heart has hope.

Regina kept reading until he finished. She heard a commotion from outside, which the man did as well. They all went outside to see the cause of the stir.

"Master Balthazar, a caravan approaches from the north," one of the servants expressed.

Regina saw a large caravan approaching. Several men on foot carried packs guiding beasts of burden, and two men, dressed regally, rode a camel and a beautiful horse.

Balthazar and his men waited silently, but Regina had many questions.

"Gabriel, where are we and who are these people?"

"We are a good distance east of Judea at the crossroads of several trade routes to distant countries. They will make their names known shortly," he answered.

The desert breeze blew across their faces as they waited. As they drew near, Regina could tell the nationalities of the men differed. Some of the men had darker skin and different facial features than the others. The man on the camel had lighter skin and wore expensive jewelry. The one on the horse had a black beard and dark brown skin. He wore the most colorful clothing out of them all.

When they got close to the camp, the two men alit from their beasts and handed off the reins to their servants. They walked together towards Balthazar, who made gestures of greeting.

Regina moved closer to hear what they had to say. They spoke a new language which they all seemed to understand as she did.

"What language are they speaking now?"

"They are speaking in the ancient Persian language. The Persian empire has spread its influence so far that most learned people in the area know it to travel more easily."

"I am Caspar. This is Melchior," the brown-faced man said. "We met on the road on the way to Judea."

Regina saw Balthazar's face light up. "My name is Balthazar, and I am on my way to Judea as well."

Caspar and Melchior looked at each other in wonder.

"We are drawn on a quest to see a child. We believe this child is a sign from God," Melchior said.

"I, too, am looking for a sign from God. Please, have your men set up camp and let us go into my tent to talk of these things," Balthazar said.

After they established camp, they got comfortable in Balthazar's tent.

"I have studied every science since my childhood. I look at mankind and wonder why the order I find in science does not exist in my fellow man. I marvel at how the Almighty arranged for everything to have its place. All of the elements, the creatures of the world, the stars in the sky, they all move with a design beyond my understanding."

The others nodded in agreement, but Regina said, "What does he mean by order?"

"Have you heard of the Law of Gravity?" Gabriel said.

"Yes."

"Balthazar knows that you can call gravity whatever you want and you can believe in it or not, but if you throw a ball in the air, it will fall down. Science can determine this kind of order in nature. Keep listening to see where he goes with this."

"I am bothered that the same order I see in science does not exist in mankind," Balthazar said. "But somehow the stars have called me on this journey to find an answer to my concerns."

Melchior nodded. "My friend, I am humbled by your mastery in the sciences. I can claim no such knowledge. I have been led from my youth to the four corners of the world to gather information on all religions. I have always been fascinated about how God revealed himself to different peoples in different ways. I say there is a law written on the hearts of men and women everywhere. It binds us into societies and the violation of this law leads to the demise of nations. I have read scriptures and studied prophecies from around the world and they have led me on this journey."

"What is this law?" Balthazar said.

"It is a natural inclination written in our hearts that allows us to live together in harmony, but every religion acknowledges that darkness can creep into our souls and corrupt the truth dwelling within us. Many prophecies speak of a child who will be born to a virgin. I have come to find this child who will expose the darkness and vanquish it once and for all."

Caspar jumped in. "A virgin? That's impossible. My life has been dedicated to learning everything man knows about mathematics and reason. Balthazar, you are a man of science, you know what Melchior says cannot be, right?"

"Scientifically it is not possible, but the stars have aligned in a way I could have never imagined. I don't imagine it very likely that Melchior and I would be on a similar pilgrimage and meet here in the desert. Why are you here?"

"I always thought life's questions could be answered with reason and logic, but then I started feeling a call in my heart which I could not explain. I kept hearing in my dreams that I needed to travel west to Judea. I could not make sense of it. When I ran into Melchior and learned of his similar call, I realized reason had abandoned me," Caspar said, hanging his head.

"It hasn't abandoned you. You have only constrained it," Melchior said.

"What do you mean?" Caspar asked.

"You assumed the postulates of your logical system were limited to only what you can see and examine," Melchior said. He didn't continue.

Caspar could see Melchior waited for him to come to a conclusion. He looked at Balthazar, who shrugged his shoulders. "Do you mean I could use my capacity for reason without a tangible starting point?"

Melchior smiled. Balthazar still looked confused. Regina shared his puzzlement. She gave up. "What are they talking about?"

Gabriel laughed. "I'm sorry my child, these are very wise and learned men talking about very deep topics, I should have explained some things sooner. What do you already know?"

"I am pretty sure these are the Three Wise Men, right?"

"Good, and?"

"And they clearly come from three different countries."

"Very good. What else?"

"Balthazar says he is a scientist, Caspar likes math, and I don't know what to call Melchior."

"I think people of your time would call him a theologian, a person who studies religions."

"Okay, that's what I know. Now, what are they talking about?"

"The Lord led them here by touching them within their own disciplines. They devoted themselves to their own fields but still remained open to divine inspiration. They represent a world that doesn't know God, but yearns for him, all the same."

"What do you mean?"

"Many people in the world do not get the gift of faith from their parents. These men show that God can always reach you, as long as your heart remains open to receiving him," Gabriel said.

"Then what is Melchior trying to get Caspar to see?"

"Caspar believes all reason must begin with human senses. Melchior wants Caspar to see God can act as the beginning."

Regina thought about this for a while. The wise men continued their conversation without her, but she knew they discussed what

Gabriel told her. She began to understand the mysteries they discussed.

"So, are you saying believing in God can be the starting point of reason?"

"Yes. Believe that he loves you and wants you to love him in return," Gabriel said. "The Lord imprints this knowledge deep in the heart of every person. Philosophers call it the Natural Law. From it, you can reason all the truths of life, but you must accept such a thing can exist, which is the essence of faith."

Regina felt a strange sense come over her. She believed in God, but this opened a whole new world to her. She felt overwhelmed and excited. She could know God with her mind as well as her soul. She wondered how she could use this reason further.

Gabriel read her mind. "Regina, when you are ready, you can see what some of the greatest minds the world has ever known reasoned about God: Augustine, Thomas Aquinas, Therese of Lisieux, and John Paul II, to name a few. These geniuses used reason to explain the beauty and glory of God and the faith. Many people feel believers have to sacrifice their intelligence to have a relationship with God, when they remain ignorant to the truth in both its simplicity and complexity."

"It is so much to take in," Regina said.

"The beauty of faith is you can appreciate it at so many levels. Start off small and simple, and then take on more as you are ready. You will find the more you experience, the more there remains to learn." The wise men discussed Gabriel's summary about faith in their own way. They moved on to sharing about their lives and cultures. Regina enjoyed their tales about their homelands and traditions. They continued their discussion late into the night, until a bright light filled the room and blinded everyone.

After a moment, Regina once again beheld the past Gabriel standing before her, visible to the wise men. They trembled in fear. The angel held up his hands. "Peace is to you. My friends, the Lord called you here to become brothers in faith. Now you must travel together to find what you have searched for all of your lives."

"What is that, spirit?" Balthazar said, his voice shaking.

"The splendor of truth. You will find it in a newborn child in the town of Bethlehem. He is the king of kings and the prince of peace."

The wise men looked at each other, amazed. The prophecies they discussed were true. Their journey had not been for naught. This creature dashed away their doubts, but still they had questions.

"Will he be born of a virgin?" Caspar said.

"How will we find him?" Balthazar said.

"Will he become the king of the world?" Melchior said.

"Follow the star I illuminate for you. There your questions will be satisfied," Gabriel said. With this, he ascended into the western sky and darted into the distance, lighting a star into a brilliant beacon. Regina gawked at the wondrous sign.

"Gabriel? How can everyone not head towards this star? It is the most amazing thing in the sky."

"Remember, the Lord makes his signs visible to only those he wills. The wise men can see it, but even their servants cannot. Jesus worked the same way during his public ministry. Some people got to see his miracles but others believed purely on faith," Gabriel said.

Regina nodded and watched the wise men discuss the angel's visit like children at an amusement park. She enjoyed this because she saw her own excitement mirrored through them. She didn't even notice when the past began to vanish.

Mark Andrews went to school early to catch up on work he pushed aside before Christmas Break. He told Katherine he wanted to get everything done that day so he could relax with the family for the rest of break. He worked for several hours alone until one of his coworkers, Rick Jenkins, came into the office as well. After some small talk, both men attended to their own business for several hours when Rick broke the silence. "Can I ask you a personal question, Mark?"

Mark looked up from his grading. "Sure, go ahead."

"You probably know where I stand on religion and such," Rick said.

"I think I can guess from the opinions you've shared."

"I hope I didn't offend you, I sometimes speak my mind too freely," Rick said.

"No offense taken. The scandals of religious leaders are particularly damaging to people of faith. I don't agree with your assertion that these failings display an inherent flaw in religion, but I can see how they would negatively form your opinions."

"Well, I have been wondering for a long time how someone as intelligent and logical as you can be religious."

Mark wondered what had touched Rick to open this door. He prayed for guidance on what words to use. He felt confident in starting with a question of his own. "Why did you phrase your question like that?"

"What do you mean?"

"Well, you presumed intelligence and logic preclude you from faith. Do you think that?"

"I guess I would say that, but then you are a contradiction to me. I suppose that's why I asked you about it."

"Some of the most intelligent people in history were deeply religious and very devout. Two mathematicians you know, Rene Descartes and Blaise Pascal, wrote extensively about faith, logic, and reason. Wouldn't you agree that their genius would blow my intellect out of the water?"

"I would agree, but many geniuses were atheists as well," Rick said.

"True, but I didn't say intelligence and atheism were mutually exclusive," Mark said.

"That's true. Okay, so let's say it's possible you can be both. I still don't get it. Can you explain why you believe?"

Mark looked at the clock. His wife expected him home in a bit. He had burned up most of the day working, with still much to do, but here a soul searched for truth. He wondered if this was part of his mission. "How much time do you have Rick?"

"I am at your disposal."

"Well, let me start at the beginning. Stop me if you have any questions."

"Okay."

"In high school, I shared your thoughts on faith and religion. Looking at the world around me, I doubted God could exist at a very young age. Even if he existed, I was angry at him. Do you know what I am saying?"

"I can relate," Rick said. "I mean, my childhood was fine, but I remember thinking things were really too screwed up in this world for there to be a God."

"Well, those moments came for me in high school. Through my angry lens, I studied history, science, and mathematics and convinced myself God did not exist. I openly doubted him in school and mocked those foolish enough to give their allegiance to this false ideal."

"Sounds like you were quiet a peach in high school," Rick said.

"You don't know the half of it. If I had the right set of phone numbers, I would be spending a lot of time apologizing. Trust me." Mark smiled and Rick nodded. "Moving on, after high school ended and I went to college, I met several people who challenged my belief system, or lack thereof, like I must challenge yours."

"Do you mean these people were intelligent and believed in God?"

"Exactly. Very intelligent and very faith filled, but more. They lived every moment with a joy I found infectious. When I spent time with them, they didn't judge me or try to get me to think their way, but they honestly answered my questions and invited me to share in their joy."

"Even though you didn't share their faith?"

"Yes. They knew about my curiosity; they wanted me to experience their world. They invited me to attend their social gatherings and observe their religious events. I asked my questions and they challenged my mind with amazing answers. One day, a friend invited me to go on a retreat for a weekend."

"For a whole weekend? That seems like a big commitment."

"I know. That's what I said, but my friend said everyone hesitates to leave campus for a weekend, but everyone sees its worth afterwards."

"Wait, you had to leave campus for a weekend? With a bunch of religious nuts? That would have sealed the deal for me."

"Maybe now I wouldn't have gone, but in college I had less fear. This was my experimentation. I never had a crazy partying phase in college. I took this risk, which eclipsed drugs and alcohol for me."

"Interesting, okay, so you went. What happened?"

"Someone's dad drove us out to a camp site about thirty miles outside town," Mark said with a smile on his face.

"Ha, I'm surprised you are still here."

Mark laughed and continued. "You'd think I would have felt nervous, but the funny thing is, once I got in the car and joined the other passengers in conversation, I felt more at peace than ever before. We talked about our majors and our dorms, you know, basic small talk. When we got to the camp, we put our stuff away in our cabins and met in a big room for opening warm-up activities like you might do on the first day of school."

"It sounds like a teachers' conference."

"The structure of the weekend was pretty much exactly like that: talks, food, and prayer time instead of workshops. The first night, they gave us a couple of hours to reflect on any sins we were sorry for or things we wanted to change about our lives. I didn't believe in sin, but I wanted to live in constant joy, like these people, so I tried my first genuine prayer."

"That was your first prayer?"

"Why? Is that hard to believe?"

"It seems a little late in life," Rick said.

"I thought you said you weren't raised in a religious family."

"I wasn't, but I remember being very little when my grandma was sick. I prayed for her to get better, but she died. I loved my grandma and felt God wouldn't let a good woman like her die. When she did, I couldn't believe in God," Rick said.

"Forgive me if I sound too critical, but the postulate that you formed your belief system on seems pretty childish," Mark said. He wanted to challenge his friend and hoped he wouldn't turn him off to the conversation.

"When you put it that way, I have to say it sounds a bit childish. You started in the same place, what caused the change?"

"Well, there I was wondering where to begin. I had at least an hour and not much to say. Finally, I remembered what one of my friends told me before the retreat when I asked him to prove God existed. He told me saints like Augustine and Thomas Aquinas had written long, complicated proofs for the existence of God, but I should really look at faith as a gift from God that I should ask for. At the time, I didn't understand what she meant, but that night I prayed 'God, if you exist, I want to believe in you, but I need a sign you are there. I want to accept the gift of faith because I know I can't keep searching for you intellectually."

"You prayed that?"

"Pretty much. I didn't say it out loud so there is no recording."

"So what happened then? Did a bush burst into flames?"

Mark dropped his smile and ended the joking. "No, the sky did."

"What?"

"There I was, thirty miles from campus, in the middle of the state. After the reflection time ended, we walked out of the lodge to go to our cabins. Several people had stopped in the path and looked up at the sky, so I turned my head and saw my sign."

"What was it?"

"The aurora borealis. The entire northern sky glowed with brilliant ribbons of spectral green light. I never saw anything so majestic in all of my life. Chills went through my whole body beyond the coolness of the November night. Something changed within me."

"Sounds pretty cool, but it could have been a coincidence."

"I pondered that all night myself, but I resolved myself to take the advice of a priest I met at the retreat. He said there are no coincidences, there are only God incidents."

"What is that supposed to mean?"

"He said God always nudges you to live the life he wants you to lead, using small events which you often dismiss as trivial." Mark changed gears. "Do you want to hear a joke he said?"

"What? Now?"

"Sure, it applies."

"Okay?"

"A faithful old man lived alone in his house. A great rain storm overflowed the river so his neighborhood started flooding. He prayed out loud, 'Oh God, what am I going to do?' he felt through the Spirit that God would provide. After a while, his neighbor came over and said, 'Quick, hop in my SUV, we will be able to drive through the flood waters and get out of town.' The old man said, 'I trust in God. He will save me.' A little later, the waters filled the first floor of his house and a man in a row boat came to his upstairs window and offered him a ride to safety. The old man said, 'I trust in God. He will save me.' Still later, the flood completely submerged his home. He sat on the roof of his house and a rescue helicopter came by. The old man said, 'I trust in God. He will save me,' and sent the chopper on its way. Well, unfortunately, it continued to rain and the old man drowned. He went to heaven and met his maker. The first words out of his mouth were, 'Lord, why didn't you save me?' God answered, 'I sent you an SUV, a boat, and a helicopter, what more did you want?'"

Both men laughed, and Mark returned to point. "The priest used this joke to point out that God uses every day ordinary things as sign posts for us, not always the miraculous."

"God incidents," Rick said.

"Exactly."

"Well, you got a little more than that," Rick said.

"I know. I feel extremely blessed for that, and there is still much more to the story, but I think what I shared should give you some glimpse into my madness."

"It's a lot to think about, but you are saying you have built your faith logically from this first moment of belief?"

"Essentially, I just had to challenge my assumptions about my first principles. Can you believe God exists? Are you willing to legitimately open yourself to his voice?"

Rick glanced at the clock on the wall. "That will have to wait, I'm sure you need to get home as well."

"I do."

"Thanks for the chat, Mark."

"Thank you for the challenge."

The men shook hands and went their separate ways. Mark thanked God and was excited to share the story with his family when he got home.

Chapter 26
Dark Counsel

Monday, December 30th
7:03 PM

Paul sat down at his dinner table looking at the Chinese food he picked up on the way home from work. He realized it was Maggie's favorite dish, beef with broccoli. He ordered it over the phone and didn't realize, until this moment, he really didn't like it. He always got it for her. He looked over at the chair she used to sit in and longed to see her pretty, smiling face.

You can call her and apologize. You know she will forgive you. The faint voice barely grazed his heart, but touched him enough. Paul took out his phone and pressed the green call button. Maggie's number showed on the screen. He realized he hadn't talked to anyone since she left. In fact, he didn't talk to many people except for her. Her easy going nature and loving spirit drew him out of the shell he spent most of his life in. Now that he had pushed her away, he wondered what he would do with his life.

You had your fun with her. There are plenty of fish in the sea. His mind turned to the carefree days he spent with his buddies when he dropped out of college. They flirted and partied with a different group of girls every night. His tempter successfully turned his mind from Maggie. Paul considered calling some of his old friends to see if they wanted to hang out. He thought of his best friend Doug and remembered they hadn't talked since he and his wife welcomed a daughter into the world in the spring.

The baby! Maggie is having a baby. She needs you. Paul felt an appeal to his manhood. Chivalry called to him but darkness squashed it.

The baby is what got between you and Maggie. You should call her and convince her to get a late term abortion. They are still legal in this state. Paul thought of the day Maggie told him the fateful news.

Paul came home to find Maggie sitting at the kitchen table dressed in her waitress uniform, which he liked. He remembered everything about her was attractive, and the feeling hurt deeper still. She looked like she had seen a ghost.

"We need to talk," Maggie said.

"Okay, something wrong?" He didn't need to hear her response. She expressed her distress very clearly on her face.

She paused for a moment and collected her thoughts. "I'm pregnant."

The words hung there for several seconds. Their eyes connected but their emotions did not.

"That's impossible. You're on the pill."

"It's not fool proof. I didn't miss any days or anything. The doctor says he sees it a lot," Maggie said.

"Well, that's not fair," Paul complained. He saw the disappointment in Maggie's eyes. She hoped for better than whining, but he could only think of what this meant to him. He didn't realize it at the time, but his tempter always successfully kept Paul thinking like a child. He displayed this through his petulance.

"What are we going to do?" She knew, deep down, what she wanted. She thought about it all afternoon. She considered what she wanted in her life and how Paul fit in. She knew he had strength in him. She saw glimpses of it, now and then. Even though she didn't have a profound spiritual life, she strongly thought that God meant for them to be together. Maggie could see a life for them as husband and wife, but that vision would soon be severely strained.

"I can take off work tomorrow and we can go take care of it," Paul said. Again, he could tell in Maggie's eyes she looked for a different answer. She didn't say anything and she didn't need to. "What?"

"How can you say that so easily?" Her eyes shimmered with tears.

"What?" He knew he had offended her, but remained obtuse.

"You would kill our child without even thinking about it?"

"How far along are you? It's only a little blob. It's not like it even looks human at this point." He heard his own words and realized how juvenile he sounded, but he knew the immense responsibility of having a child and he could barely take care of himself.

"This 'blob' is at least 6 weeks old and already has a beating heart. Something you wouldn't know anything about!" She got up out of her chair and walked into the bedroom, locking the door behind her. He heard her crying and begged her to open the door, but eventually figured he needed to wait her out on the couch. During that time, his guardian angel defeated his tempter with the help of Maggie's agonized prayers. His spirit softened and he opened up to the idea of being a father. He vowed long ago he would be better than his own abusive father. The Holy Spirit worked in him, without his knowledge, pushing him to strive to stay true to his promise.

When Maggie came out of the bedroom, Paul apologized for his insensitivity, and they talked late into the night about their situation. Paul accepted Maggie's determination not to terminate the pregnancy, and they agreed to talk about keeping the baby or putting it up for adoption.

Weeks passed and Paul's tempter slowly ate away at his resolve. He became more and more concerned that Maggie would insist on keeping the baby and they would live in squalor forever. His guardian angel and tempter pulled him in different directions. He began to drink heavily to relieve his stress. It got so bad he couldn't hide it from Maggie anymore.

"Paul, how much do you drink every day?"

"Not much, it's no big deal."

"I can smell it on your breath all the time. I'm concerned for you."

"Don't worry about me; I can take care of myself. Worry about your baby." She had decided she wanted to keep the baby and be a family together. He tried to convince her to give the baby up for adoption but she wouldn't budge.

"She's our baby." Ever since she found out the gender of the baby, she intentionally used "she" and "her" and "daughter" in their conversations. He resented it. It made him angrier and more frustrated, which gave his tempter fuel to lead him further into despair.

He found himself in a very dark place the day Maggie finally left. He thought of their last conversation, which ended as a battle.

He remembered drinking all afternoon. He couldn't speak without slurring his words. "That kid is going to ruin our lives, you know."

Since she had found about his drinking, Maggie made him promise to stop several times, but his tempter never quit torturing his spirit. "You're drunk Paul. I don't want to talk to you about this right now."

"Well, I want to talk about it." Paul teetered and caught himself using the wall. "I can't believe you would throw your life away for something that's not even alive."

Maggie wanted to ignore him, but her motherhood responded. "She is alive, Paul! Her heart is beating. I can feel her kick and turn. I can even feel her hiccups. Don't you think for a moment she isn't alive!"

"Well, I wish she weren't. It would be a shame if *she* didn't make it," he said, making a fist. Thinking back, Paul wondered what monster overtook him at that moment.

Maggie gave him a horrified look. "Is that a threat?" She stared at Paul, waiting for him to answer.

The demon alcohol would not let him back down. "What if it is?"

Maggie had heard enough. "I can't stay here Paul. I don't know who you are anymore."

Her last words to him still stung. Maggie grabbed a few things and left. He didn't know where she went and he didn't try to call. *Be a man. Let her come crawling back.* She didn't. The next day, when he returned from work, he found Maggie had taken all of her belongings and left her key sitting on the kitchen table. She left no note.

Finished with the bitter memories, he sat looking at her empty seat and the open box of Chinese food sitting on the table where she left her key. He got up, grabbed the food, and threw it in the trash.

In a moment of darkness, he felt emboldened to try one more time to get Maggie to get a late term abortion. *She must be desperate without you. You can convince her to do the smart thing. Then you get on with your lives together.* Paul admired the brilliance of the plan.

He picked up his phone and saw a missed call from Maggie. *How did I miss that?* He also saw he had voice mail. He pressed play and heard Maggie's sweet voice.

"Paul, I had the baby. She's beautiful and reminded me of you. I thought you should know." She stopped speaking but the recording continued. Paul thought he heard crying.

She had the baby. His plan got ripped from him before it had a chance. *Now you can't be together. The child will always be in the way. It will always be a burden. What if she sues you for support payments?* All of these thoughts hit Paul at once. The news of his child's birth stung him and he turned to his dark crutch. He reached for the bottle of whisky, already three fourths empty from the beginning of the week. He didn't use a glass.

"Status report!" Miseros said. He stood in a meeting room at the head of an immense desk. All around him, dozens of grisly characters sat. Each horrifically ugly, none matched the grotesqueness of their leader.

"Sir, The Job Rule is still in effect on the Andrews girl, but somehow her brother accepted the spiritual dryness in her place," one of the lower demons said.

Miseros glared at his minion. "How is that possible?" He turned to Emmanuel's tempter. "What do you know about this?"

"Sir, humans can offer themselves up to join in the suffering of the Enemy…," the demon started.

"I know that, you idiot. I want to know how this child does!"

The demon recoiled from the scolding. "Uh, uh, the child seems very simple, but I am unable to influence him. I have filed reports to see why he has special favor with the Enemy, but I haven't gotten an answer."

"This is worse than I thought," Miseros said. "What about the rest of you? What are you doing to shatter the spirits of the people in this girl's life?"

Maggie's tempter smiled. "I have been able to keep my human confused and worried about her future with a new baby and a broken relationship with its father."

"Scouts tell me she has rediscovered her faith thanks to the Andrews woman," Miseros said.

The demon's smile vanished. "Well, I have kept her confused and distracted from prayer."

Miseros gave him a suspicious look and turned to the others. One after the other claimed small victories with their humans, but Miseros knew victory slipped slowly away.

"I don't like what is happening here. You must continue to fight. Keep your people from spending time in meditation. We can't let them figure out what the Enemy wants of them. Keep them talking about prayer and making plans to read Scripture, but keep them from actually doing it. It's your greatest weapon." The demons nodded to their leader. "At least the girl suffers through her brother and the infant."

"Soon, another will join their suffering," Atramors said.

"Oh, really? I'm glad I assigned you to her case." He smiled at the image of an increase in Regina's suffering, but a sneer soon came to his lips. "We can't let these victories turn to defeats. We must double our efforts to keep her from the Enemy. Remember to fool her with busyness or fatigue. Do not let her sense the trickery we present."

Miseros looked into the distance. *Something is important about this one. We have to get this right. He* felt a bit of fear in his own gut. He knew it would be his turn in torment if this went wrong.

Louise Roland's head bobbed, suddenly waking her up before she fell out of her chair next to Frank's bed. She looked at her son. He looked so peaceful. *I asked for this.* The thought frightened her. *I asked that he have peace.* She prayed those words. She couldn't deny it. *No, that's not what I meant.* These dark thoughts haunted her until a knock came at the door.

"Mrs. Roland, can I have a moment?" The serious expression on the doctor's face disconcerted her.

"Sure," she said.

"I have the results of Frank's recent brain scan." He held up a multicolored picture, pointing to several locations while saying, "As you can see here and here, major parts of Frank's brain show limited to no function."

"I don't understand."

"I am afraid he may never wake due to the damage. You should consider alternatives ..." He continued to drone on in a voice colder than the words he spoke.

She didn't hear the rest of his explanation. She only knew he had suggested killing her son. When the hollow voice stopped speaking, she said, "No thank you."

The doctor nodded and walked out. She suddenly felt the need to share a piece of her mind with him. She jumped up to catch him. When she looked in the hallway, the doctor had vanished. She felt a frightening chill. She returned to her chair and her torment continued.

Chapter 27
Suffering

Maggie sat in her bed, waiting for the doctor to come and clear her to go home. She had been weakened by an infection for the last few days, but it finally cleared. She thought back to her feverish state and thought she remembered calling Paul in her delirium. It seemed like a good idea at the time, but now she regretted it. Her tempter took this moment of regret and sneaked in a disturbing thought. *What if I had gotten an abortion?* She thought of all of the good times she and Paul had before she found out about her pregnancy. The fantastic plans they made for their life together had died. Her mind wandered to this impossible dream world until her guardian angel rescued her. *Vita!* She saw her baby's face and her heart melted. She wanted to raise this child more than anything else. She knew God placed this miracle in her life for a reason.

She brought me my mission, Maggie thought. Between fever spikes, she spent the last two days thinking about helping girls like her. She knew what it felt like to be alone in the world without a choice. She had experienced abandonment from her family and pressure to abort from her partner. God called her to share her story and serve her sisters in need. She planned on talking to Katherine about this as soon as she returned home.

A doctor walked in. She got excited about leaving, but recognized the obstetrics expert working with Vita.

"Good afternoon, Miss Rowen."

"Good afternoon, doctor. How is my little girl?"

"The surgeries have gone well and her vitals are good. Her heart condition has stabilized, but her temperature is above normal, so I am concerned she may have picked up an infection. I have her on some antibiotics and we will monitor her closely. She should be fine."

Maggie's weariness kept her from responding. She simply nodded and the doctor bid her a good day and left. The doctor spoke positively, but she could tell he spun the news to make her feel better. She prayed to God for mercy. She wondered when her trials would end and asked for strength to endure the test. Her guardian angel rejoiced and fought her tempter from her presence for the moment so she could rest and enjoy some peace. Maggie got a feeling she should call Katherine.

"Hello, Katherine. It's Maggie, I'm better. I was hoping you could say a prayer for Vita. The doctor says she has an infection, and I'm worried." She choked up with emotion. "Thank you so much Katherine, I don't know what I would do without you." She hung up.

"Was that Maggie, mommy?" Regina said.

"Yes, sweetheart."

"What did she say?"

"She said she is doing better, but Vita has an infection and she needs our prayers."

"Okay, let's do it after…" Regina didn't get to finish her statement. Emmanuel heard their interchange, suddenly fell over on the couch, and shook violently.

"Manny!" Katherine ran to him but could only watch as Emmanuel seized.

Regina prayed for her brother's release from his torment. She heard Lucy's voice in her heart.

"Emmanuel offered himself to suffer for the health of Vita Plena. God hears your prayers but will honor his sacrifice."

"He's burning up again," Katherine said. This shook Regina from her trance and she ran to get a bowl of ice water and a wash cloth. By the time she returned, his seizure ended.

"Here, mommy."

"Can you sit with Manny and mop his forehead. I am going to call your father."

Regina sat by her unconscious brother and prayed.

"When will he be free of his suffering?"

She listened for Lucy's response but heard nothing. She ministered to her brother while Katherine called her father, then the doctor. Her mother hung up the phone and came back.

"I can take it from here. Your father is on his way. The doctor said to give him some fever medication when he wakes up and then bring him to the office."

"No, I want to do it," Regina said. The newfound tenderness for her brother surprised her, but she wanted to stay by his side. She knew his sacrifice freed her to receive her visions and protected Vita. She owed him this token of thanks.

"Okay then. You're in charge, nurse Regina." Katherine patted her shoulder and went to get ready to go to the hospital. Regina prayed over her sleeping brother.

Mark Andrews had much to think about over the last few weeks. Stress from school lessened over break, but his mind constantly jumped from the governor's actions, his failure to live his mission with the Knights, his daughter's visions, and now the health of his son.

Mark raced home as fast as he could. He focused on his little boy who already had been in the hospital once. His tempter kept Mark thinking about his son's illness. He reminded Mark about the earlier seizure and the doctor's explanation. Mark spent his car ride thinking about how he could best heal his son and provide strength for his family. He worried about his wife and daughter's health. All of the other issues in his life also swirled around in his head, and it became a maelstrom of confusion.

Mark's guardian angel encouraged him to bring his pain to the Lord in prayer. His Rosary sat on the middle console of his car, but his demon convinced Mark that he needed to concentrate on the road on this difficult drive.

The demon enjoyed this torment immensely and took satisfaction in this short term victory. He didn't know if he could continue this distraction for very long, but relished it for the time being.

Frank Roland's body remained motionless on his hospital bed in the ICU, but his soul did not rest. Frank healed in spirit while his body lay broken. He prayed constantly and could feel his guardian angel's presence. He thanked God for his company. Raphael had not appeared to him again.

After what seemed like an eternity of stillness, he sensed a spiritual change. A vision of an old man appeared in his mind. The man had graying hair and a long gray beard. He wore a brown robe which reached the ground and he kept his hands hidden in the sleeves.

"Ciao, mio figlio," the old man said. Frank did not speak Italian, but he understood the words, "Hello, my son."

"Hello. Who are you?"

"My name was Francesco, like yours," he answered, "But now, most people call me Padre Pio."

"Are you a priest?"

"Yes."

"Are you a monk?"

"Yes."

"Why are you here?"

"Jesus sent me here to teach you, Francis." Frank bristled at first when he heard his given name. Only his mother called him that, but after the initial annoyance, he enjoyed the reverent way the old priest said the name.

"Is it about my mission?"

"Yes. You could say your mission is very dear to my heart. The Lord called me in very much the same way."

"What was your mission, Padre?"

"To be like the one I love."

"What does that mean?"

"To show mercy to the weak and the poor, to love and instruct the sinner, and finally..." Padre Pio paused and looked at Frank.

"What? What else?"

"To suffer so the world can be redeemed through his grace."

"Suffer? Why suffer?" He had seen his share of suffering in his life: physical, mental, and spiritual. His father's death and his mother's health had led Frank to question if God existed. That pain still haunted him, despite his return to faith.

"I know you have already suffered much in your life, my son. It is the vocation of every Christian. You must not look at your pains and sorrows as something to avoid. You must embrace them as Our Lord embraced his cross. He needed to carry it to Calvary to complete his saving act."

"You want me to embrace my suffering? You mean enjoy it?"

"Enjoy is not the right word. Accepting it as a gift from God would be a better way of looking at it."

"A gift? Who wants a gift like that?"

"Do you know anything about my life?" Padre Pio said.

"Not really."

"I was baptized Francesco Forgione, named after Saint Francis of Assisi. My father did not die when I was young, but I basically lost him when he left Italy for America to work so I could become a priest. I grew up without him and missed him just like you miss your dad."

Frank looked at the priest, feeling a new connection. "I became a Franciscan monk, a Capuchin, to be exact. Very early in my priesthood, I felt a deep call to offer myself as a vessel for the Lord to suffer for sinners as he did. This was my constant prayer."

"I still don't understand why he would want us to suffer."

Padre Pio smiled. "To love the Lord is to walk with him, to be one with him. Prayer and study can only take you so far on this journey. A disciple of Jesus must carry their Cross and walk the very steps to Calvary if they want to live life in Christ. I prayed for the Lord to use my body as an instrument to bring grace to the world. In 1910, three years after becoming a priest, I began to feel the pains of Our Crucified Lord."

"How?"

"My hands and feet throbbed as if pierced by nails and I felt a sharp, stabbing sensation in my side, where Saint Longinus ran the Lord through with his spear to make sure he was dead."

"That must have hurt a lot."

"It did, but I happily shared in Our Lord's Passion. I celebrated Mass more fully because of the closeness I felt with Jesus. God gave me a great blessing."

"How long did that last?"

"The pain never left me. Five years later, I also felt the pains of the scourging at the pillar and the crowning of thorns."

"Wow, is that it?"

"No, three years later, in 1918, the Lord decided he would use me as a spiritual sign to others. I prayed he would spare me from the humiliation, even though I already accepted the physical pain."

"The humiliation of what?"

"Jesus made the wounds of his passion visible on me to the world."

"Do you mean …?"

"Yes, the nail marks appeared on my hands and feet. I bled from those holes and a wound in my side for the rest of my life."

Padre Pio withdrew his hands from his robes to show his pierced, bleeding hands. A chill went through Frank.

"What happened then?"

"I felt the Lord graced me when he let me share in his pains, but when news of my wounds spread, people came to the monastery in droves."

"To see you?"

"Yes. I prayed daily that the Lord would remove the signs from my body. The attention I received challenged my humility, but gradually I realized I needed to suffer the cross of notoriety so souls could be saved. I found out it wasn't the last gift the Lord would give me to show the wonders of his love."

"What else did you get?"

"He gave me the ability to read souls."

"Read souls?"

"People would come to me for confession, and the Holy Spirit would tell me the sins on their heart. If they failed to reveal the whole truth to me, I would confront them and tell them to come back when they wanted to tell the Lord the truth."

"That's amazing. Is that all?"

"No, God gave me many more, but I will end with the gift of bilocation."

"What's that?"

"My vows didn't allow me to leave the monastery grounds, but the Lord allowed me to visit people who prayed for my intercession in distant locations."

"Like a ghost?"

"No, he allowed me to physically minister to my spiritual children, while still in San Giovanni Rotondo. By his grace, I could touch those who asked for my intercession. I was present in both places."

This left Frank speechless.

"Why does this surprise you, Francis? Didn't our Blessed Lord do miracles far greater than these? Didn't Jesus walk on water, feed multitudes, and raise people from the dead? Didn't he promise his Apostles the same gifts?"

"I guess I figured that stuff happened in the Bible, and it's weird to think it happened to you so recently."

"The power of God is real, Francis. The cynicism of my time needed to be countered. So when I offered to be the Lord's vessel of suffering, he chose me to be a sign for his people and nonbelievers. Now, he is calling you to be a sign for your generation."

Somehow, Frank expected this. Saint Raphael had alluded more of his mission would be revealed.

"Padre, does Jesus want to give me his wounds?"

"I don't know, my son. Even if he did, you are not ready. You will first need to prepare yourself to accept suffering to help others with theirs. The Lord has many gifts in store for you if you accept your call."

Frank wondered if he would ever be ready to suffer in the way Padre Pio described. He wondered if he even wanted to, but the Lord called him. He reached out to his father.

"Dad, what should I do?" Frank begged for his father's guidance. No words came, but he felt a warm hand on his shoulder squeezing firmly. He remembered his dad doing this when he taught Frank to ride his bike. He squeezed his shoulder right before he started running alongside of him to ease Frank's fears. Then they would begin.

"I'll do it," Frank said.

Padre Pio nodded, showing his pleasure in Frank's acceptance. "Then we will begin right away." The pain began slowly at first and then came like a tidal wave. In his coma, Frank realized his brain had been freed from feeling the pains of his injuries. Now he began to feel the agony. Broken bones, a cracked skull, bruised flesh all screamed out to Frank at once. He felt and accepted all of it and the Lord showered him with graces. His tempter screamed in rage.

Chapter 28
All for One

Tuesday, December 31st
6:01 PM

Mark's heart pounded as he waited for the meeting to begin. John Jameson had called the Knights of Columbus together to discuss how to challenge the governor's plan to silence churches. He approached the podium.

"Thank you for coming to this emergency meeting, even though I know many of you have plans you are delaying. I promise to make this brief. Men, you all received the packet of information from Brother Wilson via email. I assume you had enough time to read through the news articles and have a good grasp of what the governor is trying to do to people of faith in this state."

Murmurs of agreement spread through the crowd. Mark read every word of the material and he felt a strong call to come to this meeting and actually deliver his message about his mission. The crisis in their state needed men of action, and these men wanted to act.

"Does anyone have any suggestions?" John said.

"We could make some flyers summarizing the information and hand it out at Mass this Sunday so everyone knows of the danger the governor's attitude poses to the church," a short man with glasses said. Mark recognized him as someone who had older children in the parish.

"Do you know how many flyers like that I pick up in the pews after each Mass? People don't read that stuff, beyond a glance anyway," a tall man said. Mark remembered this man from the first meeting but did not know him.

"Well, what do you suggest?" the first man said. The second did not respond. The hum of the neon lights filled the silence in the room. Mark felt called again to speak, but the same voices of doubt came back. *They won't listen to you, you're new. You haven't earned their respect.* He started to believe them again. He managed to pray for guidance.

He pictured himself in the chapel in college. He remembered looking at the statue of Mary positioned behind the tabernacle, the Holy Mother standing behind her Son. "My Lady, your knight awaits his orders."

"I have something," Mark said, standing suddenly. All eyes turned to him.

"Brother Andrews! Please, share with us," John said. He welcomed Mark with his immense smile.

Mark had not prepared a speech. He hadn't planned on having an opportunity to speak at this meeting but courage found him. He hoped the Lord would guide him, but as he started to speak his mind blanked. *Lord, help me. I want to do your will.* His mind flashed to the prophet Isaiah, who felt unworthy to speak God's words. An angel touched his mouth with a burning coal from the heavenly altar and loosed his tongue to speak the message of God. Mark abandoned himself to the Lord and began to speak.

"Brother Knights, I come before you, sinful and sorrowful. I did not assist you in performing the corporal works of mercy to those in our parish and in the community. God called you each by name and you answered him. He called me many times to service opportunities, but I ignored his voice. I only saw an obstruction to my own will. So, I apologize and am grateful you have so graciously accepted me back into your fold."

Mark looked around the room and saw everyone paying attention. A few nodded in agreement. He knew he had intrigued them. Mark finished with his sorrows and turned to his mission.

"I am also grateful to the Lord above. Though I denied his call for many years, he never stopped searching for his lost sheep. He didn't leave me for dead, but kept calling my name. I am humbled that he called me again, and this time, he gave me enough grace to stand. Brothers, he has called me on a mission to bring true manhood back into the world, in the model of Saint Joseph. God chose him to teach his own Son how to be a man himself. There can be no greater model, yet the men of this world look in every other direction to find someone to emulate: athletes, musicians, and movie stars, many with lifestyles contrary to God's plan. To be a man of God requires prayer, sacrifice, and suffering. We must consecrate ourselves to Our Lady, like Saint Joseph, to be a Knight in her service, to fight the evil one in her name. I come to you first because you have already heard his call and answered. Now I ask you, will you walk with me, even though I, myself, don't deserve your allegiance? I hope my words and my mission inspire your support. Thank you."

Mark nodded and sat down in his chair. He closed his eyes for a moment and thanked the Lord for the words he spoke. Now he waited to see what kind of response came, if any. He looked around the room and saw all of the Knights looked down, eyes closed. No one seemed ready to say anything. Mark looked at John Jameson. He seemed to have something on his mind.

After what seemed like an eternity, John stood up. The others took notice. "Mark, thank you. Since last summer, many of us have discussed how we felt stirred to make a spiritual change. We prayed for guidance but nothing came up." Mark looked around and saw many of the knights nodded. "I think you just answered our prayers. What did you have in mind?"

This stunned Mark. He didn't realize how easy this would turn out. *Thank you, Jesus.* He wondered how to begin, but simply decided to cut to the chase. "I propose that we consecrate ourselves to Our Lady in the manner suggested by Saint Maximilian Kolbe. We should make ourselves Knights in the Militia Immaculata."

"I don't see the point of that. We already are Knights," the tall man who challenged the other suggestion said. A chill went through Mark. "With all due respect, John, this gentleman shows up here, after blowing us off for years, and starts telling you what to do? I think you should show him the door."

The tall man had a bitter look on his face. He stared at a few of the others until they nodded in agreement. Others shook their heads. Mark felt worried. What seemed like a simple process had suddenly turned. The chill hit him again.

Satan does not want this crowd to move closer to Jesus through Mary. He likes them right where they are. Mark knew the voice of his guardian angel. He recognized the intense spiritual battle going on here for the minds and souls of the men present. Mark stood again.

"I don't speak here because I deserve your respect or your allegiance. I speak because the men of the world have forgotten what it means to be men. The epitome of manhood was Our Lord, followed by Saint Joseph. Give your respect and allegiance to them. Too many men want freedom from responsibility and hunt for pleasure. The saints have shown us otherwise. We are responsible to God, who calls us to love: love our wives, love our children, and love our neighbors. We are to do this heroically, to the point of death. Consecration to Our Lady requires that. That is how Saint Maximilian lived and how he loved. The devil doesn't want us to live our lives that way."

Mark felt the Holy Ghost pass through the room and shake the men in his wake. His challenger's face released the defiance it held. He stood up again and said, "I'm sorry, I don't know what I was thinking. I retract my objection."

"If no one has anything else to say, I move we have a vote on whether we should suggest the consecration to the Knights of Columbus of Saint John's parish," John said.

"Second," a voice said.

"Third," others said in unison.

"Passed," John said. "Who favors offering the consecration to the whole council?"

There was a shower of "Ayes".

"Anyone opposed?"

Mark looked to the tall man who voiced the original disagreement. Neither he nor anyone else voted "Nay".

"Well, Brother Mark, when should we do this?"

"Preferably on a Marian feast day, like tomorrow, January 1st, or January 8th," Mark answered. "The second one would give us enough time to prepare ourselves with prayer and fasting." He could see some confused looks.

John asked the question many of the Knights must have had. "I know tomorrow is the Solemnity of the Mother of God, but what is January 8th?"

"Oh, it is a little known feast day we used to celebrate in college because we usually started second semester around then. It is the feast of Our Lady of Prompt Succor," Mark said.

"Really, what does that mean?" John said.

"Succor means help. In the early 1800's, the sisters of a particular convent in New Orleans prayed to Our Lady using that title. Many miracles were attributed to that intercession. Two major ones were the saving of the convent from a fire that destroyed most of the city and the American troops being saved from defeat during a major battle of the War of 1812."

"It would be appropriate to turn to her for prompt aid in our situation as well, yes?" John said.

"I guess you are right," Mark said.

"What do we do after that with regards to the governor?" John said.

"I think this will be an important beginning. By consecrating ourselves to Jesus through Mary, we will prepare for the battle that will come. I think our heads will be clearer and our hearts more stout for any decisions we make."

"Very well, if there is nothing else, let us adjourn. Enjoy your New Year's festivities. I'll send a recap and a plan for next week via email."

The meeting ended and several of the men came to thank Mark for his words. Even the tall man shook his hand. He went home full of hope and thanksgiving.

Chapter 29
Theotokos

Regina waited with her mother in the car for Maggie to come out of her house. Her doctor sent her home on Tuesday morning and Katherine went over to check on her twice that day. Katherine's energy in taking care of both Emmanuel and Maggie impressed Regina. If Maggie could have brought Vita home, she probably would have taken care of her as well.

Mark Andrews went to the eight o'clock Mass to fulfill his Holy Day obligation so he could come home and tend to Emmanuel, who still had a fever. He hadn't eaten anything and drank very little over the last few days. His parents discussed taking him in to the hospital this afternoon if nothing changed.

Looking out the window, Regina saw snow drifts piled high against the house. She lost herself in the beauty of the whiteness until she saw Maggie come out.

"Thanks for taking me with you," Maggie said, climbing into the front seat.

"Thanks for coming," Katherine said.

"I talked to a nurse this morning and she told me Vita's temperature has stabilized and she really looks like she has improved."

Regina knew Emmanuel's suffering led to this improvement, but still couldn't share that with her mother.

"That's fantastic. Are you going to go see her this afternoon?" Katherine said.

"I was hoping to. Do you want to come with?"

294

"If Emmanuel hasn't improved, we are going to take him in to be looked at again."

Maggie heard the sadness in Katherine's voice and didn't reply. They rode to church in silence.

After the Gospel reading, Father Joe stood up to begin his homily. "Our Lady was the Mother of God."

He paused and looked around to let the words sink in. "We say the words, 'Holy Mary, Mother of God' every time we say a Hail Mary, but do we think about them?"

"How can Mary, a human, be the mother of God? How is that possible? Well, historically, she was mother of Jesus, and we profess as Christians that Jesus is God, which logically leads to the honorific Mother of God. I apologize for getting too theological, but some heretics throughout history proposed that Mary was only mother to Jesus' human nature but not his divine nature. So the Jesus she carried in her womb was only the man Jesus."

The priest looked directly at Regina with a questioning look. *Why did he look at her like that?* She thought about it for a moment. *Because she knew that wasn't the truth.* She saw Mary carry the Holy Infant Jesus in all of his heavenly glory within her. Children, animals, and Saint Elizabeth all recognized his divinity within Mary during her pregnancy.

"I bring this up because we do not have separate natures. Our bodies and souls don't come together at birth. God creates us as complete persons from the moment of conception, whole from the beginning. The Church teaches us that with authority and as Christians you must believe it."

He looked around the church and saw some nods, but also some confusion.

"This morning, Governor Incredo and his supporters, pushed a bill into the state legislature that would specifically, legally protect sex selective abortions."

The congregation gasped together. Tension gripped the room. Regina didn't understand. She hoped Father Joe would explain.

"We already know many people turn to abortion in dire circumstances because we, the body of Christ, are not there to help. But, the state allowing a mother to kill her own child, merely because of his or her gender, is an abomination."

Regina realized the issue. She remembered the conversation she had with her mother about abortion and the horror she felt. She could see why Father Joe made such a big deal about this.

"The Governor would have the Church remain silent in the face of this travesty. He doesn't want religious organizations to guide their members on how to think about political issues, but he doesn't understand how the church is our mother. A mother warns her children about the dangers of the world and teaches them to lead lives in truth and justice. She fulfills her mission only when she can speak about evil and what Christians must do to answer it."

Father Joe's energy had filled the seats in the church, and now it filled the souls in those seats. Regina looked at the adults absorbed in the priest's homily.

"As Christians, you have the obligation to turn to God, your father, and the Church, your mother, for sound guidance in moral questions. When the state turns against our morality, we can't step aside and say we will stay quiet as the laws of God get trampled."

Regina looked at her mother and Maggie. They listened intently to Father Joe speak.

"This action by the Governor opens the door to a host of moral dilemmas. If the state will allow a woman to choose the sex of her child, how long before it tries to suggest the sex of her child? When the state denies the humanity of its populace, what stops it from encouraging certain genders over others, certain races over others, certain intelligences over others?"

He paused as his questions sank in. "Our Lady had a crisis pregnancy. At the time of Christ, the Blessed Virgin would have been stoned if found guilty of adultery. She feared for her life when Gabriel spoke the words of the Annunciation, but trusting in God she accepted her call. As a church, we have to provide for our sisters in crisis. I encourage you all to think about what you can do to help the women in dire need of your love, your aid, and your prayers. Be vocal about your opposition to the Governor's plans. Let your coworkers and neighbors know your position about this and the deadly consequences of silence in the face of this evil. Let us now spend some quiet time contemplating the gift of motherhood on this feast day of Mary, the Mother of God."

After several minutes of quiet time, Father Joe continued with Mass. Afterwards, Katherine convinced Maggie to go out to lunch with her and Regina. They agreed on a place and ordered their food before starting to talk.

"What do you think about Father Joe?" Katherine said.

"I could listen to him speak all day," Maggie said.

"Me too," Regina said.

Katherine smiled at her daughter. She turned back to Maggie. "I bet you can't wait to bring Vita home, huh?"

"Yeah, I never thought I could love someone so much. I would give anything to ease her suffering and make her well. I kind of feel helpless watching her in her little incubator."

"I know the feeling," Katherine said, running her hand over Regina's head. "You will have many long days and nights to spend worrying about her. I still do. I suppose it will never end." She smiled at Regina, who blushed and smiled back.

They talked about motherhood for a little longer. The topic turned to relationships and as Maggie started talking about Paul, Katherine's phone rang.

"Excuse me," she said, looking at the screen, "It's Mark."

"Oh, go ahead," Maggie said.

"Hello?" She listened to what Mark had to say. "Okay, I will meet you over there," she said after a few moments. "Bye."

"What's wrong?" Maggie asked.

"Manny vomited up blood. Mark is taking him to the hospital now." Katherine looked at Maggie, "Can I take you too? You wanted to see Vita, right?"

"Of course, you have been there for me, Katherine; it's my turn to return the favor. Let's go."

Regina got up and clung to her mother in fear. Katherine hugged her back and helped her get ready to go out into the cold world.

Chapter 30
The Presentation

Thursday, January 2nd
9:02 PM

The Andrews spent New Year's Day in the hospital with Emmanuel. With a second incident in a week, his doctor became more aggressive and subjected him to vast battery of tests. Deep in her heart, Regina knew they wouldn't find anything, but she had no way to explain her knowledge and prayed to accept some suffering herself. She felt guilty that she did not feel any pain at all while her brother looked terrible.

Noticing the time, Katherine prepared to take Regina home while Mark took his turn at Emmanuel's bedside. Regina asked if she could make a quick trip to the chapel to say a prayer and Katherine agreed. The moment Regina hit her knees a vision overtook her.

Regina found herself outside the cave of the Holy Family. She went inside to see that Joseph had packed up some of their belongings. He stacked the bundles by the entrance. Mary held the Holy Infant, who slept soundly, wrapped in blankets.

"Are you ready, my dear?" Joseph said.

"Yes. Do you have the money to purchase the offering?" Mary said.

"Yes. I also packed some food for the trip."

They came out of the cave. The sun barely poked through the clouds in the east. They walked down the hilly path to get to a main road.

"Where are they going?" Regina asked.

"Jerusalem. The time has come for Mary's purification after childbirth and the redemption of their firstborn child. These are ancient Jewish traditions done according to the Law of Moses," Gabriel said.

"How long will it take for them to get there?"

"Probably about three hours. It will depend on whether Our Lord needs to eat or if he sleeps the whole time."

Until they reached the main road, Joseph made sure Mary kept her footing and found safe passage over the rocky ground. Once on the main road, he kept checking on her comfort.

"Are you okay with this pace? We could slow down."

"No, Joseph, I'm fine. The Lord has strengthened me. I can keep up. Don't worry."

They walked for a while. "Joseph?"

He slowed and turned towards her. "Yes?"

"I finally understand how my parents must have felt."

"What are you talking about?"

"I loved my parents dearly, and even though I spent very little time with them, I remember them fondly. They offered me to the temple as a young girl according to their promise to the Lord. I saw the sorrow on their faces when they left me there, but I didn't know what they felt."

"But we won't leave Jesus there," Joseph said.

"I know, but we still must present him back to the one who gave him to us. Right now, he's our baby. I can hold him in my arms and not let him go for anything, but when we hand him over to the priest…, oh, Joseph." Mary wept through the end of her words.

"There, there, Mary. What is it?"

"Joseph, I only wanted to know the Lord all my life. Now that he is with us, I want to keep him all to myself. I know I shouldn't be greedy, but I can't help myself." Mary's sorrow pained Regina.

"I can feel her pain, Gabriel. How?" She welled up with tears.

"You feel a mother's pain. Whenever a mother parts from her child, she experiences this. Mary is the Mother of God. She feels a particular anguish," Gabriel said.

Joseph put his arm around Mary as they walked. He thought of words to comfort his spouse.

"You have done God's will. You still do it. He wills that you love him and want to be with him. The Father has put this child into our care. You honor the Lord by wanting to keep Jesus close to you always."

His reason found its mark. She smiled and nodded. Wiping away her tears, she kissed the sleeping baby on the forehead. He slumbered on, letting his parents make good time towards Jerusalem. With the issue resolved, time shifted forward.

The Holy Family entered Jerusalem and Joseph haggled with a peddler.

"For two turtle doves? I paid half that price last year." Joseph said.

The peddler flashed an innocent look that Regina did not believe. "My friend, costs have gone up."

Joseph looked up and down the row of similar peddlers and gave Mary a look of sorrow and disgust.

"Gabriel, why is he so upset?"

"The temple has become a place to take advantage of the poor," he said.

Joseph went to a few more vendors and found them to be pricier than the first.

"He is trying to get two turtle doves? Like in the song?" Regina said.

"Yes, a young ram would be a customary sacrifice, but the poor could offer two small birds instead."

Joseph turned and gave Mary a mournful look. "What has this place become? Our fathers would be ashamed. I will go back to the first vendor. It will take all of our remaining money, but we agreed to offer everything to the Lord. He will provide for our journey home."

Mary nodded. Joseph returned to the first vendor. "Alright, I will pay your price, sir."

"The price is now five more," the vendor said.

"Five more? I was here only a moment ago."

"You have found for yourself my original price was more than fair, and my new price is still lower than what the others charge. So pilgrim, what do you say?"

Up to this point, the man kept his focus on Joseph. He glanced at Mary long enough to figure they had come with a newborn for a presentation, but now the infant started to make a commotion, catching his attention.

Jesus wriggled free from his wrapping, looked directly into the eyes of the vendor, and began to wail. Regina never heard him make this sound before and neither had Mary and Joseph. Regina felt sorrow and accusation in his piercing shriek.

The vendor's face went white. His eyes began to tear up. "Please friend, have the doves for five less, no, no, ten less than my first price. Please."

Joseph didn't know what happened, but he couldn't turn down the deal. He didn't ask questions, he simply paid the distressed businessman, took the birds, and led Mary away. Mary comforted Jesus, and he calmed back down to his usual blissful self.

"What was that all about?" Regina said.

"My dear, you have witnessed something that Jesus will wait more than thirty years to finish," Gabriel said.

"What's that?"

"The cleansing of the temple." Regina remembered the gospel story. "Jesus touched someone else through his cry. Come, let's go."

Gabriel transported Regina to another part of the temple and slightly back in time. She remembered the small bedroom from one of her first visions but barely recognized the frail figure lying under a thin blanket. She heard the same shrill cry Jesus made at the dove vendor's.

The old man awoke from his sleep with a start. "What is this noise that both disturbs my sleep and awakens my spirit?" He threw off his blanket and struggled to rise. His emaciated body swam in his nightshirt. "Oh Lord, how long will you let me waste away?"

As if in response of this query, a beautiful angel appeared in the room. The little man gasped but then smiled. "You have come to take me home?"

The angel held out his hand. "Come father Simeon, Our Lord will fulfill his promise to you."

"The promise? The king has arrived? The anointed one?"

Simeon took the angel's hand and struggled to his feet. The angel attended the old priest as he vested himself one final time. When he finished, Regina joined him on the slow walk to the sacrificial area of the temple. The excitement in Simeon's face made her giddy.

When they entered the courtyard, Simeon looked around disappointed.

"Where is my King?" he asked the angel.

"He comes to you now, faithful servant," the angel answered and vanished.

At that moment, the Holy Family entered the court yard. Simeon squinted, trying to see who approached. They got within twenty feet before Mary finally recognized the ghost of her old master, and Simeon saw Mary clearly.

"You?" he said, looking at Mary smiling. "From the moment Joseph took you from the temple, my strength has left me. Now, you have returned with…," he paused, finally noticing Mary's precious bundle. He held out his hands towards Jesus.

Mary felt great joy seeing her surrogate father again. She didn't hesitate, as she had feared, to step forward to hand over her child. Simeon took him into his arms. The priest's body seemed to grow an inch and pulse with sudden strength. "Lord, now let your servant depart in peace according to your promise. For mine eyes have seen your salvation which you have prepared before the face of all the people, a light to the Gentiles, and the glory of your people, Israel." (Luke 2:29-32)

Others in the courtyard heard this commotion and came closer to investigate. Simeon held the child tenderly in his arms. Joyful tears fell down his face as he stared into the eyes of Jesus who was awake and attentive to the holy man. Then, turning to Mary, Simeon exclaimed, "Behold, this child is set for the fall and rising again of many in Israel, and for a sign which shall be spoken against." He paused for a moment and added in an ominous tone speaking directly to Mary, "And a sword shall pierce through your own soul also, that the thoughts of many hearts may be revealed." (Luke 2:33-35)

Mary heard these words and turned to Joseph. He mirrored her fear and couldn't offer any explanation or consolation.

"What do his words mean?"

"Simeon prophesies that many will be born again after they fall on their knees before God and Jesus will be a great sign."

"The cross."

"Yes, a sign that will be adored but also spoken against."

"What about that sword stuff?"

"You have seen that God has chosen to closely link the Blessed Mother with Jesus, yes?"

"Yes."

"The Father created her to be the New Ark. She acted as his tabernacle for nine months. Then, she became his first disciple. Now, he reveals she will even suffer with her son, so hearts may be opened to God, sharing with his holy life until the end."

"Why? Isn't Jesus' dying enough?"

"Yes, his sacrifice will be perfect in completing the New Covenant, but her suffering will be a sign for all holy men and women to emulate. She perfectly lived discipleship. She held his body first upon birth and last before he was laid to rest, but most importantly, she always held him in her heart. When he was pierced upon the cross, she was pierced deep within her soul."

"How can I hope to have that kind of faith?"

"You must hold Jesus in your heart so closely, that when someone attacks Jesus or his Church, a sword pierces your heart as well. In this way, you can share in the discipleship of Mary."

Simeon led them forward for the consecration and Mary's ritual purification according to the Law. A small group gathered to witness the ceremony, but the sight of one excited Mary. There stood the prophetess, Anna, the daughter of Phanuel of the tribe of Asher. Advanced in years, having lived with her husband seven years from when she was a virgin, and then as a widow until she was eighty-four. She did not depart from the temple, worshiping with fasting and prayer night and day. (Luke 2:36-38)

Anna smiled at Mary and stepped forward saying, "Thanks be to God. He sends his salvation to Israel to us on this day." She took great care not to look at the child. "All who are awaiting the redemption of Israel will not have to wait any longer. The savior is at hand. Joyful are those who live in his midst."

The crowd applauded at this exultation, apparently ignorant of the connection between Anna's words and the infant before them. They had missed exactly what Simeon said minutes before.

Joseph stayed with Jesus and Simeon, while Mary stole away to speak to Anna. "It is so good to see you, Anna."

"And you, child. All those years as your teacher, I saw you working tirelessly and without complaint in this temple. I knew you would always be close to the Lord, but I never knew…," she abruptly ended, tears in her eyes.

"What is it?" Mary asked.

"All those years I watched the other girls torment you because of their petty jealousies. I didn't say anything because you bore your suffering with a smile, and I saw you used the pain to help you grow closer to God. I dreamed one day you would live in peace."

Mary smiled and Regina could tell the old woman's compliments touched her. But then, Anna continued, "I received a vision confirming Simeon's words. You will have the Joy of the Lord, but your life will never be free of the pain he calls you to. I'm sorry, Mary."

Mary looked at the old woman who gave her the dour news. Although Anna marked her future with a dark cloud, Mary held her own sorrow back and consoled her friend.

"Dear woman, when I accepted the Lord's will, I knew in my heart the road would be difficult. I knew I would have to give myself over to his protection to make it through my days. Do not weep for me. Let us rejoice today, sister, the Lord is with us, our day has come."

Anna looked at Mary with great pride. She realized the girl she knew only a year ago had returned as a woman. Privately, she thanked God for creating this woman to bear and raise his only Son for his earthly kingdom.

Amid the excitement, Regina did not miss two slimy characters hanging out in the shadows at a distance, capturing all that occurred. She and Gabriel moved towards them to capture their interchange.

"We should tell the master about this," one of the men said.

"About what? Do you remember what King Herod did last time someone troubled him with trifles?" the other said.

"That fool should have known not to interrupt him while he was being pampered."

"Really, what part of the day is left?"

The two shared a laugh.

"Who are those guys?" she asked.

"These are two of King Herod's court advisors."

"What are they arguing about?"

"The usual for them: how to find profit in any situation. They can't be sure if there is any advantage in telling King Herod about this excitement in the temple."

"What could happen?"

"King Herod would lavish rewards on those that pleased him, but brutally punished others who annoyed him. He even killed those who betrayed him," Gabriel said.

"He is that bad?"

"He gained popularity in his youth, working with the Romans to improve the city of Jerusalem with new buildings and public works, but in his old age he became extremely paranoid. He even had his own son killed for treason."

Regina shuddered, wondering how taken by evil a man would have to be to commit such a heinous crime. She took one final look at Simeon and Anna with the Holy Family before the vision began to fade. The Holy Spirit gave her the knowledge that Simeon would pass away shortly after Mary and Joseph left with Jesus, but she knew Anna would survive until… The thought got lost as the present vision vanished. She found her mother and walked out of the hospital.

A man walked by them, entering the hospital as they left. They did not know each other by face, but they had entered each other's lives recently. As Katherine and Regina walked to their car, Paul McCorvey walked up to the neonatal ward. He stood in the shadows, unnoticed for quite a while as he surveyed the sparse staff moving about. Since visiting hours had ended, the activity of the unit decreased dramatically.

Paul chose his mark carefully and moved in. He walked up to the night shift nurse who sat alone at her station.

She saw him out of the corner of her eye. "Visiting hours are over."

Paul's life had not gone according to his plans in many ways, but he could always count on getting a good read on everyone he met. He could tell this nurse barely made ends meet by the worn out uniform, cheap haircut, and poorly done makeup and nails. He felt he could sweet talk her into what he wanted. He held out a wad of money so she could clearly see it.

"Come on," Paul cooed. "I work two jobs all day long and this is the only time I can come and see my baby. I want to look at her for a little bit. I told her mother, Maggie Rowen, I wouldn't come at this time because you guys weren't supposed to bring the babies out at night. She didn't want you to get into trouble. That's why I want you to keep this between us."

The young nurse looked at the money. "What's your name?"

"Paul McCorvey."

She looked at the name under "Father" on Vita's information. He checked out. Maggie didn't have the heart to leave the blank empty.

Her nurse had told her, "You can leave it blank until he mans up and does his duty." His name was there and his ID looked valid. He did look like a sad father who simply wanted to see his baby girl after a long day of work.

"I don't see how it could hurt, but only for two minutes." The nurse left her station and walked back to the nursery. She brought Vita's incubator into the viewing room and turned the lighting up slowly. As she walked away, she marveled at the beauty of a grown man crying in joy at seeing his precious infant. She left him alone for a moment to run back to check on her station.

Paul did not cry tears of joy. His tempter had overpowered his guardian angel in combat and now the only voice in his head pounded away any paternal love remaining.

You will never be free to live your life the way you want.

When Paul told his mother about Maggie's pregnancy, she said. "A baby would be good for you. It will make you grow up and stop living like there is no tomorrow." The words resonated with him at the time, but now their impression dissipated with the force of the demon's tongue.

This child will be an economic and social burden on you. Your money will go up in smoke. You will have to stay home every night.

No voice countered. Paul had fallen away from God and damaged his conscience for so long his angel did not have the strength to fight back. He wept for himself. His selfishness created a barrier between his heart and his own daughter only a few feet away.

The nurse returned and took the bassinet back to the common nursery, and Paul walked away in silence. He felt the world coming apart around him. Maggie would help him stay afloat in a situation like this, but now an obstacle stood between them. He could never have Maggie back. *Not with it in the way.* Paul stumbled to the car, fumbled with his keys, and managed to start the engine. He pulled out of the parking space and drove off. He failed to notice the black sedan that rolled out behind him.

Chapter 31
The Wise Men

Thursday, January 2nd
10:12 PM

Regina prayed as she waited for sleep to claim her. She meditated on the Presentation as the room began to swirl. When her sight came back, she spent several days in the wise men's caravan in a few short moments. The wise men encountered two Roman scouts when they entered the borders of Judea. They explained their story to the scouts, who decided to take the travelers to the king's court. The soldiers worried that the crazy nomads would cause a problem in Jerusalem. They figured they had themselves covered.

The wise men stood in the courtroom when a man entered the room. He approached and said, "My master is busy with others in the dining hall. He asks you to state your business to me and I will relay it to him, to avoid insulting his prior guests." He finished his statement with a greasy smile.

"We humbly request that your master tell us where we may find the newborn king of the Jews," Balthazar said.

King's Herod's advisor looked amused at first, but then he thought of something and appeared troubled. "Why do you think King Herod would know where he is?"

"I have studied the faiths of the world for all of my life, and I have concluded salvation will come from the Jews. Your religious leaders must know the location of the Messiah," Melchior said.

"I see," the courtier said. He lost his smile. "I will inform King Herod and return."

The wise men waited for the courtier to talk to the king. He lied when he said King Herod had guests. Most people feared Herod the

Great. His fiery temperament and crippling paranoia caused people to avoid him as a general rule.

When his advisor entered the King's lounge, the corpulent ruler blurted through a mouthful of sweets, "Well? What do they want?"

Cringing, afraid Herod might throw something at him as usual, he answered, "They say they want to see a new born baby."

"What? Who travels to see a baby? They are obviously insane. Is that all?"

The servant gulped. "They say the child is a king and the prophesied messiah."

This caught Herod's attention. "The messiah? The fools must have lost their minds in the desert." The king laughed to himself, but then Regina could see a darkness envelope the King. She heard a voice speak into his heart. *This child will be a king. He is a threat, do not take him lightly.*

The thoughts took hold and he struggled to rise from his lounging position. "I am king in Judea. There is no other," he said. The servant looked terrified. Regina found she could read his mind. *He killed his own son out of fear for his throne, what will he do to these travelers in his rage? Worse yet, what will he do to me?*

Herod paused for a moment and schemed. Regina could tell he came up with a twisted plan but could not discern it. The evil that helped bring it about sent a chill down her spine. "Bring me the chief priests and scribes, and tell these travelers to wait. Make sure they are comfortable, I don't want them to be worried."

"What should I tell the priests and scribes?"

"Tell them to make haste if they want to live."

The servant rushed from the room and Regina followed. He ordered other servants to tend to the wise men while he ran to the temple.

Upon hearing the king's orders, the religious leaders hastened to the palace in fear for their lives. They composed themselves before they entered the King's presence.

"Tell me what you know about the coming of the messiah, the so called promised one. Where will he be born?" Herod said. The priests and scribes looked at each other in shock. No one guessed the king would ask about this topic.

One of the elders gathered up enough courage to answer. "The prophet has written:

But you, Bethlehem Ephrathah, in the land of Judah,

Are by no means least among the rulers of Judah;

For out of you will come a ruler

Who will shepherd my people Israel." (Matthew 2:6)

"Bethlehem? Only peasants and riff raff live in that hole," Herod said.

"That is the prophecy, your highness," the priest said.

"Very well, you may go," Herod said.

"May I ask why the sudden interest in your faith, sire?" The sarcasm did not elude the ruler.

"No, you may not. Leave now, or the next time the Romans want to impose a new tax on the Temple, I won't dissuade them." His fierce political skill roared.

The religious men left and the King's demeanor calmed. His eyes turned dark and a cruel smile crept onto his lips. "Bring me these *wise men*," he said.

The doorman led Balthazar, Melchior, and Caspar into the lounge. They noticed no evidence of guests. Regina could feel their disappointment with the state of the ruler of this kingdom.

"My friends," Herod started, "Would you like some wine?" He gestured and some servants stepped forward with a tray of goblets and an urn.

"No, thank you, sire," Balthazar said. "We only request your blessing to travel through your land to our destination."

"I hear you wish to see a child, is that correct?"

"Yes, your highness. We wish to pay him homage to complete our pilgrimage, and then we will depart to our homelands."

311

Again, Regina felt the same dark chill and saw the shadow on Herod squeeze words out of him. "I believe you will find your messiah in Bethlehem. Go and search carefully for the child. As soon as you find him, report to me, so I too may go and worship him." (Matthew 2:8)

The wise men looked at each other and could not find a reason to disagree. "Yes, of course, your highness, we will return on our way back, thank you for your graciousness," Balthazar said.

"Very well, give these men a letter with a royal seal so they may move about undisturbed throughout our land," King Herod said, a greedy smile still on his lips. He crept out of the room while his advisor prepared the paperwork. The wise men waited for the document and then left to finish their voyage.

The king watched them leave from a window. "Send our fastest riders to Bethlehem. Tell them to obtain whatever news they can of a messiah. If they find this child, I want him killed."

The servant's eyes displayed his shock. "But, I thought you wanted these travelers to return with news."

"Fool. If my troops cannot find the child, maybe these pious ninnies will find him for me. Either way, I can rid myself of a possible usurper." He smiled again at the beauty of his own villainy.

The servant walked away and Regina took her fear to Gabriel.

"Will these troops find the Holy Family?"

"No, Regina. They will get there long before the wise men, but the location of the cave, already difficult to see, will remain hidden from their eyes by the Holy Spirit. The only people in town who know about Jesus' birth would never give up that secret," Gabriel said.

This news calmed her. Regina's vision blurred and she returned to the Holy Family. A single, small candle burned. By its dim light, Regina could see Jesus swaddled tightly, lying before Mary. She caressed his cheek and cooed. Joseph took a break from packing their belongings and enjoyed the scene with Regina.

"Joseph, I am still bewildered by the wonders we have seen since Jesus has been with us."

"I am also. The day my branch sprouted the lily, I knew my life would never again be the same." He tightened the straps on a bag. "At least we have had some peace and quiet for a while. When we get back to Nazareth, maybe he will be able to live a normal childhood after all."

At that moment, Joseph heard a commotion in the distance outside the cave. They shot nervous glances to each other. He crept towards the entrance to peek out. Regina could hear the wise men asking their servants to calm down. She moved out of the cave to get a better look.

Looking down the path, to the foot of the hill, Regina could see all of the animals had bowed down to the ground towards the cave where Jesus lay. This flustered the servants. The wise men tried to calm them down and restore order. Everyone relaxed, and the wise men started up the hill carrying objects wrapped in fancy cloth.

Joseph did not know what to make of the wise men. He stepped out of the cave and Balthazar spotted him. "Hello, we are sorry we startled you. We mean you no harm. We have been called here by an angel of the Lord. Please tell us we can find a Holy Child here, so our journey can be at an end."

Joseph gave a surprised look. "You say an angel sent you? How did you know to come here?"

"The star above this hillside marks the location of the Holy One. We have followed it nightly, and its memory in our hearts guided us during the day," Balthazar said.

Joseph turned to look up at the sky. He saw the brilliant star that the shepherds had followed to get to the cave before.

"You need not be concerned, my friend. Our servants cannot see it."

"I know. You are not the first to come." He beckoned them forward and entered the cave. The wise men shared looked surprised looks and made their way up the rest of the hill until they came to the entrance of the cave. Joseph went inside to tell Mary the news of their guests.

Regina entered the cave before the wise men. Joseph lit a few more candles in the cave to provide more light for their guests. The travelers came in one at a time, and each gasped before falling to his knees at the sight of the Christ child.

Upon their arrival, Jesus began wriggling around in his wrappings until Mary felt compelled to release him and hold him up. He held his arms out towards the strangers. The sight of the Lord beckoning reduced them to tears. They looked to Mary for permission to come closer. She assented and they crawled forward on their knees, leaving their belongings behind.

Mary placed the child on a blanket in front of the wise men so they could see him. They took turns kissing his feet and hands. Jesus seemed amused by the visit and grabbed each of their beards in turn. The Lord tired and started to doze after several minutes. Together, Mary and Joseph marveled at the joy evident in the faces of their visitors.

"How long can they stay like that, Gabriel?"

"They feel the ecstasy of a life's work coming to a fruitful end. They searched for answers to their questions and found more questions until now. The Lord answered them with the truth of his Love. They feel the Joy of the Lord."

Caspar stood first. He bowed, nearly to the floor, before getting up and getting the package he had left at the cave entrance. The others followed suit. Caspar returned to Mary and Joseph bringing his gift. As the wrappings fell away, he displayed a handful of gold coins.

"The kings of many nations paid me these coins to solve their problems using mathematics and reason. I offer these riches back to you Lord, the king of kings, who has revealed yourself to me on this day."

Joseph and Mary bowed their heads and accepted the gift.

Melchior came next. "To the one who will enlighten us all, I bring you this collection of incense I have obtained on my travels. The priests of many faiths have raised their prayers to heaven with this incense. I now offer it to the high priest who will unite us with Our Father in Heaven."

He handed his gift to Joseph and Mary. Regina could tell they struggled to make sense of what they saw.

"Do you recognize yourself in Mary and Joseph, Regina?"

"What do you mean?"

"They feel the same sense of wonder you have felt in the last month. God gave you a spiritual gift, and you have been overwhelmed by it. God gave them the duty of taking care of the greatest gift he ever gave the world."

Regina saw the angel's point. She looked again at Mary and Joseph, who looked at the gifts, each other, and the little baby before them with puzzlement.

Finally, Balthazar came forward with his gift.

"I have studied the properties of many plants and chemicals for my entire life, and I have never found anything as worthy to anoint the Lord as this myrrh. In his life, he will teach us the path to holiness, and in his death, he will give us everlasting life."

This stunned Mary and Joseph. Regina saw their concern.

"What did he say?"

"This stranger has spoken of their child's death only a short time after his birth. Parents do not like considering the mortality of their children. They dream of growing old and leaving their children behind. There is no greater sorrow than for a parent to grieve the death of their own child."

Joseph accepted the final gift. "My esteemed guests, I thank you deeply for what you have brought us. Please, stay with us until you are content. I am sorry I have nothing to offer you. As you can see, we are preparing to depart from this dwelling to return to our home in Nazareth."

"My brother, we have paid our respects and the time has come for our return home," Balthazar said. Regina noticed something come over him. Caspar and Melchior froze as well. Joseph noticed the pause but did not say anything. Balthazar continued, "Peace be to you."

Looking at Jesus, he said, "Lord, you have blessed us well. We depart in great sorrow, but great joy we carry with us having seen you."

The wise men bowed in unison and headed back to their caravan. Regina wanted to stay with Jesus, but she felt herself being drawn by Gabriel to follow the wise men.

"I want you to hear this, Regina. It is important."

As they descended the hill, Regina heard their conversation.

"Did you feel that message?" Caspar asked.

"Yes, I heard a voice tell me to avoid King Herod," Balthazar said.

"Me, too. It told me to return home on a route far around Jerusalem," Melchior said.

"Then let us depart at once. I feel we must make haste," Balthazar said. The others agreed.

"What are they talking about?" Regina said.

"Remember the awkward pause in the cave?"

"Yes."

"Angels told all three of them the same message to ignore Herod's request. He wanted to know the location of Jesus, not to adore him, but to kill him. His evil plan has been thwarted."

Regina watched the wise men get onto their animals and begin their trip back to their homes. A few moments later, she was on her own voyage back to hers.

The man in the black car followed Paul carefully down the street. He stayed far enough back that he wouldn't get noticed. He didn't know that Paul wouldn't have noticed him if he rode on the hood of his car. Paul could only think of the little body underneath all the machinery he had seen. This led to a torment inside him he had never known.

What does this mean? How will this affect my life? His tempter kept him focused on his own needs and problems, while his guardian angel nudged him to think about Maggie and the baby.

While Paul's mind wrestled with the difficulties of his life, the man who followed him mused about the simplicity of his. He took only the jobs he wanted and made good money. He excelled at carrying out his tasks and not asking questions. That led to various employers hiring him often. He had no wife or children nor relatives he kept in contact with. He didn't need friends. Human interaction bored him. He had a passion for hunting, and this kind of job brought him the same thrill. He thought he suppressed his conscience long ago, but now and then, he wondered how his work led to people getting hurt. *I only gather information and pass on messages.* He knew the dirty nature of the information, the messages, and his employers. *I never see them hurt,* he thought. *So it doesn't matter.* Conscience cleared, the chase continued.

After a tearful car ride, Paul made it to his apartment. He opened the door, reflecting on the emptiness Maggie's absence brought about. *I made her leave.* His guardian tried to make him examine his own conscience to see that he needed to turn from his ways, but again the demon prevailed and his thoughts turned. *She completely overreacted.* This set his mind at ease as he threw his keys on the counter and went to the cupboard. Not a moment passed before the doorbell rang; preempting the drink he wanted to have.

He opened the door to see a man in a plain suit standing outside the storm screen. The man smiled. He appeared mostly normal, but Paul sensed something not right about him.

"Can I help you?"

"No, but I can help you, Paul."

"Do I know you?"

"No, but I have an offer for you that you want to hear." Despite the time of day, Paul didn't find the man threatening.

"What kind of offer?"

"It would be better to discuss it inside, in private. You have an opportunity to make some serious money," the man said.

Paul didn't want to let a stranger into his house, but the allure of a large payday swayed him. He looked at the man. Paul figured he could overpower him in a fight, but he considered the man might be concealing a weapon.

"Take off your jacket and show me you aren't packing," Paul said.

The man nodded and did as told. He had a plain, white dress shirt on with a tie. No guns. Paul opened the door. "You better not try anything. I wrestled varsity in high school."

"Do not worry Mr. McCorvey. You have nothing to fear and much to gain."

"Again, how do you know my name? And what is your name?"

"My name is Mr. Smith," Paul assumed it wasn't. "And my employer is a man of impressive means. He knows much about you. For example, your girlfriend has given birth to a child, and that child clings to life. Is that not so?"

This man's knowledge stunned Paul.

"Yes, but…"

"Let me cut to the chase, Mr. McCorvey. As I said, I am employed by a very rich man. This man also has a little girl and she desperately needs a transplant. You could provide him help with this."

"What? You want one of my organs?"

"No, not you, your child. Through my client's connections, he has discovered your child can provide the transplant that will save his daughter's life. My client will pay you one hundred thousand dollars if you can convince your girlfriend to elect to suspend life support on the child and let it pass away peacefully. She will free her child from her torment and my client's people will do the rest."

"You want me to ask Maggie to kill her baby? For money? She would never do it."

"Mr. McCorvey, you saw your baby. You would be doing her a great service by sparing her from a life of misery. A child that premature always has developmental problems. You can save her from the stigma of being handicapped, and you and Ms. Rowen from the giant burden of parenting a child with special needs." Paul's demon made the dark logic seem reasonable to him, while a distant shout from his guardian angel asked him to open his heart to a precious love that could transform his life. While spirits battled for his soul, the man continued, "And you will also be saving the life of another child who can have a normal life with wealthy parents who want her and can provide for her."

A flood of questions and emotions rushed through Paul. He wondered how this stranger knew he had been at the hospital. *Was he following me?* Did it matter? *One hundred thousand dollars!*

"Think of what you could do with the money. You could start a life with your girlfriend and live out the dreams you had."

This is a child's life, your child. The voice in his head caused him a twinge of anguish, but a second voice ameliorated the pain. *You deserve to be happy. Think of how your father stole your childhood from you. You have a chance to have the life you deserve.* The sin of greed sneaked into him in a most devious way.

"So all I have to do is get Maggie to pull the plug?"

"Yes, we have people in the hospital to do the rest."

"I'll try." Something cried out within him at this choice, but before he could register it, a more powerful force drowned it out.

"Very good. As I said, our people will do the rest, and then I will bring you the money. Take this as a sample that my client means business. If you choose not to go through with it or fail, I hope you don't spend any of this." The threat registered with Paul as the man handed him an envelope he took out of his pocket. The man moved to the door, preparing to leave, but turned around after he touched the knob. "Remember, Mr. McCorvey. Time is of the essence. If you are unable to fulfill your end of the deal before your child passes, you will not get your money." Paul liked the sound of "your money", but something bothered him.

"Wait. Why can't I get Maggie to sign over the baby's organs like a normal organ donation, why does she need to stop the respirator?"

The man gave Paul a dead, blank stare. "I gave you the instructions from my employer. I can offer you no further information and you are in no obligation to us. If you want the money, you must fulfill your part of the bargain and not worry about the details. Good night." He walked out into the darkness.

Details? The detail is they want the baby alive. Paul spent the rest of the evening in torment. Even though he had dulled his conscience, he knew he didn't like thinking of giving up a living body to an unknown man and "his people." Unfortunately, the sins of his past, along with the greed that held his heart, clouded his judgment. His tempter led him to focus on the money and his desire to be with Maggie. Greed and lust both tortured him into the darkness of the night.

Chapter 32
Flight

Katherine Andrews decided her daughter deserved to have some fun during Christmas Break. They spent the morning putting together a jigsaw puzzle, and then she took Regina to lunch and a movie.

"I know Manny can't be with us right now, but I want you to enjoy this for his sake. Have fun like he would," Katherine said to Regina.

Regina thought about her brother and how happy little things like going out to lunch made him. She tried hard to enjoy the atmosphere around her. Keeping her mind on Emmanuel, she appreciated tiny details about the restaurant and the movie theater she normally never would. She smiled at the circus theme at the restaurant, thinking about the big smile Manny would have looking at the different clown statues. At the movie theater she dried her hands in the high powered air blower in the bathroom. Manny would always tell her about this dryer whenever they came here.

After the movie, Katherine and Regina were both ready to go and see Emmanuel in the hospital. He rested on his pillow with his eyes half open trying to stay awake without his usual effervescence. Regina smiled at him hoping to convey her gratitude for his sacrifice. She felt the grin he returned sent the most forceful response he could muster. Emmanuel had more to him than she imagined. After a while, Emmanuel fell asleep. Regina asked to visit Frank in his room. She felt bad she had not made a point to see him in her last few visits to the hospital.

Mark Andrews walked her up to his room where they found Louise. Again, she expressed her thrill at seeing Regina. They talked for a little while, and then Louise excused herself to get some coffee. Mark left with her, leaving Regina alone.

Regina looked Frank over. It seemed like some of his scratches and bruises had healed, but he was still a mess. He told her he forgave her in the exciting moment when he came out of his coma, but it didn't fully relieve her guilty conscience. She sat down on the chair by his bed and immediately felt the familiar call.

Regina recognized the Cave of the Nativity again, as she stood outside it. She contemplated that God entered the world through this lowly point. She looked at the darkness of the cave mouth and pondered how the Almighty would choose to come from this place.

"All people come from this kind of darkness, Regina. From the secret hiddenness of your mother's womb, you stepped into the world. God chose to walk the earth as you do. He would not deprive himself of that same experience. He chose this humble abode to start his life. That will change," Gabriel said, stepping into the cave.

Regina followed, expecting to struggle in the darkness. She found she could see in the pitch blackness. In the early part of the cave, she found Joseph asleep on his mat. His staff, a candle, and a tinder box sat by his side. He could rise and serve the Blessed Virgin and the Divine Infant at a moment's notice.

Regina and Gabriel watched as the old Gabriel stepped into the cave. He went to Joseph and spoke into his dreams.

"Get up. Take the child and his mother and escape to Egypt. Stay there until I tell you, for Herod is going to search for the child to kill him." (Matthew 2:13)

Joseph awoke from his slumber in panic. "Mary!"

"What is it?"

"The Lord has sent me a message in my dreams. We must run for Egypt tonight." Joseph lit a candle and got their belongings together.

"Someone comes for Jesus," Mary said. Joseph froze.

"How did you…?"

Mary looked down in thought. "I don't know, but let us make haste." She got up and wrapped up the Lord.

Regina watched the holy couple quickly gather the bundles Joseph made before the Wise Men arrived. They left the cave as they found it. Mary held Jesus while Joseph carried two large bags across his shoulders. They made their way down the path to the road. The Christmas star still shined to illuminate their way. They travelled all night, pausing only to feed Jesus.

Joseph thought to stop at Yigal and Adina's house, but he decided they couldn't afford to be seen in town or waste the time.

Regina watched them struggle on in the cool desert night until they found another cave hidden from the sight of the road. Here they decided it would be safe to rest before breaking out once again.

Regina moved to King Herod's palace. From her vantage point, she saw a man race up on camelback. He stopped the beast, leapt off, and handed the reins to a man by the door. He rushed inside.

Gabriel moved in after him, prompting Regina to do the same. They followed the man to the inner room where the King's butler met him.

"I have urgent news for King Herod."

"Our master sleeps."

"This news cannot wait; do you want to be responsible for delaying its reception? Do you know what will happen to you if he finds out you kept it from him?"

"Are you certain of its importance? Do you know what will happen to you if he feels it is insignificant?"

Both men stared at each other and pondered the consequences in silence.

"Well, what is it then? What is this important news?"

"I was on patrol east of the city and I saw the strange foreigners leaving in the cover of darkness. I didn't think it important, but when I mentioned it to another scout; he told me the king ordered them to return to him with news of a child."

The butler's eyes opened wide and his face lost its color. "How can we wake him without incurring his wrath?" the door keeper said.

The two men tried to find a way to buffer themselves from a violent retribution if their master woke up in a sour mood. Finally, Regina saw the steward's face light up.

"I know someone who can wake him." He scurried off on an unknown mission without explanation. Regina stayed with the scout outside the king's door until the butler returned with a young boy.

"Who is this?"

"Behold the son of the King's eldest daughter, Salampsio. He's the king's favorite grandchild."

The scout looked over the sleepy child as he rubbed his eyes with pudgy fingers. His chubby cheeks made it hard to see his red eyes.

"Because he is so energetic?" the scout said.

"No, because he has no claim to the throne," the steward said. He turned to the child. "Now, I will give you some sweets later if you go wake up the King nicely and play with him for a few minutes."

The child woke up, his eyes brightening at the prospect of food. The steward opened the door and let the boy in. Regina followed him as he dashed through the sitting room into the King's bedchamber.

King Herod still slept. When the boy woke him by leaping onto the bed with his bulky frame, Herod first displayed annoyance, but then softened when he saw the child.

"Cypros? What are you doing up so early my boy?" the King said, tousling the boys hair.

"I wanted to see you papa!" Regina saw the steward had also entered the room.

"I hope you don't mind your highness, he begged to see you and I know your fondness for him."

The cherub softened the king. "No, that's fine. It was a pleasant surprise. Hand me my robe."

The steward handed it over and the king crawled out of bed with some effort. "What do we have on the docket for today, after breakfast of course?" Herod said.

"We have the trial of your brother-in-law and a meeting with the Roman curate, your highness."

The king made no reply. He stretched out his arms and yawned. A knock came at the door.

"Now, who could that be?" the steward said in his best surprised voice. He left the room, leaving the King to play with his grandson. Regina looked at the softness of the King with this child and wondered where his cruelty came from.

The steward returned, looking concerned. "Your highness, a scout has arrived with some very troubling news. Should I tell him to wait for you to fully dress?"

"What is it?"

"I think you should speak directly to him," the steward said. Regina could tell he wanted to avoid the wrath that would soon spew from his master.

"Fine. I will see him now."

The steward left and returned with the scout. The scout did not possess the acting skill of the butler and looked very uncomfortable. He stepped forward and stood with his head down, waiting for the king to call upon him.

"Go on, speak your news."

"Your highness, I came from a patrol of the roads east of Judea. From a distance, I spotted the train of the mysterious visitors from the east. It appears they head back to the lands of their origin," the scout relayed, wincing at the end.

"What?" the King said. "First, my best men fail, and now I am betrayed by these foreigners. That messiah will not take my throne!"

"Maybe it was all a mistake, your highness. Maybe the foreigners didn't find him either and left frustrated," the steward said.

Regina sensed an angelic power attempting to save Herod from the treacherous road he travelled. Light broke through the King's dark heart. This force of goodness made the King look at his grandson to get him to take in the beauty of children and the sanctity of life, but his sins clouded him from the saving hand of God. His heart turned to stone and he replied, "No. He's there and I will get him." He looked away from the child and turned to his servant. His eyes burned with rage.

"Should I send out more scouts to search for the child?"

Silence filled the room and the crushing blackness enveloping Herod brought Regina to tears. She anticipated the horrid words before they even left his lips. "No. The time for pinpointing the child has passed. I want a garrison sent to Bethlehem. Have them kill every boy under the age of two."

The scout and the servant gasped at this command. They trembled in fear of their king and God almighty.

"Surely, your highness…," the servant said.

"Silence! If you can't send out the order, I can find someone who can. And you." He thrust a finger at the scout. "You will join the garrison and carry out my wishes."

The scout thought to protest but did not have the gumption to bring forth his voice.

"And to be safe, I want all of the infant sons of the priests to be killed as well. It wouldn't surprise me if Bethlehem wasn't a ruse to throw me off the real trail."

The two men left the room in shock and Regina moved to the garrison who had gathered, awaiting their orders. The king's best soldiers stood ready and willing. She watched the scout, who the king put in charge of the grisly mission, go to the captain and explain the orders.

"Are you sure?" the captain said.

"Those were his orders."

The Holy Spirit allowed Regina to see the battle for the captain's soul. The forces of good and evil arrayed themselves against each other across the battle ground.

"He knows the inherent evil of this request," his guardian angel said. The angel thrust at the demon.

"He has never been religious," his tempter replied.

"The formation of growing up during a religious time has not been lost on him. He can resign his post."

"Herod would never accept his resignation. He would rather take his head."

At this point, dozens of angels and demons materialized across from each other. This startled Regina.

"What is happening here?"

"When the gravity of a situation reaches this level, the spiritual conflict within one's soul goes beyond one's own angel and tempter. You see before you the guardians and tempters of the soldiers present and the infants at risk. Heaven and hell both know the significance of this moment. Behold its effect."

Regina saw the armies collide in a battle of fists and steel. She knew she pictured the battle in this way, but it didn't mean it wasn't real. The conflict raged on, in one soul, for the souls of many. The captain's guardian and tempter continued to parry.

"He will accept death rather than lead his men to carry out the heinous act," the guardian said. The captain's heart leaned towards good and the angel army seemed to surge.

"You forget about his wife and children. Her pretty face greets him when he returns home and their sweet voices sound like an angel choir to his ears," the tempter said. The option of a noble death blurred away and the demon horde advanced.

Both armies brought heavy artillery onto the battlefield. Bombs and missiles of every type lined up on both sides.

"What is going on now?"

"Regina, the Lord has allowed me to let you see the wages of sin and the fruits of mercy play themselves out in a spiritual battle."

"Wages and fruits?"

"The force of the goodness this man has done will aid his conscience while the effects of his sin will work against him. Watch."

The captain's thoughts turned to how he bathed his own children as infants, washing their heads and kissing their feet. How could he deprive families of their most innocent members? He received the laud of many for his honest service to his country, and his honor and esteem led him to desire being remembered in a good light.

Then the darkness came to bare. The weapons against him numbered fewer, but they were monstrous. Hadn't he massacred entire villages of enemy combatants in his youth? Women and children fell by his sword. He relegated those weeks of bloodthirsty havoc to the deep recesses of his mind. He justified it all by saying he followed orders and had no choice. Couldn't he do the same and return to his warm home? He would put aside this memory while he enjoyed his life, family, and post.

Here, the captain's heart fell. He had orders and he needed to obey them. *A soldier only has honor when he fulfills his duty.* He lost his connection to truth and justice. The angels cried out in anguish and retreated from the victorious darkness. Regina wanted to raise the battle flag again herself but knew she couldn't.

"Men. Today, you will have a chance to prove yourself to your king." The men already at attention stood stiffer still. "We will march to Bethlehem. There we will carry out our orders. Who will answer the call?"

"Hai!" Every soldier answered in unison. The scout rubbed a hand over his white face.

"Who will remain behind and leave our company?"

No one moved or even blinked. Regina received the knowledge that having known the nature of their mission, several of the men would have chosen escape or even death, but now their oath had sealed them in darkness. No one would turn back. Some would not do the dirty work themselves, but no soldier would put themselves between their fellow's sword and an infant on this campaign. They would all share in the guilt.

Regina moved with the company on its march. Their march pounded in her mind like a horrifying drum which would end its beat when the last child lay in his weeping mother's arms.

The soldiers arrived in Bethlehem, and although the images of the soldiers grabbing infants from their wailing mothers flashed quickly through her mind, the force of the horror crushed her heart. Her body wretched with the pain of what she witnessed. This progressed from Bethlehem to the surrounding towns as well. Regina could see the souls of the soldiers blacken during the raid. They quashed the qualms they had about their task quickly and did their duty, leaving a wake of desolation.

The vision waivered and Regina thanked God for relieving her of this torment. She moved to the house of Zechariah and Elizabeth. She stood outside and saw a man approach on a camel. She recognized the same scout who Herod ordered to carry out the horrible assault on Bethlehem.

He alighted from the camel and ran to the door. He banged his fist on the door and waited. A servant came to the door.

"Can I help you?"

"Please, I need to see my uncle Zechariah."

The servant ran to get his master. Zechariah returned with him, moving with urgency. He examined the scout and recognized him.

"What can I do for you, son?"

"Uncle, you must hurry and take your child into hiding."

"Easy, boy, easy. What's happening?"

The scout ran his hand through his hair. Regina could see his guilt tormenting him.

"Herod issued a decree to kill all baby boys in the area of Bethlehem and for all priests with infant boys to come forward for questioning."

"What on earth for? Has he lost his mind?"

"It has to do with some foreigners who came through Jerusalem looking for the messiah. They left in secret and now Herod is on a rampage. Take your family and run. Soldiers could be here any minute."

The news of the messiah warmed the old man's heart. He figured Mary must have given birth by this time. Elizabeth told him his birth should come soon. Would Herod really kill all the infants in a town? Would Herod dare to kill the sons of temple priests? *He killed his own sons.*

"Come in, have some bread and wine," Zechariah offered.

"No, no, I don't deserve your hospitality. I must run as well, for my treason." He started to back away and head for his camel. "Please, go now and don't look back." He jumped on his ride and galloped away from Jerusalem.

Zechariah went back into the house. He thought about the young man's words as he went to find Elizabeth. She played with John in their bedroom. Their eyes met.

"What's wrong?"

"King Herod has lost his mind and means to take John's life. You must take him into the wilderness. Go to the caves where we went for picnics in our youth. Tell only your most trusted servant where you are going. She can bring you supplies as needed. I will face Herod and tell him he will not have John."

"Zechariah, come with us. He will kill you for sure."

"Woman, I do not fear death for the Lord has come to us. Mary has delivered her child." Despite her fear, Elizabeth drew strength from this news. "I am a priest. I will serve Israel until my death. You and John will live on for me. Take him and go."

Elizabeth and Zechariah embraced. He tearfully kissed John. "I spent my whole life waiting to see you. I am sorry I won't get to see the man you will become. Receive my blessing my son and walk in the path of righteousness." He laid his hands on his son and prayed solemnly before he left the room with one final look at Elizabeth.

Regina left the room with him confident Elizabeth and John would escape free of persecution. She traveled with Zechariah to stand before the throne of Herod.

"Where is your child, Zechariah? I have heard about the miraculous circumstances of his birth. Some call him a wonder," Herod said.

Zechariah looked at the haughty king with contempt. "A voice is heard in Ramah, weeping and great mourning, Rachel weeping for her children and refusing to be comforted, because they are no more." (Matthew 2:18)

"Hand over your child or I will have your head." Herod motioned to his guards. They surrounded Zechariah.

"Do you think you can intimidate me like your trained dogs? You sent them to butcher the innocent, but I obey the living God and his commandments. Take my blood; you will never have my son's." Zechariah offered his arms to the guards.

Herod fumed. "Take him away. Make him suffer until he tells us the location of his son."

God granted Regina the knowledge that Zechariah accepted his torture without betraying his family. He remained faithful until the Lord relieved him of his agony. The vision lifted.

Regina found herself holding Frank's hand. He had strength in his grip. "Frank?" he didn't respond. She checked his hand again and it weakened. She hoped for something, but when nothing changed she said goodbye and went back to her brother's room. They prayed together and eventually Regina and Katherine went home. Mark insisted on staying with Emmanuel.

At home, Regina and her mother finished dinner as the phone rang. Normally, Emmanuel would run to get the phone for a parent. He took pride in his job. Regina and Katherine both felt his absence on the second ring. Katherine got up and saw her sister's name on the caller ID.

"Hi Ronnie, how are you?" Regina watched her mother's face lose its color as she listened to her aunt speak.

"I'll be there as soon as I can." She hung up the phone and looked at Regina. "Grandpa took Grandma to the hospital. I need to go." Katherine froze in place. Her mother hadn't been herself with Emmanuel in the hospital, but she looked even more lost now. Several seconds passed. Regina remained silent. "You need to go with me. Daddy will stay with Manny."

They went upstairs and started packing. From her room, Regina heard her mother on the phone.

"Her blood pressure dropped really low and she became unresponsive. Dad called the ambulance and Ronnie met them at the hospital. She says her vitals are all over the place. I'll take Regina with me. It's only a couple of hours so I can bring her back sometime, if I need to." She paused. "Tell Manny I love him." She choked up over the last few words.

They had driven several miles before Regina finally asked the question burning inside her.

"Is Grandma going to die?"

"I hope not, sweetheart. Let's pray while we go." They prayed the Rosary meditating on the Joyful Mysteries. Regina kept up with the prayers, but her meditation never left the Visitation. All of the times they visited her grandparents, her grandmother epitomized health and energy. She flitted about the house tidying up, making food, and keeping her and Emmanuel entertained. She didn't know if she would recognize her grandmother sick in bed.

At the hospital, several people stood in line at the check-in station.

"Andrew Walden. I am here to see my mother, Rose," the man in front said.

"Andrew," Katherine said.

"Katie?" The man turned around. He smiled and hugged Katherine. "I'm so glad you're here."

"Hi, Regina, how are you?"

"Fine, how are you Uncle Andrew?"

"I've been better."

The admitting clerk checked in Katherine as well, gave them visitor tags, and directed them to the critical care waiting room. Regina had grown accustomed to hospital life over the last week. She thought this hospital seemed like hers, only much smaller: fewer floors, less rooms, and less chairs in the waiting room. They found her Aunt Veronica. She flipped through a magazine.

"Ronnie," Katherine said.

"Katie." Veronica could not say anymore before she burst into tears. Katherine held her until she could sit and talk.

"Dad's in there with her now. Kevin's here, too. He went to get coffee," Veronica said.

"How is she?" Andrew said.

"They gave her medicine to regulate her blood pressure and they're running tests. We won't know anything for a while."

Katherine reached in her purse and gave Regina a book to read. She had read it before, but the television had news on and none of the magazines interested her. She put the book down after a few pages and closed her eyes to pray.

In a few minutes, Kevin arrived with coffee. "Hey guys, I'm sorry. I should have gotten you some."

"That's okay," Katherine said. They greeted each other with hugs. After some time, Regina's grandfather, John, came out to see his kids. Usually the jolliest person Regina knew, his spirit seemed crushed. He had been crying.

"Dad," Katherine said. She stepped forward to greet him first.

"It's cancer." The words hung like a thick fog. He pursed his lips and took a deep breath. "They don't have the resources to treat her here." Veronica started crying again. "Katie, he suggested your hospital. Can I stay with you during her treatment?"

"Of course, dad." She hugged him and he wept. "When will it start?"

"They are coordinating with your hospital. Once she's stable, we'll get her over there. Maybe a couple of days," he said. Regina recognized the helpless look on her grandfather's face a lot this week.

"Can we see her?" Kevin said.

His father looked into the distance. "Huh?"

"Can we go see mom?" Kevin asked again.

"Oh, she's sleeping right now. The nurse told me to get some rest while she did. She's gonna get me when mom wakes up. You guys can take turns going in."

They nodded. Regina's grandfather sat in a reclining chair and soon fell asleep. Katherine looked at her family gathered there and her soul stirred. God spoke to Katherine in the silence. He called on her to take the faith that kept her strong all of her life to help her family through this tough time. Regina would help. *Pray with her.* The voice shouted out to her soul. She could not disobey.

"Regina, come sit with me." She came over and sat in her mother's lap. "Regina and I are going to pray for mom. Anyone want to join us?"

Kevin looked disgusted. "Mom prayed all of her life and look where that got her. All that time spent at church didn't save her from getting sick like anyone else. I'm sorry Katie. We've had this conversation before. You can waste your time if you want." He got up and moved to the other side of the room.

"He's just upset about mom," Veronica said.

"I know," Katherine said.

"Katie, you always had mom's faith. I know Ronnie and I don't go to church anymore, but we'll pray with you," Andrew said. Veronica nodded.

"Holy Mary, I offer my mother to your care," Katherine said. She started the Joyful Mysteries. Regina responded, Veronica and Andrew bowed their heads but kept their prayers silent. Kevin shook his head from the other side of the room. John woke up, noticed the prayers, and joined in.

Regina got deeper into her meditation. Suddenly, a new feeling came over her. A vision began to appear but the world around her remained. "Mommy?"

"Yes, Regina." Katherine paused. The others noticed.

Regina whispered, "I can see something in my mind."

"What is it?"

"I see a little girl. She fell off her bike. She skinned her knees and is walking into her house."

Katherine sat up in her chair. She didn't recognize Regina's scene but felt something special happening. "Regina, tell everyone what you told me and be as descriptive as you can."

Regina raised her voice. "I can see a little girl walk into her house crying. Her mother sees the blood on her hands and knees. She drops a vase she is holding. She runs to the girl and hugs her. She says she will be alright. The vase shattered and there is glass everywhere."

Her Uncle Andrew and grandfather showed some curiosity but her Aunt looked like she had seen a ghost. "How did you know that happened, Katherine? Did mom tell you that story?"

"What are you talking about?" Katherine said.

"That was me and mom, exactly how it happened. You guys were in school and I was riding my bike. Mom told me to be careful, but I tried to copy some tricks the boys did the day before and I wiped out. I shocked mom so badly when I walked in, she dropped the vase. I thought she would be mad, but she cleaned me up and held me for much of the morning until I completely forgotten about my pain. How could you know that, Regina?"

"I don't know. I just saw it in my mind," Regina said.

Kevin walked over. "I can't believe you would use your daughter like that Katherine. Is it really necessary?" Before anyone could respond, another vision formed in Regina's mind.

"I see two boys fighting in their yard. They're screaming and punching at each other. A woman comes out and yells at them to stop. She scares them and they both start crying. She makes them sit on the porch and tells them that they are brothers. They don't have to always like each other but they have to love each other. She makes them forgive each other and also promise to try to be the first person to forgive when they get mad."

Kevin and Andrew looked at each other, stunned. Neither one could say anything. "Did that happen to you two?" Katherine said.

Kevin recovered from his shock. "Yes, I suppose mom didn't tell you that either?" He shook his head. Regina didn't pause.

"I see a man walking up to a building. He seems upset. He grabs the handle of the door but is unable to open it. It isn't locked; he can't bring himself to open it. He wants to go in and he wants to go home. He's just standing there. Wait, he banged his head three times really hard on the door frame. Blood is pouring down his forehead. He laughs at the blood and goes back to his car to go home." Regina stopped. "I don't understand, mommy."

The siblings looked at each other in confusion. Finally, they heard the quiet sobs their father made.

"I never told anyone that story, not even your mother." He bent down and parted his hair to show them a very faded scar. "I told mom I hit my head at work. I was still bleeding badly when I got home and she took me to the hospital to get stitches. That woman saved my life twice that day."

"What are you talking about dad?" Veronica said.

"Before we had you kids, your mom and I went through a real rough patch. We didn't have much money and I was a weak fool. I drank heavily and your mother was at her wit's end with me." He looked at Regina. "You saw me in your vision, sweetheart. I wanted to go into a bar to drown my sorrows in liquor again. When I grabbed the door handle, the love of your grandmother stopped me. I swear the devil himself told me to go in, but your grandma's faith kept me out. I finally realized the only thing I could do to make sure I didn't go in there was smash my head against the door. I figured if I knocked myself out, I couldn't drink. The massive head wound had the same effect."

No one spoke. Katherine explained, "I have to tell you all something amazing that has been happening for the last few weeks…" She told them about Regina's visions. She told Maggie and Father Joe's stories as well. When she finished, even Kevin seemed touched. The others had tears in their eyes. Regina felt embarrassed but didn't mind that the truth was out. She could see what Father Joe meant when he said her mission was to simply have the visions.

"We don't know what will come, but we know God has touched our lives. Regina only saw the distant past before, but now she reminded us all much mom touched our lives. We should put aside our own issues and pray for her as a family in the way she would want us to. Together." Katherine looked at Kevin. He nodded and joined them.

They prayed the Rosary together, as one family.

Chapter 33
Far, Far Away

Saturday, January 4th
9:23 AM

Rose didn't wake up on Friday to see her family before visiting hours ended. A doctor came and told them her vitals had stabilized. Everyone went home and planned to come back in the morning.

After breakfast, the family headed back to the hospital and waited while John Walden checked with the nurse about his wife. He came back and sat down by Katherine.

"We can go back in a bit. Can you pray with me again, Katie?"

"Of course, dad," she answered.

Katherine said only a few words before Regina left them.

The Holy Family struggled through the desert for several days. At one point, a wind storm pelted them with dust and debris. Blinded, Joseph and Mary stumbled along until they found shelter behind a large rock formation. After several tortuous hours, the storm passed. Stepping out of their enclosure, they discovered they had lost track of the road leading to Egypt.

Joseph climbed on top of the largest rock to get a better look. He still didn't find the road, nor did he see any other travelers. He climbed back down. "I don't see the way."

You can run from my servant, Herod, but you cannot run from me. The voice sent a chill down Regina's spine. She knew Mary heard the voice as well, but Joseph did not. The vast emptiness of the desert seemed to crash in on them. It frightened Regina but it appeared to embolden Mary.

The pressure swelled. Regina could see a demon army close in. *Without the road, you will be lost in the desert. Without food or water, your child will surely die.*

"My friends, aid us in our need," Mary said. Joseph joined her in prayer. For a moment, the pressure swelled, but then Regina saw an angelic army burst forth. They clashed with the demon hoard, sending them off. The dark haze that had enveloped them lifted and in the distance, a train of camels walked along. Mary and Joseph shared a look of surprise.

"I wonder if they are walking along the main road," Joseph said.

Mary closed her eyes. "They are."

Joseph led them toward the camel train. Nearing the animals, they discovered the road. The moment Joseph stepped onto the road; the camels ran off into the distance and out of sight.

"Give thanks to the Lord, for he is good; for his loving kindness is everlasting," Mary said. (Psalm 136:1)

They continued on the road. Joseph kept looking behind them.

"What worries you, Joseph?"

"My father told me that highwaymen plague these roads. He said to always travel in caravan, especially to foreign lands."

Before long, they spotted three men on camelback in the distance. They galloped closer. The largest of the men jumped from his mount. Regina noticed they wore clothing like desert dwellers of her time.

"You are a long way from home."

"Please. We don't want any trouble," Joseph said.

Ignoring Joseph, one of the other men asked, "What have you got there madam?"

Mary held Jesus closer and glared at the man. Mary's strength had amazed Regina before, but she never saw the Blessed Virgin more determined.

"It is only our child," Joseph said, stepping between them.

"I don't believe you, let me see," the large man said.

Joseph nodded to Mary. She opened the blanket to expose Jesus. She held him out for the robbers to see. Jesus's face shined in splendor before them.

The men froze in place, unable to speak.

"Are you satisfied?" Joseph said. Regina didn't think Joseph saw the wondrous sight.

The head thief came to, shaking his head. "My friends, I swear by the heavens you have revealed a treasure greater than gold to me. You have nothing to fear from us." The others nodded.

This confused Mary and Joseph, but they also felt relief. "You must stay with my family as our honored guests. I live a short distance from here. You look weary and hungry. Please say you will come."

"Please excuse us for a moment." Joseph led Mary a little distance away from the men. "What if they intend to enslave us?"

"They could have taken us already." Mary closed her eyes and listened for the Lord's voice. "The Lord provides us the help we asked for. We should go with him."

Joseph agreed to go with the thief. Regina missed his name but heard his life story as they walked to his home. From outside, Regina could smell food cooking.

The man's wife saw that her husband brought guests and started to protest. The man took her aside and explained the situation to her. His wife looked at Mary and Joseph curiously and didn't argue any further.

"Is there anything I can get you?" she said.

"Could I please have some hot water? I would like to bathe my baby," Mary said.

"I will make you some." The woman walked away and returned with two buckets. One had steam rising from it. She showed Mary a basin she could use.

"Thank you," Mary said. She prepared a bath for Jesus.

Regina looked at the water in the buckets. It didn't look like the crystal clear water she took baths in. *Gross*, she thought in her mind.

"This is what the water these people could find looked like," Gabriel said. "Many people, in your world, use water like this to bathe in, cook with, and even drink."

Regina thought about her complaints of having to drink the metallic tasting well water at her grandparent's house. At least she could see through it. She lamented taking for granted the ease of her life and felt pity for the poor.

"Remember them in your prayers, always," Gabriel said.

Regina vowed to and returned her focus on Mary bathing Jesus. She watched in wonder as the water around him actually got clearer as Mary washed him. Regina looked at Gabriel, who simply smiled. Mary continued to tend to Jesus as the thief walked into the room and looked at the marvel before him. He hurried away, prompting Regina to follow him into the next room.

"Get Dismas, quickly," the thief told his wife.

"I think he's sleeping."

"Wake him and bring him here." The thief returned to Mary and Joseph, who washed their hands and faces in the water which now sparkled.

"My guests, would you permit me to bathe my child with this holy water that your child has blessed?" The man looked at the floor as he spoke. "My son, Dismas, has suffered with leprosy for a long time and we fear he will not live much longer."

As he finished explaining, his wife came in with a little boy, about four years old. Sores and lesions covered his shirtless body. Several bloody bandages barely covered his blackened extremities.

His mother looked at her husband, wondering what he wanted their child for. Waiting by the bath water, he said, "Come here, my son." He held his son for a moment, looking at Mary with hope. He took a handful of water and rubbed his hand along his son's arm. The sores vanished as the water poured over them.

Mary and Joseph shared a look of wonder. The child's mother gasped before running over to join her husband in the bathing. The parents wept as they washed their child clean of his infirmity. When they finished, the family remained in a long embrace. Mary and Joseph left the room to give them privacy.

After a few minutes, the thief rejoined them with his son, now clean of illness. "When I first laid eyes on your child, I knew God walked with you. Now, he has cleansed this house." Again, he dropped his eyes to the floor. "My father was a thief and his father was a thief. It is all my family has known for generations. Please pray my son, Dismas, follows a different path and knows the way of the Lord."

Mary closed her eyes and prayed for the little boy. Moved by the Spirit, she opened her eyes. "I can't promise you what kind of life he will lead, but I know he will be with the Lord in paradise."

The men wept tears of joy and left the room. The rest of the time the Holy Family spent there blurred by. While she watched, Regina said, "Will this boy be a thief?"

"You don't know who he is?"

"No."

"I won't spoil the surprise, you'll see eventually."

Regina gave him a frustrated glance but let the issue go.

They left the home of the thief, stocked with provisions for a long trip and made their way farther into Egypt. They made a home in the land of Egypt, far from Herod's reach.

Regina saw Jesus take his first steps and speak his first words in a foreign land. He cut his first tooth and got his first scrape falling on a rocky path. He had a normal infancy, aside from Mary singing psalms to him morning, noon, and night. They lived simply. Joseph bartered his carpentry skills for food and seeds to plant on the small land they found.

At first, their neighbors looked at them suspiciously, but the humility and holiness of these foreigners disarmed their hostility and they welcomed them into their community. Mary and Joseph both offered their service to the poor and weakest around them and they garnered the love and respect of all.

Everyone loved Jesus. When Mary brought him outside, people would line up to see him and kiss his little feet. His smile would brighten people's days and, little did they know, his presence brought them the best two years of crops the region ever knew.

Regina saw all of this in a very rapid speed. She had yet to see several years play by at once and the sensation made her head throb with pain. When it subsided, she found herself again with Joseph as he slept.

Joseph dreamt of running through the desert. He looked back and saw a serpent chasing him. It gnashed its teeth and spat venom towards him.

You aren't worthy to raise Jesus. He will die because of you. The serpent's taunts stung worse than its venom ever could. Joseph tossed in his sleep. Cold sweat covered his forehead.

Gabriel appeared in the dream and banished the serpent. Joseph's relieved soul prostrated itself before the messenger of God.

"What does my Lord ask of me?"

"Get up, take the child and his mother and go to the land of Israel, for those who were trying to take the child's life are dead." (Matthew 2:20). The dream ended and Joseph awoke. The darkness of the night still encompassed them so he began to pack what he could without disturbing his family.

Despite his best efforts to keep quiet, Mary woke up. "Joseph, what is it?"

"The angel of the Lord appeared to me again and said we may return to our homeland."

"Thank the lord. Our Son will get to grow up in the Promised Land."

The next day, they said tearful goodbyes to the friends they made in Egypt and set out for home.

"Out of Egypt I called my son," Gabriel said. (Hosea 11:1 and Matthew 2:15)

"What?"

"It is a passage from Hosea also mentioned in the Gospel according to Saint Matthew."

"Why did you say it?"

Gabriel smiled. "Have you ever heard Jesus called the new Adam?"

"Yes, and Mary is the new Eve. I remember Father Joe talk about it one Sunday. I couldn't really follow what he talked about, but I know the story of Adam and Eve."

"Good. God created Adam and Eve in his own image, but they fell into sin. Due to their transgression, God punished them to pass their sinfulness onto their descendants. Many generations passed and out of love, God intended to send his Son as the new Adam. This time, Adam would come from the flesh of Eve, in the person of Mary."

"Oh, like Eve came from the rib of Adam?"

"Yes, and Jesus could also be called the new Moses," Gabriel said. "Can you see why?"

"Does it have to do with Egypt?"

"Good thinking, that's part of it."

"I also remember Father called Moses the Chosen One."

"How about the Deliverer?" Gabriel said.

"Oh yeah, I never understood that name." She thought about her lessons from Sunday school.

"Someday I will show you the link between Jesus and Moses in the celebration of the Passover, but not right now. Let's get back to the present." He paused. "I mean the past. Well, you know what I mean."

Regina smiled and they returned their focus to Mary and Joseph's trek. They crossed paths with a caravan headed into Egypt. Joseph stopped a man.

"Excuse me, friend. What news can you tell me from Jerusalem?"

"King Herod has died, his son Archelaus sits on the throne."

"What about Antipater, his first born?"

The man looked queasy. "Herod had him executed for treason."

Joseph and Mary looked at each other in alarm. Joseph thanked the man for the information and they walked on. After some distance,

Joseph said, "We can't return to Bethlehem for what we left behind. The son of Herod may still hold his father's fears."

"Do you think we can go back to Nazareth?"

"Yes, we should stay far from Jerusalem. There, Jesus will be safe."

"She will be perfectly safe during the trip," a voice said. Regina's blurry vision cleared enough so she could watch a doctor explain how they would transfer her grandmother to the hospital by their house. She couldn't follow the medical details, but understood she would sleep at home that night.

After the doctor left, Regina finally got to visit her grandmother. She and Katherine went to her room and found her lying in bed, plugged into several machines. Regina's visits with Frank hadn't prepared her for this sight. Her heart broke to see her grandmother in this state.

Katherine went over to her mother's bedside and held her hand. "Hi mom," she said, barely above a whisper. Regina saw the pained look on her face as she struggled not to cry.

"Katherine," Rose said. Katherine started to cry.

"I love how you say my name, mom."

"Why's that?"

"I don't know, but when I went to college, I had everyone call me Katherine, because it reminded me of being home with you." Katherine barely got through her explanation. Rose smiled. She opened her eyes for the first time and looked at Katherine and then Regina.

"Hi, sweetheart. I hear I am coming to visit you for a change. That's exciting, huh?" Regina knew her grandmother wanted to be strong for her. She appreciated it but didn't know how to answer.

"Come here darling, grandma can still give hugs." She held her arms out and Regina filled them. To Regina, her hug felt as wonderful as always. "Regina, can you find your way back to the waiting room? I want to talk to your mommy for a little bit."

"Sure." She walked out and left the two women alone.

When Regina left, Rose turned to her daughter. "Katherine, please sit down."

Katherine pulled up a chair to the bed. She could tell by the look on her mother's face she had something important to say.

"I want to be cremated when I die," she started.

"Stop talking like that, you can beat this," Katherine said. Her mother had never failed to step up to a challenge in her life.

"Whenever the end comes then, that is what I want."

"Why?"

"I don't want people to see me all wasted and worn away."

"You look fine, mother," Katherine said.

"Stop it Katherine. You know I could always tell when you were fibbing." She smiled, forcing Katherine to as well.

"Sorry mom, is that all?"

Rose paused. "I want you to get me a Do Not Resuscitate order I can sign."

"What? Why me?"

"Because my sickness has already taken its toll on your father, and I don't have the energy to fight him on this. When the Lord calls me home, I want to go to him. I don't want to be held in this world. Promise me you will do this."

Katherine pictured her family's response to this and hesitated. Her mother counted on her to be strong despite her fears. "I promise."

"Finally, I want you to take care of your father, your brothers and sister. I prayed they would all know the Lord and love him like I did, but their hearts have not been ready. I want you to continue praying for them and make sure you all continue to get together on holidays and for reunions when I'm gone."

"I'm sure we will mom, I don't think you need..." Katherine started.

"No, *you* have to hold them together, Katherine. I know it happens all the time. When their parents die, siblings drift apart because their lives get in the way. You need to keep the family together and never stop praying for them. I won't ask for anything else."

Rose's rare outpouring of emotion humbled Katherine. "Of course, mom, I promise."

"I always told you to listen for God's voice and follow his will. Now, I hear him, but fear has me in its grip. Pray for me, too."

Katherine began to tear up and hugged her mother. She felt like a little girl again. Together, they wept.

Christina Wilde sat on the guest bed in her mother's house. She stared at her neatly folded clothes lying next to her. She looked in the mirror at her matted hair. She tried to find the will to replace the pajamas she had been wearing for several days when her mother appeared at the door.

"Sweetheart, you have to move past this. You didn't do anything wrong. I told you that place was no good."

"I know you did, mom. I just feel so helpless. I can't pay my rent, afford my car, or pay any other bills."

"You'll find another job, and until then, you can move in here with me and I'll take care of you."

"You barely can make your own payments. I promised myself in college I would get a good job and take care of you. Now you have to keep taking care of me." Christina started to cry.

Her mother sat down next to her on the bed and held her.

"Can I make you some tea?"

"Thanks, mom."

Christina forced herself to get up and put on her clothes. She went to the bathroom to brush her teeth and hair. Her mother knocked on the door as she finished.

"Your friend Matty's here. Can you talk to him?"

"Matty? Tell him to hold on a second." She made herself somewhat presentable and headed out. She found Mateo Luchesi standing by the front door.

"Christina, I had to see you. Can we talk?"

"How did you find me?"

"It's a long story. Maybe we can step outside?" He nudged his head towards the door.

"Mom, it's okay. I feel better already," Christina said to her mother, who seemed to approve.

They stepped onto the front porch. Matty had a wild look in his eyes.

"Sorry about barging in like this, but you weren't answering your phone."

"It's probably dead. I haven't felt like talking to anyone since I got fired."

"Yeah, I heard. Can you tell me exactly what happened?"

Christina pictured back to what happened on the previous Thursday.

"I was doing my usual lab work. I put the reagents in the vials and set the timer like normal. I read a few pages of my novel when the timer went off. When I looked down, I dropped my novel. I couldn't believe what I saw."

"What was it?" Matty said.

"All five of the vials glowed in a goldish color."

"What?"

"Seriously, they were glowing. After months of seeing clear tubes, I knew something had happened."

"Wow. Then what?"

"I didn't remember what to do. I only remembered that we had a protocol to follow if a reaction occurred. I opened my drawer where my pad of paper with the instructions they gave me on my first day were. I wrote everything down after the first few weeks when nothing ever happened."

"I did that too," Matty said.

Christina smiled. "My heart was racing. After logging the result, the final step was to call this number. I told the person that answered that I had a positive result. A cold voice told me that someone would be with me shortly. After a few minutes, a team of technicians arrived. They had carts of storage equipment. One of them said, 'Congratulations on your success. As a reward, you can take the rest of the day off.'"

Christina stopped and tears filled her eyes. She wiped them away. "I went home. I was so excited to have gotten a positive result and the day off, I didn't even think to ask why they were packing up everything from my lab station."

"Then what happened?"

"I drove to my apartment, thinking about what I would do with the rest of my day. I planned on going for a jog. By the time I changed into workout clothes and had a small snack, the doorbell rang." She looked at Matty. "A man gave me a big envelope with the few personal effects I had at my station and a small envelope with a month's pay and a letter of termination. They attached a legal notice explaining how I would be sued if I ever disclosed anything about that job or the company."

"Unbelievable." Matty shook his head.

"I went straight to my mom's house and cried for the rest of the day and most of yesterday, too. I have felt like a complete loser, getting fired from my first job."

"You are not a loser. Something isn't right here and we need to do something about it."

"You heard me, Matty. They told me they would sue, remember?"

"For what? You don't have anything." She nodded in agreement. "When you didn't show for lunch, I texted you. When you didn't answer, I thought I would say hi in person, but your lab space was cleared out. I asked the security guard about you, and he said you had resigned. When you didn't answer my calls, I knew that was a lie."

"I'm sorry about that," Christina said.

"It's cool, I understand. I've been depressed, it's not fun. Anyway, I figured they had fired you, so yesterday I got nosy."

"Oh Matty, what did you do? I don't want you to get fired."

"Without you, I have no reason to work there." Realizing what he said, Matty blushed and looked down.

Christina smiled. "Thanks, Matty."

He recovered. "Anyway, I probably broke some rules and laws, but I got this." He held up a computer printout.

"What is it?"

"It's the shipping manifest detailing where all of the vials of blood you worked on this week came from."

"Oh my goodness. Where did the positive test vial come from?"

"Illinois. The manifest only has the name of the hospital, a patient number, and the department where the blood came from. Which is rather interesting."

"Why?" Christina couldn't hide her curiosity.

"The blood came from the patient in neonatal."

"A newborn?"

"Yeah. We need to go to Illinois."

"What?"

"Right now. Let's go. Don't you want to know what got you fired? What do you have to lose?"

Christina thought about it.

"I can't do it, Matty. I lost my job; I can't go afford to fly to Chicago right now."

"Let's do a road trip. With short breaks, if we drive through, we'll get there Sunday. I'll pay for gas and we can make a ton of sandwiches. I have a cousin we can stay with in Milwaukee. What do you say?"

"My mother won't like it, but if I explain that it might hurt the company, she probably won't mind."

"Well?" Matty asked with hope.

"I haven't felt this excited in six months. Let's do it." She laughed and hugged Matty. He had a huge smile on his face.

Christina went inside and explained the story to her mother who surprisingly backed their decision. She began to make up a huge travel basket full of food for their trip. While Matty helped her mother in the kitchen, Christina took a shower and packed. Soon, they hit the road.

Chapter 34
Reconciliation

Saturday, January 4th
6:49 PM

"Hi Katherine, it's Maggie. I am a little annoyed that you cleaned my house for me, because now I have nothing to do. Seriously though, I really appreciate all of your help. I know you are busy with your mom. Call me if you need to talk. Thanks again."

Maggie put down her phone. She cleared the kitchen table and looked around the immaculate house. With nothing to do, her tempter did not waste any time.

You are all alone. Maggie realized she hadn't stayed in this house without Vita inside her. The demon took the empty feeling and led her to consider the hole Paul left in her heart. Maggie didn't know her and Paul's tempters had concocted an evil plan to confuse their souls. She also did not know Paul stood outside her house.

Paul stood with his finger on the doorbell, unable to push it. Both his guardian angel and his demon urged him to go and see Maggie, but for very different reasons.

Apologize to her and beg for forgiveness. Accept your child and love her. Pray for her life so she may endure these difficult times. Deep within, Paul's heart moved to consider the possibility of fatherhood. Could he be a father, unlike the one who abandoned him?

No. The child stands between you and Maggie. Remember the offer. Get her to agree and they said they will do the rest. You will have enough money to have a life together. Together!

Paul wrestled with his thoughts, finally giving way to the darkness. *Together!* He believed he could make her see things his way. He pushed the button and waited for her to answer.

Maggie opened the door. Her eyes lit up. "Paul!" She took a deep breath and forced the smile from her face. "Would you like to come in?"

He had the same reaction in his heart when their eyes met. He longed to embrace her, but the awkwardness between them acted like a steel curtain. "Yes, please," Paul said as he followed her into the living room. "How have you been?" Immediately, he closed his eyes and shook his head.

"Oh, pregnant and alone, and then in the hospital alone."

He is making an effort, offer him your forgiveness. Maggie looked at Paul's reaction. He stared at the ground, a frown on his face.

"I'm sorry, Paul. It's been hard, you know?"

"I'm sorry, too, Maggie. I should never have made you leave. I was scared."

"I was scared, too. I still am a little, mostly for Vita."

Once the baby is gone, the two of you can be together.

"I saw her in the hospital," Paul said.

"You did? When?"

"Yesterday. I saw her lying there in the incubator and could only guess how much pain she must be in."

"I know, but she's a fighter, Paul. She's strong and has so much life within her."

"How can you say that, Maggie? She's suffering. She's tied to a bunch of machines. She might be for a long time, maybe forever. What kind of life is that? Have you even held her?"

"No. Why? What are you trying to say?"

Their angels and demons struggled in battle. Paul's words about Vita's life support struck Maggie's heart. She choked back tears when she envisioned her poor little body overshadowed by tubes keeping her alive. *How can you be so selfish to keep her alive? Death would relieve her of this torment.* Her tempter tried to twist her mind into Paul's plot.

"Maggie, a man came to me and said if you take the baby off life support, he would give us one hundred thousand dollars." He hadn't planned on bringing the offer up so soon in the conversation. It sounded ludicrous now that he said it.

Through tremendous effort, her demon allowed the allure of money to briefly touch her mind, but her guardian angel took her motherly love and used it to crush the evil attempt. "What? You want me to kill my baby for money?"

"Maggie, she may not even make it. We can save her from a life of suffering and help a rich man's baby. He can give us our one chance at happiness together." Paul knew by Maggie's expression he had lost his case. The tempters did as well. They decided that they could at least extract some wrath from the situation.

"I don't want his blood money!" She looked at Paul's regretful eyes and softened for a moment, but anger overcame her again. "Get out! You make me sick!"

"Maggie, please. I need you."

"No, Paul. Vita needs me. She needs a father, too, but you don't want to be that man. We have both made so many mistakes in life, but she isn't one of them." She moved to the door in swift steps and opened it, exposing the dark night.

Paul looked at Maggie one last time. She looked away. He walked out without a word and headed to his car. Driving away, Paul realized he wanted to tell Maggie he loved her. He slammed on the brakes and pounded on the steering wheel.

Mr. Smith saw Paul's angry display through binoculars. He had pulled over several hundred feet behind him. He pulled out his phone.

"It's me. She didn't bite." Smith listened as Paul pulled away again. "I understand. I'll take care of it." He started to follow Paul again.

"Poor fool. Now, we will need to do things the hard way."

Maggie sat on her couch with tears running down her face. The devastating spiritual battle ended, leaving her in pieces. She longed to hold Vita and Paul. Loneliness crept into her again. She grabbed her phone. "Katherine, please answer."

"Hello?" Regina watched her mother answer her cell phone. They sat in the waiting room, which had become all too familiar to her over the past week. "Hi Maggie, Regina and I are at Good Shepherd right now. Can I come and get you? We are going to be here for a while. You can visit Vita." She listened to the response for a few moments and said, "Okay, I'll be there in a few minutes." She hung up the phone.

"Is she all right?" Regina said. She saw concern on her mother's face.

"Yes. She's just lonely. I'll go get her and come right back. Can you wait here with Aunt Veronica?" Katherine looked at Veronica to confirm. Veronica nodded, as did Regina.

Katherine's brothers both returned to their homes for the evening but her sister remained at their father's side. She and Regina sat there quietly for a while after Katherine left.

"Never fight with your mom, Regina."

"What?"

"Never fight with your mom, and if you do, you will probably be wrong, so make sure you apologize as soon as possible."

"Okay?" Regina looked confused. *Did mommy tell Aunt Veronica that we fight?*

"I'm sorry. I guess I'm trying to save you from the pain I have, from causing my mother a lot of grief when I was younger. I was a terror in high school and college. I caused your grandmother to lose many nights of sleep."

"What did you do?"

"I can't tell you that. Let's just say I wasn't a good girl, and my mother loved me too much to let me continue to hurt myself with my bad behavior."

Regina thought about her battles with her mother and realized she usually caused their issues.

"I have never apologized to grandma for my behavior. When I finally grew up and stopped acting like a brat, she treated me like an adult and never brought up my past against me. I feel bad about it, I guess."

"Why don't you apologize to her now?"

"It's not that easy."

"Why not?"

Veronica looked at Regina defiantly. "You don't understand, you're just…" She hesitated. "You're right, Regina." She laughed to herself. "You know, you're something else. As your Godmother, I am supposed to be teaching you about life, but you have taught me so much in the last two days. Thanks." She hugged Regina. Regina's grandfather walked into the room.

"Hey kiddo," he said to Regina. "Your grandmother wants to see you." He patted her on the head and gave her the best smile he could muster. She followed him back to her room. Her grandfather left before she walked in.

When Regina entered her grandmother's room, she noticed the distinct fragrance of roses. She looked around and didn't see any flowers in the room.

"Come closer, Regina," Rose said. She approached the bed and her grandmother took her hand. "Regina, when your mother was a little girl, I prayed God would call her to become a nun. As the years went by, I knew it wasn't his plan for her. So, I changed my prayer. I asked Jesus to give her a daughter as lovely and wonderful as she was to me." Rose smiled at Regina. "That prayer came true."

Regina blushed.

"Regina, something happened to me that I know you will be happy to hear about." Regina listened. "When I got here, before your grandfather arrived, a boy came to my room. He said his name was Frank."

Was Frank out of his coma? Why would he visit my grandmother? Many other questions raced through her head. Regina couldn't hide her amazement. Noticing this, Rose smiled and continued, "He told me about Manny and the baby of your friend. He told me Raphael, the archangel, would come and heal me if I wanted him to."

Regina's face brightened, but her grandmother's look remained serious. Rose paused for a moment. "I have prayed that Jesus would allow me to serve him in a special way." She waited to let Regina think about her prayer. "Frank said I had another choice. He explained the Job Rule to me and told me how Manny offered himself for you and the baby." Again, she took a break. She took deep breaths to build her strength. "Manny is going to be fine now. Don't worry, I took care of it." She closed her eyes and rested.

"What do you mean, grandma? I don't understand."

Rose's eyes remained closed. "The Lord heard my prayer and asked me to take the suffering from the Job Rule. I chose not to be healed, but to heal others instead. Regina, pray I will stay strong."

Regina realized what her grandmother meant and began to cry. "But what if you die? I want you to get better."

"Everybody dies, Regina, but I will be helping your brother and that little baby live. I want this Regina. I am scared, but the Lord is calling me and I want to serve him. I know you can understand, and I need you to be strong for your mother and our family."

Regina had nothing more to say. The smile on her grandmother's face said it all. The Joy of the Lord shined through her.

"Regina, I am so proud of you. We will still be together for a while. I will allow the doctors to treat me so I can offer up my suffering for as long as possible, but, in the end, the Lord will take me. Frank told me about your mission from God as well. If we do our parts for the Body of Christ, the will of God can proceed, and many will be brought to healing and faith. Don't cry for me, darling."

Regina realized she was crying profusely. She wept for her grandmother, Frank, Manny, and Vita. She wiped away her tears. They embraced for a long time.

"Has your mother ever told you the story of Saint Bernadette and Our Lady of Lourdes?"

Regina laughed. "We just talked about it the other day."

"When your mother was a little girl, I told her about Bernadette Souberou many times. I loved to talk about Bernadette's honesty and obedience to her parents, her trust in God, her humility in the convent, her service to the sick, and her joy through her suffering. Your mother and I talked about the lessons of Lourdes for hours…" She trailed off, a distant look in her eyes. "You know how Our Lady gave Bernadette a miraculous spring with healing waters to show everyone the visions were authentic?"

"Yes, I remember that part of the movie. Lots of people saw it."

"She is going to give a similar sign to show that your message is from God." Rose snuggled into her sheets and closed her eyes.

"What kind of sign? What message?" Regina realized her grandmother had dozed off and could not hear her questions. She wondered what all of this meant. *Pray,* she heard Lucy say, and she planned to, right after she saw Frank.

Chapter 35
Homecoming

Regina found Mrs. Roland sitting by Frank's bed when she walked into the room. Her sad face brightened when she saw Regina.

"Regina, I was about to go home for the night. I'm glad you came. How are you?" Louise said.

"Good, how's Frank?"

"There's no change. He's still in a coma."

"What?" Regina clearly showed her confusion.

"He might be like this for a while. What's the matter, sweetie?"

"Nothing." Regina felt bad about lying, but she didn't know what she would tell Mrs. Roland anyway.

"Is your mom here?"

Regina realized Mrs. Roland didn't know anything about her family's health issues since they hadn't seen each other in days. She explained all of the dramatic events surrounding Emmanuel, her grandmother, and even baby Vita.

"I need to see your mother. Your support has meant a lot to me. I want to see what I can do for your family. I'm glad you are here for Frank. Bye, Regina."

"Bye," Regina said. Mrs. Roland kissed Frank's forehead and left.

Regina waited for Mrs. Roland to leave her sight. Then, she leaned in close to Frank. "Frank, can you hear me?" She didn't really expect a response, but she couldn't really be sure what would happen.

"My grandmother says you visited her. I don't understand how, but if you did, thank you. There's so much going on right now. It seems you are the only person who I could talk to, even though you are still in a coma."

The silence didn't offer Regina any answers or comfort. She prayed for his healing. Inside this prayer, she saw the walls began to waver.

Regina saw the Holy Family arrive at Nazareth early in the evening. They immediately went to the house of Rachel and Malachi. Joseph knocked on the door. Malachi opened it. "Joseph! Mary! Thank God you are alive. We heard no news of you after you left for the census. We didn't know what to think. Rachel, come here."

Rachel came to the door carrying a young infant. Both couples expressed their joy for each other's children. Jesus watched the reunion silently. Regina noticed Jesus did not reveal his divinity to Rachel and Malachi.

"Why does Jesus reveal his true nature to some people but not others? These are his family members, aren't they?"

"The Father's appointed time for Jesus's public ministry has not arrived. He allows Jesus to touch individuals privately, but the news of his wonders doesn't get out. You saw the healing of the girl at the well, the saving of John the Baptist, and cleansing of the leprous child. No one heard of these miracles. The people Jesus sees daily during his childhood will consider him to be completely normal. Of course, he will be righteous in all his ways, but little about his youth will be recorded in history. When he enters into his ministry, the people of this land will ask, 'Isn't this the carpenter's son? Isn't his mother's name, Mary?'" (Matthew 13:55)

Regina felt good. She genuinely understood something for once. The Father wanted his Son to experience a normal human life, but he also wanted to touch some people through his presence.

Mary and Joseph returned to their home after dinner. Rachel and Malachi did a decent job of keeping their home in shape during their flight to Egypt, but it needed work. They fixed the place up and settled into their lives in Nazareth. After that, the vision transferred to a point in the future.

Regina figured a couple of years had passed, judging by the growth of Our Lord. He played while his parents talked.

"Let's leave early for the Passover Festival. I would like to go to the hill country and visit Elizabeth. We've heard nothing from her and I'm worried," Mary said.

"That's fine," Joseph said. "I will finish up my contracts and not take any new ones until we return."

Mary and Joseph finished preparing to make the trip to Jerusalem for their annual pilgrimage. Regina traveled with them on the long journey and shared their dismay at finding someone else living in Elizabeth's house.

"Please tell us what you know about the old masters of this household," Joseph said to the servant who answered the door.

"I know the old priest was executed by Herod several years ago when he refused to turn over his son."

Mary and Joseph shared a sorrowful look. "And his wife and son?" Regina could tell he hoped for better news.

"I don't know about them. They haven't been seen here for years."

Mary took Joseph's arm. She couldn't hide her sadness. The servant saw this. "But one of their servants still comes by here for work. She can be found in a small house down the hill to the east." He smiled, hoping they could use the information.

"Thank you," Joseph said. He led Mary and Jesus down the hill to the small house located there and knocked on the front door.

A woman answered, recognized Mary, and squealed with delight. Seeing Jesus, she fell to her knees. "Blessed be the name of God forever and ever." (Daniel 2:20) Jesus walked to her and she embraced him. She wept with him in her arms before she turned to Mary. "My mistress told me you would come one day and I was to take you to her. She said your child was the Chosen One of Israel and only for you should I ever expose their hiding place."

"We are ready to see my cousin."

The servant got off her knees and prepared a bag of provisions to take into the wilderness where Elizabeth and John hid. The trip took several hours. When they neared the cave of seclusion, John spotted them from afar.

He turned around and ran to his mother. Regina sped across the plain with Gabriel to follow John back to Elizabeth. She reclined on a bed of soft grass. "He's coming, mommy. Prepare yourself, the Lord is coming."

Regina thought Elizabeth looked like her grandmother in the hospital. She didn't look like she had much longer to live. John's news lifted her spirit and gave her energy. She managed to get out of bed, put on a robe, and a mantle to cover her head. She walked out to the entrance of the cave in time to see Mary bringing the Savior to her. She wept soft tears of joy while she waited to hold him.

When Mary got close enough to Elizabeth, she put Jesus down. He ran into the waiting arms of his aunt who held him tenderly, continuing her weeping. Regina saw her praying but couldn't make out her words.

When Elizabeth released Jesus, Mary approached and embraced her.

Regina moved in closer and heard Elizabeth say with a wink, "But why am I so favored, that the mother of my Lord should come to me?" (Luke 1:43)

"Cousin, won't you return with us? I will take care of you. King Herod has died, you can live your last days in peace," Mary begged Elizabeth.

Elizabeth replied, "I live my days in peace with John. When I heard about the death of the King, I was prepared to return, but John would not go. He loves living out here and I have everything I need in him."

"What do you eat?" Mary said.

"John gathers fruit for me. He insists on eating locusts and honey. We are happy here, Mary. The Joy of the Lord is our strength."

Mary smiled. Several hours into the reunion, Regina watched Jesus and John walk into the distance.

"Let them go Regina. Mystically, Jesus will share his mission with his cousin. Neither child's young mind will understanding what is happening, but their souls will share the knowledge of God's vocation for each of them. Years from now, when God calls out to John, his soul will remember this moment. He will know to leave the wilderness and begin his work. Jesus will know his day has come when John makes his appearance. Until then, they will not see each other again."

John knelt. Jesus blessed him and then had his cousin stand up so they could embrace. The adults did not see this behavior, but it touched Regina. After this, the scene advanced rapidly. The Holy Family tearfully said their goodbyes. Regina received the knowledge that Elizabeth passed away peacefully soon after. When she died, Mary learned of it from God, and prayed for some of her guardian angels to go and tend to little John while he grew up in the hills by himself. Regina felt comforted that John had heavenly company out in the wilderness.

Regina got to see the Holy Family enter Jerusalem before the vision dissolved and she returned to her own time.

"G, I thought you might have come here," Mark said. He hadn't seen her in her trance. He looked at the broken body of Frank. "Poor kid."

"I thought I would stop by and spend some time with him."

"That's very thoughtful of you. Are you finished? The doctor said we can take Manny home. All of his tests came back negative and he seems completely normal."

Regina smiled. She knew her grandmother's words had come true. She believed God would take care of Emmanuel and Vita's health now.

"Yes, let's take Manny home."

Regina went home with her father and an ecstatic Emmanuel. They left her mother behind to stay with her family and Maggie. Katherine waited with her sister while a doctor gave Maggie an update. As the doctor spoke, tears started to fall from Maggie's face. The second he left, Katherine approached her friend.

"Oh no, what did he say?" Katherine said.

"No, no it's good news. I'm so happy."

"What did he say?"

"He said they did a complete set of tests on Vita and she is completely free of all of the complications that threatened her life. They can't explain it. It's a miracle." Maggie started to cry again.

Katherine smiled and hugged her.

"Well, what does that mean? How long will she still be here?"

"She was still really premature, but she won't be attached to all those machines and stuck in isolation. I'll get to hold her soon."

"That's wonderful, Maggie. Come on. Let's see if we can tell her goodnight."

Paul slammed the door behind him as he entered the house. He took off his coat and threw it across the room. The chaotic mess around him matched his mental state. He had gone straight from Maggie's place to the bar by his apartment. The drinks he pounded back did not help him erase the memory of his failure from his mind. Instead, he became increasingly agitated as he thought about how terribly he screwed everything up, again.

He stumbled to the cabinet and opened the door. Finding it empty, he took a dirty glass out of the pile in the sink and opened his liquor cabinet.

"Damn it." He forgot he had finished his last bottle of whisky the night before. He whipped the glass against the wall. The knock at the door stunned him from his frenzy.

Paul looked out the window to see the stoic face of Mr. Smith. It frightened him a little.

"Mr. Smith? What…"

"Mr. McCorvey, I take it your attempts at persuasion were unfruitful?"

"You already know the answer to that question, don't you, Sherlock?" Paul eyed Mr. Smith. He wanted to fight the man, hoping Mr. Smith would pummel him. He deserved that.

"I surmised the meeting did not go well by your reaction. I have to tell you that my employer's need has reached a critical level. He will now pay you one million dollars."

Paul's mind shifted from fighting this shady character to the staggering number he quoted.

"One million dollars?" It didn't sound like his voice asking the question. He felt like he observed the scene as an outsider. "Maggie won't take any amount of money."

"My employer realizes that. You will need to take care of this yourself."

"What do you mean?"

"Get the child out of the hospital and take it to this address." Mr. Smith handed Paul a scrap of paper. The address had been typed out.

"Mr. McCorvey, my boss will not be happy if you don't come through. Trust me when I say, you do not want to make him unhappy."

Mr. Smith left. Paul's tempter used Paul's fear, intoxication, and depression to erase Vita's humanity from his mind. Greed and self-preservation helped him begin to form a dark plan. His tempter weaved the images before him. *One million dollars.*

Chapter 36
The Holy City

Sunday, January 5th
10:21 AM
The Solemnity of the Epiphany

Father Joe Logan stood before the congregation, ready to preach his homily. He saw eagerness in his parishioners he hadn't seen before Regina's visions began. Despite his early hopes of a rapid transformation in his people, the priest knew the zeal in their souls hadn't caught up with the interest on their faces. He knew something had to change. He had to do more.

"Today we celebrate the Solemnity of the Epiphany of Our Lord. Epiphany means manifestation. This is the day we remember that God revealed his Son to the world. In the western church, we meditate on the coming of the magi, who represent the non-Jewish world. They show us that Jesus was not only born to save Israel but the whole world. From even earlier in history, the eastern churches recalled the Baptism of the Lord in the Jordan, where the Father announces from the heavens that Jesus is his beloved Son, with whom he is well pleased." (Matthew 3:17)

Having seen the wise men with the Christ child, Regina thoroughly enjoyed this homily. She knew what seeing Jesus meant to Balthazar, Caspar, and Melchior. Her memory of that particular vision brought great joy to her heart.

"In both situations the world faced a decision. God made himself available to us, in the flesh. What would humanity do in response?" The priest shot a quick glance at Regina and continued.

"The wise men brought the Christ child gifts of gold, incense, and myrrh. All symbols of what mankind can produce using God's gifts and of whom Jesus would be. In gratitude, when his time came, the Lord sent out his apostles to all nations to make disciples of them, and an entire world saw conversion to a faith in the Son of God."

"In the Jordan, the Holy Spirit descended onto Our Lord like a dove, marking him with Divine Right. Many people witnessed this amazing prodigy and followed him, but then some scattered when times got tough."

"So who are you then? Are you like the wise men? Will you bring your gifts to the Lord and then carry his love in your heart? Are you like the apostles who Jesus called, soon after his Baptism, to build the early church? Or, are you like his followers, who he touched by his words, but couldn't stand behind Our Lord when the test became too difficult?"

"Friends, the truth is, the time has come where you can't be another body in the pew. God manifests himself in our presence and we can't pretend like it isn't happening. We can't sit idly by and hope someone else will answer his call and do his work."

The priest could not see the state of each soul before him, but angels and demons clashed in an epic struggle. Many of these tempters had accepted that they couldn't stop their humans from going to church on Sunday. No temptation could dissuade them from going to Mass, but the demons convinced them that simply fulfilling their Sunday obligation made them friends of God. Some of their humans wouldn't sing or even join in the common prayers. When they left the building, they would forget about the Lord and the mission of the church until the following Sunday. The priest's words sounded like a horn in the battle and an angel cavalry began to stir the hearts of the people.

"When Jesus entered Jerusalem on Palm Sunday..." Father Joe began to explain something about the temporary joy of the crowd who would soon abandon Our Lord, but Regina did not get to hear the rest of his homily as she departed from her time.

Regina marveled at the festivities occurring around her. Before Passover, the city of Jerusalem pulsed with excitement and captivated Regina, who consumed the spectacle with her eyes. Vendors and craftsman jammed the streets to market to the throngs of pilgrims flocking to visit the temple in the Holy City.

"What is going on here?" Regina said.

"This is the City of David rejoicing over Israel's escape from Pharaoh's bondage," Gabriel said.

"What?"

"Sorry, Jerusalem's Passover celebration always looked like this back in the time of Jesus. Pilgrims come here from all over Judea and the surrounding lands."

"It's like a carnival."

"Most of these pilgrims work hard all year. They come here to indulge themselves a little. Others come to somberly remember how the people of Abraham spent 400 years in slavery before Moses delivered them."

"It's Mary," Regina said. The Blessed Virgin came out of the crowd, followed by Joseph and a boy. He had a handsome smile and a wiry frame. He clearly enjoyed the festival occurring around him. "Is that...?"

"Yes, he is twelve years old, Regina, like you."

The vision of the Lord at her age stirred Regina's soul. She couldn't take her eyes off him. His face brightened even more.

"James!" Jesus ran to another boy who appeared to be about his height. They hugged and laughed, enjoying their reunion. "Mother, can we go explore the city?"

Mary smiled. "Okay, but make sure you come back to your Aunt Salome's house for dinner on time. Don't be late!" As she said this, Salome, her cousin, approached with a little boy in tow.

"That's right, James, don't get your cousin into any of your usual trouble." Salome and Mary hugged.

"Don't worry, mom, he won't let me," James said.

The little boy tugged on his mother's cloak. "I wanna go, too." Regina smiled at the adorable way he said this.

"No way, you'll slow us down," James said. The little boy frowned and tears filled his eyes.

"Hey," Jesus said. "I can't leave my favorite cousin behind. Come on John, you can ride on my shoulders. You won't slow us down."

A huge smile broke out on John's face, and he looked up at his mother. She gave him a nod to go ahead. James shrugged his shoulders, accepting the little companion. John ran to Jesus, who hugged him and then lifted him onto his shoulders so they could explore the city.

Mary watched them go and then turned to Salome. "It is so good to see you. I am sorry we missed seeing you for the last few years." She looked at Joseph, who talked to tool vendors, and then to the ground.

"Yes, how is Joseph these days? Better, I hope?"

"He has been strong of late. It's hard to tell because he never complains about his pains. He continues to work and help everyone that asks, but his body is weakening. Jesus does so much to help him. He never gets to play with his friends. He prefers to help Joseph with his work."

Salome nodded. "I am sure he is proud of Jesus, as Zebedee is of James. He has become quite a fisherman. But come, have something to eat." They told Joseph to come to Salome's house to rest when he finished his business.

"They will stay with Salome during their Passover pilgrimage. This is a tradition for their family and an honor for Zebedee and Salome," Gabriel said.

Gabriel took Regina to follow the boys as they wandered the streets, playing and telling each other stories they hadn't shared before.

"Won't their parents worry about them?"

"Life was different back in Jesus' time. James lives here and Jesus has come to Jerusalem many times. They know the streets very well.

Adults would take care of them if they got in trouble and Jesus will ensure they won't cause problems. Watch," Gabriel said.

"What do you want to do, James?" Jesus said.

"Let's play follow the leader, you can be the leader."

"Why do you always want me to be the leader? Why don't you be leader for once?" Jesus said.

James smiled. "I like it that way, brother."

"Well, let's go the temple."

"Okay."

Jesus led the way with John still on his shoulders. They headed out, away from the lower part of Jerusalem, up toward the temple mount. Regina wondered if she would think of going to church as one of the first things that came to her mind when she could freely play.

"These are not two ordinary boys, Regina." Gabriel said.

Regina accepted this, but realized they still had a lot of boy in them because of the way they skipped around, climbed on things, jumped off others, and kicked rocks as they made their way towards their destination.

When they arrived at the temple, a large crowd had gathered near the entrance. Regina could hear shouting and crying. As Jesus approached, the crowd parted and they easily walked through to the middle. Regina followed. She saw that a wooden construction scaffold had collapsed, trapping a man under a large beam. A young boy, about the same age as Jesus and James, cleared away smaller bits of debris, but couldn't lift the massive wooden bar. No one in the crowd stepped forward.

"Why won't anyone help that boy?" Regina said.

"He is a foreigner. It was considered unclean for a Jew to touch a non-Jew, especially during Passover."

"Please, someone help my father. He's dying," the boy said. Jesus put John down and walked forward inside the invisible circle the crowd had created. Everyone gasped. James and John followed him. Jesus looked with compassion at the fallen man, pinned by the large plank of wood. Regina guessed it weighed hundreds of pounds.

Jesus turned to face the crowd, which eagerly awaited his next moves. Jesus fixed his gaze on a man dressed in religious garb. "Would I be unclean if I touched this man?"

"Yes, he is not a Jew."

"Would it be unclean to touch this wood?"

"No, it is only a piece of wood, you may touch it. But it is too heavy to lift and you risk touching the foreigner or his child. Besides, he is a dead man anyway, look how the beam has crushed him."

Jesus scowled at the crowd. He turned to the boy. His face, streaked with tears, moved Jesus with pity. He had cried for Joseph's pains many times. He wheeled back to the religious man. "What would shock you more? If three boys could lift this massive block of wood or if I touched the foreigner?"

"If you lift the wood, but you can't. I couldn't lift that beam with three of my strongest friends."

The pinned man coughed and blood spewed from his mouth. Jesus walked over to the boy. "Let me help you bear this burden."

The boy looked at him with profound gratitude. Jesus bent down in unison with the boy. James joined his cousin and together they lifted the immense weight and moved it to the side. The crowd emitted sounds of amazement.

The man still lay crumpled on the ground. The son knelt by his dying father and wept, speaking to him in a foreign language. Jesus also knelt by him, across from his son, and placed his hand on the man's chest. The crowd inhaled sharply and murmured. Jesus closed his eyes and prayed silently. "Rise, my friend."

The man opened his eyes and looked at Jesus. Jesus and the boy helped the man to his feet. Again, the people indicated their disbelief. The foreigner, seeing the crowd's agitation, quickly thanked Jesus and said to his son, "Simon, we need to leave, now. Come on." He took the boys hand and left.

The crowd started having an argument about what they should do next. Amidst the shouting and chaos, Jesus grabbed John and

James and they slipped away unnoticed. Regina said, "How did no one notice Jesus leave?"

Gabriel laughed. "It's another one of his gifts."

The boys ran down an alleyway and walked to the north.

"Let's go to the garden outside the Sheep's Gate," Jesus said. James nodded. As they walked, Jesus stopped all of a sudden and looked out between some buildings to a hilltop to the west. A chill went up the spine of Jesus. Regina felt it.

"Jesus, why do you always stop when you see that place?" James said.

"Do you ever wonder how you are going to die?"

James gave Jesus a surprised glance. "No, why?" James suddenly started to feel an itch at his neck. He started to scratch it.

"No reason. Come on, let's go." Jesus started walking at a brisker pace. John ignored their conversation and enjoyed the new speed.

They exited the city through the Sheep's Gate to the north and walked around to the Garden of Gethsemane. Here they walked through the trees and looked at different plants and bugs. James walked off in a different direction from Jesus to explore. Jesus continued to carry John on his shoulders. Regina smiled as she watched how the little boy would rest his head on Jesus, now and then.

Jesus saw a young girl sitting by a tree. She whimpered as they approached. Jesus put John down and sat by the girl. "Why are you crying?"

Dirt and tears had made a mess of the girl's face. "I dropped my water jar and it broke. Now I have no water and my mother will punish me for being clumsy."

Regina could see the broken pieces of the clay jar. Jesus moved to obstruct the girl's view and worked in the dirt. He soon turned around and held aloft a perfect jar. "See, good as new."

The Lord continued to amaze Regina. The girl yelped in joy, not questioning how Jesus produced this new jar. He put it down. Water filled it to the brim. He took some and washed her face. Then he took the edge of his cloak and wiped her dry. When he finished, the girl's face shined.

"My name is Jesus."

"I'm Veronica."

Jesus smiled. "Now go home and give your mother her water."

"How can I repay you?"

"Maybe someday you'll find a way."

"I'll never forget you." She kissed Jesus on the check and carefully carried the jar down the path.

Regina saw Jesus feel something come over him and he fell to his knees. *You are my son, I am well pleased.* The voice spoke into Jesus' soul, yet Regina could hear it clearly. She could tell he felt even more, but she didn't know what.

"What's happening?"

"Jesus has always been the Son of God, and though fully human, he is also fully divine. To protect him, Mary has never spoken of it."

"And now?"

"His father chose this as the time where his Son would know the truth and carry it in his Sacred Heart."

"Isn't it a lot for a kid his age to deal with? I have trouble keeping small secrets. I tell my friends not to share anything confidential with me."

"Yes, but for all the normal things Jesus does, he has always had a profound interior life as a child. He inherited this from his mother. She taught him about faith in the God of Israel, and he will understand fully who his Father is."

Regina watched Jesus in prayer. His intensity amazed her. John didn't say a word and knelt at his side. At this point, James returned from his own adventures. "Praying again?" He smiled at his simple tease. Jesus did not respond. He remained in his trance.

"It's one of these, huh?" James said.

John opened his eyes. "Shhh," he said. He went back to his own prayers. James reclined and made himself comfortable.

372

Time flashed forward for Regina and when it returned to normal, Jesus lost his deep connection with his Father and came to. He looked exhausted. He turned to see James, asleep on the ground, and chuckled. "Hey James, asleep already? There is still so much left in the day." He rose to his feet. James and John jumped up as well.

"Well, let's get moving then," James said.

Regina watched them play in fast forward, noticing Jesus never said anything about what happened during his time in prayer. They spent the rest of the day as three average boys doing everyday things.

"Thanks for your help with my homily, Regina." Father Joe said after Mass.

"What did I do?"

"Your visions inspire me to challenge the parish with what the Lord challenges you with."

"Oh, cool, but I didn't hear all of it. I had a vision during part of it."

Regina explained her trip through Jerusalem with Jesus, James, and John. The details of her story fascinated Father Joe. Mark and Katherine shared the news about Emmanuel, Rose, and Vita with their priest.

After thinking for a moment, he said to the family. "Thank you for sharing your updates on your personal missions. Stay strong together. As they say, 'Blood is thicker than water.'"

Chapter 37
Blood

Sunday, January 5th
11:21 AM
The Solemnity of the Epiphany

Christina and Matty scarfed down their breakfasts at the first diner they found when they pulled into town. Neither one spoke. The food disappeared before the waitress came by to refill coffee.

"You two were hungry," their server said. They both nodded, mouths full of food. They smiled at each other.

"I told you the food would taste better if we hunkered down and drove right through to Illinois, instead of stopping in Saint Louis," Matty said.

"Did I taste the food?" Christina smiled. Matty laughed. "Matty, I don't think I have laughed that much in my entire life."

"Me too, it was fun. Hey, we still have to go back."

Christina nodded. The waitress brought the check and Matty paid. When they got in the car, Christina said, "What are we going to do when we get to the hospital?"

"I thought we would figure out a plan on the ride out here." He gave her a worried look.

She looked at him and burst out laughing. He hesitated and then started laughing too. Their guardian angels had done the first part of their job in getting Christina and Matty out of their sorrows. Now, the Lord needed more from them.

"Let's go in and be honest," Matty said.

"Okay, I trust you." She put her hand on his. He smiled and they spent the drive to the hospital in silence. When they got there, they found the Phlebotomy Lab.

"Hello, can I help you?" a woman in white coat said.

"Hi, Jody," Matty said, looking at her name tag. He wore his most charming smile. "My name is Matty and this is Christina. We are both lab technicians at a biotech company in California."

"Oh, what brings you here?"

"Actually, we have a mystery that you could help us solve."

"Really?" Jody looked at Matty and then Christina. "What is it?"

"We have been testing blood samples for a long time, looking for a very specific reaction, and we finally got one."

"What were you testing for?"

"That's the thing, Jody. We don't know. Have you ever been asked to do lab tests without knowing the point?"

"No, I can't say that I have."

"How would you feel if you did?"

"I can honestly say I would be very uncomfortable."

"Well, our company didn't tell us what we were screening for, swore us to secrecy, and when Christina got a positive result, she got fired. What do you think about that?"

Jody raised her eyebrows and squinted. "That all sounds terrible." She looked to Christina. "I am very sorry, but that still doesn't explain why you are here."

"Well, when Christina got fired, I decided to snoop around to get some answers. I found out some interesting information about the source of the blood sample," Matty said. "Do you want to guess what hospital sent it to us?"

"Ours?" Jody said.

"Yes."

"What company did you say you were with?"

"PermaLife."

"What's the mailing address there?" Jody asked. Matty told her. She entered it and looked at the screen. "We send them blood every day, but we never get any kind of results from them. That's weird. What else do you know?"

"I have is a patient number," Matty said. He handed Jody a piece of paper. Jody typed the number into the computer. Her eyes opened wide.

"What is it?" Christina spoke for the first time.

"The blood came from a baby," Jody said.

"We know," Matty said.

"What would be so important about a baby's blood that I would get fired?" Christina asked Jody.

"I don't know," Jody said.

"Jody, I understand confidentiality and I don't want you to get fired too, but I think that this baby's parents need to know something weird is going on. Can you help us?" Matty said.

Jody thought about it for a while. "Okay, I don't like what I'm hearing, but I also don't know you two at all, so the best I can do is contact the baby's mother and see if she is willing to hear your story. How's that?"

"You would do that?" Christina said.

"Like I said, I don't know if I can trust you, but this really bugs me."

Christina and Matty shared a smile. They waited patiently in the waiting room for Jody, who made the phone call. She reappeared and told a coworker, "I am going to lunch." They walked away from the ward. "The mother said we could come over."

As they walked out of the hospital, Jody ran into a man going in, making her drop her purse. The man mumbled an apology and helped her gather the items that fell out, including the paper with Maggie's address. He didn't notice it because the whole time he looked down and never made eye contact with anyone.

Soon, Jody, Christina, and Matty were on their way to Maggie's, and Paul McCorvey made his way to the neonatal ward.

Father Joe Logan knelt in the rectory chapel. He gazed on a replica of a painting of a priest holding up a host that glowed. His mind went back to the time he saw the original painting on a trip he took to Italy with his family. He pictured himself sitting in the pew of a church listening to his tour guide.

"Welcome to the church of Saint Francis. In the early eighth century, our city of Lanciano was called Anxanum. A young priest doubted the Real Presence of Our Lord in the Holy Eucharist. When he held the host aloft at the moment of consecration it turned to visible flesh. The wine in the chalice changed to blood."

No way, Father Joe remembered thinking. This whole trip had been boring and now he had to listen to outlandish stories.

"The flesh and blood remains intact today. Behold," the tour guide said moving aside to reveal a silver reliquary which held the coagulated blood and a monstrance which displayed the fleshy host.

Father Joe remembered the Holy Spirit moving him at that moment. His spirit stirred and he felt the Lord's call. He leaned over to his mother and said, "Mom, when I grow up I want to be a priest."

His mother smiled and cried. They prayed together that day for his vocation, as he prayed today for it.

"I believe you are present in the Holy Eucharist, Lord, but that poor priest did not. You dispelled his doubt by turning the bread and wine into flesh and blood. Please help me with my doubts."

He thought about all of the events surrounding Regina, her visions, and her family. He wondered if he had provided them with the guidance they deserved.

"Most Precious Sacrament of the Altar, I offer myself to your will." He remained on his knees, in silence.

Maggie changed her clothes after Mass and got ready to go to the Andrews' house for lunch before heading to the hospital.

"Thank you, God, for putting Katherine and her family in my life. I don't know what I would do without them." They helped her find her faith again, and while she wished Katherine's mother a speedy recovery, she rejoiced for the opportunity to return some service to Katherine for her love.

The doorbell rang. *That must be the lady from the hospital.* She walked to the door and opened it. Three people faced her.

"Ms. Rowen? My name is Jody Stevens. I spoke to you on the phone. I work in the Phlebotomy Lab at the hospital and these are my friends Christina and Matty. I'm sorry I couldn't tell you more over the phone."

"You promised Vita was alright?"

"Yes, your daughter is fine, but we think you will find what we have to say very interesting," Matty said.

Maggie looked at the three of them. "Okay, come in."

When the Andrews returned home, Regina went up to her room and Emmanuel went to the den to play. Her parents prepared lunch for Katherine's family and Maggie. Katherine set the dining room table when her father walked into the dining room.

"I like your friend, Maggie. We talked after Mass while you spoke to your priest," John Walden said.

"We do, too. She is part of the family now," Katherine said.

"That's good." He reached inside his suit coat pocket and pulled out a paper. "Katie, I signed this." She looked at the paper and saw tears in his eyes. She didn't need to ask what he held.

"Dad, I'm sorry. Mom told me to get it and …,"

"It's okay, sweetheart, I'm not mad. Your mother was right. I wouldn't have been able to ask the hospital for it. I have to accept that I could lose her without a fight. It's what she wants, but it's still hard." It pained Katherine to see her father this way.

"What's hard?" Veronica said, walking into the kitchen.

Katherine looked at her father, who returned her glance. Then, they both looked at the paper. Veronica saw where their eyes went.

"What's that?"

Katherine couldn't say the words out loud so she handed the document to her sister. Veronica eyes widened. "This is a DNR order. Why do we have one of these?" Her voice trembled. "Dad, you signed it? Why?"

Her father remained silent as Katherine tried to console her sister. "Veronica, it's okay…"

"No, it's not okay. We are not going to give up on mom." Her voice escalated and before long, all the adults came to the kitchen.

"That's not what it means," Katherine said.

"What does it mean then?"

"It means mom doesn't want to be kept alive using extraordinary methods. She said if the Lord calls her, she wants to be able to go with him and not be held back. Dad signed it because he wants to respect her wishes."

Regina heard the commotion from her room and listened from the top of the stairs. She heard her uncles chime in and offer their two cents. They made suggestions about specialists to research and treatments to try.

"Guys, the most important thing is that mom told me we need to be here for each other." Regina heard the next words clearly, "We need to stay together as a family," before she went back in time.

Chapter 38
Gone

The Passover celebration ended. Jesus, James, and their families said their goodbyes. Zebedee helped Joseph make preparations with the other men of Nazareth in their caravan. Despite Joseph's health, he still had a great deal of strength and helped tie several sacks to their donkey.

Mary helped Salome clean her house when she noticed Jesus outside looking restless. She put down her broom and walked out to see what troubled him.

"Did you enjoy the celebration?" Mary said.

"Yes, mother." He didn't sound convincing.

"What's wrong?"

"Why doesn't everyone love the Father the way we do?"

"Why do you say that?"

"I don't know how, but I can feel the love and hate in the hearts of people."

Mary didn't know how to respond.

"What is Jesus saying?" Regina asked.

"Jesus is God, but he is also a boy. What knowledge the Father gave him about his divinity is a mystery. He is trying to explain his conflict to his mother, who will guide him on his journey."

"I never thought about how awkward this must be. Mary knows he is the Son of God and Jesus does too, right? But they don't know what the other knows. Wow," Regina said.

"The Lord has graced you in many special ways, and he has graced me with you, my love. Listen to his call; let it be your guide. I will always be there to help you," Mary said.

Jesus smiled. "I know you will."

"Mary? Jesus? It's time to go, the caravan will leave soon," Joseph said.

"We're ready," Mary said. She turned to go, but Jesus quickly moved to embrace her. He held on tightly. The fierceness of his emotion surprised the Blessed Virgin, but she welcomed it. They parted to finish their preparations.

"You promise you'll stay with me?" Jesus said.

"Always."

Regina moved to the large caravan. Hundreds of people prepared to move out from the city.

"The celebration will continue on the way back to Nazareth. The caravan provides safety, but also entertainment," Gabriel said.

"Entertainment?"

"As you can see, the men and women form their own packs according to custom. This allowed each group to behave more freely, not constrained by having the other gender around. The younger children would be allowed to wander and play between the groups." Mary and Joseph went to their respective groups after agreeing to meet up in the town where the caravan would arrive at the end of a day's journey. Jesus stayed with his mother.

"When will Jesus have to go with the men?" Regina said.

"When he turns thirteen, he will be considered a man."

Jesus walked, talked, and played with the children around him. He teased the younger children playfully, but also made sure no one got mistreated during the games. He even taught them lessons.

One little boy got angry and tried to punch another. Jesus caught his hand before he could connect. "Though shalt not kill."

"I wasn't trying to kill him; I only wanted to hurt him a little."

"Truly, if you have anger or hatred in your heart towards your brother, you have murdered him already. Forgive each other and return to your play." Jesus crossed his arms and waited.

The boys shook hands and went back to their play. Our Lady watched this display with pride. He looked up to see her watching him and smiled to her.

After several hours, the caravan stopped for a break. People sat, ate, and drank water or wine. Jesus played where Mary couldn't see him. He suddenly froze.

I need you, my Son. Come to me.

Jesus turned to look at the speck of Jerusalem in the distance.

"Did you hear it?" Gabriel said.

"Yes," Regina replied.

"Now listen to the voice Jesus will hate for the rest of his life."

You have to tell your mother. Tell her everything. The slimy voice hissed into Jesus' ear. Regina shared a shiver with Jesus. *Tell her you are hearing voices and she will know you have lost your mind. Maybe they will stone you for being possessed by devils.* The voices continued and they found their mark.

"Why doesn't he banish the demons?"

"What would you do in his place?"

"I don't know, I would be … I was scared." Regina remembered facing her tormentor. She couldn't fathom being taunted by the devil, himself. "Doesn't Jesus have a guardian angel to help him?"

"Of course, behold."

At Gabriel's pronouncement, Regina's eyes opened to a multitude of angels. They adored Jesus. She could also see darkness close in on Jesus.

"Why don't his angels intervene?"

"They act in accordance with the Father's wishes. The Father wants to challenge Jesus's faith and resolve."

Each member of the angelic assembly readied to jump. Each awaited the signal to come to Jesus's aid, but no word came.

Tell your mother and father you hear voices. Tell them you think about your death. Tell them you speak to God. They won't believe you. Each word stabbed at the Savior's heart. Tears welled in Regina's eyes. She begged for his torment to end.

"Deliver me from my enemies. I trust in you, Oh God," Jesus said. The voice stopped, the darkness vanished, and the angels stood down. Jesus, himself, relaxed and looked up with determination.

He walked to Mary who spoke to another woman. She smiled at his approach. "My Father has need of me."

The Blessed Virgin nodded. "Then go to him."

"She thinks he's going to Joseph, right?" Regina said.

"Yes," Gabriel said.

Mary went back to her conversation and did not watch Jesus head off in the direction of Jerusalem. No one did. Regina moved with Jesus and heard his thoughts. *Father, I am coming.*

Time flashed forward as Our Lord raced back to Jerusalem. Regina could not tell if Jesus knew his angel companions helped him on his way, but she could see them lighten his step to help him make better time. He never stopped to catch his breath.

When he arrived in Jerusalem, he went straight to the temple. Once inside, weariness and thirst overcame him, and he stumbled to his knees. Only a very elderly woman, asking for alms, noticed his struggles. She got up from her stool and approached him.

"Are you alright?"

"I thirst," Jesus said. He looked into the woman's eyes and their souls connected. Through this, Regina recognized her.

"It's the prophetess, Anna, Mary's teacher."

"Good job, Regina."

Anna saw those same eyes twelve years earlier when she held the Lord as a baby, not far from where they sat now. Unable to work in the temple any longer, she begged for alms near the entrance. She looked to the heavens. "Thank you Lord, for allowing me to see your Chosen One again."

Jesus did not catch her words but her behavior astounded him. She gave him the little water she had and wiped the sweat from his face. After she tended to him, she said, "Please help me to sleep."

Jesus gave her a funny look but helped her back to her spot. She stretched back on her mat. "Now, give me permission to rest."

"But, why do you need…"

"Please, do this for me."

Although he didn't understand her request, he had gratitude for the love she showed him. Putting his hand on her head, he said, "You may rest."

She smiled and closed her eyes. Jesus left her.

"He doesn't know that Anna will pass away in a short time. He gave her a final blessing," Gabriel said.

Jesus felt drawn to the public meeting area on the temple grounds. Priests, scribes, and other men had gathered here in intense discussion.

"Haven't you heard the rumors? The year King Herod had the infants killed, travelers from the east searched for a newborn king. Certainly it was a sign," one man said.

One of the priests stepped forward. "No one here can testify to actually seeing these foreigners. It's all hearsay."

"I was there when Simeon announced he had seen the messiah, on the day he died."

"Did he actually say those words?"

"Well, he… basically."

"What exactly did he say?"

Twelve years had passed since Mary and Joseph brought Jesus to the temple. "I don't remember the exact words," the man said.

"Exactly as I thought. You people need to stop dwelling on the Messiah. His coming will be obvious to all. He will be a great king and rule our people in justice. No one will question his authenticity."

"What about King David?" a young voice said.

All of the men in the assembly became silent and they parted to the sound of the voice. Jesus stepped forward. "Forgive my intrusion, but what about King David?"

Some of the men seemed annoyed that a child would wander into their meeting, but his question caught their attention. A murmur went through the crowd until the high priest responded. "What do you mean about King David?"

"When Samuel asked Jesse to present his sons, he brought them forth. They were strong and righteous before the Lord, all fit to be king, but Samuel examined each of them and declared the Lord had not chosen any of them."

The men nodded and agreement went through the audience. "When Jesse brought forth the boy David, he was not an obvious choice for king. When he went to face Goliath, everyone mocked David and counted him as a dead man. Some look at that battle as a triumph of cunning over strength, but surely, it is a triumph of faith over godlessness."

"Are you saying that God's chosen one wasn't obvious to everyone?" one of the men asked.

"Yes," Jesus said.

"You have spoken well. What else do you have to say?"

Jesus looked over the crowd. They hung on his next word. He first spoke on the strength of the Father's call, but now his nerves stunted him. After checking the encouraging faces around him, he continued.

"When the Lord called Moses, our deliverer asked to be pardoned from his summons by saying 'Behold, I am of uncircumcised lips, how shall Pharaoh listen to me?'" (Exodus 6:30)

"What do you take this to show?" one of the chief priests asked.

"Moses also reminded us that the Lord does not show his power through leaders as we would imagine. Israel may not recognize the Messiah when he comes, but he will yield the power of God and speak with his authority."

One after another in the audience began to applaud the answers of Jesus. Time moved forward into the evening and as darkness approached, Jesus slipped away. The dismayed congregation did not know the identity of the boy but longed for him to unravel more of the scriptures to them. They shared their disappointment.

Jesus walked away from the temple as night fell. He had no idea where his parents would be at this point, but he could feel his Blessed Mother's heart breaking.

"Father, I have obeyed your call to come to Jerusalem. I beg you to give my mother comfort. Though I am lost in her sight, let her be at peace knowing that I am safe and in your care."

"Gabriel, his love warms my heart," Regina said.

"Come and see what it does for Mary." Gabriel whisked Regina back to the where the caravan had stopped.

The small village reminded Regina of Bethlehem and Nazareth. The houses looked similar and the streets and paths had the same kind of layout. The caravan rested on the edge of town. The men outpaced the women for the last few miles of the journey to arrive early and prepare camp. Regina found their setup interesting. In the distance, she saw the women approaching.

Joseph had finished work on their tents, so he helped others with theirs. As the women arrived, they made their way through the camp to find their husbands.

"Joseph?" Mary said.

"Here I am."

She smiled as she approached. "Where's Jesus?"

Joseph's smile vanished. "I haven't seen him all day. I thought he was with you."

"I haven't seen him either; I thought he was with you and the men."

Regina felt a sharp, stabbing pain in her heart. She looked at the terrified eyes of Mary. "Is this what she is feeling?"

"Yes."

"It's awful. Can you make it stop?"

"No. God wants you to feel the meaning of Simeon's words to Mary, about a sword piercing her heart."

"He was talking about this?"

"He was referring to her life as the first and closest disciple of Our Lord. Because of her strong and intimate connection to Jesus, the loss of his presence causes her the pain you feel now. God wants you to understand this is what the effects of sin are on your soul."

"I don't see how Mary sinned here."

"She didn't. In fact, due to God's plan, she never did."

"I'm confused."

"Let me start at the beginning. Every person has been marked with the stain of original sin since the fall of Adam and Eve. Do you know that story?"

"Yes."

"God so loved the world he sent his only Son that the world might be saved. Remember when we talked about the Ark of the Covenant?"

"Yeah, the place where they kept the Ten Commandments," Regina said.

"Correct. God had the Israelites build it perfectly to his specifications so his Word would have a fitting resting place and his Spirit could overshadow it. Do you understand why he would want a perfect dwelling for his laws?"

"Yes."

"For this same reason, when he decided to send his Word into the world in the form of Jesus, instead of having the Israelites create an ark of gold, he created Mary as the new Ark of the Covenant. She would carry the Word within her and the Spirit would overshadow her. Remember my words to Mary, 'The Lord *is* with you'."

"God made Mary without sin *so* she could have Jesus?"

"Exactly. Jesus could not be flesh of Mary's flesh unless she was free from sin-period, end of story."

Mary's terror made her fall to her knees.

"I don't see how this is supposed to teach me about the effects of sin. You just said Mary never sinned."

"When you remain in the state of grace, you remain in contact with Jesus. He remains present to you. Mary's loss of Jesus cripples her. That is a sign of what happens to you when you sin. You lose Jesus like she did. Look what it does to her."

Regina saw that Joseph understood the situation. "I am sure he is around here somewhere. We will find him." He set out to look for Jesus.

Mary and Joseph called out for Jesus to no avail and asked everyone in their party if they had seen him.

"I'm sorry, I haven't seen him all day," their fellow travelers responded, one after another. With every passing denial, Regina felt Mary's heart sink further. The agony grew as they went from one traveler to the next. Mary's mind spun and she felt faint.

"The Joy of the Lord has been her strength for her entire life. Even before she had Jesus with her, in the flesh, the Father and the Holy Spirit accompanied her closely. If you loved the Lord like his mother, this is what you would feel when you turned from him," Gabriel said.

"But, Mary didn't turn from him," Regina said.

"Regina, you must understand. This is the most important lesson for you to learn. Jesus chose Mary to be your model. Not because she had any divine power, but because she loved him above all things. Jesus was everything to her and she submitted herself completely to him. Have you heard the expression 'What would Jesus do?'?"

"Yes, I have a bracelet that says that."

"A better question would be 'What would Mary do?' The Father sent his Son to save the world, but you can't do that. In Mary, you have the model of the perfect disciple: in her humility, her devotion, and even her devastation at the loss of the Lord."

Regina understood that her visions had made this message clear. She began to understand what her mission was now, but before the concept fully materialized, a sharp wail escaped from the mouth of Mary.

"Where is he?" Mary's voice faded and another one took its place.

"Where is he?" Regina emerged from her vision making the voice sound distant and alien.

"Regina, do you know where Manny is?" Regina came to. Her mother's face became clear. It had the same pained look as the Blessed Mother's two thousand years ago.

"What?" Regina said. She realized she hadn't moved from the top of the stairs. Her mother sat next to her and the rest of the family waited at the bottom of the stairs.

"Manny isn't here, Regina. He left foot prints outside the back door. Did he tell you he was going out to play or something?" Katherine voice wavered. "We don't see him anywhere out there."

"I'm sure he just wanted to play in the snow after being cooped up in the hospital for so long," Mark said. Regina could tell from his expression he didn't believe his own words.

"Are you sure he didn't tell you anything?" Katherine said.

"Yes, I'm sure," Regina said. She wanted to tell her mom about her latest vision, but the time didn't seem right. The doorbell rang.

"Maybe that's him," Mark said. He went to the door to find Maggie, along with three strangers. "Maggie? Did you see Manny out there?"

"No," she said. "Is everything all right?"

"I don't know. He isn't here," Mark said. "He's probably around the neighborhood. We didn't think he should be out there so soon after his illness. Who are your friends?"

Maggie introduced everyone to the lab techs. Mark and Katherine's brothers excused themselves and left to look for Emmanuel. The techs explained their story to the rest of the family. Regina listened, still sitting at the top of the stairs. Their tale took several minutes to complete and in that time the men returned.

"I followed his footsteps. They lead from the back of the house to the sidewalk. From there they head east. I am going to take the car and see if he went to one of his friend's houses up the street," Mark said.

"Why would he do that?" Katherine said.

"I don't know," Mark said.

A cell phone rang. Maggie recognized the ring tone and opened her purse. "Hello?" Maggie smiled. "Yes it is. Is Vita alright?" The smile on Maggie's face disappeared as she listened to the voice on the other end. "What? How can that be?" Her eyes displayed her horror. "Okay," she said. Her hand shook as she put her phone away.

Regina felt her stomach sink. Her grandmother said Vita would survive. Katherine assumed the worst. "Maggie, I'm so sorry."

"No," Maggie said. Everyone waited for her to break into tears. "No. Katherine, Vita's been kidnapped." Before Regina could share in Maggie's grief, God took her back to Mary.

"Where is he, Joseph?" Mary's desperation had not subsided. Joseph tried to comfort her.

Suddenly, Mary relaxed and her tears abated. "He's alright."

"What?"

"I felt him call out to me. He's okay and he's still in Jerusalem. Come, Joseph, I must be with him." She started towards the road.

"Mary, it's too dangerous to walk in the dark. There is barely a moon to give us light."

"Joseph, I will crawl to Jerusalem if I have to. Even though I know he is safe, I cannot bear to be apart from him."

"She spoke as a mother and a true disciple. She wished to be with her Lord and nothing could keep her from her pilgrimage," Gabriel said. Regina understood.

Joseph believed her. "Then let me get some torches and a few supplies."

In a few minutes, Joseph obtained what he needed. Their closest friends bid them good luck on their trip back to the holy city. They did not make good time in the dark. After a lengthy walk, Mary heard the call of Jesus bidding her to rest, and she obeyed.

Jesus, having asked his mother to rest for the evening, made his way back to the Garden of Gethsemane. Regina watched Jesus drift off peacefully to sleep, bathed in the warmth of his Father's love, protected by a legion of angels. Before he fell asleep, he prayed that his mother would feel his peace. Regina knew Mary and Joseph slept soundly, even though they went to bed with heavy hearts.

The next day, Jesus spent the morning visiting the sick and the elderly around Jerusalem. The Father moved him with pity to make these trips and he never stayed long enough to see the wonders he left behind.

Regina walked with Jesus as he strolled through the city. At one point, he walked past one house when the Holy Spirit ushered him inside. There, he found a man on a bed with heavily bandaged leg. The man moaned and sweat drenched his body. Jesus went to him, prayed over his leg, and left. The man's delirium left. He opened his eyes and sat up. He removed his bandages, slowly at first, but then frantically. Looking at his leg, he laughed.

"Mother, come here and look. My infection is gone." He stood up to test his healed leg as his mother walked into the room. She saw him standing on his own and put her hand over her mouth. She wept and her son embraced her. Gabriel took Regina back to the wandering Jesus.

He walked by a blind beggar. "Have pity on me."

"I have nothing to offer you but my prayers," Jesus said.

His voice moved the beggar and Regina as well. She never wanted anything in her life as much as Jesus's blessing and she could tell the beggar felt the same way.

"Then pray for me, please."

Jesus put his hand on the beggar and walked away after imparting his blessing. The moment the Savior had left, the old man opened his eyes and found his sight restored.

"Does Jesus even know he is healing these people?" Regina said.

"Jesus followed the will of the Father. He calls Jesus to touch these people and move on. The time for his public ministry has not come. These people won't attribute these wonders to this holy child, but will know that God has touched their lives."

After his morning errands, Jesus returned to the temple, where the assembly enthusiastically welcomed him. Regina could feel that many men had a question in their hearts. *Are you the messiah?* Regina wondered if Jesus even knew the answer to the question.

Jesus began the day's discourse with the fall of Adam and continued to explain all of salvation history. The child's memory of scripture and his ability to explain theological concepts continued to amaze the learned men assembled. Jesus weaved a connection between the heroes of the Old Testament, the words of the prophets, and the coming of the messiah.

"How does he know all of this?" Regina said.

"Mary has taught him about the Law and the Prophets from his youth. She sang the psalms to him since birth. When Joseph gave Jesus free time, he talked with Mary about faith and justice. Add the mystery of what the Father lets him know, and you get what you see here."

The lesson lasted for hours, but no one seemed to mind. Jesus jumped from story to story and deftly answered the questions the audience battered him with. The excitement in the room rose to a fevered pitch. Regina grimaced when the scene began to fade and she got pulled to a new location.

Mary and Joseph had walked for hours already. The previous day's travel took its toll on Joseph, but he suffered in silence. Mary balanced her desire to find Jesus with her loving care for Joseph.

"I am sorry you have to wait for me."

"It's alright. I'm comforted with the knowledge that Jesus is safe. I want you to be well also," Mary said.

"Mary, I have loved him as my own son and I want to desperately find him, too, but I can tell in your eyes you want something more. What is it?" He stopped a moment to catch his breath.

Mary turned to look at her most chaste spouse. "I treasure each moment with him knowing God is with me. Everything in the world seems right, but without him I am lost. I feel like I have a hole inside my heart which grows with each moment."

Joseph pondered her words and Regina could tell he wished for the same relationship with his foster-son. "Okay, I am ready to move on." Regina felt Joseph's tremendous pain.

"What's wrong with him, Gabriel?"

"He suffers from a disease that wears his body away, causing him a lot of pain. Joseph wanted to bring his Son the most honor and protection he could. He asked for suffering as an offering to God, and he bears it as his own cross to be a living sign for Jesus."

"Can Jesus understand this?"

"Your parents teach you many small lessons when you are young which you will not appreciate until you are older. Joseph's suffering and Mary's piety, prepare Jesus to be the public figure you know from the Gospels. Remember, God could have chosen to come as a grown man to save the world, but instead he chose to come as a baby, born into a family, to share in the fullness of our lives."

Mary and Joseph arrived in Jerusalem late in the afternoon and immediately went to Zebedee's house to ask about Jesus. No one had seen him, but they all went to look around the neighborhood.

They only made it a short distance when Roman soldiers came crashing through the streets. "Curfew, curfew! Everyone get back to your homes."

Joseph stopped a running soldier. "What is happening?"

"Several prisoners have escaped from jail, and we don't want any people in the streets as we look for them. Get back to your home."

"But we must find my Son," Mary said.

The angry soldier turned in rage but softened when he looked at Mary. "If we find a lost boy, I promise you we will get him home or hold him until morning so he is safe. Please, return home."

Brokenhearted, Mary returned with Joseph to stay at her cousin's once again for the night. Regina wanted so much to console the Holy Mother, but could only stand idly by and watch her cry. The scene shifted back to Jesus.

Jesus once again sneaked out of the temple without anyone noticing. Regina asked, "Why does he keep doing that?"

"The Heavenly Father wants Jesus to teach the council the truth about salvation, but not for his identity to be discovered at this time."

Regina nodded and they followed Jesus through Jerusalem again. He walked straight into a Roman prison complex, completely unnoticed. Before Regina could ask Gabriel the question, he answered.

"At times, you can see a miracle, at others it is miraculous that you can't be seen." Gabriel smiled.

Jesus approached a cell holding three men. Regina did not find them to appear threatening but she did notice their forlorn faces. "Brothers, what brings you sorrow?" Jesus said.

The oldest of the men looked up. "We are in prison because we tried to rob Caesar's tax collection box. My sons and I will never be able to return to our town again. I am an old man, but my sons have yet to marry. Their lives are ruined, and it's all my fault." The father hung his head.

"Please father, stop. We are all guilty. We knew what we were risking," the elder boy said. He put his arm around his father. The other son did the same.

"Did you need the money?" Jesus said.

"No, it wasn't for us. We have a small farm and we grow enough to live happy lives, but the well that supplies the water for our town has run dry and there are many people who go hungry each day. Still, Caesar taxes us to the point of death. We saw the money sitting there and thought we could save the poor of our town," the old man said.

Jesus looked at the family with pity. "The poor will always be with you. Remember to follow the commandments so your riches, as theirs, will be waiting for you in Heaven. Render unto Caesar what is Caesar's and unto God what is God's."

Jesus walked away, amazing them with his words. The father knelt and his sons joined him. "O Lord, if we ever return home, I promise to obey your commandments and share whatever we grow with the poor so all may be able to eat."

At the end of the prayer, Regina saw angels appear and put all of the prison guards to sleep. The door unlocked and opened. The three men got off their knees, raised their eyes to heaven, and made their escape.

Regina would never see them make it back to their distant town where they fulfilled their promise to take care of the poor. The Lord blessed their farm so they always had enough to share. The sons got married and the town prospered. One day, they would host a feast for a prophet that would come to their town, not knowing he had freed them from a Jerusalem prison.

Chapter 39
The Finding of Jesus in the Temple

Sunday, January 5th
5:13 PM
The Solemnity of the Epiphany

The bishop got out of his car and walked to the door of Saint John's rectory. He made the drive from his house very quickly. The excitement of his plan bubbled up inside him.

He had received more complaints about Father Joe and his challenging homilies. Simultaneously, two chaplain positions had opened at the large prisons in his diocese. It didn't take much prodding from his tempter to make a convenient connection between Father Joe and these new positions.

"I think your passion will serve these men very well. Lord knows they could use the light you feel called to bear." The bishop's words didn't make the shocked priest feel better about the news of the transfer.

Father Joe thought he had cleared this hurdle of the prelate's discomfort with him, but could tell his boss genuinely felt his mission to challenge the hearts and minds of his flock would go well with the prison population. The priest wished for the Lord to intervene and explain his will to the bishop.

What if he is right and you are wrong? It was a legitimate question. *How can I be so arrogant to think I must be correct about the Lord's call? This is the bishop, my superior. What if the spirit guides him and the devil guides me?*

Father Joe's tempter had learned from the best and had unleashed this attack at the most opportune time. Throughout history, many people have assumed they had pure intentions but actually followed the wrong path against the advice of a superior.

The priest weakened at this doubt, but a voice resounded sharply in his mind. *Pray. Invite him to the chapel to pray and God will provide.* Father Joe's angel gave him a new confidence.

"I will obey your will, Excellency, but first, please pray with me in the chapel. I would consider it an honor," Father Joe said.

Surprised at the ease of the meeting, the bishop accepted and the two men left the rectory.

The baby wrapped in the blanket in the passenger's seat whimpered like a kitten. Paul McCorvey continued to aimlessly drive. His head spun with so many emotions he had no idea where he was. He looked at the next street sign to gather his bearings and went back to trying to sort out his feelings.

What do I do now? One million dollars sat next to him, but he was now a wanted man. He couldn't believe his plan at the hospital worked, but he didn't know the number of tempters that had distracted their humans enough to let him slip through the hospital security. He got no answer to his question.

"I am following him right now," Mr. Smith said. "He is not going where I told him to go, so I am waiting for him to stop somewhere so I can grab the package." He felt a twinge of disgust towards himself. *It's only a job, get a grip.* His guardian angel hadn't given up and never would, but the man's soul kept hardening with each job, and the task got ever more hopeless.

Paul felt sick and pulled over. Smith assessed the opportunity but noticed several people in the parking lot around Paul's car. He wondered how he could get to Paul without being seen.

Paul rested his head against the steering wheel and wondered how his life could have arrived at this nadir. The baby whimpered again. Paul's eyes filled up with tears and a prayer escaped his soul. "God help me."

The simplicity of the words did not match the depth of the anguish that spoke them. His soul, crushed and separated from the love of its Creator, cried out to God. Paul spent his life not believing in God. He would have repeated his beliefs only hours earlier, but his guardian angel made his move right at rock bottom and something clicked.

Paul, why do you run from me?

Who are you?

It is the Lord, your God.

Paul shook his head to clear it. Instead, a location appeared in his mind.

Why should I go there?

No answer came, but the call overwhelmed him with hope. He couldn't have explained it, but he knew where to go, and to get there immediately. He put the car in drive and started to move. Mr. Smith followed.

The short trip ended. Paul softly grabbed his daughter and ran into the building. Smith cursed himself for leaving too much room between his car and Paul's. He didn't have a chance to catch Paul before he got inside. He slammed the car into park and calmed himself down. He contemplated his next move.

Mark Andrews burst into the house. "Is he back?"

The look on his wife's face answered his question. Maggie turned away so he knew not to ask his next question. She had finished talking to the policeman assigned to her case. She explained the technician's story about Vita's blood but refrained from mentioning Paul's offer. She wondered if the officer noticed her tension about Paul. *Could he have done this?* The officer didn't say anything indicating his doubt, but he said he would follow up with "Mr. McCorvey."

Mark and Katherine's brothers had driven around the surrounding neighborhoods for hours while Katherine called everyone in their school phone book. The police officer assigned to Vita's case took information down about Emmanuel as well.

"Do you have any reason to think the disappearances are related?"

"No, I can't see how they could be," Katherine answered. She didn't think to share anything about Regina's visions or the fact that she sat entranced at the top of the stairs.

"I will do what I can for your son, Mrs. Andrews. Normally, it would take more than a few hours for a child missing from his home to become a police matter, but since I already have your information, I will do my best." The policeman had been gone for several hours already.

Mark rummaged through the closet and found his heavy snow boots and started putting them on.

"What are you doing?" John asked.

"I am going to walk through the woods. We have driven around the neighborhood ten times already. I can't just wait here." Mark's voice strained with emotion. His anguish broke the façade he tried to maintain.

No one stepped in to deny him his shot in the dark. Before he put on his coat, the doorbell rang. Mark opened the door and found Katherine's mother, Rose standing there, along with two other people.

"Hello, Mark." Rose said.

Katherine heard her mother's voice and jumped off the couch. "Mom? What are you doing here?" Everyone else exclaimed their shock as well.

"I'll explain later, but I brought someone here who needs to tell to you something important." She stepped aside, allowing a boy to enter.

"Regina knows where Emmanuel is," Frank Roland said.

Jesus spent the night in the Garden of Gethsemane, undisturbed by the patrolling Roman soldiers, and awoke with the sunrise. He made his way back to the temple, where the assembly anxiously hoped he would reappear. He rejoiced at his arrival and he immediately began to speak of the Messiah. He connected the numerous prophecies that spoke of his own coming. The gathered men asked him new and more challenging questions. He answered them all.

Meanwhile, Mary and Joseph woke up early and scoured the town, asking people if they had seen a young boy with Jesus's description. Unfortunately, no one had seen him. They made it through the part of Jerusalem that would have been most familiar to Jesus, when one of Mary's guardian angels received permission to relieve her sorrow.

"My Lady, the Lord says Jesus will be where you offered him to his Father."

"I know where he is, Joseph."

Mary led Joseph through the streets. Regina moved back to Jesus.

He continued to speak of the messiah. Finally, Mary and Joseph arrived at the temple. Hearing a boy's voice, they made their way through the crowd. As Mary broke through and had the joy of seeing her Divine Son, Jesus said, "Behold, a virgin will be with child and bear a son, and she will call him Immanuel." (Matthew 1:23)

"Regina? Can you hear me?" a distant voice called.

Regina's vision wavered between two worlds.

"Do you know where Emmanuel is?" Katherine asked.

"Emmanuel?" Regina managed to say before going back to Jerusalem.

A hush fell over the crowd when Mary and Joseph entered their midst. Mary stepped forward, ran to Jesus to embrace him, showering him with kisses. When her passion for Communion had been satisfied, she spoke from her heart, saying, "Son, why have treated us in this way? Your father and I have been terrified and restless looking for you." (Luke 2:48)

Jesus looked tearfully at Mary and Joseph who stood behind her. Regina could tell it hurt him deeply to see Mary's distress, but with confidence he said, "Why were you looking for me? Did you not know that I would be in my Father's house?" (Luke 2:49)

This astonished the congregation. *Did he claim to be the son of God?* They started asking each other about this heresy when Jesus, along with his parents, slipped away. Witnessing the reaction of the holy men, Joseph led Mary and Jesus quickly away from the temple and back to Zebedee's house.

"Get me into a car," Regina heard her own voice say in a distant world.

Jesus never left the embrace of Mary on the trip. Mary forgot about her sorrows as she melted into Jesus for strength.

Regina asked Gabriel about something that bothered her. "In Saint Luke's gospel, it says Mary and Joseph did not understand what Jesus had said to them about being in his Father's house. Didn't they know he was the son of God already?"

"Yes, Regina, they knew that. What they didn't understand was why they didn't know where he would be. This whole episode happened to prepare Mary for the crucifixion. The Father understands Mary's profound love for Jesus and wants her to know, when Jesus leaves her, it will be to go to his Father's house. She will not fully come to this understanding until right before the end, but this knowledge will prevent her from truly dying from sorrow when Jesus leaves her on Good Friday."

"She knew he would come back to life on Easter?"

"These three days serve as a sign of those three, but she didn't necessarily know the exact hour of his return, like you don't know when Jesus will return now. She believed Jesus when he said he would return. You need to believe him the same way, because," Gabriel's voice ended.

"You know where he is?" Mark's voice replaced the archangel's.

"At his father's house," Regina said.

"Where?"

"At church, at St. John's," Regina answered. She became fully alert. She sat in the back seat with her aunt. Her father and mother were in front.

They arrived at the church in a few minutes. Her father helped her out of the car. Her mother ran into the church. They followed. She saw the rest of her family getting out of cars as well. She saw Frank Roland, causing tears to fill her eyes.

"Frank!"

He smiled at her. "Later."

They ran inside and saw an incredible sight. Emmanuel stood by the altar, speaking to Paul McCorvey, who sat on the steps clutching a bundle in his arms. Paul rocked the weakly crying baby. Emmanuel seemed to be preaching. No one knew what to do.

Maggie and Katherine broke from the collective trance first and ran forward. Frank followed closely behind.

"Emmanuel!"

"Paul!"

The women ran forward to claim their children. Paul relinquished Vita to Maggie. She found the child pallid and broke into tears.

Frank Roland came forward. "Please, let me help you."

Maggie handed Vita to him in desperation. He took her in his arms and breathed into her face. Vita opened her eyes and her tiny body stiffened for a moment and then relaxed. Her face turned to a healthy pink and she seemed to swell in size. Frank handed her back to Maggie.

Emmanuel ended his sermon when his mother called his name. This also broke the trance controlling Paul. After Maggie got Vita back from Frank, Paul fell at her feet and broke into tears. "I am so sorry for everything, Maggie. I don't deserve your love, but I beg for your forgiveness."

Maggie anguished between her anger and her love. She wanted to call Paul out for all of his transgressions in front of everyone gathered. Paul and Maggie's tempters both knew this and worked in concert to get her to go for his spiritual throat. They knew it would push him into the precipice he stood over. His soul neared a breaking point, and a rejection from Maggie would solidify his damnation.

The Holy Spirit did not intend this for Paul. He expressed his will to Maggie's guardian angel and she encouraged Maggie to ask for God's grace. Somehow, Maggie responded with a prayer in the silence of her heart. *Lord, what should I do?* Through this openness, the Lord responded with an outpouring of love. Showered with grace, Maggie said, "Paul, I forgive you."

The immense weight crushing both Maggie and Paul lifted. Maggie touched Paul's head with her free hand. He took it and kissed it tenderly, still unable to look at her. It would be a while before he could. Then, he finally looked at his child with the love of a father.

Mr. Smith sat in his car and fumed at the number of people who had entered the church. He still tried to form a plan for completing his task. The phone rang. He looked at it in disgust. *Disgust for my failure or disgust for my job.* The moment of soul searching allowed his guardian angel to penetrate the crack in the stone surrounding his heart. He shut off the phone. He looked up and saw two more men walking towards the entrance of the church. The younger of the men looked in his direction. Their eyes connected across the great distance for only a moment. *You are lost, come home.* He shuddered. The sensation made him realize this mission was over. He started the car and drove off, the battle for his spirit only beginning.

Father Joe and the bishop entered the church to find it surprisingly active. The bishop looked at his priest, ready to question him about the meaning of this gathering, but saw Father Joe's face transfixed on something.

Father Joe glided towards the statue of Our Lady in the front left corner of the church. Everyone noticed his strange behavior and watched. He went to the kneeler and dropped to his knees. He looked up at the statue of his mother.

"Thank you for hearing my call, my son."

Chapter 40
The Joy of the Lord
Part 2

Sunday, January 5th
6:10 PM
The Solemnity of the Epiphany

Father Joe looked at Our Lady and his eyes brimmed with tears. He felt unworthy to look upon her beauty, but the Holy Spirit willed him to gaze upon the fairness of His spouse. The significance of the world vanished and he felt joyfully lost in this moment shared with the Blessed Virgin. She smiled at him.

"Call the one who bears my name."

"Regina Marie, Our Lady calls you." Everyone gasped. They fell to their knees. Regina looked at her father for guidance. He nodded and she made her way to the priest, never taking her eyes off the unmoving statue. When she arrived at his side and knelt, she too, shared his vision. Her heart fluttered.

"My child, do you know who I am?"

"You are the Joy of the Lord," Regina said. Her parents glanced at each other. Everyone stared at the statue but didn't see anything out of the ordinary.

Our Lady smiled. "You have learned well, my child. Saint Gabriel showed you how Our Lord blessed me with more joy than a lowly handmaid deserved. You must share the story of my joy, Regina." Her name never sounded sweeter.

"Blessed Mother, how can I share this story?"

Our Lady reached into the folds of her clothing and pulled out a gorgeous rosary. "Humanity has chosen to serve false gods and lives in misery. You must remind everyone that those who serve God live in the Joy of the Lord. By meditating on the Joyful Mysteries, every Christian can share in the joyful wonder Saint Joseph and I felt long ago. Through your mission, all of my children will find their missions."

"Mother, I am scared. I want to do his will, but I feel weak and unworthy."

"Do not be afraid, my child. You will not do this work alone." The Blessed Virgin gestured to her friends and family. Regina looked around and realized God had touched their lives through her. "The Lord will provide, and I will always be with you."

The vision ended with a flash of blinding light. When they regained their sight, everyone could see that the statue of Mary now held the beautiful rosary only Regina and Father Joe could see in their vision.

Father Joe and Regina stood and faced the others. No one could speak. A legion of angels came upon the Blessed Virgin's departure and dispersed the tempters of everyone in the church. The clarity that accompanied the heavenly thunderclap before Gabriel's first visit returned, but this time, the Creator maintained his connection to all present and bathed them with his grace.

"Go, Regina," Father Joe said. She rushed to her parent's embrace. Emmanuel joined to complete them.

Freed from his tempter, the Bishop warmly embraced Father Joe. "Father, forgive me for doubting your mission."

"I forgive you, Your Excellency."

"We will need to call in someone from the outside to explore today's events, but clearly something heavenly has blessed this parish. I will want you to help bring this blessing to the rest of the diocese."

"Can I come and see you tomorrow? I think I need to minister to my flock."

"Yes, of course." Bishop Roberts walked to Regina. She bowed her head and received his blessing. The bishop shook hands all around and left without saying more. He walked out of church full of energy and excitement.

Mark walked to Father Joe.

405

"What do you think about all of this, Father?"

"I'm going to need your help, Mark."

Mark nodded. "Anything you need, I'll be your right hand."

"Mark, I want you to help me make real disciples in this parish. Men and women, totally dedicated to God's call, do you think you can do that?"

"Yes, I do. How do we start?"

"Before you leave today, I want you to take two books I recently finished reading."

"What are they?"

"*Rebuilt* by Fr. Michael White and Tom Corcoran and *Forming Intentional Disciples* by Sherry Weddell. They lay out a path that Our Lady wants us to follow to do the work of Jesus. Read these as soon as you can and we'll start laying out the framework for parish renewal."

"What about Regina?"

"Our Lady spelled out Regina's mission, but left it to me to help keep her moving forward. We will have to discern it, together."

They shook hands and Mark returned to his family.

Katherine still had not let go of Emmanuel. "What happened, Manny? How did you know you should come here?"

"Mother Mary told me to come."

She stared at him with wondering eyes. She opened her mouth to ask another question, but something told her he had nothing more to share. She hugged him tightly and over his shoulder saw her siblings with her mother. They all knelt together in prayer. Rose's smile made Katherine happier than any kind words from her mother could. They finished their prayers and John helped his wife up. Katherine went to her mother.

"Mom, tell me what happened," Katherine said. Everyone gathered close to hear the story.

"That boy, Francis, came to my room again." Rose described the encounter.

"You're back." Rose said.

"Yes, ma'am," Frank said.

"Why?"

"When I visited you last time, I was in a coma. God gave me the gift of bilocation to come to your room. This time, he healed me of my injuries so I could bring his healing to you."

"I thought I was to suffer," Rose said.

"The Lord is honoring your prayers for your family. Your healing will be temporary, as a sign to them that he wants them to know him. In addition, you will give a message to Regina."

"What message?"

"I don't know. The Holy Spirit will reveal it to you. Have faith."

"Okay, I'm ready," Rose said. The family listened in awe. "You know the rest of the story."·

"Incredible," Katherine said. "Will you go back to the hospital now?"

"I'm afraid you know the answer to that question already, Katherine."

Katherine gave her mother a melancholy look and hugged her. She didn't want to let go, but did. The others did the same. When Veronica's turn came, she sobbed into her mother's shoulder.

"Mom, I'm so sorry for my childish behavior all of these years. I, I…" It was enough.

"Thank you, dear. You don't have to say anymore. I love you. I always have and always will, may God be with you." She blessed all of her children in turn. "I want you to know that I accept all the suffering that will come my way from here on. Don't pray for my release, but for my strength and that the fruits of my labors will go to those who need Christ's mercy."

The seeds of faith planted in her families' heart in Baptism flowered at that moment and would blossom in time. Her husband put his arm around her and they prayed together again.

Paul still hadn't left his place on the ground at Maggie's feet. When the vision ended and the light from the miraculous rosary flashed, Regina and Father Joe regained their earthly sight, but Paul lost his.

Paul, I have need of you. Repent and seek me, and you will see again.

"Paul, look at your daughter," Maggie said. She knelt down to Paul's level and held the child before him. Vita moved vigorously.

"I can't Maggie. I am not worthy to see her or you. The Lord took my sight until I repent of my sins."

Paul's conviction startled Maggie. She never heard him speak with such confidence.

"I have to turn myself in to the police."

"No, Paul. I forgive you. It's alright."

"Thank you, my love, but I need to accept the consequences of my actions. I hurt you and risked the life of our child for nothing but my own selfishness. It's okay. The Lord is calling me to this."

"I believe you, Paul. I know what that feels like. I will ask for leniency on your behalf. Our daughter needs her father." Vita continued to squirm. "I wish you could see her. We'll take her back to the hospital, but I've never been surer that she will make it."

"I'm sure she will," Paul said.

Louise Roland knelt in one of the pews. Tears of joy ran down her face. She watched her son, joyfully, in silence. Frank went to join her.

"Mom, are you alright?"

"Frankie, I've never been better." She hugged and kissed him again. "I never thought I would get my little boy back."

"Mom, I saw demons trying to get you to lose hope, but I knew you never would. Your faith helped to bring me back, but..."

"But what?"

Frank explained what happened when Padre Pio returned to him.

"Francis, the time has come for you to return to continue your mission."

"Padre, what does the Lord want me to do?"

"First, the Lord will heal you of your injuries. You will still feel a great deal of pain, but your healing will break the hardness of many hearts."

"Will it be worse than the pain I have felt so far?"

"It won't be more than you can bear."

"Then what?"

"When you awaken, your mother will want you to rest, but you must tell her the Lord healed you for a specific purpose." Frank paused.

"I believed you, and then we came here, but why do I feel like there is more?" Louise said.

"I will be with you, but I won't be your little boy anymore. Padre Pio didn't tell me exactly what God wanted of me, but I know it will be hard. I need your support, no matter what it is." Frank's conviction scared Louise. A sword pierced her heart.

"Francis Xavier Roland, you have my support," she said. Her eyes moistened, but she managed not to cry.

"Thanks, mom." He hugged her. "I need to talk to Regina."

Regina said very little after her vision of the Virgin Mary. She hugged and accepted kisses from her family, but now she waited to speak to Frank. She still looked at him in disbelief as he approached.

He saw the look on her face. "It's a long story."

She hugged him. She no longer feared him as the dark spirited bully. She had a kindred spirit; someone who could relate to her spiritual experiences.

Regina pulled away. "What happens to us now?"

"What did Our Lady say?"

"She told me my mission was to share the Joyful Mysteries with everyone."

"The Joy of the Lord is my strength," Frank said.

"Why did you say that?"

"I don't know," Frank said. He smiled and shook his head. "I have many things to figure out, but I'm glad that we're friends."

"Me too."

"Hey, what do you make of that?" He pointed towards Emmanuel who knelt in front of the statue of Mary. His lips moved but he made no sound.

"I don't know," Regina said, and the world disappeared.

Regina saw Jesus kneeling outside his house. She heard what he heard in his prayers.

My Son, wait for my call. Until then, honor your father and your mother. Trust in them. I made them for you.

"Yes, Father," Jesus said. He rose and went inside. Mary and Joseph embraced him and got ready to share a meal. The vision ended and Regina went home.

Miseros smashed the last object remaining on his desk against a wall. He finished destroying his office by flipping the desk over and kicking a hole in the side. A knock sounded on the door.

"What!?!"

The door opened and a frightened demon walked in. "Sir, I have a memo from Dark Command." She held a note in her trembling hands.

Miseros's chest heaved as he gulped in air. He held out his hand; the demon gave him the paper and scurried away. He collected himself and began to read.

His scowl slowly turned to a horrible grin. "Yes. That will work. That will work just fine." He looked around. He reached out his hand and a broken intercom unit jumped to it. It reformed like new at his command and he began to bark orders. "Summon the Elite Council. The master has given us a job to do."

Miseros reordered his room and sat down at his desk. He took a piece of paper and wrote the name *Regina* in the middle of it. A moment later, it burst into flames. Miseros shook his head, unsatisfied.

"What are you thinking about, Matty?" Christina said. Matty focused on his driving.

"What?"

"You haven't said anything since we left the church," Christina said. Jody nodded, in the back seat. "What do you think about the Virgin Mary appearing to the priest and that girl?"

"I don't know what to make of that. I've been thinking about Paul's story about that Smith character."

"What do you mean?" Jody said.

"Do you really think there is a rich man with a sick child that needed Vita's organs?" Paul said.

"Who does Mr. Smith work for then?" Christina said.

"I don't know, but I am pretty sure I am going to need to do some more snooping around at PermaLife," Matty said.

Christina tensed. "That sounds dangerous. Right, Jody?"

"They did fire Christina for a positive test result. What would they do you if you got caught?" Jody said.

"What do you suggest? I'm not going stop here," Matty said. His resolution showed clearly in his eyes.

"Why don't you two crash at my place tonight?" Jody said. "I have a guest bedroom and a pullout couch. I need to finish up some stuff at the hospital, but we can talk this through some more. I agree that we can't stop here, but we need to be careful."

Matty and Christina looked at each other. Matty nodded.

"Let's do it," Christina said. "Best road trip ever."

Matty smiled.

Consua prayed while he waited for Lucy. She arrived, but he didn't break his concentration. Without opening his eyes, he smiled. "Are you having fun yet?"

"Yes," Lucy said.

"I have asked you here to show you something."

"What is it?"

"Come with me." Consua took Lucy's hand and they transported to a rocky mountaintop. Smoke filled the sky and the smell of sulfur filled the air.

"Why did we come here?" She grimaced as she looked about.

"Come closer to this edge and look." Consua stepped to a space in the rocks and pointed out. Lucy walked up to him and gasped.

Thousands upon thousands of demons lined up in rows. They held weapons and armor, primed for war.

"What's happening?" Lucy could not hide the fear in her voice.

"Behold hell's response to Regina's mission."

"This is all for her?"

"No, but the enemy knows he has to go on the offensive. He has a plan to sink many souls, and this army is only waiting for its orders. They will be on the attack very soon."

"What should we do?"

"Do what we always do. Pray."

Do you want to help Regina with her mission?

Share this story with your friends, family, and fellow believers

Look for the sequel to The Joy of the Lord, The Light of the World in 2016.

Visit http://www.facebook.com/TheJoyOfTheLordRM to like Regina

Follow ReginaMarieMOH on Twitter

Ask God to bless your mission and vocation

Get involved in your church and community

Pray, pray, and pray